CRIMES AGAINST HUMANITY

CRIMES AGAINST HUMANITY

Paul Michael Dubal

iUniverse, Inc.
Bloomington

CRIMES AGAINST HUMANITY

This is a work of fiction. All of the characters, names, incidents, organizations, and dialogue in this novel are either the products of the author's imagination or are used fictitiously.

iUniverse books may be ordered through booksellers or by contacting:

iUniverse
1663 Liberty Drive
Bloomington, IN 47403
www.iuniverse.com
1-800-Authors (1-800-288-4677)

Because of the dynamic nature of the Internet, any web addresses or links contained in this book may have changed since publication and may no longer be valid. The views expressed in this work are solely those of the author and do not necessarily reflect the views of the publisher, and the publisher hereby disclaims any responsibility for them.

Any people depicted in stock imagery provided by Thinkstock are models, and such images are being used for illustrative purposes only.

ISBN: 978-1-4620-4533-4 (sc)
ISBN: 978-1-4620-4531-0 (hc)
ISBN: 978-1-4620-4532-7 (ebk)

Library of Congress Control Number: 2011913967

Printed in the United States of America

iUniverse rev. date: 08/26/2011

CHAPTER 1

As she lay chained to the bed in the squalid Montreal flat, Marisa Dimitrov reflected on the events that had brought her to this terrible life. Travelling to a country that offered so much opportunity, she would never have believed the cruelty she would suffer.

Marisa had endured abject poverty living in a remote village in South-western Bulgaria at the base of the wonderful Pirin Mountains. At least there she had her cherished family.

Despite everything, Marisa's family had always been close and pulled together even when things appeared desperate. When her father Vasil lost his job at the Petar Dodov steel mill in Satovcha the family did not give up.

"We will get through this," he urged his family. "I will find another job, and soon." Her mother, Marisa and her younger brother and sister nodded in agreement but with very little conviction. Even her father did not really believe it, but he was a proud man and would not let his family see the worry that twisted him inside. A strong but simple man, his voice boomed across the bare wooden table as if the louder he spoke the more likely it was to come true.

As Marisa looked around the bare walls of their crumbling stone cottage, she realized her father, at forty-six years of age, would probably never work again. All of her seventeen years had been a fight to keep the family's head above water, but this time there was no escape from the merciless claws of poverty. Later that evening, she heard her father quietly sobbing in the coal bunker, the only place where one could find any privacy in the small cottage. She wanted to rush in and comfort him, but her father would never allow his children to see him like this. A Bulgarian man's duty was to his family, to provide a shelter and food for the table. Once the man of the house lost the ability or means to do this, he was somehow emasculated, less than a man. Marisa knew her father's tears were as much to do with his wounded pride as the bleak future now staring them in the face.

As she took the long walk back from her local college the following day, stepping between the muddy potholes on a drab, cloudy day, she reflected on her family's desperate situation. So many families in the village had been affected in the same way, yet that did not make it any easier. The village was so poor, it only survived through sheer determination that its people would have some kind of life, despite the humiliating effects of poverty. Tonight her family would huddle together in their living room, afraid even to light the log fire for fear their meagre stock of wood would soon be depleted.

She thought about her friend Deyana, who had talked about earning a living abroad. Marisa had confided in her, and while walking to their next class, Deyana had suggested the possibility of working abroad.

Marisa was sceptical. "Working abroad? Where? To do what?"

Deyana replied, "Have you not seen the posters at college, or heard the radio adverts? You can work as a nanny or au pair in somewhere like America or Western Europe and earn ten times as much as you would get here. You could have a brilliant time and still have enough money to send home. That's what I am going to do when I have finished college."

This had set Marisa thinking hard. Why wait to finish her education? The only reason she was studying now was because she could not find a job locally and her social studies course was incredibly boring anyway. Her family needed the money now. With her father out of work, her brother and sister too young, and her mother occupied with supporting the family, only Marisa really had the chance to bring some money to the family. The more she thought about it, the more the idea grew. Her brain nurtured the idea into a plan of action and the next day she decided she would find out about the opportunities available.

The college library was a useful source of information, but it was a small, amateurish poster which drew her attention. Against a backdrop of a poorly drawn Rocky Mountains scene, the poster proclaimed "Work in Canada" and gave a contact number and few other details, except a list of jobs—waitress, au pair, nanny, or a customer service rep, whatever that was. She knew very little about Canada, but had heard of its vast and beautiful scenery, and she could not stop thinking about it all day.

When she arrived home that evening, she peered at her parents' exhausted faces, every line of which revealed the abject poverty that haunted them day by day. It was more an existence than a life, a battle for survival that gradually eroded their willpower like waves beating endlessly against a cliff. With the loss of the family's sole income, the battle had just become much harder. Her father smiled weakly at her as she entered, but it was the hollow expression in his eyes that betrayed how he really felt. She saw fear, for his family and for their future.

By then her mind was made up. "I have decided to work in Canada," she blurted out to her parents.

Her father's smile faded rapidly and her mother stopped her kitchen chores and came to the table.

"Canada?" exclaimed her father. "Why?" His voice had the disapproving air she knew so well.

"Papa, look at us! We cannot live like this. We have no money coming in to the house."

"I told you before Marisa I will find a job!" he replied. "It just takes time, that's all." His tone of voice fooled no-one, not even himself.

Her mother looked concerned but said nothing.

"Papa, I know you are trying but look at us. Look at the people in the village!" She felt her voice rising. "There is nothing here for us. Deyana says they earn really good money in Canada. If I can find a job in Canada I can send money back."

"What job will you do in Canada?"

"I can be an au pair or waitress, anything, it doesn't matter!" she said.

"You are still at college. You must complete your studies," he replied flatly.

"What good is a college education if there is no job at the end of it Papa?" she screamed.

Her father banged his fist on the table in a rare moment of passion. "No I will not hear of it. We will be okay. We will get some money somehow." His voice had an air of finality to it, but Marisa's mother, having observed silently, decided to intervene.

"Listen to the child, Vasil. We have nothing here," she said, gently squeezing her husband's hand.

He pulled away from her and stood up. "No, I will not break up this family," he shouted and stormed off to the coal bunker to smoke another roll up, even that remaining pleasure threatened by their financial situation.

She could still picture the expression on his face, his stubborn refusal to accept what had happened to his family. Her mother had not liked the idea, either, but she also knew how obstinate Marisa could be and had finally agreed to speak to her husband.

As Marisa lay in bed at night shivering in the room she shared with her sister and brother, she had decided to enquire about Canada with or without her parents' blessing. Marisa had rarely left this region of Bulgaria throughout her life, and she was tired of the village. She did not want to be around to see it slowly dying in front of her, while her family stayed here helpless. Her mind was made up as she drifted into a restless sleep.

CHAPTER 2

Marisa's friend Deyana had agreed to accompany her to the international recruiter's office. Marisa felt rather guilty that she was skipping lectures, especially when her mother had cheerfully waved farewell with a "Have a good day at college!" She did not like deceiving them and her unease at having to do so increased when Deyana sent a text just before they were due to meet to say she had remembered a late assignment and had to submit it that day. The message ended with an embarrassed apology which only served to reinforce Marisa's sense of unease about this venture.

As she took the long bus ride through the picturesque mountains southwest to Sandanski, she scanned the address of the international recruitment agency she had copied from the poster. She had called the previous day from a pay phone at college and the voice at the other end had been effusive and helpful, urging her to come in and talk about the "opportunity of a lifetime." The man at the agency had been highly persuasive and had urged her to come in and see him immediately. After having talked to him she was convinced she was doing the right thing, but as she sat alone on the bus, watching the mist creeping over the sweeping valley below, and the rain start to drum against the windows of the bus, she began to feel some nagging doubts.

She arrived in town by late morning. She had never been to Sandanski and her enquiries at the bus station for directions to the office yielded only blank stares. She asked a taxi driver who offered to take her there but he turned away in disgust when she explained she wanted directions only and could not afford the ride. He vaguely pointed in the general direction of the streetcars and she headed to them and checked the route. She took a streetcar to the edge of town near the street where the office was located. It was the last stop and when she arrived she was the last one to alight. As the streetcar circled back to repeat its journey in the opposite direction, Marisa walked briskly through the quiet street of run down grimy looking buildings, and was relieved to quickly find the address she was looking for. The tall, dingy building had the number scratched on the inside and a few peeling nameplates, one which showed the agency she was looking for was on the fifth floor. The stairwell smelt damp and banished all light from outside, and the wall light had long since been vandalized. She carefully climbed the narrow stone steps, spotting graffiti in the gloom and knocked timidly at the door.

She heard movement within the office and the click of a spy hole. The door opened and she was greeted by a pockmarked, scowling face which instantly broke into a wide grin at the sight of Marisa.

"Ah, you must be Marisa," the man smiled, extending his hand. "I am Georgi—we spoke on the phone. Come in, come in. Follow me please."

Marisa smiled back and shook his hand and followed him through the outer office into a small room stacked with boxes and papers. The office felt bright after the gloomy stairwell, but the windows were grubby, as if they had not been washed in years, and the office untidy. She had expected to see an array of consultants and secretaries but it was clear Georgi was alone. Maybe everyone was at lunch or the secretaries had the day off, thought Marisa. He cleared a chair of boxes and beckoned her to the seat and he squeezed his obese frame behind his large desk, grunting as he did so.

He regarded Marisa across the desk, saying nothing, just a lecherous grin on his face, revealing broken yellow teeth, his double chin wobbling. Marisa smiled weakly in return, trying not to show her discomfort. It felt like he was mentally undressing her, and she could not meet his steady gaze.

Georgi broke the awkward silence. "So tell me Marisa, why would you like to work in Canada?"

As Marisa explained her circumstances, Georgi listened with real empathy, letting her talk but gently interrupting now and then to clarify something. He scratched at some of the spots on his cheek as he listened and nodded approvingly, and Marisa's initial sense of unease wore off. She began to feel more relaxed as Georgi seemed supportive.

"A beautiful girl like you would have no trouble finding a good position as a nanny or au pair in a good Canadian home. Canadians are good people and they will treat you well. All of our clients prefer to have live-in nannies. That means you will not have to worry about accommodation or transport when you get there. In fact, my colleagues will even take you to your place of work when you arrive in Canada. Everything will be taken care of for you. We can even arrange your working visa."

He gave a leering grin again. "I think someone like you will be just the person the clients want. I do hope you will join our project."

Marisa blushed. Despite being flabby and full of acne, with an odd leer, he had a certain charm. It was a long time since anyone had been so complimentary to her. It felt good for her self esteem. Even her parents had forgotten how to be really nice to her.

As she thought about her parents, a twinge of guilt stabbed at her. "I don't think my parents would approve of me doing this."

Georgi leaned across the desk and took her hand in his sticky, fleshy palms. Although repulsed by the gesture, she did not move her hand away. "Marisa, let me tell you. We have hundreds of girls like you working all over the world making a good income and sending money to their families so they can survive. Many of their mothers and fathers objected at first but they soon saw the benefit because the money those girls sent back became their lifeline. They may not understand at first but when they start receiving money from you—then they will understand and they will love you for it. You can make them very proud of you." He squeezed her hand before letting go, still grinning in that disconcerting way.

"Well I have made up my mind, I want to do this."

Georgi's face brightened. "Good, good, let me get the papers." He quickly delved into a drawer and pulled out a crinkled bundle of papers. "I took the liberty of preparing the documents before you came. I knew you were a sensible girl when I spoke to you on the phone. Please sign at the bottom."

Marisa scanned the papers. It was full of small writing and grouped into numbered paragraphs full of legal jargon. She could feel Georgi's eyes boring into her, waiting expectantly for her to sign. "What is this charge—one thousand Euros?"

Georgi forced a smile. "Oh, did I forget to mention? It is the agency's fee for finding a position for you, arranging the visa, and it even covers the airfare. It is really good value."

"But I don't have one thousand Euros," replied Marisa.

"Don't worry," he assured her. "There are no fees up front. My agency will cover it. You just need to pay us back in stages when you are settled in Canada. It is much easier for you this way and you will have it paid off before long. If you are lucky sometimes your employer will pay toward it."

Marisa shrugged. Did she really think that travelling to Canada and getting a job would be free? Georgi was right—for the work his agency was doing, it did not seem too much. Once in Canada, she would pay it back as quickly as possible so she could start putting money aside for her parents. She barely gave it another thought as she signed the contract, thinking instead about what she would say when she got home.

She spent the next hour discussing the logistics with Georgi. He took copies of her passport to get her a visa and set up bank accounts, or so he claimed, and also gave her details of the flight she would take. Instead of landing at Toronto as she expected, she would fly to London and take a connecting flight to Montreal. From there she would take a local flight to St. John's and then go by land to Toronto. Marisa did not really understand the journey but it did sound rather strange. She thought it was possible to fly direct from Sofia to Toronto.

"Oh don't worry," he assured her. "It's all okay—you will be taken good care of. We do it this way because the air fares are cheaper. We have a good deal with the airlines. This way we can keep the costs down for you. We recognize how hard it is to get to

Canada in the first place. It is a slightly longer journey I agree, but it will be worth it. You will love Canada!"

His explanation sounded genuine enough and they agreed Georgi would finalize the travel details and also fix her up with a nice family he knew with two young girls, aged four and two. He would call her in a few days to confirm the arrangements. Within a week she would be on her way to Canada.

As they parted he gave that disgusting grin. "They love brunettes in Toronto." It was an odd comment and one she never really paid much attention to at the time. Also it only occurred to Marisa later that he never once asked if she had ever worked with children.

Marisa travelled home in a pensive mood, still uncertain she had done the right thing, and the hefty agency fee weighed a little on her mind. When she arrived home she decided to confront her parents with the news immediately. Her father was furious but her mother managed to calm him down, holding him and softly talking to him so his initial temper subsided. However, as he left for the coal bunker, apparently resigned to the situation, he turned to Marisa and said the words which now haunted her. "Will we ever see you again?"

All the time her younger siblings stood silently at the kitchen door, impassively observing the argument. When Marisa left to pack her few belongings, they stared at her mother and little Goran asked, "Is Marisa going away?" Her sister said, "We don't want Marisa to go. Make her stay."

Her mother replied in a trembling voice, "Marisa has to go away, but she will be back soon."

It was all she could say without collapsing in tears. She would support Marisa and realistically it was the only way the family could survive. If they lost the cottage, as seemed likely if they did not get some money fast, the family would break up anyway. She had heard some horror stories of children put in orphanages and subjected to brutal treatment by the owners, while their parents were barely surviving on handouts, moving from one homeless shelter to another like unwanted cargo.

Emotionally, it was a different story. It was hard to accept that even if they could keep a roof over their heads, it was at the expense of losing their precious daughter, who had been such a source of comfort and maturity in difficult times, yet was so impulsive. She prayed Marisa would be fine and make a better life than she ever could in this dying village. Her daughter had the hope of a happier life ahead—things would turn out well for her, but as her two younger children ran into her outstretched arms, she could stem the flow of tears no longer.

Two days later, Georgi rang Marisa to confirm the travel arrangements. She would be leaving on a Wizzair flight from Sofia to London in five days. During that time, her father barely spoke to her. Although his initial anger had subsided into a resigned acceptance, he felt a sense of betrayal that she was abandoning the family. He could not yet accept he was no longer the breadwinner in the house and that his daughter, still only a child, had usurped his role. Although he never told Marisa, he loved her deeply and was very concerned about her living in a foreign land. Marisa did not have much life experience. That was partly their fault, but they had never had the money to travel. He had done all his travelling before they had kids. Even the battered old Skoda they had for trips was now a luxury they could no longer afford.

Marisa found his silences distressing, but her mother was a source of comfort. She understood her reasons for leaving and even helped her pack her few possessions, although much of the time she was in tears as she did so. Her brother and sister could barely comprehend why Marisa was leaving, and their persistent demands that she stay tore at her heart.

Going into college in those last days was a relief to escape the tense atmosphere at home, but even there her announcement she was starting a new life in Canada brought a mixed response. Most surprising of all was the reaction of her friend Deyana, who had first proposed the idea. As they walked out of the drab concrete college block for lunch, she flicked back her long blond hair and turned to Marisa.

"So you are actually going through with it then?"

"Yes," replied Marisa. "It was your idea!"

"Not so soon though. At least finish college."

"Deyana, I can't wait that long. Papa has lost his job at the steel mill. We have nothing coming in. We are broke. At least this way I can send some money back. They are a good agency. They will get me the visa and set up all the payments I want back here to the family, and they will set me up with a really nice family in Toronto."

Deyana peered at her friend with her penetrating hazel eyes. "Are you sure they are genuine Marisa?"

"Why shouldn't they be? They are putting me on a plane to Canada and I have not had to hand over any money. How can they be dishonest?"

"I'm sure it is fine Marisa. I just wish I had come with you to Sandanski."

"Yes well so do I. Maybe they can find you a job and you can join me in Toronto."

"Maybe, but not until I have finished college."

Marisa felt guilty about prematurely finishing her studies, and her tutor was not impressed. However, she reminded herself that circumstances had given her no choice. It seemed no one was genuinely happy for her and this reinforced her sense of isolation. However, she had always prided herself on her strength of character, and this made her more determined to seize the opportunity.

The day she left Sofia was one of the hardest days of her life. The family was already grieving her loss and the atmosphere around the house was like a funeral home. Her father barely left the coal bunker when she was around, and when he was, she could see her betrayal in his eyes. Marisa preferred him shouting and arguing to the stony silence he now greeted her with. When it was time to go, he had refused to accompany her on the bus to Sofia. He mumbled an excuse to her that it was too difficult, and he could hardly meet her gaze. However, he did hold his arms out to her and as they embraced she could feel the dampness of his tears in her hair. He gently whispered "***добър щастие ту любов***" (good luck my love) and then he disappeared up the lane toward the village.

There were more tears as she hugged her mother, and then Goran and little Iva before setting off on the bus for the long ride into Sofia. As she left, she gave them a rueful wave, not knowing when she would see them again. Had she known just how long, she would have never passed the gate from her house, but as she did so and her house and the life she had known passed out of sight, all her thoughts were focused on the unknown challenges which lay ahead.

CHAPTER 3

Marisa arrived at St. John's airport exhausted and bewildered after a long, arduous journey of over two days. The journey from Sofia to London had been tiring, but she had little time to rest as her instructions told her she was then required to run to the transfer area at Heathrow to board a flight within the hour. She barely had enough time to check through the long lines at passport control before grabbing her rucksack full of her worldly possessions from the baggage reclaim and sprinting across the airport to transfer to a transatlantic flight bound for Montreal. Fortunately her English was good enough to follow the directions and she made the flight breathless with minutes to spare.

The flight to Montreal had been long and uncomfortable. The seat the recruiter had obtained for her was cramped and squeezed next to an overweight, elderly man who said little and seemed to spend the whole flight retching as if he was about to throw up. The sparse pre-packaged meals they served were at odd hours just as she was trying to sleep, and she had barely touched them. However, as she waited for her luggage she wished she had eaten more, as the pain of hunger gnawed away at her tired body.

The next flight from Montreal to St. John's, with a stopover in Halifax, had been little better. The plane was an old propeller driven bucket which reminded her of some of the decrepit military aircraft she had sometimes seen flying low over her village. The roar of the engines and the constant shaking as the plane was buffeted by strong winds had made sleep impossible, even though her body craved it by then. As the plane descended for landing in St. John's, she peered out at a bleak and colourless landscape, a sprawling town huddled against the coast, squeezed between deep ocean on one side and rugged land stretching to the horizon on the other side. The wind was howling and the place felt cold and hostile even from the plane.

As the aircraft skidded to a halt on the oily tarmac, she regretted not having checked on a map exactly where this place was. She felt disorientated and could not even be sure she was still in Canada. It was like the edge of the world, and as she stepped out into the biting March air she had never felt more alone.

The tall, uniformed immigration officer had thumbed through her passport and glared at Marisa for a full minute while furiously tapping away at his keyboard. He was probably wondering what had brought an Eastern European girl to these desolate shores, something she was beginning to wonder herself. He asked her what she was doing in Canada and her explanation of working as an au pair appeared to leave him unconvinced. However, he finally stamped her passport. After collecting her pack and clearing the small customs area she emerged into the arrivals lounge and sat down to rest for a while. A number of people waited to meet the flight, several with name boards but none of them for Marisa. She could not even get a coffee as she waited, because she had no local currency. Georgi had told her not to bother as everything would be taken care of upon arrival. As she waited, her dream of a great new life in Canada was fading already.

As Marisa slumped in the chair clutching her backpack, her exhaustion overcame her and she drifted off into a dreamless sleep. She did not know how long she slept but she was awakened by a steel-like grip on her upper arm, roughly shaking her awake. She flinched and grabbed at her pack, and when she looked up a large, angry face peered down at her. The man had the build of a professional bouncer and he hauled Marisa to her feet by her arm with ease. He grunted her name and she nodded dumbly, still half asleep. She detected a faint Russian twang. His scowl accentuated an ugly purple scar across his left cheek, and deep set blue eyes carried a glint of suppressed aggression.

He jostled her briskly out of the arrivals lounge, ignoring a few curious stares, and into the biting cold late afternoon wind. Outside the building, he waved to a vehicle parked further up the airport approach road, still gripping Marisa's arm, and a large Land Cruiser pulled up beside them. She was too startled to protest, and he bundled her into the back seat, threw her pack unceremoniously in the trunk and sat down opposite her.

Despite the spacious interior, his bulk seemed to fill the car. However, crammed into the corner were two frightened looking girls about Marisa's age. One had wispy blond hair, attractive but with a tiny, almost emaciated frame. The other girl had a fuller figure and short cropped black hair, but with very soft features and large green eyes that had a pleading look, as if she was silently begging Marisa for help. Like Marisa, they were not dressed for the bitter Canadian weather and were shivering.

The beefy Russian spoke to the driver in front. "Go, we have no time to waste. We have to make the rendezvous tomorrow morning."

The driver slammed into gear and with a furious lurch, the vehicle lunged forward and screeched out of the airport exit road.

Marisa decided to introduce herself. "Hi, I'm Marisa," she said in her best English to the girls.

The girls merely stared impassively at Marisa and said nothing. Despite the silence, she sensed their fear.

The Russian scowled at her, and his scar throbbed. "No talking," he growled.

His expression and tone carried enough of a threat for Marisa not to argue and she slumped silently into her seat, cold and hungry, and stared out at the dreary landscape. The airport was north of the main town and it was not long before they had left the wooden whitewashed buildings on the outskirts and were on a winding road which skirted a sweeping lake on one side and green open fields on the other. The driver lurched around each bend in the road as if he were fighting the steering wheel, and Marisa began to feel sick with the constant sharp turning. Her empty stomach did not help. She closed her eyes and mouthed a silent prayer. This was not how she had imagined it. She desperately wanted to sleep but as they were constantly thrown one way then the other, any chance of relaxation was impossible. Only the big Russian held steady, his bulk keeping him upright as the Land Cruiser roared and bucked around another bend. Fortunately there was no traffic on this small road as the driver insisted on using the full width of the road, particularly on blind hairpin turns.

Despite the noise of the engine, the atmosphere in the passenger seats was heavy with a tense, dead silence. At last she could bear it no longer and turned to their guide. She smiled faintly at him.

"You did not tell me your name," she said in a friendly tone.

"No I did not. Now be quiet."

"So what is your name?" she persisted.

"It is not important. Now be silent!"

There was something in his expression and his narrow blue eyes that told Marisa it was best not to push it. She glanced at the two girls and they both looked down at their feet to avoid catching her eye. The Russian yelled something at the driver in a language she did not understand and the driver accelerated, the beautiful wild scenery blurring past.

The journey continued for several hours. They skirted the coast for a time but then moved inland. After a while the rugged landscape had become monotonous and Marisa longed to stretch her legs, and was relieved when finally the driver pulled over by a small culvert and got out. They stretched their legs and allowed the girls to do so as well, but only one at a time and for barely a minute each. As Marisa gingerly stepped out from the heavy door into the bracing air, her legs were throbbing. She looked around and for a fleeting moment considered whether to make a run for it. She quickly dismissed the idea. The Russian was breathing down her neck and, despite his bulk, he looked like he could run fast. He was all muscle. Even if she escaped him, where would she go? They had not seen another human for over an hour. Only the magnificent osprey gliding overhead provided any company. This place was about as remote and desolate as anything she had known. Anyway, she was not sure what she would be running from. She still held onto the optimistic hope they would get to Toronto and she could start the promised au pair job as soon as possible. She was not a prisoner as far as she knew—the two men had not hurt her. They had just shown a complete lack of courtesy and respect, something which unfortunately happened more and more often in her own country.

She got back in and now the driver was sitting with them. He was darker, his olive complexion framed by a dark goatee beard. He just gawked at them, his thin lips upturned more in a sneer than a smile. He was not as bulky as the Russian, but his body still looked athletic and powerful. "I am Nasim," he announced proudly, smiling. A hostile grunt from the Russian discouraged any further conversation.

The journey continued on in silence, Marisa every so often drifting off in exhaustion before she was jolted awake, until the gloom descended and the twilight quickly turned to darkness. Nasim turned the vehicle off the road down a dirt track into a wooded area, where the trees pressed in and amplified the black night. After ten minutes bouncing down the rough track, they found a small clearing and parked under a large overhanging tree. The men quickly and skilfully assembled two large tents. The Russian pointed to the smaller tent and ordered the girls into the tent.

"In there, in there," he barked. They were all desperately cold and hungry by now and complied without argument. Nasim brought a few dirty blankets from under the seats in the car and threw them into the tent. He then passed them a bottle of water and a hunk of dry, hard bread for the girls to share.

The girls settled in for the night. Despite its size it was fairly cramped for three people. Marisa tried to start a conversation with the girls but they did not reply, just looked even more frightened, and Marisa was cut short by the harsh voice of the Russian right outside the tent.

"Silence!" he screamed.

Lying shivering in the tent, Marisa listened to the night sounds of the forest, the rustling and hooting of strange animals, noises she had never heard before. She heard the men talking and they had soon set up a camp fire, shadows flicking across the thin fabric of the tent, but too far away to provide much needed warmth. The men were talking, but she could not hear what they were saying. Every so often their conversation would be punctuated with a deep, throaty laugh. Rather than showing the two men as human, it sounded like a cruel, mocking chortle. She heard a mechanical clicking and managed to find a small tear in the fabric to peer at them. The Russian appeared to be loading a gun. He snapped the barrel shut and took aim directly at their tent and made a mock firing gesture. Once again the two men guffawed.

Why did they need guns? This was becoming more and more sinister. It was certainly not the way she had expected to spend her first night in Canada. She wrapped the thin blanket as tightly as possible around her, closed her eyes and drifted into a troubled sleep.

It seemed like Marisa had only just closed her eyes when a strident shouting of "Get up, get up!" invaded her dreams and she jerked awake. The men pulled the tent from around the girls and the cold rushed in. It was still dark, but in the east a faint glow beginning to spread across the clear night sky signalled the coming dawn. Marisa held the blanket to her for warmth but Nasim, with a crooked smile, whipped it away and began loading everything quickly in the truck. The other two girls, whose names Marisa realized she still did not know, also got up quickly, and they were herded back onto the Land Cruiser. As Marisa climbed in from the icy wind, she saw the glowing embers of a camp fire. The men had clearly been up for a while and had already eaten. It reminded Marisa of how hungry and parched she was. Having slept in her clothes and not washed for days, she felt dirty and bedraggled. The Russian roughly pushed her in to the vehicle and she turned angrily to him.

"Let go of me you dirty Russian!" she protested, slapping away his hand.

At first the Russian said nothing, just gave her the most malevolent glare, his eyes like coals. His face seemed to throb with anger and he bared his yellow teeth. For long tense moments they sized each other up, and as they did so Marisa's courage wilted under his savage glare.

"Don't ever call me a Russian," he said slowly but menacingly. Then, with lightning reflexes, he raised his palm and launched a stinging slap across Marisa's cheek in the blink of an eye. The blow was so hard her head snapped backwards and the pain shot through her like an electric surge. Her eyes blurred with tears and as she clutched at her cheek she felt the blood trickle from a split upper lip.

"I want to go home," she protested weakly, her tears now coming in floods.

"Your home is here with us. Get in. Now!" shouted the Russian, or whatever nationality he was.

She obeyed, still clutching her face. The girls were cowering in the corner and still said nothing, but they were clinging to each other for comfort. Their eyes held a mixture of pity and fear but they still did not speak. Nasim merely grinned and finished loading the vehicle before they bounced along the dirt track out of the forest and back onto the tarmac road.

Marisa really had no idea where they were going and how long it would take to get there. This place was more remote than any place she had ever been, and surrounded by these hostile strangers, she had never felt so isolated. This dream of a better life had so far been a nightmare. Her cell phone did not work here and there was no one she could call anyway. As she cried softly to herself, she realized she had no choice but to see where this terrible situation would end up.

The journey continued in silence, the Russian's threatening presence in the back ensuring no-one, least of all Marisa, would start a conversation. The sun soon climbed above the horizon and bathed the surrounding forests in a pale glow, as Nasim threw the vehicle round the bends and curves of the narrow road.

They passed through a small town on the edge of a vast lake. Marisa saw the sign flash by—Gander, population eleven thousand, but they sped right through the clean white store fronts of the main street, as if the proximity of other people was an unwelcome distraction. There was little traffic at this time and they jumped several lights where they could. Marisa saw the blinking lights of aircraft coming into land at the nearby airport, silhouetted against the rising sun. They stopped at a gas station on the edge of town and Nasim filled up as the Russian kept a close and baleful eye on the girls to make sure none of them were foolish enough to attempt an escape. Even Marisa felt her courage slipping and just stared out of the window at the vast lake shimmering into the distance.

They were soon on their way and Nasim passed the girls a bottle of water each, which they gratefully accepted. Marisa swigged the bottle in one go, her thirst overcome but her hunger pains sharper than ever. They soon left the lake behind and were in deeper forest, the traffic more sparse and the tall skeletal trees closing in, forming a canopy over the road in some places. Nasim continued to thrash the car around the winding roads, even where the road was bordered by a crash rail beyond which the ground dropped away into steep valleys or in some cases, prevented them from plunging into icy blue lakes.

They passed swiftly through several more small settlements, firstly Grand Falls Windsor, and then Badger, taking no time to stop. However, when they crossed a small river feeding one of the many lakes they were allowed to get out and wash, again one by one only, and always closely watched. Marisa felt dirty and scruffy and plunged her hands into the swiftly flowing brook to wash her face. She gasped in surprise at just how cold the water was, numbing her forearms, and she quickly withdrew them from the water and rubbed the circulation back into her arms.

Several hours later, by mid-morning, they arrived at a fairly large settlement called Corner Brook, a bustling town set in a broad valley at the mouth of a wide river. As they did so, the Russian brought out his cell phone and muttered something unintelligible. They still did not stop but they did leave the main highway and began bumping along a rutted track which ran parallel to the open river heading out toward the sea. Nasim had slowed down and was looking around anxiously as the Land Cruiser continued to bounce along, the girls inside being shaken around.

They drove further up the track, which soon widened out into a broad ledge that skirted a steep line of cliffs on one side. On the other side, about forty feet below, the waves crashed against the rocky shore and seagulls drifted in circles around the outcrops of rock, and sometimes veered toward the Land Cruiser out of curiosity. The track ran dangerously close to the edge at times and the girls hung on as they bumped along, the engine racing as it ascended around the imposing cliff face.

Before long, however, they were heading back down toward the rugged shoreline and the track suddenly ended adjacent to a series of caves, most of them above the waterline. The Russian got out and clambered over a series of rocks while Nasim got in the back and watched over the girls, still grinning inanely. Within fifteen minutes the Russian was back and the girls were ordered out of the vehicle and handed their packs, and he grunted at them to follow him.

It was hard work carrying their packs over the wet rocks, and Marisa, her light shoes totally unsuitable, nearly slipped several times. The Russian offered no help, just looked back and barked at them to hurry up. Marisa finally cleared the rocks and jumped onto a small sandy beach near a large cave entrance where the sea rolled in. Within the gloomy shadows of the cave Marisa could see a small wooden motor boat moored against the rock and two older men with weathered faces standing by it. They looked like fishermen, dressed in long waterproof trench coats and woollen caps. They greeted the Russian with a perfunctory nod and they shook hands as he strode up to them. Marisa saw him hand one man a brown envelope and he immediately ripped it open and thumbed through the contents. He grinned to the other man and they began preparing the small boat. The Russian grunted at the girls and pointed to the boat.

"We go for a boat ride, girls, yes?" he said. His face gave a perceptible flicker. It was the most he had spoken to them on the whole trip.

The girls stepped onto the boat and were herded down steep narrow steps into a tiny cabin, just enough room for them to huddle together with their packs, but at least it provided a respite from the icy wind that whipped in from the sea.

The Russian and the two fishermen stepped onto the deck and one untied the mooring rope and the boat was soon roaring out to the open sea. Out of the small porthole Marisa could see Nasim driving the Toyota back up the dirt track. Unfortunately the Russian had stayed close to them and his looming, threatening presence still clearly intimidated the two girls squeezed in with Marisa.

With the Russian on the deck talking to the two fishermen, his voice just audible over the drone of the engines, Marisa attempted conversation with the two girls. This time they plucked up the courage to speak in hushed tones, still wary of being heard.

The tiny blond girl introduced herself as Olivia. She lived in Macedonia with her sick mother and alcoholic father and had run away from home to work in Canada. A friend had introduced her to a very friendly man who arranged her passport and said he had arranged a job for her in Toronto as a waitress. They had even paid for her flight here. She had hoped to be able to send some of her money over to her mother when she was settled here. Everything seemed fine even though the flight had been long, but the Russian, whom she had heard Nasim refer to as Alexi, had been "scary" as she put it. She was even younger than Marisa, just turned sixteen, and if it was possible, Olivia's situation seemed even more desperate than her own.

The dark haired girl, Eveline, was older, at nineteen, and had no family to speak of. A Romanian gypsy girl, she had also been seduced by the promise of a better life in Canada rather than working in the chicken processing factory on a subsistence wage and living in a variety of hostels before she was moved on. People in Romania, she said, were too concerned about their own troubles, the poverty and the daily scraping to survive, to think about anyone else outside their immediate family. In her short life she had always been moved aside or ignored or frowned upon. Romanians hated travellers anyway, and this prejudice had coloured the way she had been treated. She had heard Canadians treated people of all races equally and with respect, so she had planned her escape for over a year. Now she was wondering if it was such a good idea.

"I have seen men like him before," she whispered. "It is the way he looks at us. I am afraid what may happen."

Marisa confidently assured her they were all on their way to a better life, even if Alexi their guide was an ignorant brute. When they reached Toronto they would take their jobs and be rid of him.

"Look at what he did to you," she said, pointing at Marisa's still puffy lip. "This man is very cruel." She had heard rumours when in Romania that sometimes girls recruited for work in other countries could be exploited, and the jobs did not really exist. She had never really believed this, especially in Canada, but now she was not so sure.

"I asked him about a job when we get to Toronto and he said he would make sure I was put to work. I wasn't sure what he meant and then he ordered us not to ask any more questions. He has a look I have seen before—he is a very bad man."

They lapsed into a fearful silence as they heard the clanging of boots on the metal stairs to the cabin. Alexi's huge bulk blocked any light from the open hatch and he surveyed the girls silently.

Marisa glared at him, her throbbing lip fuelling her contempt. "When do we get to Toronto?" she said. For all they knew, they were being taken by sea to another country.

"Soon," he scowled. "No more questions."

The girls lapsed into silence and Marisa peered out of the small porthole. They were out in the open sea, but the waves were mercifully subdued, as her still empty stomach would not have survived a rough journey. They heard the men upstairs laughing and caught snatches of their conversation above the drone of the engine.

"You have good produce here. Very attractive," they heard one of the fishermen say. The other one laughed and said this was much better than fishing. Alexi joined in a little, but it was mainly the voices of the fishermen they heard.

The journey lasted the whole day. At no time were the girls allowed on deck and the cramped and noisy conditions hardly allowed any room for sleep. They had barely had a few hours the previous night and despite the discomfort, Marisa's head bowed and she dropped off into an exhausted slumber. Her lumpy bed at home in Bulgaria felt like a distant memory, the last time she had really slept properly.

She woke from one of these troubled naps to the sound of the Russian barking at them to get ready. As she became fully awake, she felt her body aching with stiffness. It was an effort to move her legs, but Alexi was demanding they hurry up. It was now early evening and dusk was spreading across the sky. The engines had stopped and as she climbed stiffly up the stairs onto deck, she saw they were drifting about twenty yards from shore in shallow water by a small beach enclosed on all sides by steep rocky outcrops, bordered by trees, barely visible in the gloom.

Alexi ordered the girls onto shore and Olivia, seeing the distance to the beach, looked at him pleadingly. He just pointed and when she still hesitated he picked up her tiny frame with the ease of a doll and threw her over the side. She stood up in the shallow water, gasping and sobbing, and the Russian threw her pack in after her. She grabbed it and waded to shore as quickly as possible. The fishermen merely smirked and dragged on their cigarettes. Alexi then turned to Eveline and Marisa, and they did not need any further persuasion. Marisa took her pack and gently plunged into the water, holding her pack as high as possible. As she hit the water it rose past her waist and she gasped as the icy black water stabbed at her like a thousand sharp knives slashing every part of her lower torso. She quickly waded to the shore as fast as her rapidly numbing legs would allow and when she flopped onto the beach breathless, she rubbed them vigorously to bring back some feeling.

With the girls on shore, one of the fishermen started the engine and the boat swung around in an arc and idled close to shore. The Russian clapped the two men on the shoulder and grabbing his own pack jumped off the boat and onto the shore. The motor revved up and the boat circled back toward the open sea and was soon lost in the gloom.

Alexi cast furtive glances around him and silently pointed toward the steep rock face surrounding the beach. He slung his pack over his shoulder and headed to the base of the rocks, eyeing the girls cautiously. They had no choice but to follow—the only way off the beach was to climb.

The climb up the rock was an arduous one, punctuated by Alexi's barked commands to hurry up, while the girls struggled, weighed down by their backpacks and fatigue from lack of food and sleep. It was clear the Russian was anxious for them to leave the beach, and he urged them up the steep, slippery outcrop. They scrambled up as quickly as possible but it was slow progress. Marisa was at the rear and gently encouraged the two girls above her. Olivia was directly ahead and at one point she looked down. Her eyes widened in fright at how far up they were and she lost her concentration. Her right foot slipped and her whole body slid a few painful metres, almost knocking Marisa from her narrow ledge.

"Are you alright?" cried Marisa.

Olivia steadied herself. She had scraped her right knee as she slipped, and her torn trousers revealed a small gash from which blood trickled lazily. Balanced precariously on the ledge, Marisa ripped some cloth from her thin vest and tied it around Olivia's trembling knee as the girl sobbed softly, her breath in short gasps.

"Never look down!"

Olivia, still shaking and her eyes filled with tears, nodded in agreement and Marisa helped her off the ledge onto the next foothold. As they ascended, Marisa watched her very carefully, trying to quell her own fears. One slip could send them tumbling back to the rocks at the bottom, which was now a long way down.

It was slow and painful progress, but eventually Olivia and Marisa managed to scramble over the summit of the rock face. Eveline was already up and resting close by, and as they reached the top, Alexi hauled them like a sack of potatoes onto the grassy verge, and they collapsed on the cool, wet ground, breathing heavily. They hardly had time to catch their breath before the Russian was shouting at them again to get moving. Marisa felt her anger rising, but she saw the Russian's challenging look, and felt her swollen lip. Now was not the time. She quickly checked Olivia's knee. The blood had ceased trickling and she was able to move her knee freely.

The dusk quickly turned into a black night. In the distance they could see the shadows of a group of trees, and they stumbled on toward the trees in the darkness. Alexi stayed close to them, making sure none of them ran off in the gloom. She could feel his looming presence and his bulky silhouette. Their eyes adjusted quickly and Marisa could see they were headed for a large forest. The Russian had forced them to jog along and he urged them forward, cursing and occasionally lapsing into his native language. Marisa sensed that he appeared very tense but as they reached the forest and the canopy of trees closed in, he allowed them to slow down. However, as they staggered through the trees, a set of moving lights pierced the darkness. The lights swung round and they heard the drone of an engine not far away. Alexi instantly pushed the girls to the ground.

"Get down and stay down!" he spat at them.

The lights seemed to be aimed directly at them, and they were bathed in the glow of the vehicle's lights.

"Don't move," ordered Alexi, feeling for something in his pocket. He pulled out a small hand pistol and in the pale light he saw the Russian checking the barrel. However, the lights swung away from them, and they heard the vehicle move away into the distance, its tyres skidding on the dirt track.

Alexi breathed a sigh of relief. "We stay here for now." He pulled two thin blankets from his pack, and passed them to the girls. There would be no tents tonight. It was too dark to assemble, and Alexi was keen to ensure they could get away quickly if they needed to.

Marisa and Olivia huddled together for warmth in one blanket, and Eveline settled beside them in the other blanket. Marisa could see the black shape of Alexi peering at them in the blackness. It was clear he was on guard and would not be sleeping tonight. Despite the cold, Marisa soon heard Olivia snoring gently next to her and within minutes, she fell into a deep sleep.

CHAPTER 4

It was still the middle of the night when Alexi whipped off their blankets and ordered them to move. Marisa, still groggy, jerked awake with the cold and scrambled to her feet, quickly followed by the other two girls. The Russian rummaged into his backpack and hurled a half loaf of hard bread at them. The girls tore hungrily at the bread. As Marisa chewed rapidly on the tasteless bread, she thought how degrading this was, but by this time she was starving, much too hungry to care.

They barely had time to finish when Alexi growled at them to move on quickly. He was still as taut as a coiled spring and his tone had an underlying menace. He beckoned them to follow and they hoisted their backpacks on and followed him through the damp, soft undergrowth of the wood. He moved at a considerable pace and they found it difficult to keep up, but he did shine his flashlight behind him every so often to make sure the girls were close by. Marisa was tempted to make a run for it but she had no clue where she was, and without proper shelter, could easily perish in this cold. As it was her bones ached and protested against the cold, the hunger and the interrupted sleep.

She could see in the gloom the Russian glancing at his watch. She had no idea of the time as her watch had slipped off and crashed to the ground when she was climbing the cliff from the beach. The thin crescent moon provided a weak, thin light. Dawn was far off, however, and there was a cacophony of nocturnal howls and whistles from the woods.

They soon reached a clearing and in the pale light Marisa could see a tarmac road that wound its way past the trees. After twenty minutes of waiting they heard the distant rumble of an engine and

Alexi pushed them down onto the damp earth and listened carefully, his senses ablaze.

"Keep still," he urged them.

He took out his gun and held it steady, aiming carefully at the set of lights which swung round a bend and headed down the road toward them. They were barely ten feet away from the road.

Marisa was convinced they had been seen as the lights illuminated their prone bodies, especially as it slowed down very near them, its headlights dazzling. Alexi shielded his eyes and stood up. This was not another patrol car. The vehicle came to a halt and flashed its lights three times, waited a minute and repeated the action. Alexi gave a visible sigh of relief and headed toward the vehicle, still holding the gun.

He looked into the driver's side window, gun still poised, but as the driver stepped out of the car he slipped the pistol back into his pocket and embraced the driver. They chatted excitedly. It was the most animated Marisa had seen the Russian. Alexi pointed toward the girls on the ground, and the driver beckoned them over. Like Alexi, the driver was a stocky, muscular man who seemed to have no neck, just a meaty head on huge bulky shoulders and a frame distorted by too many strenuous workouts. He had almost shaven blond hair, and from their discussion it was obvious they were countrymen. Marisa could only make out the odd clipped word of Russian, but little more.

The vehicle was a small van that had a large grill over the back windows, like a dog catcher van. As the girls nervously headed toward the van on Alexi's instructions, the other man grinned at them, more like a snarl.

"I am Serge," he announced as he opened the back doors of the van. The girls began to climb in as he held the doors, prompting them in. There were no seats in the back and the stench was suffocating, as if the dogs that no doubt were usually transported had urinated in there. As Marisa climbed in, Serge put his hand under her butt, his chubby fingers digging into her buttocks as she paused gagging in the doorway.

"You have a firm arse," he leered. "I will try you out later."

Marisa could take no more. She spun round and slapped his hand away. "Get off me you creep," she spat.

The driver's face went very red. He did nothing for a full moment, but Marisa could almost see his temper rising through his body like a kettle coming to boil. The other girls sensed this too and despite the smell in the van, they cowered into the corner. Serge slowly raised his hand and was just about to bring it slamming down onto Marisa when a strong hand caught his wrist.

"No, Serge, we need the goods undamaged. Strict orders my friend."

Marisa felt her panic rising and instinctively tried to make a run for it. She evaded Serge's clumsy grab at her and was suddenly running blindly into the freezing night to nowhere, just to get away as far as possible. Her breath came in short, wheezing gasps but as she ran her legs protested and began aching quickly. Her body, weak from lack of food, would not respond to her mind's urgent demands, and as she heard the gentle but urgent padding of footsteps on the soft ground behind, her legs felt like they were wading through treacle. She kept going, trying to ignore the feeling that her throbbing legs were about to burst, and she was in the forest, blindly thrashing through the undergrowth.

Breathing hard, she tried to dart for cover but the undergrowth dragged at her light shoes. As she ran blindly she came to the horrible realization that even if she escaped she would never survive the night in the frigid temperatures, not in her light cardigan and thin trousers. She paused slightly and as she stepped forward again a trailing vine caught her foot and she was sent sprawling onto the soft earth. She clawed at the ground to get up but as she did so a pair of huge, rough hands spun her round and she faced the Russian, his face twisted in anger. He said nothing, just growled like one of the area's resident bears. He hoisted her over his shoulder like a sack of potatoes and strode back to the dog van where his colleague was waiting.

"She is a feisty one," he said to Alexi. "Should we teach her a lesson in obedience?"

"No, Serge," he replied. "I told you. The goods reach the rendezvous in best condition. I have seen your "lessons" before. We want her earning right away. How would I explain it to the boss if she arrived all black and blue?"

He pulled her down from his shoulder and slammed her against the side of the dog van. Marisa groaned and sobbed, and the hostile voices of the two Russian thugs echoed through her, but she did not understand their meaning.

"What will we do with her?"

"I think you know Serge."

Serge nodded knowingly and grinned as he took out from the passenger foot well a large black hold-all. He unzipped it and rummaged inside and then produced a large dirty looking needle filled with a clear liquid. He tapped it gently with his finger and squirted a little of the liquid to test the syringe. Then Serge began advancing menacingly toward Marisa.

Her eyes widened in terror and she struggled frantically, but Alexi had her in an iron grip, his fingers digging deep and bruising her thin arms. He held her right arm steady as Serge, with another malevolent grin positioned the syringe.

"This is the part I love best," he said as he plunged the syringe deep into Marisa's arm. She bit her lip with the sharp agonizing pain and her eyes rolled back and she went instantly limp as a dark oblivion overtook her.

She could not be certain how long she had been unconscious but she awoke with a raging thirst. She was still dressed in the same clothes which by now had become totally ragged, and her body felt soiled and filthy. She could not remember the last time she had washed properly. She was lying on a lumpy bed with a metal rail like a hospital bed. She remembered the needle and the pain as it was jabbed and pushed into her arm and she instinctively tried to raise her arm. As she did so, she met with solid resistance and there was a sharp clang of metal on metal. She realized immediately that she was chained to the rails. Her surroundings gradually came into focus and she looked around her.

The small cell-like room in which she was imprisoned had ashen plastered walls that were heavily stained and damaged, bare brick showing through in places. There were various messages and graffiti scrawled on the walls and a pair of thin, torn curtains were draped across the window. A single light bulb hung despondently from a frayed wire but its pale light barely reached all of the corners of the room. There was no other furniture except a tiny, battered wooden dresser table and a soiled chamber pot. On the table was a cup of dirty looking water but she reached out with her free hand and gulped it down. She felt her bruised lip. The swelling had gone but it was still tender.

A pallid light filtered through the curtains but did little to dispel the gloom. The room had the smell of stale sweat and desperation. Her head felt as if it had been squeezed in a crusher. Whatever drug they had injected to knock her out had some very unpleasant side effects, and she did not know where she was or how long she had been in this squalid room. She began to feel a rising panic and tried to prise her wrist out of the manacles, but they were tight and the metal rail was unyielding. She began shouting for help in the hope that someone outside might hear her cries, and within minutes she heard the click of a bolt being opened outside the door.

Her two captors, Alexi and Serge both entered the room. Their combined bulk filled the doorway and she shrank back in the bed. They both grinned at her, baring their tobacco stained yellow teeth.

"Welcome to Montreal," Alexi said. "I thought you would be up sooner but you have been out for nearly two days. I must apologize for my colleague Serge. He is very enthusiastic with his, ah, needles. You might do well to remember that."

Serge gave another nasty grin and made a motion of injecting with an imaginary needle.

"What do you want from me?" she said as forcefully as she could. Her voice just sounded weak and reedy and she was almost shaking with fear. Without the other girls for company she now felt isolated and vulnerable.

"We don't want anything from you. But our boss does. You will see him soon enough," replied Alexi. His smile now disappeared and his expression was hostile. He quickly unchained her and pulled her to her feet. "Now get undressed."

"What?"

"You heard me. We wish to look at you."

She gave a short gasp of panic and for a split second thought about fleeing but they barred the doorway completely and began to close in on her. She stepped back against the wall and the men waited expectantly. She slowly pulled her sweater and torn vest off and then her trousers. Serge's breath came in short excited gasps as she stood there in front of them in her ragged underwear.

"All of it please." Alexi pointed to her bra and knickers.

She stood there shocked, unmoving. "Quickly, or I shall do it for you myself and I will not be so gentle."

Marisa's head was throbbing and she was choked with humiliation as she unclipped her bra and let it fall to the floor. She then slipped off her knickers and stood there naked in front of them, one arm over her small breasts and the other protecting her middle.

"Hands behind your back," he ordered her.

Marisa had no choice but to comply and as she stood there for what seemed an eternity of humiliation, Alexi merely looked her up and down and appraised her as Serge continued to wheeze and began perspiring.

"Easy Serge," said Alexi. "You will maybe get your chance soon, yes?"

For a horrible moment Marisa thought they were going to attack her there and then, but Alexi merely gave an approving nod at her long legs and slim figure and ordered her to put her clothes back on.

"Now you can eat."

Her two captors allowed her to wash and change her clothes in privacy although she could not look them in the eye without a sense of shame. She felt that when they looked at her, the men were picturing her naked again. She was exposed and vulnerable and could sense the looks passing between them.

Alexi informed her she was being taken to Toronto to meet "the Boss" and they would be driven to Toronto that afternoon. She could tell they were in an old deserted house in a run down street in an old part of town. It was very quiet apart from the howl of stray dogs. All the rooms were locked or had bolts and there was no way to escape the house. In any case the two Russians maintained a very close presence and it was hard to escape their attention. As she waited in the graffiti stained hallway, another girl entered. She turned and saw it was Olivia. Marisa broke out into a huge smile of relief at seeing her and she hugged Olivia tight. The tiny Macedonian girl gave her a weak smile and as Marisa looked into her eyes she could see Olivia had suffered the same humiliation. They did not need to speak. Marisa hugged her again to show she understood. Olivia was not as strong as her and Marisa wanted to protect her as much as she could from these brutal thugs.

Alexi began to push them roughly to the door. "We go now," he growled.

He led them out of the rear entrance of the house into a dark, narrow alleyway strewn with rotting garbage. Serge's dog van was waiting and Alexi bundled them in and sat in the front with a stern warning to Marisa not to cause any more trouble. Marisa looked around but the high walls of the alley blocked any natural light and it was so long that the street at either end was just a distant shaft of light. No one would have seen them leave, and there was little point in shouting for help. The truck sped out of the alleyway and flowed into the traffic heading out of the city southwest toward Kingston. The traffic was light and they made good progress out of the sprawling metropolis before hitting the auto route over the vast Ile aux Tourtes Bridge and heading swiftly onwards. It was clear they were anxious to leave Montreal as quickly as possible. Alexi spoke quietly into his cell phone. In the roar of the traffic she could only hear snatches of what he said, but his tone was respectful, almost polite. She guessed Alexi was briefing the Boss he had spoken of earlier.

The journey was tedious and long across vast unbroken stretches of highway. The dog van was extremely uncomfortable and the powerful stench of sweating dogs was still there, leaving them gasping for fresh air. Marisa could only catch brief discussions with Olivia before the Russian ordered silence.

Marisa stared out at the landscape rushing past but even this was through the wire mesh of the dog grill. Whatever drug they had injected her with had left her limbs feeling heavy and lethargic and her head was still pounding, made worse by the awful dog smell. Her last proper shower had been at home in their village and the dog smell probably masked her own body odour. Her body felt dirty and defiled, not just with the hardship of the journey, but with the terrible humiliation she had suffered. She found it difficult to banish from her mind the dissolute expressions of the two Russians as they had studied her exposed body.

As she stared outside, trying to claw the images from her mind, she saw the coastline of a vast, placid lake shimmering in the weak light of the late afternoon sun. It stayed with them for several hours as the road followed the coastline and it was dusk when they began to enter the outskirts of the city. She peered out and recognized the impressive skyline immediately. Marisa had smuggled out a book on Toronto from her local library and had studied the photos of her destination. She recognized instantly the vast spire of the CN Tower twinkling in the distance, and the towers of the business district were lit like beacons in the fading light of dusk.

At last, after an arduous and painful journey, she was arriving in Toronto, where her dreams of a better life for her and her desperate family lay. Marisa could never have imagined arriving in these circumstances, and somehow her dream was being slowly squashed by bitter reality.

CHAPTER 5

Akhmad Timayev's plush penthouse condominium on the top floor of one of the many uptown Toronto apartment blocks displayed all the trappings of a successful businessman, and in a sense he was exactly that. He never tired of viewing the Toronto skyline, especially at dusk, when the sun drifted gently below the horizon in the west, silhouetting the distinctive downtown view. Every time he gazed out from the large window that took up the whole external wall, he was reminded of how far he had come in the five years since he had fled Grozny and sought political asylum in Canada.

The first year had been the most difficult, when he was not certain whether he would be sent back by the Canadian immigration authorities to face certain persecution and possibly death. As a separatist rebel fighter, Timayev had been at the heart of the war for independence against the Soviets, a relentless and bloody fight that had claimed so many lives of his fellow countrymen—not just soldiers but his own family. His mother had been killed in the Russian raid on Caucasus, when the Russians sent over one hundred thousand troops to free the Dagestan region and quite literally flattened Grozny in the process. He could vividly remember the bombs and the fighter planes roaring through the scorched sky, shooting indiscriminately as civilian women and children scattered in all directions in total panic, fleeing buildings which were crumbling around them.

With the Russian army closing in, he had come back from the fighting with his unit to help the people in Grozny to escape, although it had been a futile effort. As the fighter planes and bombs pounded the city, the Russian ground troops had waited on the fringes, ready to finish the operation and root out the rebel fighters. His unit had reached the city without confrontation, but had been powerless against the bombardment. He reached his mother's apartment block and saw the concrete structure in ruins, the whole front of the building ripped away to reveal the inside of each apartment, grey and lifeless. In blind hope, he had reached his mother's apartment on the sixth floor, and had forced his way past the rubble into the apartment. Even after all this time, he still burned with anger and grief at the memory of seeing his mother's crushed and lifeless body trapped under a fallen concrete beam, her hair still swaying in the breeze that drifted in from the huge tear in the outside wall. His grief was compounded because he did not even have the chance to give her a decent burial. If ever he was to revenge her death, he had to make sure he was alive to do it, and survival had been his first priority as the Russian army closed in.

By some miracle, Timayev had slipped through the huge Russian assault squad and escaped from the city, but with so many of his compatriots captured and killed in action, his band of rebel fighters were decimated and powerless against the Russian onslaught. For the near future at least, the Chechen uprising had been crushed in a savage manner, with countless women and children dead or dying amongst the ruins of Grozny.

He fled to the countryside but it was only a temporary respite as the Russian army continued to quell any further uprising, killing rebel soldiers mercilessly and in brutal fashion. Staying in Chechnya under Russian occupation could only end one way, and so he made the desperate decision to exile himself from his beloved nation and to avoid the fate of his brother a few years earlier, one of the thousands of Chechen "disappeared."

He had managed to secure passage to Canada, and although he knew very little about the country, he knew it was a land of democracy, an alien concept in his homeland. With no passport or documentation to support his cause, he had fought bitterly to stay in the country as the threat of deportation back to Chechnya had seemed a real probability. He had, however, been lucky enough to be represented by a brilliant immigration and human rights lawyer who had managed to persuade the government he represented no threat and would almost certainly be put to death if he were sent back to his homeland.

It had taken over a year of legal argument and counter arguments, but during that difficult time he had developed some very useful contacts. Those contacts were able to give him glowing testimonies which helped persuade the authorities to allow Timayev to stay.

What had helped Timayev in the first year, and the four years since, were two specific qualities. The first was a surprising entrepreneurial ability to seize opportunities when they arose and to establish contacts and associates who could help him achieve his goals. The second was a complete disregard for the value of human life, a trait instilled in him as a frustrated teenager unable to live freely in his country of birth, and later as a rebel fighter when killing became his stock-in-trade.

Living on the streets in Toronto left one vulnerable, but also provided an avenue to the underground economy, the shadowy world of drugs and vice few people saw. Most homeless people took drugs eventually, if only to help them escape the miserable daily struggle for survival, and for many it was an even faster route to self-destruction. Timayev had himself taken amphetamines and progressed to crack cocaine. His supplier had mistaken him for just another feckless and vulnerable client, a fatal mistake. When he began to dilute the drugs to increase his profits, he assumed his miserable clients would be too stoned or too weak to object. He was badly wrong, and Timayev, suffering another injustice, decided retribution was needed, not just for himself but for the dealer's other clients.

With the same lack of mercy he had seen from the former Communist soldiers, he slit the dealer's throat and left him to bleed to death in a deserted back alley. With the skill of a seasoned soldier, the act took barely seconds and he left no clues. The police had another unsolved mystery on their hands, and given the victim's track record, did not try too hard to find the killer. As far as they were concerned, the streets were cleaner as a result and even if they found the culprit, a medal rather than prison would have been the preferred result.

As always, the rumour on the street was closer to the truth than any half-hearted police investigation, and Timayev suddenly found he had earned a grudging respect amongst the city's finest drug lords, pimps and criminal fraternity. From being another petty thief heading for drug induced oblivion, he had been promoted to someone who suddenly had a reputation, someone not to mess with. In true Romanesque fashion, he took over the mantle of his vanquished opponent and his career in the drug trade had begun.

That career proved to be very lucrative in a very short time. His business acumen and negotiating skills helped him to achieve some reductions in the unit costs for the range of drugs he was peddling. These were mainly cannabis, cocaine and crack but as his network expanded, he graduated into the supply of heroin and methamphetamine. Before long he was operating not on street corners but in a small rented office with a loyal list of clients who he treated with respect and never ripped off, unlike the previous dealer who had bullied and defrauded his clients until he met Timayev. The respect was mutual, not only because he had killed, but because he provided his clients with fresh needles every time, an innovation which also impressed the middle men who supplied him. He figured that a client who had died from an infected needle was no longer of any financial use to him. It was better to keep his clients "healthy" so they would come back for more.

However, the competitive nature of the street drug industry meant inevitably he would suffer the indignity of someone muscling in on his territory, especially as his street presence was limited by the fact he was working from an office. A second brutal slaying cemented his reputation, although he could claim self defence, as his opponent had attacked him first. His lean frame made him look an easy target, but his military hardened body was wiry and flexible, and he had been thoroughly trained to kill with his bare hands in a variety of ways.

Even so, he realized after this incident that he could not build his business alone. He needed a bodyguard in case he was caught by surprise, and as his supply chain customers increased, he recruited several of his own countrymen, the only people he could really trust, to help with the deals. He took on more of a management role, and he was good at it.

With his growing reputation as a tough but fair negotiator and his highly trained security team in place, his network of dealers began to spread rapidly. This meant he needed to encroach on the territory of other street dealers. Few of these were by now as well organized as Timayev's small but elite band of operatives, and when they met resistance, his team crushed them with ruthless efficiency. He made a point of being personally present at any interrogations or elimination of competitors, even where his growing army had the authority and ability to carry out his orders. He felt it was important to give a personal touch to such matters, and this further enhanced his fearsome reputation amongst the underground drug fraternity.

The middlemen were happy to deal with Timayev, even when he established control of key strategic areas with impunity by eliminating the competition. They were not really interested whether it was a small time drug dealer or Timayev they did business with, as long as they had an outlet on the street. However, even the middlemen respected his strong negotiating skills and his ruthless, psychotic approach and made some price concessions, further strengthening his balance sheet and his status. Suddenly Timayev was starting to make some serious money and he used this to help his neighbours in what was a poor and troubled area of Toronto. He had many clients from this group, and he always treated them well, offering fair prices and only supplying enough drugs to keep them addicted but not to overdose. He and his team helped with neighbourhood disputes, fighting for old widows with officious landlords trying to evict them, or mediating petty quarrels such as unpaid debts. All of this was done with a gentle persuasive hand but with an implied threat that if his directives were disobeyed, the gentle hand would become an iron fist. He also offered protection to his community. When some young punks in the neighbourhood attacked a disabled client of his, they suddenly disappeared before their dismembered remains turned up in a city dumpster in a back alley on the east side a couple of weeks later.

However, his almost legendary reputation in the criminal fraternity was inevitably going to bring him to the attention of the mainstream police. He was careful to ensure that few of the disappearances could lead back to him, but he remained a suspect in a number of unsolved killings, and he had been called in for questioning by the local homicide squad several times. He had been too shrewd and skilful to be outmanoeuvred, especially when it was clear the police often had no real admissible evidence. Even so, he decided he needed to buy off a key officer and his team researched and selected a couple of them.

It was an audacious and risky move, kidnapping a high profile police officer in the narcotics unit, but a great success. It was amazing how the immediate threat of a grisly death while talking to your young family on the telephone with gruff foreign voices in the background focused the mind. The officer agreed to Timayev's requests and his promise of loyalty was cemented with a considerable supplement to his police pension and the threat that if his loyalty wavered, his family, who Timayev made sure were frightened but unharmed, would be targeted.

This tactic had proved valuable and with inside help, he was able to diversify into the lucrative trade of human trafficking. This business opportunity arose when a client offered the services of his "girls" in part payment for a drug debt. He took up the offer out of curiosity. By now he was earning so much, another few thousand dollars would not be missed, and he was keen to explore this vice, especially as he had been somewhat abstinent since he arrived in Canada. He enjoyed their company and quickly developed a real liking for the company of prostitutes, and became a regular user of the escort services. As he talked to the various girls who shared his bed for cash, he found they all had pimps who would be making lots of money.

He decided to research the business, and with his considerable network of contacts, was able to set up a number of brothels unmolested by the police with the appropriate payments. It was clear in Toronto the appetite for escorts was insatiable, not just from the underground but from the working class and white collar middle class sections as well. The demand was mainly for Korean, Japanese and other oriental girls, but Timayev decided to diversify the market by introducing mainly Eastern European women. He set up supply chains in Bulgaria, Macedonia, Romania and several other Eastern bloc countries through a network of recruiters, and now had a highly profitable business running alongside his core activity of drug dealing. In fact he had just received a call from his faithful and loyal compatriot Alexi with the good news that the human cargo was on its way, having safely negotiated the tricky journey from St. John's. They would be arriving in less than an hour, and he wanted to be at the house to greet them.

The house was in one of the poorer neighbourhoods north of downtown, where crime and vice was part of the social fabric of the society and violence was always lurking in the background. As he cruised toward the house in the dark, there were few people about. Most of the sensible law abiding citizens would have shut themselves away from the cold hostile outdoors as darkness fell, hoping tonight their house would not be chosen, or if it was, their flimsy locks would repel any would-be burglars. When night fell, a different breed suddenly appeared. There were the whores and the kerb crawlers, the park prowlers and the drunken hoodlums, or the small time dealers peddling their stash, some of them working for him. After five years, this was his patch, his stomping ground. Although he had long since escaped the deprivation for his plush condo, most of his daily business was still done here, and people knew and respected him in this area. Sometimes the respect was born out of fear, but Timayev would not have it any other way. He always kept a Russian made Baikal MCM pistol and a German combat knife handy just in case, and could use them skilfully. He had tired of the lack of privacy in having a constant bodyguard and figured he had the ability and the means to fend off most attacks, except from a sniper, where a bodyguard would be useless in any case.

He pulled up by the house and waited for Alexi and Serge to arrive. Despite the cold, he decided to get out and take a walk along the neighbourhood before taking a call and entering the house to check on business.

The dog truck pulled off a major route into the city and seemed to weave in and out a number of dark and narrow back streets before it pulled up outside a large but tumbledown Victorian house. Marisa could not see too well outside of the truck and it was now dark, and there were few street lamps in this area to pierce the gloom. She had no idea where she was, but it was a great relief to get out of the disgusting truck. The smell seemed to cling to every fibre of her body and she felt as dirty as a farm pig after several days travelling from St. John's. As she stepped out, Alexi handed her a black piece of cloth and motioned to her eyes.

"Put it on," he ordered gruffly.

"No way," she protested.

"I am not asking you," he responded, drawing closer in a threatening way.

He handed one to Olivia and she hesitated and then placed it gingerly over her head. Serge straightened it and began to lead her into the house. Alexi waited expectantly, and she decided there was little use in protesting unless she was prepared to risk another slap. She put it on and Alexi roughly guided her into the house. She stumbled up a set of stairs and was herded into a dank smelling bedroom. As the girls took their blindfolds off, the two men disappeared from the room and they heard the click of a lock behind them. They were imprisoned in the small room. Marisa immediately went to the window but it had been blacked out and was barred. She tried the lock but it was sealed tight. The room was lit by a single threadbare light bulb, a large double bed and dressing tables, and the room was covered in bright but sickly looking flock wallpaper in a vain attempt to add cheer to this drab room. The girls were left waiting for nearly half an hour before the door opened, and in walked a lean, muscular, tough looking man with close cropped brown hair and haunting grey eyes.

"Ladies, good evening," he said graciously. "My name is Akhmad Timayev."

CHAPTER 6

Following behind Timayev was a huge, hairy mountain of a man with dead, expressionless eyes, a long, straggly beard and wearing a flowing Moroccan style caftan. He had a large Kalashnikov rifle slung over his shoulder, and huge military style hiking boots. In fact he looked to Marisa as if he was about to join an insurgency there and then. He stood in front of the doorway, an irresistible object against which any chance of escape would be impossible. His arms were thicker than Marisa's thighs and she suspected he would probably be able to crush her neck with one hand, expending hardly any effort.

The huge man held both of the girl's backpacks and he slung them down beside Timayev.

"Welcome to Toronto," began Timayev. His smile disappeared. "I believe you have not had a very pleasant trip. A little precaution on my part, having you fly into Newfoundland. A lot more difficult for you to be traced than if you had arrived directly into the city." He paused and added ominously, "But then you are not here for your comfort."

The huge soldier had already been through their packs and he handed Timayev the passports for the two girls. Timayev held them up for the girls to see. "You will not need these anymore. You are now my property. I purchased you both for ten thousand Euros each from my European suppliers. With the additional cost of bringing you here I have made a considerable outlay and I am looking for a return on my investment. You are both in debt to me for twenty thousand Euros and I expect the debt to be paid off. The good news for you is you will be able to start doing this immediately by servicing my clients."

Marisa glanced over at Olivia who was looking very frightened and started to weep. Marisa herself felt weak, not just from the hunger and exhaustion that had marked her journey to this depressing house, but from the confirmation of what she had suspected ever since the slap she received from Alexi. She was a prisoner, but worse still, a slave. She rocked slowly from side to side.

Timayev's tone became serious, almost threatening. "I should warn you that any refusal to do your job will be dealt with swiftly and painfully."

Timayev shot a meaningful glance in the direction of his enormous associate. The man gave a menacing grin to the girls, and it chilled Marisa to the bone. His twisted smile held more threat than any words.

"I am from the glorious Republic of Chechnya, but Rahmon is from Tajikistan. It is a country which has known its share of conflict, but I have never come across a man from the region that has such a propensity for violence. He does seem to enjoy inflicting pain very much, especially for some strange reason on women, and he is good at it. You shall work for me and you will enjoy doing so, and if I hear of any dissatisfied customers you will be punished." Still clutching the passports, he held them up again and ceremoniously ripped them to shreds with his powerful hands.

His tone relaxed slightly and smiled. "I am not being a very good host. You must be hungry and you both smell like the dog truck Serge brought you in. Rahmon will show you where to get a shower and then you can eat before you start work."

By this time Olivia was crying openly and Marisa was numb with shock. They were made to follow the Tajik through a long, dimly lit landing with locked doors on both sides. They could hear through the thin walls the soft moaning and grunts of other clients, but the noise barely registered through her shock. Everywhere was a maze of locks and barred windows, a depressing and seedy place. Even the bathroom was locked but Rahmon opened it and pointed to a dingy communal shower, with dirty white tiles and stained floors. There were two thin towels on the floor by the shower.

As Marisa showered she could sense the Tajik's menacing presence in the doorway. When they had finished drying off he handed each girl a cheap looking camisole and ordered them to put it on. The lingerie was thin and see-through, its bland pastel colours doing little to hide their bodies underneath. Marisa felt degraded and vulnerable in this horrible outfit, especially under Rahmon's impassive stare. They were herded toward separate rooms but as he tried to push Olivia into one room she clung onto Marisa, afraid that if she let go she would be truly alone to face this nightmare they had found themselves in. Rahmon tore her grip away from Marisa with effortless ease, as if he were swatting a fly, and roughly pushed the sobbing girl into the room and locked the door.

Rahmon quickly bundled Marisa into another sparsely furnished bedroom and as he closed the door she heard the turn of the lock and his heavy steps thudding down the hallway. The room had a double bed with an iron frame and patterned but dirty sheets. The room was decorated in a deep red, and the lounge seat in the corner of the small room was a gaudy patterned scarlet. The diffuse light from the single light bulb hanging limply on its fraying cord reflected off the walls to give the whole room a garish red glow in a poor attempt to appear alluring. It felt superficial and cheerless, especially as there were sturdy steel bars on the windows. It had a door to a small bathroom with a toilet and closet, and a tiny bath with a shower attachment.

After a time a plate of cold chicken and vegetables was pushed under the door and she took a glass of water from the chipped and stained sink in the bathroom. She hungrily devoured the food and lay on the bed emotionally drained, thinking about Olivia, so vulnerable and innocent. How had they come to be here? She lay on the bed but despite her fatigue sleep would not come, although it was nearly midnight.

She heard the lock turning and the tough looking Chechen man entered.

Timayev strode in and immediately began undressing by the side of the bed and got in beside her. She could see his body was wiry and muscular but had ugly purple lacerations across his chest and legs. He also had an intricate set of dragon style tattoos across his upper chest and powerful arms.

He turned to her as she cowered away from him. "You are my property now. If you do what you are told and you please me then you will find it is not so bad here. We will treat you well, and you will make lots of money for me. You are a beautiful girl and you will satisfy my clients. I think you know what will happen if you do not. No one knows you are here and no one will miss you."

As soon as he had seen the Bulgarian girl, Timayev had decided he wanted her. Despite her dishevelled appearance when he had first seen her, she was tall and slim with long, tanned legs, just the way he liked them. Her olive complexion, accentuated by her dark eyes and golden-brown hair held the hint of untouched, exotic beauty. He had to have her. He began groping at her thin camisole, his thick powerful fingers probing her body. "I like to test the goods first," he murmured as he began to move on top of her.

Marisa had no choice but to let this brutal soldier run his rough hands over her body and allow him to remove her flimsy lingerie. He was clumsy but not aggressive and she submitted to him.

She said nothing and drew into herself, as if her mind at least could escape the abuse her body was suffering.

As he lay on top of her grunting and pushing his hard body down on hers, she forced her mind to drift away, as if her docile submission belonged to some other person. It could not be Marisa, because she was strong and independent and would never allow such a terrible thing to happen to her. Through all the difficult times back in her village, which now seemed an eternity away, she had been the strong one in her family, the one who would save them from the poverty that threatened to engulf them. Now she was a prisoner, and a slave of the worst kind, one which insulted her morality and her strict upbringing. How had she come to this? What had led her to this terrible place?

Timayev finished with one final cry of ecstasy and then silently dressed and left. As he did so, Rahmon peered into the room, again giving a twisted, chilling grin before he closed and locked the door.

Marisa lay naked on the bed, not moving. An overwhelming sense of shame and guilt washed over her and she began sobbing with grief for the innocence and purity she had lost, something that could never be replaced. A part of her had died and she would never feel the same. Her body convulsed with sobbing for a long time before she composed herself and took a shower in the cramped bathroom. She scrubbed hard to wash away the filth, but it was not outside her body, and no matter how hard she rubbed, it did not help.

Before the night was over, Rahmon brought in three more men and she discovered what it was like to be a whore. As each of these overweight, repellent men lay their sweaty heaving bodies on top of her to fulfil their twisted desires, she lay there silently as they declared how beautiful she was, as if she were there of her own free will. After each session she showered and furiously scrubbed her tainted body, trying to scrub away the dark memory of what she had experienced. She knew, however, that she would never forget the humiliation and the degradation of this night. She felt cold and dead inside, as if the violation she suffered had torn out her very soul.

As the last man left, and the first faint fingers of a breaking dawn slowly began to filter through the barred windows, Rahmon's huge bulk filled the doorway. He wiped his beard on his caftan and spat on the floor.

"You sleep now. There will be plenty of men to look after tomorrow," he taunted. He shut the door and she heard the metallic click of a lock being turned. Her exhaustion allowed her to sleep, but it was full of dark and fitful dreams full of rough looking men waiting their turn, and she woke several times covered in sweat, her heart pounding.

Later that day she was allowed to visit the kitchen area in the house, always closely supervised, where other girls forced to work as prostitutes, a few very young but their faces drawn and haggard beyond their years, regarded her with a disinterested, resigned expression. Amongst them she saw Olivia, her eyes red as if she had cried all night. She spotted Marisa and she ran to her and began to cry again. They hugged each other, saying nothing, understanding what each had been through, knowing their lives had been irrevocably changed.

CHAPTER 7

Over the next few days and weeks, Marisa's miserable routine established itself. The large rambling Victorian house was actually two townhouses knocked into one, a detached property with eight bedrooms, at least six of which were currently occupied with other girls. They were kept under close supervision at all times and the only time Marisa saw them was during meals in the kitchen, where they were supplied with meagre rations and expected to cook for themselves. The other girls in the house were not unfriendly, but they were a little distant, and were reluctant to disclose anything about themselves other than their names, especially with Rahmon or another guard looming close by, listening to their every word.

Marisa did not know how the other girls had arrived here, but she could guess they had suffered a similar deception to Marisa and Olivia. The poor Macedonian girl was particularly affected by her ordeal, and every time Marisa saw her she looked so depressed and withdrawn that Marisa's words of comfort and encouragement sounded empty even to herself.

The girls were ordered to sleep during the day so they would be ready for entertaining clients from the early evening. This meant they were effectively imprisoned in their rooms for most of the day, emerging only for meals and cleaning, and even then they were forced to ask for permission to leave their rooms. The bars on the windows only increased Marisa's sense of imprisonment and isolation. There were no phones in the house and although her backpack had been returned to her, the cell phone she once had was missing.

The days were tedious and routine, but the nights were simply unbearable. A procession of men would enter her room throughout the night, up to eight men every night. They ranged from young to old, and some were fat, disgusting men who drooled over her.

They ranged across all the diverse ethnic backgrounds, reflective of the multicultural society of Toronto. There were husbands, soldiers, bankers, and even religious men. It seemed no corner of society was immune to the oldest profession, and even those with a good reputation in the community were happy to give their business, with no real concern for whether the girls were there voluntarily or otherwise. She washed and showered after each one but could not wash away the stench of humiliation.

There were a few clients who looked sympathetic, and she would ask them if she could borrow their cell phone so she could call her family and let them know she was still alive. She missed them badly and they would be frantic with worry as the weeks passed with no communication. However, even the kinder ones refused, saying it was against the rules but promising they would not tell Rahmon of her audacious request so she would not be punished.

She was expected to satisfy them and if she did not they would make a complaint to Rahmon or to Alexi if he was around. When this happened, Rahmon would come lumbering toward her, his thick neck wobbling, and silently deliver a stinging slap across her face. As she recoiled in the corner of her room, he would tell her she had been fined, which would be added to the money she owed for the journey to Canada.

On no occasion did the clients leave any money and Marisa assumed they paid Rahmon or whichever guard was on duty directly for her services. She had no idea how much they paid, and she did not have a clue how much was left owing on her account. She concluded that Timayev and his band of thugs were not really counting anyway.

To make matters worse, the Chechen had shown an unhealthy interest in Marisa. He declared a weakness for olive-skinned Eastern European girls and he seemed to find her particularly attractive, always commenting on her long limbs and slim figure. He would force himself upon her on his frequent visits to the house, as if she was his personal concubine. She had no idea whether this degrading submission went toward payment of her debt, but she somehow doubted it. If the other girls discovered his obsession with her, they would probably hate Marisa.

Sometimes after he had satisfied himself, he would not leave, but lie next to her, smoking marijuana and rambling on about his time in the Chechen military, how he was carrying on the fight. She barely answered, feeling quite threatened in his intense presence. He carried an air of raw aggression that Marisa felt bordered on the psychotic, as if one wrong word from her could cause him to explode in anger. She said as little as possible, and even his probing questions were met with one word answers until he got tired of talking and left.

Occasionally there was a trip out where they were allowed to hang out on street corners touting for business. This was usually late at night when the bars were closing, and it was on one such evening that Marisa made a desperate lunge for freedom.

Despite the chilly breeze, she stood on a dimly lit street corner dressed in a provocative miniskirt, high heels and stockings, heavy with make up. She looked and felt cheap, but it was an order from Rahmon and his thugs who controlled the brothel. Timayev viewed the street business as an opportunity to expand his client base and particularly felt that Marisa, with her looks and figure, would be good for business. He was keen to get her out on the streets as soon as possible.

She had been in the house for just over three weeks and Timayev felt she had adjusted well enough to her situation not to be a threat if she was allowed out. For the other more experienced girls, a night on the streets was like an outing, a welcome relief from their confinement, although it was more dangerous as they were required to approach possible customers, many of them high from the drink or drugs they had consumed in the club, and therefore more volatile. Although the girls were closely watched by one of Rahmon's men, partly for protection and mainly to ensure they did not attempt to escape, there was still danger. One of Timayev's girls had once been bundled into a car with four men and she had been beaten badly by the time she was rescued. After that, she was of little use to him.

As it was Marisa's first time on the street, she was watched closely by one of Rahmon's men, a bald, powerfully built man with dark Arabic features who called himself Hanif "the believer" and who like most of the men who guarded them was a fanatic for the Chechen cause. He said very little to the girls, regarding them with a sneering contempt, as if they were foolish to have allowed themselves to be exploited, and had hardly spoken to Marisa since she arrived. Fortunately he kept a discreet distance. As she waited on the corner, the clubs beginning to spill out with groups of men of all ages, some with girls, but mainly without, she could feel his brooding presence lurking in the shadows. Sometimes, when the girls were approached, the pimps would step forward and begin negotiations, but often this scared potential clients and Timayev preferred to let the girls talk while his men stayed in the background.

A group of men passed by her and let out some drunken wolf whistles.

"Come on, darling, show us what you got!" shouted one drunken youth who lurched toward her, hands flailing and grabbing at her before he was hauled back by his boisterous friends.

She swore at him in Bulgarian and they walked off laughing. Moments later a more sober trio of men passed by and actually smiled at her. Encouraged by this, she approached them and after a short exchange a price was agreed with one of the men. His friends gave him an encouraging slap on the back and disappeared.

As he followed her back to the brothel, she said nothing, but looked around carefully. She guided the man into a dark, deserted alleyway first and gently steered him against the wall. A screeching cat darted across their path but there was no sign of Hanif. Her hands felt up and down his body and he lay back against the wall, smiling rapturously, excited by her very direct approach. She quickly found what she was looking for and gently felt in his jacket pocket while her other hand rubbed between his legs. Eyes closed and gasping with pleasure, he was too distracted to notice her expertly lift the cell phone out of the jacket. She surprised herself at how easy it was, fuelled by her desperation. Marisa immediately kicked off her stilettos and went sprinting down the dark alleyway, stumbling over rubbish and splashing through pools of oily, stagnant water as she desperately headed for the distant light at the far end of the alleyway. The man shouted, cursing her loudly, but he did not give chase. However, she knew his shouts would alert Hanif.

As Marisa sprinted blindly down the alleyway, something sharp dug into her stockinged feet, and she yelled in pain, but continued running. She quickly glanced back and could see the dark shape of her stocky pimp silhouetted against the street lights. He was striding down the alley toward her but in the pitch black she felt certain he could not see her. She ducked into a deep recess in the brick wall and with fumbling hands, opened up the cell phone and pressed the digits for her telephone number back home in Bulgaria.

The light from the cell phone display lit her face and she quickly turned away against the black wall to hide the glow. She recalled her number in Bulgaria and prayed they would answer. There was a clicking of a connection being made and then a pleasant, calm, relaxed female voice came on the phone. "I'm sorry but the number you have dialled has not been recognized. Please hang up and try again." Tears streaming down her face, she almost choked with panic. She had the right number. Why could she not get through? Through her desperation Marisa remembered she had not dialled the international code for Bulgaria. She quickly redialled and heard the number ringing. Come on, come on, she whispered desperately to herself. It just kept ringing for what seemed an eternity. It would be early morning in Bulgaria, not even six o'clock yet.

Then, to her surprise and delight, a sleepy but familiar voice answered the phone.

"Hello," he said in Bulgarian.

She was sobbing so much it was hard to get the words out. "Papa, it's me, Marisa. I'm in Toronto—please help me—this gang—I have been taken —"

The phone was wrenched from her hand and there was a metallic snap as he crushed it under his heavy boots. Even in the dark Marisa could see the malevolent glint in Hanif's eye as he hauled her back out of the alley.

"You must be punished," he said with a relish that suggested he would personally carry out the punishment. She struggled and began screaming wildly, arms flailing, if only to get attention. She could not escape his iron grip and the crowds of night-clubbers had dispersed and the streets were once again empty. The most a screaming girl would get in this neighbourhood was a twitching of curtains from frightened residents. However, Hanif did not wish to draw too much attention, and so he used his military training to strategically pinch hard on Marisa's vagus nerve running through the neck just below the jawbone. She let out a startled cry and flopped down like a lifeless rag doll, and he quickly carried her back to the house.

CHAPTER 8

Vasil Dimitrov sat at his kitchen table, staring at the phone for what seemed an eternity. The sun was beginning to creep up in the west over the hills and the children were still fast asleep. His wife had twisted and stirred in her sleep as the shrill, incessant tone had invaded her dreams, but Vasil had instantly snapped awake and ran to the telephone. They had managed to scrape together enough money to pay the last telephone bill to avoid being cut off, as it was their only chance of communication with Marisa. He regretted his stubbornness at refusing to accept her plans and his failure to say a proper farewell. It had been over four weeks and the family had not heard a thing from their daughter until this morning.

He was highly disturbed—it was clear Marisa was in some kind of trouble. It was a desperate, strangled message, but the most disturbing fact was that it had ended so abruptly. His only comfort was that she had reached Toronto, but Vasil knew her daughter's voice well enough—she was under extreme duress. Something about a gang and being taken?

His mind churned away at the possibilities, none of them pleasant. Suppose Marisa was in great danger and there was nothing he could do about it, sitting here in this tumbledown cottage thousands of miles from a child who clearly needed him? He felt completely helpless, and that was the worst cruelty. He had always been there for his children, but now Marisa needed him more than ever.

His wife came hurrying into the kitchen and still half asleep, stared hopefully at her husband. His expression was grave, and she could feel her heart thudding in her chest.

"Tell me Vasil, what is it? Marisa?"

He nodded slowly, and she knew it was bad news.

Vasil relayed the message to his wife. He had not even had time to respond to Marisa before the call was abruptly ended. He was convinced he had heard her let out a cry as if the phone had been torn from her grasp. Had there been some kind of struggle? He knew he was torturing himself as his mind raced with thoughts about his little girl. He missed her greatly since she had gone and the family had waited anxiously night after night for news. As each night passed without contact, they had grown more concerned. Even the children had sensed things were not right and continually asked questions—"Where is Marisa? Why won't she speak to us? Will she ever come back and see us?"

They were impossible questions to answer, and, without a job to occupy him, he had spent far too much time worrying about Marisa. He looked hard at his wife. She looked so sad and dejected. He made up his mind.

"Lydia, I need to go to Toronto."

His wife looked up at him incredulously. "Vasil, how can you? We have no money. Even if you get there how will you find her?"

"I don't know but I have to try," he replied.

"Maybe she is okay and will call again soon," Lydia replied, but she sounded unconvincing, even to herself.

"No!" he said angrily. "She is in trouble. I know it. I have to find her!"

"But Vasil, we have no money. How will you get there?"

"I will find a way. I have to!" He got up and marched to the coal bunker. He had to find the money somewhere. Someone surely could help. As he smoked, he began thinking furiously about how he could raise the money to travel across the Atlantic. They had nothing to sell and very little income. He was not even sure how much it would cost to reach Canada, but he had travelled abroad when he was younger and he was confident of managing if he got there. He had no resources. All he had was his anxiety as a father to stir him into action.

It took nearly a week for Vasil to raise the money. With a new sense of purpose, he had trudged through all the major banks in the village, but all of them had firmly turned him away, most of them politely, a few of them dismissive. He had nothing to offer them as collateral. Even the small mortgage on his cottage was in arrears and when he told them the reason for using the money, they literally shut the door in his face. However, one of the smaller private banks had offered him a conditional loan, with a strongly worded suggestion that it would be in his best interests to pay back the loan and interest as soon as possible. The owner of the bank had a reputation as a dubious character, and he had heard rumours that the owner was quite prepared to use whatever means necessary to get his loans repaid. However, Vasil had no choice but to accept the loan from whomever was prepared to lend him the money. He would worry about paying it back later.

Within a few days he had arranged his visas and was ready to leave for Toronto. As he prepared for the long coach drive to Sofia airport, his wife and small children bade him a tearful farewell. He gathered up his holdall and as he boarded the coach, he gave one last lingering wave to his family. They had not heard from Marisa again in the ten days since her last frantic phone call, and this only reinforced Vasil's determination to find her. However, he did not have much of a plan except to go to the police as soon as he arrived. All he had was a tatty map he had "borrowed" from the local library.

As the coach sputtered into the distance, expelling clouds of choking black exhaust fumes, his wife held her children's hands and led them back to the empty cottage. In the space of less than two months her family had been diminished considerably, and they still faced the prospect of eviction from the cottage if they did not raise enough money in time. While Vasil was here there was always a chance he would find work again and things would return to normal, but now he was gone. She prayed that night for a time when her family would be together again, sitting round the table for dinner as they had done so recently. She could not even guess when that time would come.

When Vasil arrived in Toronto on a rainy late April morning, he felt bewildered and confused as he stepped out into the large arrivals lounge where people bustled past him, an obstacle in the way of their busy lives. He had collected his holdall and had stowed away his cash tightly in his jacket pocket. Now he had at last arrived in this unfamiliar land, he felt lost and unsure of what to do next. His English was limited but he could just about get by. Marisa had been very good at speaking English and had taught the family a lot, but he had never used it outside the sanctuary of his own home. He was soon surrounded by a gaggle of taxi drivers, all chattering to him and offering a ride, but when he looked at them blankly and did not respond, they quickly lost interest.

Eventually he found a bus that took him into the downtown area of the city, and after wandering for several hours, clutching his holdall against the chilly April breeze, he was able to find an affordable hostel. He found the huge skyscrapers of the downtown business district quite suffocating. They seemed to close in on him from all sides, blocking out the emerging sun and creating harsh angular shadows. He had only been to two big cities, Sofia and Bucharest, and although they had tall buildings they did not compare to these colossal glass fronted structures. It was a relief to find a hostel away from the downtown area and as he rested on his bed in the relative comfort and warmth of the dormitory room, he was able to decide on a plan of action.

He looked over his Toronto city map. His first stop was the police. Armed with photos of Marisa, admittedly a year or so old now, he intended to pass these to the police so they could distribute them at every street corner. Although the Bulgarian police were under-resourced and tainted with corruption, and much of their investigatory work relied on who was prepared to pay for their services over and above their paltry government wage, he had heard the North American police were very different. He was certain they would do everything in their power to find Marisa, and within a week he would be returning home with her safe and well.

He was up early next morning and left the hostel before eight o'clock. The hostel owner, a tubby, white haired man of about sixty, was friendly and gave him directions to the nearest police station, although he had looked puzzled at Vasil's request. Vasil did not wish to disclose the reason for his journey and left quickly after thanking him. When he arrived at the police station he explained at the desk in his best broken English that his daughter was missing and waved his photo of Marisa at the receptionist. She directed him to a small waiting room plastered with various leaflets on domestic violence, crime stoppers, victim services and more. Despite his barely conversational English, he had never mastered the written word, and he found them impossible to read. It therefore seemed like an eternity before he was greeted by a tough looking officer with a grim face, who curtly led him to a small, bleak, windowless room which Vasil thought looked more like an interrogation room.

The officer introduced himself as Constable Flaherty, a large red-faced Irishman whose uniform was busting at the seams. He sat down heavily opposite Vasil on the aluminum chairs, staring intently at Vasil as he teetered uncomfortably on the small chair. Marisa's father explained as best he could his suspicions about his daughter. At times he stumbled over his words, trying to express himself in an unfamiliar language, and at times he lapsed back into Bulgarian words. Constable Flaherty listened patiently but stony-faced. Vasil handed over a picture of his daughter and Flaherty took it and glanced at it. He took out a note pad and began scribbling.

"So when did your daughter arrive in Canada?" His accent was still as broad as the day he left Dublin thirty years before.

"A month ago, even longer," replied Vasil.

"And you say you received a phone call from her about ten days ago?"

"Yes, yes," said Vasil, a little frustrated. He had just covered all of this with the officer.

"Then why are you here?"

"Because I believe she is missing."

"But you don't know that for sure," Flaherty challenged.

Vasil was beginning to feel quite agitated with the policeman. "But the phone call," he urged. "She got cut off when she talk. We not heard from her since. I need to find her."

Flaherty merely looked bored. He had heard a similar story so many times before. In his experience the girl usually turned up safe after having a great time with friends, sometimes forgetting to contact their parents because—well, it was just something teenagers did all the time. He tried to reassure the girl's father. "Mr Dimitrov, do you know how many missing person enquiries we get every day just in Toronto? It is impossible for us to investigate every single case. In nearly all cases the person turns up safe and well and embarrassed they have put their family through a difficult time." He did not add that in a few isolated cases, the only thing that turned up was a body.

However, Vasil was insistent. "Please, you have to help me. My daughter could be anywhere."

"That is precisely the reason why we cannot use valuable police time in looking for her. As far as we are aware, no crime has been committed. We have enough trouble keeping up with actual crimes. I sympathize but at the moment there is not a lot we can do. However I will take the photo and keep it on file."

Constable Flaherty peered at the photo in his hand but Vasil angrily snatched it back. "It is my only photo. If you are not going to do anything then do not take it!"

"Okay, okay," said the constable, trying to placate him. "I will copy it and distribute it amongst our divisions in the Greater Toronto Area. I'm confident she will turn up alive and well and there will be nothing to worry about."

Vasil left the police station clutching his daughter's precious photograph and as he stepped out into the breezy, noisy Toronto street he looked around this sprawling metropolis. Somewhere out there his daughter was alone and in pain, he was sure of it. He had pinned his hopes on the police helping him. He had heard great stories about how the police were incorruptible and would not stop until they had found his little girl. They had barely been interested. "No crime has been committed," they had said. Of course it had. He was certain of that, just from the phone call. She was being held against her will and he was determined to find her, with or without the help of the police. However, he really had no idea of his next move. He sat on a park bench, huddling up against the wind, thinking. Across the street he saw a shop that offered copying services. He went in and paid for five hundred photocopies of his daughter's photo and spent the rest of a long, weary day handing them to any passersby.

CHAPTER 9

Dan Huberman sat in his small, grim office east of Finch Avenue in one of the seedier parts of town. He had rented the tumbledown office three years ago when he started out as a private investigator because it was cheap, and after his acrimonious and expensive divorce from his wife of eighteen years, that was what really mattered. It was in a back street and therefore he did not receive much in the way of passing foot traffic, but that suited him. Most of his business came from anxious phone calls or emails. In any event he was only in his office for a fraction of each day when he had reports to write and other paperwork to catch up on.

The majority of his clients were insurance companies requiring investigation into fraudulent claims or government departments wishing to gather evidence to use against suspected benefit cheats, the type who claimed invalidity benefits for being unable to work and turned up at the golf course on bright weekday mornings. Most of the work was mundane and boring, often hanging around spying on someone for hours on end in all types of weather, waiting for them to make an incriminating move. His clients were meticulous about the paperwork, often because it was likely to be used as evidence in any prosecution against an individual. He found this at times even more tedious than the field work, but it was an inevitable and critical part of the job. The work did not lend itself to any form of social life. The hours were long and unpredictable. He could be working eighteen hours one day and two hours the next, depending on the assignment he was on, or indeed if he had any work at all. Fortunately, in these tough times, work was picking up as austere economic times meant more people trying to cheat the system to squeeze a living. That was fine—he made a reasonable living, but not enough to get out of this ramshackle office or to hire a secretary to help him, and he had very little social life to speak of anyway. Every so often, along came a case that reminded him why he had entered this business in the first place, something that kept him going.

He had found it particularly hard to pick himself up after the traumatic events of a few years ago, and those friends he did have at the time seemed to melt away into the distance as his troubles multiplied. Before his daughter Sarah's death, he was a successful detective rapidly building a good reputation in the force's narcotics division. She was only sixteen years old when she died of a drug overdose outside a Toronto nightclub. They had been having a lot of trouble with her, and his wife had found her impossible to control. Teenagers are difficult at the best of times, but he had to admit that at times Sarah was unmanageable. He had suspected drugs for some time. As a narcotics officer, he knew the signs all too well, one of which was withdrawal and refusal to talk. No matter how much he tried, he could not talk sense into his daughter. She hid her supply well and he only found it after her death. Despite all the problems, when she died it tore a gaping wound in their lives which had never healed. Their only child, they had seen their future as a family destroyed in that one fateful night.

He was off duty when it happened and received a call from one of his colleagues at two a.m. He raced to the club and as he saw the ambulance and the paramedics gathered around a prone figure his heart sank. He burst through the small crowd of revellers and ghoulish onlookers who had gathered to witness the drama so they could tell their friends. Some were even taking pictures with their cell phones. Flashing his ID he saw beyond doubt it was Sarah, eyes rolled back and foam caked around her mouth. He stood back as the paramedics desperately tried to revive her but he instinctively knew it was no good. One of them turned to him with a deep look of sympathy and shook his head. Later that evening he had to visit the mortuary to formally identify his daughter's body. He would never forget his last sight of her, lying lifeless as a wax dummy, her big toe already tagged, and it had haunted many sleepless nights since.

It was the prelude to the gradual dismantling of his life. Her funeral was the most difficult thing he had ever been through, despite his years on the street. Of course the mourners greeted him and his wife with expressions of sorrow, but it was mixed with a degree of judgemental curiosity that a sixteen year old, especially the daughter of a police officer, could be out at a club so late at night and taking drugs. He could see it in their eyes. After the funeral and the initial period of grieving, he tried to keep things together but he just felt empty all the time, as if his insides had been ripped out and stamped on. His wife took it very badly, and when they spoke the conversation inevitably led back to Sarah, followed by uncomfortable silences, until it just became easier not to talk at all. Sarah had been the bond that had kept them together, and after her death, as they faced the prospect of a barren life without children or grandchildren, there was little reason for them to carry on.

They both suffered a deep depression and dealt with it in different ways. Both withdrew into their own private world. Dan became paranoid his wife somehow blamed him; that he should have known about the drugs Sarah was taking, been stronger in dealing with her. In the early days after her death, making love felt like a form of healing, but after a while she could not bear him touching her, and he in turn lost the will to try. It was almost a relief when one day she phoned him and said she was leaving. He did nothing to stop her, and this only increased the resentment she felt toward him—a resentment that surfaced many times in their ensuing divorce battles.

With his marriage crumbling, he buried himself deeper into his work, not only as a form of therapy, but as the best way to keep Sarah's legacy alive, to strike out at the type of scum who had caused his daughter's death. He dived into his work with an intensity that intimidated even his superiors, desperate to find and dispense justice to the hordes of parasites who made their daily living from selling drugs on Toronto street corners. In doing so, however, his judgement was impaired, never more so when on one hot August night he caught a young dealer selling crack to a group of girls not much older than Sarah and decided he could not wait for the courts. Dan had long been a black belt in karate, but had always used it in self-defence, which had been very useful in some difficult situations. This time he used it to attack and left the dealer, a lad of only twenty one, so badly injured that he was in intensive care for nearly two weeks. He was immediately suspended from his job and assigned to desk work. After a long and careful investigation under media and political scrutiny, the force, while privately sympathetic with his reasons, had no choice but to fire him, and a promising, decorated career was over.

He did not remember much of the ensuing year, mainly because he did not wish to, only that it was full of bitter recriminations and acrimony as his divorce dragged its torturous way through the courts, the only winners being counsel for both sides. It was also a period which he spent in an alcoholic haze for much of the time, when for most days there really seemed no reason for getting out of bed at all. However, through it all, he had stayed in contact with a few of his old colleagues, guys who still carried a lot of respect for the talented officer he had once been.

The divorce settlement was perhaps the turning point for Dan. At that point he could not have got any lower, but amongst the misery there was a certain relief that the acrimony was finally over and there was a sense of closure. He could never forgive his ex-wife for blaming him for Sarah's death, but this was mixed with a sense of guilt that in some way he was culpable. Looking back, he had tortured himself with the fact that maybe he could and should have done more to prevent her descent into drugs, but the settlement gave him the opportunity to move on and he gradually learnt not to attack himself over his failings with Sarah. Under the financial settlement with his ex-wife, he no longer had a home but had enough money to rent out a small, seedy bedsit in a run down part of the city. He had no job but at least he was not homeless. Even his training would not equip him for life on the streets during the cold, bitter winds that swept over Toronto for large parts of the year.

He gradually sobered up as he realized the drinking did little to ease the pain, but only created a type of numbness. One of his former colleagues, Brad Miller, one of the few who had stood by him throughout his troubles, suggested he look into private investigative work. After all, despite his drinking, Dan was still a fearsome opponent with his martial arts skills. Brad still felt a strong obligation to Dan, who had mentored him during his formative years in the force, and they had been on some challenging field operations together over the years. They had watched each other's backs and both could claim to have saved the other's life on more than one occasion. Brad had supported him in getting started as a private investigator and it had given Dan a new sense of purpose. He quit the drinking and rented an office and Brad and a few others sent some mundane cases his way. He slowly built the business by word of mouth and he found he enjoyed the challenge of solving cases. His police background was an enormous benefit in this line of work and he had a reasonable degree of success. The cases were routine and unspectacular, and certainly could not match the excitement of an anti-drugs field operation, but he had to admit to a quiet satisfaction when he exposed the cheating husband or the fraudulent benefits claimant. There were even some days now when he did not wake up thinking of Sarah.

However, he was starting to grow a little tired of the endless paperwork and boring surveillance operations and was hoping for his next "big" case to come along.

As his mind wandered, struggling with his latest report and how to justify his fees after a fruitless investigation for an insurance client, he was startled by the heavy clang of the door being opened. He looked up and saw a desperate looking middle aged man enter his office clutching a photo and a stack of papers.

Dan looked at him curiously. It was unusual for him to get visitors unless they had called in advance. The man was thin and scruffily dressed, and he had a hollow, haunted look. His eyes darted nervously to and fro. When he spoke he had a thick Eastern European accent, but his English was passable and Dan could just understand him.

"Please, please, you must help me," he blurted out to Dan. "My daughter has been kidnapped. I have to find her." He looked at

Dan pleadingly. "I have money," he added, waving a stack of twenty dollar bills in the air.

Dan guided him to a seat opposite his large battered old desk and cleared away a stack of old papers which clogged every inch of available desk space, relieved at postponing his tedious paperwork. He pulled out a writing pad and took some details.

"Let's start with your name," suggested Dan helpfully.

"Vasil Dimitrov. I come from Bulgaria. My daughter is somewhere in Toronto. Please help me." Vasil looked so bereft of hope and he stared at Dan so hard that it was difficult to return his gaze.

Vasil described how his daughter left their village in Bulgaria many weeks before and the only phone call he had since received from her, as Dan scribbled notes on his pad. Vasil was so deeply concerned for her safety that he had decided to come to Canada to look for her. He thrust the photograph of his daughter across the table and Dan studied it carefully before handing it back. The girl was smiling and radiant, as if she did not have a care in the world.

"She is a beautiful girl. How old is she?" asked Dan, handing the photo back to Vasil.

Vasil smiled weakly. "Thank you. She is seventeen." Dan could tell Vasil was fiercely proud of his daughter and she meant everything to him. He had felt that way once. He quickly dismissed the thought.

"Why have you come to me?"

Vasil struggled to understand and then nodded. "Yes, yes, I come to you because the police will not help. They are not interested. They say I cannot be certain she is missing." His voice rose in anger. "She would never lose contact like that. I know she is missing!"

"Let me think about it. I am very busy at the moment," replied Dan.

"Please, please, you must help me now. I have money." Once again he waved a wad of bills in front of Dan, as if this would entice him to act.

"My retainer is usually a thousand dollars," said Dan, looking him over. "I don't think you can afford it."

Vasil protested and pleaded in equal part and Dan thought he might have to physically throw him out of his office. He promised to find the money but Dan guessed that would be virtually impossible. He would not leave and his distress was evident. Dan felt guilty but he had a business to run. Though he admired the man's dedication to his daughter in travelling to Canada, a trip he obviously could not afford, one of his basic principles in running his agency was not to allow emotions to cloud his business judgement. He could understand why the police would not help. The girl's father had no leads as to where she might be and could not even be certain she was still in Toronto. Even if she was, there were five and a half million people in and around Toronto. A wild goose chase if ever there was one, but this little man was persistent.

"Alright," he sighed. "I will think about it. Tell me where I can reach you."

Vasil calmed down and gave him the address of a scruffy back street hostel not far from the office, and said he would come in first thing tomorrow. Dan had the feeling that Vasil, despite his small stature, would not be put off easily.

Later that evening, as Dan relaxed in his tiny box like apartment, he sipped his iced tea (he did not keep any alcohol in the place in case he fell prey to temptation) and turned on the latest CNN news. The usual wave of depressing world events flashed across the screen—Taliban insurgents were gaining ground in remote Afghanistan valleys, Sri Lankan Tamils had been mercilessly slaughtered by government troops, and another suicide bomber had attacked a Moscow subway station, the Russian government suspecting rebel Chechen zealots.

The world was a crazy place, dominated by conflict and hatred in every part of the globe, yet like most people he found it hard to really engage with unless it affected him personally. It was the individual stories of human suffering that seemed to touch people and made these terrible events seem more real. It was why he sat there agonizing over his decision to help the Bulgarian guy. He had bills to pay and this business never got any easier. He was fortunate most of his clients were corporations or public sector departments—they paid on time, although at low rates. In his experience, working for individual clients was never profitable, although he had to admit, more rewarding when it turned out well. Clearly the diminutive Bulgarian had very little to pay, although he had to admire his courage and determination in coming to Canada, which to him must seem like an alien land, in pursuit of his daughter.

His thoughts turned, as they often did in quiet moments, to Sarah. Now she would have been a little older than Vasil's daughter, but still a teenager. Sarah too had striking features, a soft round face and piercing hazel eyes framed by long brown sweeping hair. She had inherited her mother's good looks, and his own olive complexion, and the combination had always brought her lots of male attention. Dan could understand what Vasil must be going through. The thought of not knowing and fearing the worst must be excruciating for him to bear.

How could he help Vasil? Even with his skills as a private investigator, there was very little he could do. He had nothing to go on and he did not even know if the girl was still in the city. Vasil was convinced she was, but the call he had received from her had been nearly two weeks ago. Anything could have happened since then. He had worked on a few missing person cases and usually it was a succession of dead end leads and frustrating enquiries. He had never actually found anyone, although one of his cases had turned up of their own accord. He did not wish to give the man false hope but could he really turn him away? He was still agonizing over what to tell Vasil when he fell asleep in his armchair.

True to his word, Vasil was waiting outside Dan's office when he arrived at 7.30. He looked dishevelled and had dark rings around his eyes, as if he had spent the night on the sidewalk outside his office. He was still clutching his daughter's photograph. Vasil saw Dan's expression as he let him into his office.

"I do not sleep well. I worry about my daughter."

Dan got straight to the point. He had decided during a restless night. "Look Mr Dimitrov-"

"Please, call me Vasil."

"Vasil. I have great sympathy for your situation. I know what you must be going through but I really cannot help you."

Anger mixed with desperation flashed in Vasil's eyes. "How can you know what I am going through? Do you have a daughter?"

The question rattled Dan. "I *did* have a daughter," he said quietly.

Vasil did not understand Dan's use of the past tense. "Then maybe you understand. Please help me. She means everything to me."

He continued to plead, even grabbing Dan's hands in his own coarse hands. Dan could feel his defences crumbling. He had not really anticipated what he would say to justify his decision. Sarah had meant everything to him and his world had caved in when she had gone. He had to confess to a great admiration for Vasil's determination in the face of impossible odds, and had to admit that if he did not help him he would be racked with guilt. He did not know how he could help but perhaps he could figure that out later.

"Vasil, I really don't think you are going to allow me to refuse you. I will try and help you but you must realize the chances of success are minimal. Toronto is a big place—assuming she is still here—and I don't even know where to start. I will make some enquiries but that's all I can do at this stage."

Vasil's worry-lined face lit up. "So you will help me?"

"Yes, I will try."

Vasil gave Dan a huge bear hug and kissed him on both cheeks. Dan was surprised at how strong this small Bulgarian was. Vasil pressed a number of twenty dollar bills into his hand.

"I will pay you everything I can," he declared. Dan just nodded but handed the bills back. This was never going to be about the money.

"Take the money Vasil. I can't possibly take anything until I have some progress. Besides, you need it for the hostel. I know where I can reach you."

He grabbed his legal pad and scribbled furiously as Vasil explained in greater detail than the day before everything he knew, from Marisa's trip to the au pair recruiter in Sandanski to her departure to Sofia airport and then the garbled, desperate phone call from Toronto. Since then, absolute silence. Vasil explained this in slow, at times broken English as he struggled for the right words, and Dan patiently took down every detail he could, prompting with his own questions. He was particularly interested in the phone call. From his experience in this business, it was the small details that later proved critical.

"Come in tomorrow and I will let you know what I have found."

"Thank you, thank you," said Vasil, his troubled eyes suddenly brighter. As he left the office Vasil's previously sagging gait had straightened and he strode out of the office with a new sense of purpose. As Dan watched him leave, he suddenly felt a sense of responsibility he had not felt since he had become a private investigator. He had better not let him down.

CHAPTER 10

Dan had a heap of paperwork and a surveillance job on a builder suspected of stealing materials from the building site he worked on. He looked at his schedule without enthusiasm and decided to make some enquiries for Vasil. The first question was whether Marisa could be traced as having arrived in Toronto on or around the dates in March that Vasil mentioned. Flight manifests were notoriously difficult to obtain and were jealously guarded by the airlines, particularly since 9/11. Vasil said that he had barely spoken to his daughter in the last few days before she left. All he knew was that she was headed for Toronto but he did not know which airline she was travelling on. He wished he'd paid more attention, he had lamented to Dan.

He checked the Toronto Lester Pearson Airport website for incoming destinations and flight times. There were no direct flights from Sofia, which he had suspected. Most flights from Europe would originate from London, but there were many airlines which operated flights from London to Toronto, and it would be like looking for a needle in a haystack.

He made a call to the airport to explain he was looking for a passenger he believed was travelling from London into Toronto and he got the response he had feared.

"Do you know how many people we service at this airport every day?" the woman demanded, her irritation evident even over the phone. She paused for effect. "Over one hundred thousand! You don't even know which day she arrived, never mind which airline! Good day!"

His next idea was passport control. The immigration officers at the Canada Border Services Agency no longer just glanced at the passport and waved passengers through, especially foreign nationals.

Her passport would have been scrutinized and the number entered into the database with the date of entry and details of the working visa.

However, without the passport number her entry would be very difficult to trace. He decided to call Brad Miller. His old colleague had always stood by him and they kept in touch regularly. Brad was still in drug enforcement, and his career was burgeoning, but even so, he was one guy Dan could rely on. It took just three rings for Brad to answer his cell phone.

"Hey buddy, what's up?" answered Brad's cheery voice. There was a hum of traffic in the background.

"Brad, I need a favour."

"Man, how many more favours!" he laughed. "I don't think you've paid me back for the last ten yet!"

"I know, I know. I owe you. Put it on my slate. I have a strange feeling about this one. I had a little Bulgarian guy come in and see me yesterday. His daughter is missing. He thinks she entered through Toronto. He got a call a few weeks ago from her—she was desperate and said she was being held in Toronto. He has not heard from her since and he has come here to look for her. Can you pull a few strings at the Canada Border Services Agency to see if she entered through Toronto? Don't they record the passport numbers now?"

"Yes they do, and she would have needed a visa as well. Do you have details of these?"

"No I don't Brad."

Brad let out an exasperated sigh. "You know how bureaucratic they are. It would be impossible to trace without the numbers!"

"Come on Brad, you're a detective. You can crack it. I know you have contacts everywhere. Surely you know some skirt in their records team that you can sweet talk?"

"Stop right there. You know I'm a happily married man. I would never do what you're suggesting," he replied, his tone sarcastic.

"No, of course not Brad. Look I need it fairly quickly. Can I email you everything I have? We know within a couple of days when she arrived, we just don't know from where. I suspect London but I can't be sure."

"Okay, but you owe me one—again. It could be tricky. Send me the details. I will be back at the station in the hour. I will make a few calls. If you can get me the passport or visa numbers, that would really help. Even then I can't promise anything."

"Thanks Brad. I know you'll come through for me." He always did, thought Dan.

Dan decided not to wait for Vasil to come in. Knowing Brad was helping him out gave him added determination to move ahead quickly. He could not get through to the hostel so he decided to walk the few blocks in the late spring sunshine over to the hostel. On the way he saw a pile of messy blankets sprawled on a street corner, under which a shapeless figure appeared to be huddled. It was a sight becoming more and more prevalent on Toronto's streets, reflected Dan. As he passed by, he reminded himself how close he had come to being the man under the blanket.

The hostel was an old, square, characterless building, sprayed here and there with fading graffiti. It was used mainly as a youth backpacker's hostel and Vasil probably stuck out amongst the groups of transient youth. Indeed, the surly middle-aged guy with the double chin at the counter knew exactly who Dan was referring to.

"Yeah, yeah, the crazy Bulgarian guy," he said with some distaste. "You'll find him where he usually is, handing out leaflets of his daughter near the Jane and Finch mall." He did not seem to approve of Vasil trying every way he knew to look for his daughter and Dan felt like punching the man's podgy face. This guy obviously did not have his own family and did not want to understand what Vasil was going through. Dan briefly thought of his own daughter. However, now was not the time. He left swiftly and hurried to the mall a few blocks further on. He saw Vasil outside the mall diligently handing out papers to every passerby, some who took them indifferently before glancing quickly at them and immediately screwing them up. Others did not even accept them, hurrying past, too busy with their own lives. A few of the papers had been discarded and Marisa's photo flapped and drifted in the breeze, scattered by cars zooming past.

He saw Dan and looked hopefully at him. "So soon, you have news?"

"No, nothing yet, but I need you to help me."

Dan and Vasil took a cab back to the office and Dan prepared coffee. "Vasil, I need you to call home. Ask your wife if Marisa left any documents at the house, copies of her passport or something like that."

Dan handed him the phone and Vasil called his home number, relieved their telephone had not been cut off yet when he heard the distant beeping. It seemed to take an age before his wife answered and he spoke rapidly in Bulgarian. All Dan could make out was the odd reference to Marisa. Then there was a pause and Vasil explained that she was looking through Marisa's bedroom. Presently she came back to the phone and Dan could sense the excitement in his voice. He scribbled down some numbers on the legal pad Dan handed him and when he rang off he turned to Dan.

"She had a scrap of paper hidden in her drawer with two sets of numbers. On the paper was also a telephone number and the name "Georgi" scribbled on it. Vasil handed the details to Dan.

"This is good Vasil, said Dan. I will get onto this right away."

With renewed hope, Vasil went back to distributing copies of Marisa's photo to any interested pedestrians, and Dan phoned Brad.

"Hey Brad, I have some more information for you."

Brad was now back in the office. "Good, because what you've given me so far sucks. I called a contact at Canada Border Services and she nearly crucified me when I told her I had no numbers. They *need* the numbers buddy," he emphasized.

"I think I may have them." He reeled off the numbers to Brad.

"Okay Dan. I'll speak to my contact again if she doesn't chew my balls off. By the way, the piece of skirt you were referring to is a sixty two year-old grandmother weighing two hundred and twenty pounds with a fierce Irish temper."

"Just your type then," retorted Dan.

"You really do owe me this time," said Brad.

Dan was curious about the telephone number and the name "Georgi" scribbled on it. Vasil had mentioned that she had visited a recruiter in—he consulted his notes—Sandanski. He checked a Google map to get a better idea of where in Bulgaria it was, located at the foot of the Pirin Mountains in the extreme south-west of the country. He had never been to Eastern Europe, let alone Bulgaria, but the Net certainly made the life of a p.i. much easier. Within minutes he had established that the number he had from Marisa's notes contained the dialling code into Sandanski. It was worth a try. It would be nearly six in Bulgaria and it was probably an office number. He dialled the number, adding the codes to dial from Canada to Bulgaria, and the phone beeped monotonously. He was just about to click off when a breathless voice greeted him in Bulgarian.

Dan cursed himself for his stupidity. After meeting Vasil, he had not thought it through and assumed any Bulgarian would speak English. Well he was not going to learn Bulgarian now so he put on his best European accent.

"Hello, I wish to speak to Georgi," he began, not having a clue what he wanted to talk about.

The heavily accented voice switched effortlessly to English. "Yes, this is Georgi speaking."

"I have some girls for you."

There was a pause on the other end of the line. "Who am I speaking to?" said Georgi cautiously.

My name is Petrov. My daughters would like to work in America—as au pairs."

Dan could sense the tension in Georgi's voice. "Okay, where do you live?" asked Georgi.

Dan hesitated. "Near Sandanski. But I need your address to take them to see you."

The European accent was not working too well. There was heavy suspicion in Georgi's voice. "Where did you hear about me?"

"My friend—you arranged for her daughter to work in Montreal."

Another pause. "Come and see me tomorrow," he said finally.

"Okay, but your address please Georgi—?" He paused, hoping the recruiter would fill in the gap for his surname.

"I suggest you get it from your friend," snapped Georgi brusquely and promptly hung up.

Dan banged the desk in frustration. All he had achieved was to arouse suspicion in the recruiter, but at least it was unlikely an international telephone number could be traced from rural Bulgaria. He had never been that skilled at bluffing, but his experience as a private investigator had given him an insight into a person's body language and even, when talking by telephone, their pauses and nuances over the telephone. It was clear Georgi's tone had been defensive and that suggested to Dan he had something to hide. He clearly recruited more than just au pairs.

He set to work on the Internet. Despite his limited information, it did not take long for him to trace references to a Georgi Kakov, a recruitment specialist. Tucked away in an obscure social media website he found a forum which talked about recruiters in the area and he drilled down to references to Georgi Kakov. As he reviewed the forum, his frown deepened. There were several sycophantic testimonials to how professional and efficient Georgi was. One of them said they could not thank Georgi enough for introducing her to a fantastic new life in America, and another explained how he had organized everything to make her dream come true. They sounded almost too good to be genuine. These and other similar praise formed many of the postings, but hidden amongst them were some rather disturbing posts.

"Do not trust this man. He is a crook. He promised me a job with a rich American family. Instead I landed in a disgusting house with an elderly American couple who treated me like a slave. They stole my passport and hardly let me leave the house. They did not pay me any

money as they said it was being sent to Georgi first and I had nowhere to go so I had to stay with them. Eventually I could bear it no more and managed to get back home after six months begging on the streets. Georgi Kakov is a fake."

Further on there was another posting in a similar vein but it was the third negative posting that really made Dan take notice. He rubbed his stubbly chin thoughtfully as he read the note.

"Georgi Kakov promised me a dream life as an au pair in Canada. It turned into a nightmare that lasted over a year. I was taken and sold into sexual slavery to a brutal gang who forced me into prostitution to pay off the debt. They said they had bought me and treated me like their property. I was beaten and starved if I did not satisfy the customers and I was not able to contact my family in all the time I was there. They thought I was dead. The only reason I escaped was because one of my customers took a liking to me and helped me get away and paid for my trip back home. I was one of the lucky ones. I got away but I will never forget how Georgi Kakov betrayed me. I still wake up screaming some days but at least I am home."

Dan leaned back in his squeaky, battered leather office chair and pondered this new information. What was it Vasil had said about Marisa's call? The person on the forum said she had been *taken*—he had a strong fear that Marisa may have suffered the same fate. This was going to be difficult to tell Vasil.

That afternoon, Dan sat in his old Chevrolet across the road from the building site peering at his target through powerful field glasses. The site was another expensive uptown development, the kind that had started and then stalled as the local economy ebbed and flowed. The foundations had been prepared and they were now on the first level, providing Dan with a good position in which to analyze the suspect's activities. This type of surveillance he hated the most. He could spend tedious hours just watching and then turn away for a second to grab a coffee and miss a vital piece of evidence. He also had to be constantly ready with his long range Nikon to capture any suspicious activity, but right now his target was acting as a model worker. He found it hard to concentrate, and his thoughts kept wandering back to Vasil and his daughter. The more he thought about those disturbing posts on the forum, the more he was convinced Kakov had steered Marisa into the hands of someone who was exploiting her. He had carried out some routine checks and as he expected, there had been no application for a social insurance number, health card or anything else he could tell that would indicate her presence in the country. It was if she had fallen completely off the radar.

His reverie was interrupted by the high pitched beep of his cell phone. He nearly jumped out of his seat.

"Dan, it's Brad. I have some interesting news for you. Marisa came in through Montreal."

"Montreal? Okay, thanks Brad. Good work."

"No no, that isn't it. She then appeared to have taken an interconnecting flight to St. John's later that day. It was lucky her details were recorded on arrival. In most cases where there is a domestic flight, the immigration officers will just glance at the passport and let them through. Sometimes, however, they will record the entry again if there is any reason to do so. Whoever brought her to Canada took some effort to cover her tracks."

CHAPTER 11

Timayev was just wrapping up a briefing with his team in his large dining room, which doubled as a board room on such occasions, when the call came through on his laptop. He quickly dismissed his comrades and turned his attention to the computer where the strong, rugged features of the self-styled General Vladimir Medov appeared on screen. There were few people Timayev answered to, but he regarded the General with a mixture of fear and respect. Despite the official stance of the Moscow administration that active military operations in Chechnya had ceased, Timayev knew a bitter underground war continued to be fought as ordinary Chechen civilians suffered repressive and dictatorial rule under pro-Russian local government. General Medov was a key player in that war, an expert in guerrilla warfare, with a long and proud record in combat.

Adding to the aura that surrounded the General was the fact that his sister had been one of the first Chechen female suicide bombers, taking a bus full of Russian Air Force pilots with her. He was ruthless and ambitious, but totally devoted to the cause of freedom for Chechnya. However, running a brutal insurgency was a costly business, and Timayev was proud to be in a position to provide much needed finance to the resistance. His fear of the abrasive General Medov was also mixed with a degree of pride that the General regarded Timayev's contribution so highly, even though it was so far from the front line.

The General's voice echoed through the Internet connection. "Good morning Akhmad," he began. It was early afternoon in Toronto. "I trust things are going well with the preparations for tonight?"

"Yes, General, everything is planned and ready."

"Good, good." The General smiled but his voice carried a hint of threat. "This is an important deal Akhmad. We are making a hefty investment for these drugs. Make sure the cocaine is of good quality."

Timayev tried hard not to show his irritation. It was his corporation which had made the investment and his team always checked the quality of the merchandise. "Yes sir, we have it covered."

"I don't trust these Jamaican drug gangs. They are a little too hot-headed. At the first sign of trouble, they start shooting. Have your men properly armed and ready."

For all of Medov's war heroics, Timayev doubted whether he had ever dealt with a Jamaican drugs gang, but he had an opinion on everything and Timayev merely listened. They discussed the logistics of the operation in detail and also the supply chain. Timayev's team was to meet up with the Jamaican "posse" at three a.m. the next morning at a location just east of the Toronto docks. These exchanges were always tricky. Apart from the obvious threat of the authorities turning up, there was the deal itself, which was always steeped in mistrust on either side. One hostile move could trigger a bloodbath. Also, before they handed over the cash, Timayev would have to be satisfied with the purity of the cocaine. He had been assured by the gang's leader that it was of the finest quality Kingston had to offer, but of course he would say that. Timayev intended to take a number of his girls along to act as a sweetener. The Jamaican men had a weakness for white girls and it would help to relieve the tension while his team carried out the quality control checks on the merchandise.

Timayev always regarded these deals with a little apprehension, despite enjoying the adrenalin rush of a successful deal. They were fraught with danger, but that was part of the attraction. When Medov signed off, he gave a sigh of relief and began the final preparations for the evening.

The rendezvous point was behind a small promontory east of the Toronto docks. Alexi had carried out a reconnaissance of the area and had confirmed to Timayev that it was suitable for the pickup. The point had a natural shelter and over the three continuous nights that Alexi had watched the area, it had not been actively patrolled by the police on the lake. They had provided the coordinates to the Jamaican gang, and as Timayev scanned the inky black horizon, he spotted the Jamaican boat silently gliding in behind the headland, all its lights extinguished until it dropped anchor and drifted lazily on the water about thirty metres from the shore.

Timayev gave a silent signal to his men and they quickly filtered out of the two vehicles and headed toward the small rocky beach adjacent to the bluff where the land curved round. The men were heavily armed with small Russian made Stechkin APS double action pistols, selected for their capable rapid-fire accuracy in semi-automatic mode, although they stayed concealed. Timayev wondered why they even bothered to hide them as the Jamaican posse would hardly expect them to come unarmed. It just seemed to be part of the protocol for a drug deal. They also closely escorted four girls onto the beach as two large rowing boats gently slid onto the beach. The group quickly boarded and the Jamaicans rowed them swiftly and skilfully to the yacht bobbing gently on the tiny swell of the lake. The two Land Cruisers drove off with instructions to return and collect the group in precisely one hour.

Among the four girls were Marisa and Olivia. They did not protest as they were firmly guided onto the boat. It was the first time Marisa had been let out of the brothel since she had tried to escape. Timayev had let the huge monster Rahmon deal with her and he had shown great delight in living up to his reputation for violence. They had also denied her food and water for three days in an effort to break her spirit. She had been very weak and ill, and although her bruises had healed, their cruelty was fresh in her mind. She was more determined than ever to escape, but she had been closely guarded for the past couple of weeks. Olivia sat next to her on the boat, trembling with fright. They had been warned by Alexi that this was a volatile situation and they must satisfy the Jamaicans or else it could turn hostile.

As they boarded the yacht, Marisa felt the Jamaicans staring lewdly at them. They were directed down into the spacious cabin where one of the gang members kept watch over them, staring intently at them in the dim light. Marisa could hear Timayev's voice making friendly overtures to the gang, and the deep, resonant Caribbean twang of the posse's leader. There was a tense five minute silence as the exchanges were made and each side examined their booty. They heard the Jamaican leader give a raucous laugh. The deal appeared to be going well and presently Timayev, his voice high with elation, declared that the girls were an extra present as a gesture of goodwill. The gang seemed in no hurry to get away. The waters were black and empty, without a trace of a patrol vessel. The yacht had several small bedrooms adjoining the main cabin and as the men came down they began to eye the girls lustfully.

She heard Timayev speak in a friendly tone. "Enjoy them my friends. We will collect them in forty five minutes." Along with Alexi and the rest of his band, Timayev stepped off the yacht onto one of the rowing boats, and immediately the Jamaicans moved menacingly toward the girls. One of the crew first pulled Olivia toward him and she meekly submitted and allowed herself to be led away to an adjoining bedroom. The other girls were similarly grabbed and manhandled through the cabin door, their muted protests ignored, until Marisa sat alone with the gang leader. He gave a wide menacing grin. His dazzling white teeth interlaced with gold fillings contrasted oddly with his red, bloodshot eyes which peered at her callously. He grabbed her wrist. He was strong and his coarse, dry fingers dug into her skin. As she stared up at him she suddenly became overwhelmed with panic.

The Jamaican pulled her up and began steering her roughly toward one of the small bedrooms. She looked wildly round her. She could see through the porthole the rowing boat with the Chechen gang and their merchandise gently gliding toward the shore. Instinctively, she pulled away and before the Jamaican could react, her legs propelled her up onto the deck. She heard the metallic clang of the steps as her captor pounded after her and as he surfaced on the deck he began grinning at her. She realized she had nowhere to go on the small deck. Without thinking she hurled herself overboard. She was dressed only in a short skirt and camisole top, and as she hit the freezing water it felt like she was being stabbed by a thousand steely knives all at once. She gasped and the air in her lungs was forcibly expelled in the extreme cold and she plunged into the black depths. Struggling for breath she tried to kick to the surface, but her limbs, stiffened by the muscles contracting in the freezing water, felt like lead, and the weight of the water pushed her down. Her lungs felt ready to burst and she was about to lose consciousness—she vaguely heard desperate shouts, muffled by the water lapping in her ears.

On the deck of the yacht, her Jamaican tormentor stood on the edge of the handrail, snarling with fury and pulled out his handgun. He aimed it at the water where Marisa was thrashing about.

"No, no!" came a cry from the rowing boat, where the gang members had seen the commotion. Yuri, one of Timayev's most trusted operatives, dived off the boat and swam toward Marisa, slicing expertly through the water despite the extreme cold to reach her. As she began drifting further down, he dived under and grabbed her.

Marisa felt tired and just wanted to sleep, but suddenly a strong pair of hands pushed her to the surface and she jerked back to consciousness as her lungs gasped and greedily sucked in sweet fresh air. Yuri guided her to the shore and laid her on the ground. She was coughing and spluttering and bringing up a little water, and Yuri gently but persistently pushed down on her chest cavity to expel any excess.

The Jamaican on the boat was shouting and cursing in patois and his colleagues emerged from the cabin and bedrooms, a few already in their underwear, and gathered on the deck, some waving guns. The gang leader had the three remaining girls brought up onto deck. He shouted across the water to Timayev.

"Take your whores—we do not want them. This deal is finished," he spat.

There was a tense few minutes as the rowing boat turned back to the yacht and picked up the girls as the Jamaican gang members looked on angrily. Both sides had their weapons drawn, the pretence of coming unarmed completely abandoned on both sides. Timayev was furious but his face was like stone. He knew in moments like this it was critical to stay calm. It would only take one careless shot for the whole situation to descend into a deadly combat, especially where the trigger happy Jamaicans were concerned. His own team remained disciplined and collected the girls without confrontation, while Timayev offered an apology to the Jamaican gang leader. It barely registered on his face, which was set in a deep scowl, but he accepted the apology with reservation.

"We are going now. We have what we want. Get off my boat!"

He stepped away and Timayev's first instinct was to cosh the Jamaican with the butt of his gun for his insolence. However, he stayed focused and carefully directed his men back to shore where they loaded the girls into the returning Land Cruisers. The rowing boat swiftly returned to the yacht, and the Jamaicans pulled up anchor and quietly chugged away into the night. Timayev sighed with relief. It could have been worse, much worse.

While his colleagues collected the girls, Yuri stayed with Marisa. She regained full consciousness quickly and as she looked up at Yuri, she struggled to get away. However, he held her down gently but firmly. Her limbs still felt like solid blocks of ice, and she offered little resistance.

"What the hell were you doing? You could have drowned," exclaimed Yuri.

Marisa was shivering violently, a good sign, noted Yuri. Her teeth were chattering, and she could just about speak. "W-What do you care?"

"Believe me I do care," he replied. He was desperately cold himself from the water, but he took off his leather coat, squeezed out as much of the remaining water as he could and draped it over her. It was not too effective but would do for now until he could get her back to the house. Marisa was surprised at this act of kindness. Yuri worked like a nurse attending a valuable patient, with compassion and understanding. She had come to regard her captors as cruel and heartless but she had not seen Yuri before tonight. She looked up at him. His face was set in concentration as he attended to her. Although it was scruffy and unshaven, it was not an unkind face, but one that had clearly seen more than its share of death and suffering.

"Thank you," she croaked.

He smiled. "I used to be a medic in Chechnya. Not that it made any difference," he added bitterly. "When a man is badly injured in conflict and you know he is going to die you try and avoid looking him in the eye."

"Why?" asked Marisa, a little surprised at his candour.

"Because if I did they could tell just by my eyes there was nothing I could do to save them. I could only keep them as comfortable as possible until they died. They would search my eyes hopefully and realize they had minutes, sometimes only seconds to live."

Marisa felt a rapid tingling in her heavy limbs as the blood began to course through her body again. "So you gave it up to join a gang dealing in drugs and prostitution?" she challenged him.

Yuri looked at her. "We are funding a very important war. We want our people to be free to live in the land of our fathers without oppression. It is a noble cause." Even as Yuri replied he realized it sounded so hollow. How could this young girl possibly know about the sacrifices people like him had made and continued to make in the battle for freedom in their homeland?

"So would you allow your daughter to be forced into prostitution for your"—her words were heavy with contempt—"noble cause?"

"I don't have a daughter. I *did* have a son though," he stammered, tears welling up at the memory. Suddenly his face hardened. "I do not have to justify myself to you." He lifted her dripping wet in his arms with ease and carried her to one of the nearby Land Cruisers.

Timayev's elation at the deal had been subverted by the events on the boat, and as the first rays of dawn cast their shadow after a long night, he stepped into the house where his girls had been returned. As he walked in with Alexi, a few clients passed by him, squeezing by sheepishly and avoiding his eyes. Business was good again tonight. It was incredible that there never seemed to be a shortage of clients from all walks of life. When he entered this trade he could not have envisaged just how profitable it would prove to be, and it was now a key component of his business empire. But dealing in humans also had its risks. The girls were generally subservient after they had been "tamed," which was something Rahmon was good at, but there were still risks. Although the consignment had been checked and found to be pure, and the deal concluded successfully, the actions of the Bulgarian girl had jeopardized the whole operation. She was volatile and unstable. As he entered her room with Rahmon, he saw she was chained to the bed by her right wrist as he had ordered Yuri to do. The gang's unofficial medic had stayed with Marisa and had wrapped her in warm blankets to increase her body temperature. She was now conscious and alert and cowered on the bed as Timayev entered. She knew her actions would bring consequences. Timayev, however, just smiled. Rahmon stared at her, his huge, fleshy neck bulging with anticipation.

"I have to admire your spirit. You are a brave girl but a stupid one. Clearly you have not been for a swim in Lake Ontario before tonight. I really hope you did not swallow too much water. There are hundreds of toxic chemical pollutants in the lake, including raw sewage, pesticides, uranium and heavy metals like cadmium—and it's a lot cleaner than it used to be." Yuri stared at him hard as he said this. Timayev had been quite happy to order him into the water to save her.

"However," continued Timayev, "the freezing water is a bigger killer and you put one of my men at risk tonight. You also nearly destroyed my transaction and for that you must be punished."

Marisa glared at him silently, her eyes filled with hatred. She said nothing.

Slightly disappointed at her lack of reaction, he motioned to Rahmon who moved threateningly closer. Marisa involuntarily backed away as far as her chained wrist would allow as his huge bulk towered over her.

Timayev continued, "Despite your best efforts, I made a good deal tonight and I am very happy. I am also a lenient man and I will not have you beaten."

Rahmon turned to him, looking slightly disappointed. "It is clear to me you need to be controlled more closely. Fortunately, we have the resources to do this." He spoke calmly and matter-of-factly, but as he nodded to Rahmon, the man mountain grinned and produced a large syringe full of a whitish liquid.

Yuri stared hard at Timayev. "For God's sake Akhmad, is this really necessary? There must be another way," he protested.

Timayev shot a furious glance at Yuri. He was not used to having his orders questioned. "I think it is necessary. Do you wish to challenge me on this Yuri?"

Yuri hesitated for a moment. It was not the first time Akhmad had used this tactic on some of the girls—get them hooked on heroin or amphetamines and they would be dependent on Timayev for as long as they proved useful to him. As a medic, he found the practise degrading and abhorrent. At the same time, he knew how highly his leader valued discipline above all else, and now was not the right time to show dissent in the ranks. "No," he replied meekly.

Timayev gave a triumphant smile and said politely, "Thank you, Yuri."

The Chechen medic turned away, disgusted with himself as much as what was about to happen, as Rahmon, grinning inanely, tossed the blankets aside and grabbed hold of Marisa's left arm. She screamed and tried to twist out of his grasp, her chained arm clanging desperately against the bedstead, but his thick fingers were too strong. He positioned the crook of her arm flat against the bed and pressed the needle of the syringe expertly into the basilic vein.

There was nothing Marisa could do. She howled and looked pleadingly at Yuri, but he sat passively studying the floor while Timayev looked on, smiling. As the needle was jabbed into her arm, her cry became one of intense, sharp pain, and as Rahmon pushed the plunger, she felt the alien liquid begin to course through her veins. It felt warm and brought a calming, pleasurable sensation to her. She began to feel immensely fatigued and had no more energy to struggle anymore. She stopped thrashing about and gave in to her body which just wanted to sleep. The faces of her tormentors became blurred and she slipped away into black unconsciousness.

CHAPTER 12

Dan sat in a secluded booth at the corner of a small bar in St. John's, listening to the gentle twang of country music being played over concealed speakers. Although spring was in full bloom, there was still a piercing wind off the Atlantic that chilled the air, and the bar was a welcome respite from the cold. He had taken a cheap flight that morning into St. John's to follow up an interesting lead in the search for Marisa. Following up the information Brad had given him, he knew exactly when she had arrived at the airport. With Brad's help and after much persuasion, he had managed to convince the security team at the airport to release the CCTV footage around the arrivals exit for a one hour period following arrival of Marisa's flight, allowing for time to collect her baggage and pass through customs. They had emailed him the digital file with a slew of warnings about confidentiality and how the footage must be used, and the dire consequences of failure to observe these rules.

He had studied the black and white footage closely and found nothing unusual for the first fifty minutes. The camera was in an elevated position and had a wide field that allowed views of the doorway and also the road, so that vehicles could also be monitored. However, there was the usual coming and going of people filing in and out of the airport, and cars pulling up and driving off minutes later as they collected passengers. Very routine and very ordinary and Dan was growing bored, thinking all his efforts to get the footage were wasted, until something on screen had made him sit up and pay close attention.

The image showed a dark haired girl walking out with a thick set, muscular man with cropped blond hair. They had their backs to the camera but Dan could see the girl was being held firmly by the arm and guided toward the road. She was not resisting but it was apparent from the film that she was being pulled along. She was clearly not dressed for the weather, in a light frock and cardigan. It was evident from the way other people were bundled up that it was a very cold day, and even her companion wore a heavy sheepskin coat. As they turned toward the road they faced the camera for a fleeting moment. The image of their faces was quite grainy. Dan stopped the film and reversed it back to where their faces came into view. He could not make out their features clearly and as he clicked to expand that section of the footage their faces began to fill his computer screen. Although he lost clarity in doing so, he had enough to convince himself that he had found Marisa. Even from the jumble of pixels, her features appeared to match the photograph Vasil had given him.

Dan looked with concern at the pixellated image of Marisa's companion. Despite the grainy image, he could see the man had a strong, square-jawed face that held a hint of raw aggression, reinforced by his angry scowl and a long ugly scar below his left eye. Dan had seen the type before. This was no employee from an au pair agency. He carried the look of a professional soldier, and had a stature to match. He could probably kill a person with his bare hands, doubtless without a flicker of remorse.

He had continued to run the film and seen a Toyota Land Cruiser pull up quickly along the road. Marisa's companion had quickly bundled her into the vehicle, which had moved swiftly out of camera-shot. Even though the images were silent, Dan could almost hear the screech of the Toyota as it sped up the road. He could not see inside the vehicle as there was an element of glare on the windscreen. However, by expanding the image of the front of the vehicle he could just figure out the licence plate number.

It had not taken Dan long to run a check on the licence plate through one of the various online agencies to get the details of the vehicle owner. Was anything private these days, he had wondered as he brought up the full profile of the owner almost to his leg measurement in less than ten minutes. It made his job easier, at least. The Land Cruiser belonged to a construction worker who lived just outside St. John's and had reported the vehicle stolen. Dan suspected they would have dumped the vehicle very soon after the delivery as they had not even bothered to put false plates on the car.

He had made contact with the owner, Ben Franklin, and at first he had been reticent to talk.

"I've been through all this with the police," he said. Dan, however, had explained to him his interest in the matter, and eventually he reluctantly agreed to meet up with Dan. He did not want to say too much on the phone, so Dan offered to fly to St. John's to meet him. Even as Dan waited, he was still uncertain whether Franklin would show up. He glanced at his watch. It was ten past three and their meeting had been arranged for three. He looked around the bar—he was positioned so he could see the entrance but the bar was very quiet, only a few regulars slumped over their drinks propping up the counter and a couple of occupied booths. Then in walked a tall, slim man dressed in work clothes and heavy boots. His face was masked by a pepper coloured beard and a baseball cap pulled down low. He looked around suspiciously, as if he were being followed. It had to be Franklin. Dan waved him over and ordered him a coffee. They exchanged peremptory handshakes as Franklin squeezed his gangly six foot three frame into the booth opposite the private investigator.

"Thank you for agreeing to see me," said Dan.

Franklin was diffident. "Yeah, well I haven't got long. I nearly didn't come," he admitted.

"I'm glad you did."

"So what's this about a girl?"

"I believe your stolen vehicle was used by a gang to pick up one or more girls from the airport. I think these girls are being exploited within a human trafficking ring."

Franklin sat back and whistled. "Whoa. I didn't think that sort of thing happened here. Montreal or Vancouver maybe, but St. John's?"

"That's precisely why they would choose an entry port like this. It is less likely to be scrutinized," replied Dan. "So what did you do when you discovered your car was stolen?"

Franklin reached into his pocket for his cell phone. "I reported it to the police as soon as I was aware of it. I had parked it at a car lot near the station and gone to work on a contract for a few days. It was only when I came back in the evening several days later I discovered it was gone. I went immediately to the police and they took the details but warned me the vehicle could have been stolen any time and could be anywhere by now. They agreed to a look out on their patrols but they did not hold out much hope. Then the next day I got this voicemail message."

He handed Dan his cell phone. He put the attached earphones on and played the message. The caller had an accent that he could not quite place, an Eastern European or Russian twang. It was said in a slow drawl that lent his voice a menacing tone. However, it was the content which was more disturbing. It was only thirty seconds long, short but concise. There was a clear threat that any attempt to proceed with the complaint to the police would be met with retribution. They reeled off the names and ages of his two young children and where they attended school. They did not need to say anymore. It was obvious what would happen and it made the message even more chilling. Dan played it again, listening intently to the caller's accent, before handing it silently back to Franklin.

The construction worker gave an ironic smile. "I don't think these guys were messing about. I have to confess it spooked me. They must have been watching us. I was not prepared to risk my children just for a poxy Land Cruiser. In any event the police called me a couple of days later and reported that it had been found burnt out at the bottom of a ravine about forty kilometres west of Corner Brook."

"That's a long way from here. Did they carry out any forensics?" asked Dan.

"I don't think they were too interested. It was just another stolen vehicle to them, not worth investigating. I did not tell them about the message. I must admit I was too scared. They just told me to claim on my insurance and as far as they were concerned, the investigation was over.

"Probably better that way," suggested Dan.

"I don't want any trouble. I am taking a risk seeing you. They know where I live and they are serious. I really hope you find your girl but please, don't contact me again."

Dan slid his business card across the table to Franklin, but the construction worker refused it. He got up and pulled his baseball cap low, looked furtively around and quickly exited the bar. Dan paid the bill and left shortly after and took a cab to the airport.

As he flew back he pondered his next course of action. The trip had not yielded much information except to confirm what he already suspected. However, there was a growing Eastern European population in Toronto and he would need to make some discreet enquiries, because at present he had no solid leads. It would be useful having Vasil with him to help bridge the culture or language gap, but it could be perilous and he needed to confirm with Vasil he was comfortable with it.

When he arrived back at his office in Toronto he checked his phone messages and emails. There was nothing urgent and so that evening he walked to the hostel where Vasil was staying. Despite the time of year, there was a distinct chill in the air, although it was positively balmy compared to the raw but beautiful east coast of Newfoundland he had flown in from earlier that day.

When he reached the hostel, the same grouchy middle-aged man squatted at the reception desk, his head buried in a book. He glared at Dan with a trace of hostility, annoyed at having to put his book down, but did not appear to recognize him.

"I am looking for Vasil Dimitrov."

The hostel attendant's brows furrowed in irritation at the mention of the name. Oh, you mean the Bulgarian," he replied. "He's gone. He left here yesterday. Took all his things and just went. I went to collect his payment for the next few days and found him gone. If you see him can you tell him he owes me for three nights? Do they think my boss is running a free house here?"

"Yeah, I'll be sure to tell him," said Dan, a sarcastic edge to his voice. That was worrying. Where could he be? It was too late for him to be handing leaflets out again so Dan took his Chevy around the area, occasionally being tooted by impatient drivers as he slowed down looking intently for clues. It was no use. It was getting too dark and so he pulled into a scruffy car lot and took a walk. His instincts told him Vasil was on the street. There were a number of homeless people scattered round, huddled in doorways, wrapped tightly in torn blankets, as even the late spring nights could get rough. They usually just wanted to be left alone and not hassled—the police did enough of that, and when Dan disturbed them to ask if they had seen a new guy around he was usually met with blank stares or irritated cursing.

After a few fruitless attempts he asked one guy who looked more like a college student on a camping vacation, clearly a newcomer to the streets himself. He did not wear the haunted, gaunt look of a street veteran. He nodded in recognition as Dan described Vasil. He pointed in the general direction of a large tower block further up the street of flats. "Try that tower. The newcomers always camp in the entrance lobby before they realize it's too dangerous." Despite his youthful looks, he said this with the authority of bitter experience.

Dan slipped him ten dollars and quickly headed to the tower block. It was a squalid looking building, encased in crumbling, stained concrete, and as he approached he could see a number of youths loitering about the base of the building, all dressed in the street uniform of hoodies and baseball caps, and jeans halfway down their butt. A few were trying skateboard tricks as others watched them, smoking or swigging from bottles. As he walked toward them they stopped their raucous chattering and stared at him silently with an almost palpable hostility, aggrieved at this intrusion on their territory. As he headed quickly for the wide, glass fronted doorway of the tower block, one of the youths rolled at speed directly at him on his skateboard. Dan stopped and stood his ground, ready to jump out of the way, but at the last second the youth veered away and bumped Dan's shoulder as he rolled past. The other youths watched this show of intimidation with amused interest and decided he was not worth messing with, and he reached the cheerless doorway unmolested.

There were a few sets of huddled blankets scattered along the doorway, where protruding feet offered the only sign a person lay under the messy pile. He lifted them to look for Vasil, and was met with an angry stream of obscenities. The doorway itself was locked and apart from the youths and the homeless, no one else was brave enough to be around now it was fully dark. He skirted around the other side of the building to the south doorway, a similar entrance but even more dingy. He spotted another group of hoodies congregated in the doorway, clustered around something or someone. They were shouting and swearing at whoever or whatever they grouped around, and Dan saw an occasional kick aimed at the prone figure on the floor.

Dan, his interest aroused, silently drifted toward the throng. He heard a scream of protest from amongst the group and his heart missed a beat as he recognized an Eastern European accent. Without further thought he marched toward the group and shouted "Hey!" and they all turned toward him, fixing him with belligerent scowls. One youth of about eighteen produced a weapon like a piece of lead piping and moved ominously toward Dan. His pierced face was twisted in a hateful grimace and the others began to edge forward in support, their victim momentarily forgotten.

The armed youth raised the lead pipe in preparation for a strike. "You had better leave now if you want to keep your head on your shoulders mate," he threatened, edging menacingly closer.

Dan tensed, ready to pounce. He felt his anger rising as he was convinced it was Vasil who was being tormented by the gang, but there were five of them and his anger was mixed with fear. The gang members briefly lost interest in the huddled figure on the floor and began encouraging the youth. Desperate not to lose face, he grinned at his friends before lunging at Dan, swinging the pipe wildly. However, his coordination was clumsy and Dan easily sidestepped the youth whose momentum carried him to one side of Dan. Before the youth could recover and resume his attack, Dan aimed a swift kick with his flat sole which connected hard against his torso in the soft area around the kidney. The youth gave a muted grunt and dropped to the ground, dropping the pipe and clutching his torso in agony. As he lay motionless on the ground whimpering, the other gang members involuntarily stepped back from Dan. They snarled angrily at him, but no one seemed brave enough to be the next to attack. Dan had seen it before. Despite their threatening stance, he could see the cold glint of fear in their eyes. He decided to use this to his advantage quickly before they gained renewed courage.

"Who's next?" he growled, assuming an exaggerated Taekwondo posture.

No one came to the assistance of their friend, and Dan was sure the youth would be punished further by the gang for losing credibility. A couple of them began to step forward but sensibly decided Dan was not worth the bother, and they drifted away, hurling insults after Dan and threats of "watch your back."

Dan quickly headed to the doorway where the figure was huddled against the entrance, and he immediately recognized Vasil. He was shaken and had endured a few kicks but was otherwise unharmed.

"My God, look at you," exclaimed Dan, seeing Vasil's dishevelled state. He helped the Bulgarian to his feet and hoisted Vasil's holdall over his shoulder. "Why did you leave the hostel?"

Vasil staggered forward, clearly relieved at seeing Dan. "I have no more money. I have only what I can pay you. A man told me to sleep here." He produced from his back pocket a small tattered wallet that contained a number of twenty dollar notes. "This is all for you to find my daughter." He glanced at Dan. I hope it is enough."

Dan turned to him. "Vasil, these streets are dangerous. You should not have left the hostel just to save money. You were probably two minutes from losing all your money and everything else you brought to Canada and they would still have given you a nasty beating just for the hell of it. Let's get out of here."

They walked briskly through the poorly lit streets, Dan occasionally glancing warily over his shoulder to make sure they were not being followed by resentful gang members, and they stopped at a late night café where Vasil hungrily wolfed down a plate of fish and chips. Dan could tell he had not eaten that day. As they ate, he made up his mind. He had considered it from the moment he heard Vasil had left the hostel.

"Vasil, you should stay at my flat. It's not that comfortable and you will need to sleep on the sofa but at least it's better than a stinking tower block entrance."

Vasil did not protest. His short but harrowing experience of life on the streets in Toronto was enough. "Thank you," he whispered, clearly grateful.

"But Vasil, I need you to work with me. I am struggling to come up with any definite leads on Marisa but I do know she was taken by an Eastern European or Russian gang." He explained his findings on the CCTV and the meeting with Ben Franklin in St. John's. "I need you to help me make some enquiries around the local community. We need to find out if anyone knows about this group holding Marisa. They are more likely to be helpful with you around. They will not talk to me on my own. I should warn you it could get dangerous. We risk getting some unwanted attention but I don't think we have a choice."

Vasil peered intently at Dan. His eyes held a steely determination Dan had not seen before. The Bulgarian's voice was firm and his words were clear. "I will do whatever it takes to get my daughter back."

CHAPTER 13

Dan's tiny bedsit was cramped and uncomfortable at the best of times, and Vasil had to sleep on the sofa bed in the main living room, which had been untidy to start with. However, Vasil was so unobtrusive that Dan hardly noticed his presence. In fact, Vasil cleaned and tidied his flat when he was at work the following day, something Dan hardly had time or inclination to do. Dan spent the next few days catching up on his other cases, which he had to admit had been allowed to slip. He had to fend off a few angry calls from officious government employees who reminded him in no uncertain terms of their status and expectations as clients.

When Dan had arrived from work after a long day, Vasil had a steaming plate of *Gyuvetch*, a traditional Bulgarian dish of beef and peppers waiting for him. It was absolutely delicious, and as he looked around the apartment, it looked and felt cleaner than at any time he had lived there. It was like being married again, but without some obvious benefits, he laughed to himself. He also found Vasil's company very stimulating and enjoyable. Vasil talked fondly of his family and despite his obvious poverty and the poor quality of life in Bulgaria, Marisa's father had a naturally optimistic outlook. It had never once occurred to him he might not find Marisa. It was also clear that as the eldest child Marisa was particularly special to him, and he would stop at nothing in his search. Vasil had total confidence in Dan, and although it put added pressure on him, it made Dan more determined to succeed, if only to conquer some of his own demons.

Vasil was also an attentive listener and Dan found himself confiding in him in a way he had not done with anyone in years. He talked about Sarah and his anger and guilt after her death, and

Vasil showed empathy and understanding. In Dan's mind this was becoming less of a business arrangement and more of a mission.

They discussed their next course of action, and the following evening, they were ready to head out to the area around Roncesvalles Avenue, a leafy suburban area in the west of the city that housed a growing Eastern European population. They parked close by in High Park and decided to walk along the pleasant streets, Vasil armed with his precious photocopies. As they meandered along in the early evening spring sunshine, they saw people sitting out on pavement cafés reading the paper or sipping coffee. Others just sat on the steps of tall Victorian style townhouses just watching the world go by. It was a scene of complete serenity, as if this area had been insulated from the cares of the outside world. Vasil did not waste the opportunity to hand out copies of his daughter's photo to these bystanders and Dan observed as they glanced at them disinterestedly and shook their heads. He had to admire Vasil's tenacity. In this big city he was always working against the odds, and he was not confident their enquiries tonight would yield anything, but they had to try.

He had done a little research on the area and identified a few bars to try first. He explained to Vasil that this area had the highest concentration of Eastern Europeans, mainly Polish and Ukrainians, but also other ethnic groups such as Russians. Dan's experience was that the most unlikely sources could provide leads in missing person cases, and there was no substitute for this type of exhaustive enquiry. However, it was not without its dangers. Brad had provided him with some information about the drug activity in the area, which centred around a number of bars Dan was intending to visit. Curiously, however, Brad suggested to Dan not to make these enquiries. When Dan pressed him he was a little evasive, only saying it could be dangerous.

They tried several bars and restaurants as they began filling up, but were often met with antagonistic glances and a refusal to even take Marisa's photo. They had rehearsed their story—Dan was a family friend and Vasil had recently moved to Toronto with his family, but Marisa had run away from home. They were careful to avoid any suggestions that Marisa had been taken, as this could cause some unwelcome attention. As it was Dan perceived a degree of hostility and as the evening wore on, they had made little progress. However, one drinker had mumbled to them that they should try the Cavern Club, a seedy basement bar at the northern end of Roncesvalles Avenue.

It was past eleven when they arrived at the club, set back from the main avenue, only a small neon sign pointing down toward a black doorway to advertise its presence. It was so inconspicuous that it had taken them a long time to find the club, and the entrance, set below ground level, was dark and uninviting, garbage bags piled high on either side of the narrow entrance. It looked like the back way, but Dan and Vasil could not see any other way in, so they descended the metal steps toward the door. The stairwell down was like a fire escape and their feet clanged on the metal. Dan gingerly opened the door and they were confronted by a large, brooding bouncer who eyed them carefully before deciding to step aside and let them in. As Dan entered, he could see why it was called the Cavern Club. It was a cramped basement with low ceilings and subdued lighting. The driving beats coming from the DJ in the corner and the hordes of clubbers crowded around a small dance floor reinforced the feeling of claustrophobia. As they fought their way through the crowds pushing and shoving against them they made it to the bar. Dan caught the attention of the barman, a stocky man in his mid-forties with a bulbous chin and a mean expression. Dan ordered a couple of beers, raising his voice above the pounding music, and the barman gave him an irritated scowl as he slammed the drinks on the counter.

"Have you seen this girl?" he shouted, thrusting a picture of Marisa into his hand.

The barman scanned the photo briefly and handed it back. "Who's asking?" he said.

"I'm a family friend. This is her father. She ran away from home and we think she may be around here."

"Nope I haven't seen her." He began to move away as customers clamoured at the bar, waving dollar bills in his direction.

"Can I speak to your boss?"

The barman glared at him, his eyes narrowed. "Why?"

"We need to find her. It's very important. Please."

The barman impatiently pointed toward a door at the far end of the club. "The door next to the exit sign. Through there. Now get out of my face." He turned away, scowling. Dan and Vasil fought their way through the crowd and slowly opened the door into a narrow hallway which led to another room at the end. The door to the room was open and Dan could hear voices and some raucous laughing, and smoke drifted lazily from the room into the hallway.

Dan had a distinctly uncomfortable feeling and Vasil hesitated behind him, ready to turn and go. However, Dan squared his shoulders and walked into the room. There was a group of six men playing cards on a round table, laughing and joking, surrounded by a smoke haze from their thick cigars. The room was dimly lit by a single frayed light bulb and the walls and furniture were black. He was immediately confronted by a huge minder who barred his way, and the group stopped their game of cards and glared at the intruders.

One of the men in the middle of the group, adorned with a stack of expensive gold jewellery on his wrists, neck and fingers, spoke to Dan in a heavy Slavic accent. "Who the hell are you?"

Dan nodded to the doorway back into the main club. He could barely see over the bulk of the minder. "Your barman sent me here. We are looking for a girl."

The man's face cracked into a smile, revealing even more gold in his two front teeth. "Aren't we all," he joked and the group launched into a mocking laughter. He nodded to the minder who roughly frisked Dan and Vasil. Finding no weapons, he decided they offered no threat, being half his size, and pushed them in front of the table. Dan felt like a child summoned before the headmaster, the group regarding Dan and Vasil with silent suspicion.

"So who is this girl?" he asked. His tone carried a sense of amusement as if he were showing off to his guests.

Dan spoke up. "Her name is Marisa, and she has been missing for many weeks since running away from home. This is her father."

Vasil gave a weak smile and carefully laid a batch of photos on the table. The other men took one and regarded her with detached interest. One murmured that she was a real beauty. Dan carefully scanned their faces and noted one of the card players staring at the photo with a serious expression, rubbing his temple in concentration. Dan's instincts suggested he might know something about Marisa, but as he tried to catch his eye the man quickly turned away.

"So what is your interest?"

"I'm a family friend," replied Dan.

"Of course you are. Well Mr family friend this is not a missing persons' bureau. As you can see we are busy and you are disturbing us. We don't know anything about your girl although if you find her tell her she would be welcome as one of my strippers any time," he grinned, gold teeth glinting. The rest of the group laughed and Vasil's face flushed red with rage, but to Dan's relief he did not react. The odds were stacked against them and the comment was a deliberate attempt at provocation.

The club owner's gold smile quickly faded. "We have a game to finish here so get out of my club." That was a signal for the huge minder to grab both men by the arm and roughly steer them back through the hallway into the main club. As he did so, one of the card players threw down his cards and stood up.

"I'm done here. I will see them out." He followed through as the minder shoved Dan and Vasil onto the floor of the club and disappeared back through the door. The card player walked toward them and Dan noticed it was the same man who had studied Marisa's picture so intently.

He glanced around furtively and grabbed Vasil gently by the elbow, silently guiding them to a small booth in a dark corner of the club. As he did so he scanned the area again but no one took any notice of them, focused instead on dancing to the thudding beat or standing around drinking and eyeing up the talent. They sat down and the man talked low despite the background noise. Vasil and Dan had to strain to hear him.

"Listen, I don't have long," he hissed. "If they see me with you I am as good as dead." He turned to Vasil. "I know where your daughter is."

Vasil's jaw dropped in shock. "Where, where, tell me!" he said.

"Hold on. It's not as simple as that. I can't tell you now. You are going to have to trust me."

Despite the background noise, Dan could tell his accent was also Slavic, but with more of a twang than the arrogant gold-tooth. "Why should we trust you? We don't know you."

The man glared at Dan. "Because you have no choice if you want to find Marisa alive."

He took out his cell phone. "I know who you are, Dan Huberman, private investigator. Your story about being a family friend isn't fooling anyone. I want to help, but I can't talk here. Give me your cell phone number and I will call you tomorrow."

He programmed Dan's number into his phone. "Can I take yours?" asked Dan.

He shook his head. "No, I will contact you. There is one thing I will give you now. He pulled out a crumpled business card. The name on it had been etched out but it carried a company name and a logo. He handed it to Dan who studied it carefully. The company name was called rather innocuously Rebel Antiquities but underneath in italics were the words "победа в крови." He was not sure of the language. The logo was of a grey wolf sitting proudly on a raised dais with the moon behind it, an image contained in a white circle. The circle itself was encased in a green and red background. It was a curious picture.

"It's an import and export company for antique furniture and fine art, only that is not all it imports." He looked around suspiciously again and leaned even closer to Dan and Vasil.

"Friday night, the company is making a delivery of a big consignment of drugs for the East African market. I heard your girl may be there. I don't know exactly where yet. That's all I can say for now."

"Why are you telling us all this?"

"Let's just say I have a moral problem with the way the company is being run. You don't need to know any more than that."

"At least tell us your name. You seem to know me well enough," said Dan.

"Yuri."

Yuri waited a few minutes for Dan and Vasil to leave the club and he then followed. He had been wrestling with his conscience for days, but when the two men had arrived looking for Marisa, he had acted on impulse. He had found it difficult to look into her father's eyes, but now he had chosen a path from which there was no turning back. He quickly headed back to his apartment—there was a lot of work to do. As he left the club a lone drinker sat in the shadows, silently observing the short meeting from a nearby booth, oblivious to the loud, crowded surroundings. As he watched the Chechen man leave, he pulled out his cell phone and made the call.

"Akhmad?" It's me. It is as you thought." He listened intently, one hand cupped over his other ear, receiving his instructions.

"Yes, yes, I know what must be done." He gulped down the last of his drink and strode out of the club.

CHAPTER 14

Dan spent the next morning working through his considerable backlog and fending off irritated clients, but he managed to find a little time to look at the company through its public filing documents held on the Ontario provincial registry of companies. He studied the articles of incorporation, and noted the company was just over three years old. There were five directors, all with Russian or Eastern European names. He made a note of them to check their origin later. There were no home addresses, just a service address the same as the company's registered office. The public records no longer held residential addresses, a legacy of the attacks on directors in controversial industries such as pharmaceuticals. It was hard to know if they were Canadian residents, although Ontario corporate law required at least a quarter of the directors to live in Canada.

One of the directors was Yuri. The primary activity of the company was stated exactly as Yuri had mentioned, and the company's filing showed two shareholders, one with a 49% holding and one with 51%. They were both overseas trusts, one based in Liechtenstein and the other in Luxembourg. Dan had seen this type of structure before. The company probably had a legitimate business importing and exporting antiques and fine art, and no doubt if he visited the company's registered office he would see an active and honest trading entity with several employees and a modest turnover.

However, Dan surmised, behind the facade was a more nefarious activity, one that did not show up on the company's balance sheet or its taxes, yet was probably far more lucrative than its "front" business. No doubt the beneficial owners of the offshore trusts controlled this aspect of the business, and likely controlled the directors. The true personalities behind the company would probably never surface.

This veil of secrecy was a useful protective mechanism if things went wrong, as well as a useful vehicle for funnelling the proceeds of illegal activity, which quickly got lost in the complex financial system and ended up in secret bank accounts.

Vasil had been up early as usual, despite their late night at the club, on his usual mission distributing pictures of his beloved daughter. He had left the club with renewed optimism that Marisa would be found, but this was mixed with a fear of the terrible ordeal she was still suffering. In many ways, not knowing was the most difficult part. He was not complacent, and stuck to his monotonous routine diligently in the faint hope that a stranger might just turn around and recognize her smiling face.

Dan had furnished Vasil with a cell phone, and had agreed to call him the moment he received any further communication. Dan waited anxiously for the call, still wondering if it would indeed happen. He could not believe his luck. It appeared that the evening was going to be fruitless until they reached the Cavern Club. He had no reason to believe Yuri would not call. After all, he had approached them and had given them some useful information already. His thoughts were interrupted by a bleep of his cell phone. He picked it up and a text message was displayed.

"Wait by the Air India Memorial at Humber Bay Park at 7 tonight. I will find you. Come alone."

The message was not signed but it was not necessary. Dan's heart leapt in excitement as he studied the message. This meeting could prove a major breakthrough. He was confident Marisa would be found soon. However, he noted the warning at the end of the message. He called Vasil with the news and told him he would go alone. Although Vasil protested, they had to follow instructions. This meeting could go either way.

Although he was so busy, he found himself glancing at his watch constantly and the rest of the day seemed to drag. At six he was in his car and driving across downtown, fighting rush hour traffic before arriving at the park a quarter hour early. He quickly parked up and headed toward the dark marble monument, a tribute to the three hundred and twenty-nine crew and passengers of Air India Flight 182 from Toronto that was blown up in mid-air over the Atlantic just west of Ireland en route to London and Delhi in 1985. It was a tragic reminder of man's barbarity and cruelty to his fellow man. The beautiful polished shrine was reached by a network of gravel paths that ran past the monument toward the lake, serene and glass-like in the fading sunshine. As he looked toward the lake, however, he could sense something happening, and he heard the strident blare of police sirens flying past.

He walked quickly along the paths and saw an ambulance rapidly negotiate the route usually reserved for cyclists and joggers. Several of them moved quickly aside as the ambulance barged past, flashing lights and sirens in full emergency mode. It rushed toward a scene of bustling activity. As Dan moved closer, he could see a small crowd gathering by the beach area just further on from the memorial, where a natural harbour was created by a peninsula which jutted out into the lake. The water here was as still as a pond, but surrounding the beach area was the unmistakable bright yellow tape of a police crime scene. He glanced at his watch. It was nearly seven and there was still warmth in the late spring air, but Dan felt a cold chill as he moved toward the group assembled around the beach. He gently steered through the crowd and reached the yellow tape. A tall, athletic police officer stood resolutely in front of the tape and addressed the growing throng, the contempt in his voice almost palpable.

"Folks, please move back. There is nothing to see here. Let us do our job." His plea fell on deaf ears. If anything, the crowd pressed in even closer, clearly believing there was something to see. Dan addressed the policeman directly. "What's happening officer?"

He let out an exasperated sigh. "We got reports of a body washed up on the lake. Probably someone who ventured too far out and got in trouble. There is nothing to see," he repeated. Dan knew even the police officer did not truly believe that—this area of the lake was so sheltered it was like a mill pond.

The small squadron of police cars and the ambulance now parked on the beach created a poor shield against the curious crowd of people. Dan could see past them and watched a team of police divers emerge from the water. He moved back and found a more elevated position away from the main throng up the incline and remembered the field glasses in his pocket, one of the essential tools of his trade. A couple of divers gave disconsolate shakes of the head as they emerged, ripping their masks off. Nearby a body was being dragged out of the water and it appeared to be twisted at an odd angle. Then he realized why. Dan could clearly see the torso was headless and also naked from the waist up. There was a gasp from the crowd as others saw this horror and some turned away in disgust. He adjusted his field glasses further and the body filled his field of vision. Although it was bloated from its time in the water, the body looked like a white, slim, middle-aged male. Something was carved across his chest, as if by a knife. He focused his glasses to see closer. He could not be certain but it looked like the word "traitor." The body was quickly covered in a white sheet and hoisted onto a gurney and placed in the ambulance, which sped away, sirens still blaring.

As Dan surveyed this incredible scene, the stark realization swept over him. It was past seven o'clock now and he was certain now that Yuri would not be attending their planned meeting.

CHAPTER 15

Driving back toward home in the waning daylight, Dan's brain throbbed with a mass of jumbled thoughts. His overriding emotion was one of anxiety. Already the media was reporting breaking news that a headless body had been fished out of Lake Ontario. Dan had no doubt who it was, and he was gripped with the icy cold realization that this gang was prepared to kill to protect whatever information it had. The stakes had suddenly become higher. This was no longer just a missing person enquiry. He had inadvertently stumbled on what appeared to be a fairly sophisticated drug operation, one which was prepared to kill its own to protect its secrets.

Dan had also lost a valuable lead which appeared to link directly to Marisa. However, withdrawing from this investigation was no longer an option. As he turned the events of the last few days over in his mind, he realized they had probably been seen with Yuri. The radio said the body had been in the water less than twenty four hours. They could have followed Yuri from the club and killed him that evening.

His reverie was interrupted by the strident horn of a fire engine racing up quickly behind him, lights flashing, and he pulled to one side. The fire engine flew past and was rapidly joined by a police car in full siren mode. They took a right turn up Finch Avenue and he followed them. As he gazed up the long, bustling street, he saw a thick pall of smoke curling lazily into the sky just east of Finch. He had a sudden knot in his throat and drove faster, jumping a red light and receiving an angry blast from the horn of an irate driver. He ignored the man's angry gesture and raced along toward the billowing black cloud.

He turned the corner and saw the flickering orange glow of a fire that had consumed most of a two storey property. The firefighters were spraying foam and water into the guts of the building but a stiff breeze was fanning the fire and the crackling flames whipped around in a frenzy, making it difficult for the crew to control the blaze. Nearby residents had been evacuated from their homes and stood back from the blaze chattering excitedly amongst themselves.

As soon as he had seen the direction of the smoke cloud, Dan had a hollow feeling in the pit of his stomach—almost instinctively he knew where the blaze was. As he pulled up behind the banks of fire engines and police cars that sealed the road ahead, his suspicions were confirmed. His first thought was a desperate concern for the frail but cheerful old lady who lived alone in the upper floor apartment. His office had been decimated, and with it his business. He felt an odd calm as he arrived there, shielding his face from the intense heat of the flames engulfing the structure which was now little more than a shell. For a short time he stood watching with the other residents behind a police cordon as the firefighters skilfully brought the fire under control.

Within minutes the building was a charred, smouldering wreck spilling out acrid fumes that drifted over the assembled crowd. A small throng of police officers began to press the crowd back, urging them to disperse to avoid the choking air, and they reluctantly began to move away. Dan could see from the blackened interior that nothing could possibly have been saved inside. An officer was standing close by manning the cordon that surrounded the property and Dan took out his business card and handed it to him.

"My landlord is gonna go crazy," he said, "not to mention my clients. Any idea how it started?"

"Too early to say I'm afraid. Once the building has been secured a forensics team will be on the scene. I suggest you stick around. I'm sure they will have some questions."

"There was an old lady who lived in the flat above my office." His voice was heavy with trepidation. "Is she okay?"

"As far as we know, the building was unoccupied, and there were no reports of any cries for help. Lucky you were not working late sir."

Dan gave a weak smile. "I'm out of the office a lot in my line of work."

He turned away and fumbled for his cell phone. He had to warn Vasil that they could be in danger. As he did so his phone beeped at him. The number on the phone was unfamiliar.

He hesitated, a slight tremor in his voice. "Yes?"

He turned white as he listened to the heavily accented voice. Dan recalled Franklin's voice-mail message in St. John's, that slow menacing drawl. They sounded like the same person.

"I hope you enjoy the pyrotechnics show, my friend. There will be more to follow if you insist on looking for the girl." Despite the accent, his English was perfect.

"Who the hell are you?"

The voice on the line gave an ironic laugh. "I am a person you really do not want to fool with. I am sorry we appear to have put you out of business. I think spying on other people is such a dirty business anyway. Maybe I have done you a favour."

"Not as dirty as kidnapping young girls for prostitution," retorted Dan.

There was a pause at the other end and the voice was hostile. "I am giving you fair warning to stay out of our affairs. The consequences if you do not will be very severe."

"You've destroyed my livelihood. What more can you do?"

"That was just a small encouragement to stay away. There is plenty more we can do. We will be watching you."

"Are you threatening me?"

The voice on the line sighed in exasperation. "Let's get one thing clear. I am warning you. I do not make idle threats. Any retribution will be swift and deadly and I promise you will not see it coming."

"Like you did to Yuri?"

"He was indiscreet."

Keep him talking, thought Dan. "Is that how you deal with people who work for you?"

Another pause on the line. "He knew the risks. It was unwise talking to you."

Dan was indignant. "So you had him killed just for talking to me? He didn't even tell me anything! What sort of person are you?" *Keep him talking.*

"Mr Huberman, whether you realize it or not, there is a war going on out there. Loyalty is critical to me and those who do not show me loyalty must be prepared to face the consequences. Casualties are inevitable. Forget looking for Marisa or you will be part of the war and you will become one of those casualties."

"But—"

There was a click on the line and it instantly went dead.

Damn! He hoped he had been on the line long enough. His Smartphone had a built in recording facility that he had quickly utilized to capture most of the conversation. It also had a GPS tracker. All phones emitted a roaming signal even when they were on the move, and this would be picked up for transmission by the next nearby antenna tower. It was then possible to use the GSM system, the global system for mobile communications, a globally accepted standard for digital cellular communication. He could operate GSM localization using multilateration based on the signal strength to nearby antenna masts. The multilateration process, often used in military surveillance, could locate an object by accurately computing the time difference of arrival of a signal emitted from the phone to three or more receivers, based on distance.

His Smartphone had the software to calculate the time differences to each receiver and use this to determine a fairly precise position which was translated into GPS coordinates. For his system to work, it needed the caller to stay on the line long enough for the software to make the calculation. The system had cost him a fortune but it had proved useful in many cases in tracking the location of a subject.

Although the system was accurate, it did not in itself provide the answer. The person in question could be anywhere and on the move, and it had never proved possible for him to find someone immediately as a result of the technology, although he had heard the FBI and other law enforcement agencies used it for that purpose. However, it did provide him with useful information. In his experience people were creatures of habit, and they often visited the same places where a call had been made. Armed with the information on location, Dan could visit the location to make an assessment of why they may have been there. In some criminal cases a target had called from their home thinking their cell could never be traced but the landline could, and the GSM technology had allowed the authorities to locate and apprehend them easily.

Dan waited with anticipation while the software worked through the calculations until it flashed up the longitude and latitude coordinates. As the information flashed on his phone, he raised his eyebrows in surprise. He recalled Yuri's mention of a drug deal on Friday night, just two days from now. As he looked at the coordinates, he realized he had a strong intuition about where it was going to take place.

CHAPTER 16

Vasil had made Dan another speciality Bulgarian dish, this time for breakfast. Dan had decided on a late, leisurely start to the day. He had no office to go to any longer and he just needed a morning to allow himself some breathing space and think things over. He had a number of phone calls to make to clients to inform them of the fire, although it appeared several were already aware and had texted him to offer their support. His client files had been completely destroyed, and he had been unable to salvage anything from the melted wreck of his computer. However, his business was not lost, as a lot of backup information was held on his personal PC in his bedsit. He would need to undertake an arduous and intricate task of reconstructing his records as far as possible.

The police had already contacted him. The initial finding from the fire service was that the explosion had been caused by a faulty gas main and there were no suspicious circumstances. Dan of course knew differently but had decided not to share his information with the police just yet. He needed to speak to Brad first.

As Dan chewed on the Bulgarian *milinki* bread, Vasil served him tea.

"I am very sorry Dan," he said, his head bowed.

"For what?"

"For getting you involved in this. I had no right to ask you."

"Vasil," began Dan. "You had every right. Your daughter is missing and we still have a mission to find her."

"But this is not your fight."

"It is now. Marisa has been taken by some bad people and I have a much better idea of who than I had a few days ago. Anyway, it's personal now. These guys destroyed my office and would have killed the dear old lady who lives in the flat above if she had not been out at her bingo night. I am involved whether I want to be or not. We had a very important lead that turned up headless in the lake, but we cannot give up now. We find out who these guys are and we find Marisa. We know there is a drug deal happening tomorrow night and I aim to be there. Surveillance is my job and I intend to find out exactly who this gang is."

"But it is very dangerous. If they are anything like our gangs in Bulgaria, they catch you and you are dead," warned Vasil.

Dan was touched by Vasil's concern. He regarded this courageous and dignified Bulgarian with great respect, and the two men had developed a strong friendship in a short period of time. "Don't worry, I won't do this alone. I have support. I know just who to call."

Vasil looked at the floor, unconvinced. Dan reached out and gave him a reassuring squeeze of the shoulders. "I *will* get Marisa back for you." He wished he could be as confident as he sounded.

Dan reached Brad immediately. His friend's voice was full of concern. "Hey buddy, I heard what happened to your office last night. Are you okay?"

"I'm fine. I wasn't there. Do you know who did this?"

Brad hesitated. "What do you mean? I heard it was a faulty gas main that blew apart."

"I got a phone call after the fire. It was a warning to stay away."

"From who?"

"I was hoping you could tell me."

"Dan, you know I don't work in that field. What has this to do with drug enforcement?"

"Because it was from the gang that took Marisa."

There was silence on the line. When he spoke, Brad's voice was low, almost threatening. "Dan, listen to me. I think you should heed the warning."

Dan felt a surge of irritation. "Why?"

"Because you've just lost your business, something you worked hard to build over the last three years. That business saved your life.

You need to concentrate on salvaging what you can. Forget about looking for the girl. Pick the battles you can win."

"Brad, you know I am not a quitter."

"Dan, we are not talking about quitting here. It's commonsense. You don't know what this group is capable of. You worked in narcotics Dan. These are not nice guys. They do not negotiate. If they did destroy your office as a warning, what will they do next? If you keep poking around they are sure to come for you. Do you even have any leads?"

"I spoke to a guy claiming to be one of their gang. He suggested there was a drug deal going down on Friday night. I was due to meet with him last night before they fished him out of the lake."

"Where did he say it was happening?"

"He didn't get the chance to tell me, but I traced the call I received to the Montreal area."

"We get reports of drug deals happening all the time. Most of them are false alarms. Montreal is a big place. Without any definite location and any evidence we don't have the resources to investigate. You know how it is." He sounded almost apologetic.

Dan was growing more irritated. "So what do I tell her father who has travelled all the way from Bulgaria to find his daughter and who has no one to turn to but me?"

"You are not going to be of much help to him if you wind up in a back alley dumpster. Dan, you're getting emotionally involved. I do understand Dan, your daughter . . . ." His voice trailed off.

Dan was now getting angry. "What the hell do you know?" he shouted.

Brad's voice was controlled but icy cold. "Dan, take my advice, leave this thing alone. It could cost you your life."

Dan took out the battered business card Yuri had given to him and turned it over in his hands, thinking furiously. He had always relied on Brad to be upbeat and positive. Brad had been there for him at some of his lowest points in the last three years, always giving good sensible advice. There had been desperate times when he felt that without Brad's support he could not have survived. Brad had literally dragged him out of a hole of deep depression more than once. It made his negative approach all the more bemusing. He had assumed Brad would support him completely. Maybe he was looking out for him by telling him to drop this, but Dan suspected Brad was not revealing everything. Brad knew Dan too well to realistically expect him to give up after what happened. It only made Dan more determined to find Marisa and bring this gang out in the open, but it was apparent that at least for now he was going to have to do that without the support of the Toronto Drug Squad.

He looked at the company name and began trawling through the Internet. The company did not have a website as such—when he tried to access the domain name of the company, it merely showed as being under construction. However, within fifteen minutes he had found some possible link to the company's operations in Montreal. He was able to access a number of manifests for ships which ploughed the St. Lawrence River and delivered or collected consignments, several of which appeared to transport antiques from the Black Sea area of the Russian Republic. He recalled the names of the directors, all Russian or Eastern European. It was a tenuous link, but the importing of such specialized goods from such a specific area was probably a fairly unique business in Ontario or Quebec. He also noticed by cross referencing against a number of ships that the collection or delivery of these antiques always seemed to occur at a terminal in Kahnawake Mohawk Reserve. If it was Yuri's company that handled these goods, they clearly had a storage facility in Kahnawake, and as he dug further, he became more convinced it was.

If it was Yuri's company shipping these antiques, and the call he had received was from the Montreal area, it was not a great leap of imagination to make the connection with the drug transaction Yuri had referred to with the storage facility in Kahnawake. He reached for his Quebec directory and began searching for Kahnawake Mohawk Reserve. He had never been there but saw on the map how accessible it was to Montreal, an area of land of forty-eight square kilometres lying on the southern bank of the St. Lawrence River across from the city.

He spent a busy afternoon trying to reconstruct some of his case files from his personal computer, but the task was meticulous and tedious and he found he had little enthusiasm for it. Despite Brad's warnings, it was difficult to think of anything other than the narcotics transaction supposedly happening the following night, and the possibility that Marisa might be there. Yuri had hinted that she may be there, though he was not sure why. As Brad had rightly pointed out, he had no real evidence a transaction was even taking place, just the word of a person who was now dead. However, Dan could not see any reason for Yuri to have lied to him—after all, it was he who approached them, and the fact that Yuri had suffered such terrible retribution suggested his betrayal was genuine.

When Dan had served in the Toronto Drug Squad, they had sometimes carried out some field work with other units, most commonly with the Montreal office, particularly because a lot of the narcotics which found their way onto the streets of Toronto often entered the country through the St. Lawrence Seaway. His unit had worked with Montreal many times. If they could strangle the supply chain at the point of entry, the problem was eradicated before it even reached Toronto. This strategy had met with mixed success, but he had made some useful contacts in the Montreal field office before his demise. He knew from Brad that some of those guys were still there. He did not want to go through Brad again, and there were a number of contacts he recalled from those days. No doubt some of them would have moved on. He remembered a year or so ago hearing with great sadness of the shooting death in a stakeout of an officer he had worked with in Montreal several times. It was unfortunately a hazard of the job, but it was still a shock when it happened. Some just retired through burnout or stress and moved out of fieldwork.

Dan recalled a few names and contacted the Montreal Drug Squad. He spent a frustrating hour being passed around various clerks before he was put through to Carl Rodriguez, a fifteen year veteran of the Drug Squad. Few lasted that length of time and Rodriguez, an extrovert Hispanic who had been with the Montreal police a total of twenty-five years, had a distinguished reputation in the force. Dan had worked with him on one assignment, but did not expect Carl to remember him.

"Hey Dan," came his cheery voice, still heavily accented after thirty years in Canada. "Good to hear from you man. I thought you were history."

Dan smiled inwardly. "Rumours of my demise were greatly exaggerated. I'm still kicking around."

Carl's voice suddenly turned serious. "I heard about your daughter. Gee, I'm sorry. What can I do for you man?"

"Thanks Carl. What do you know about Kahnawake Mohawk Reserve?"

"We've had a bit of action up there in the past," Carl replied cautiously. "Why are you asking?"

"I've heard rumours there may be something going down there tomorrow night."

"How do you know this?" There was a pause on the phone and Dan could hear Carl reaching for a notebook.

"I work as a private investigator. One of my client's daughters was taken by an Eastern European gang operating in the Toronto area. I think they may be planning something in Kahnawake."

"Our intelligence doesn't suggest that Dan, although as you know we sometimes do get taken by surprise and only learn about it after the event. There are a few known people in the area that we have under surveillance, running racketing schemes and small time stuff, but it is by no means one of our worst areas. We did a big drug bust there about two years ago but since then the area has been fairly quiet."

He paused. "Dan, what do you want us to do?"

"Just investigate, see if you can find out anything. Think of it as a tip off," replied Dan.

"Yes, but I need you to tell me everything you know about this."

Dan provided a detailed summary of the circumstances and when he had finished there was silence on the line. After a while Carl responded.

"This is not much to go on Dan. Even if Yuri was not lying, you can't be sure it's going to happen at Kahnawake. You're making a lot of assumptions. I can do some digging around but there is no way I can commit our team to a stakeout without more evidence of exactly when and where it's going to happen. Our resources are stretched enough as it is."

"Carl, I don't think Yuri was lying," replied Dan. "He approached us and he ended up at the bottom of Lake Ontario minus his head for his trouble."

"But even if he wasn't, you are only guessing at the location. He did not even tell you it was in Montreal. Even if it was, we have a huge area to cover. We need something more."

Dan sighed in frustration. "I understand," he said. "Thanks for talking to me."

"It's good to hear from you man. I'm glad you're hanging in there. I will check it out and call you if I find anything. Leave this up to us. Promise me Dan you won't do anything stupid like going to Montreal."

"Of course not Carl," Dan lied.

CHAPTER 17

The unmarked white van with the false Quebec number plates parked in an obscure Montreal back street looked completely inconspicuous, like any other private van whose owners had neglected it, giving it a shabby, beaten look. Sometimes when he was on the road Timayev would use the Rebel Antiquities company van, complete with its striking logo, but this time, given the importance of the operation, he did not wish to draw any adverse attention to the company, a thriving legitimate business in its own right. This job was too important to take any unnecessary risks. As it was, reflected Timayev, the dangers were clear enough.

He had spent several months working on this deal. He had arranged a steady supply of merchandise from his various sources over the past six weeks in order to satisfy the requirements of a Somali pirate gang who, Timayev suspected, aimed to flood the market in that turbulent region and obtain a stranglehold on the burgeoning drugs market. General Medov had made the introductions to Timayev and they had been involved in some intensive negotiations to reach this point. The General had described the Somali gang as "brothers in arms," referring to the fact they shared a common interest as insurgents fighting against an oppressive occupying force in their country. It was part of his charm offensive—Timayev knew Medov did not really believe that nonsense, and it was likely a number of them were based in North America anyway as part of the large and growing Somali community. The fight against oppression was where the similarity ended. This gang was as volatile and as dangerous as any he had encountered in his career. From a country whose Islamic court routinely ordered amputations for convicted thieves, these gang members had barbarism instilled in them. The gang had a reputation for brutality which exceeded even the cruelty of the Russians, whose violence he had encountered first hand.

However, the risks were outweighed by the potential of this deal. A successful transaction would provide the key Chechen rebel forces with enough funding to support them for up to eighteen months. This deal promised to be the most lucrative by far, and tonight, in a deserted warehouse near Montreal, if everything went according to plan, his own personal wealth would be greatly enhanced.

In the gloom at the back of the truck, his face glowed from the light of the laptop screen as he tapped away and entered the coordinates to connect with the General. His men stayed in the front of the van. Though he was certain they were loyal and capable, he had never allowed them access to the General—their conversations were strictly private. Even someone like Alexi, a trusted associate and someone he had known for years and fought shoulder to shoulder with on the Chechen battlegrounds, could not know of the arrangement he had with the General. Alexi would lay down his life for the cause, and the notion of personal wealth was not so relevant to him. Timayev was also totally committed to the cause, but the side effect of his business activities, which he had found himself so good at, was amassing his own personal wealth. He morally justified this as the rewards of the job, just like a Chief Executive Officer.

His belief in his men had been shaken, however, by the incident with Yuri. He had never expected such disloyalty from a senior member of his team. His retribution had been swift and lethal, in order to send a clear message that anyone in his team who became a liability would be dealt with. The operative he had used for the termination, a fringe member of his team and with no friendship or allegiance to Yuri, had been over-zealous. He had also been sloppy to dump the body in the lake without even weighting it down. In spite of the body's condition, it would not take long for the police to identify it as Yuri's, and this would prompt some awkward enquiries. Although he had a number of "contacts" in the police force who would help him smooth things over, it was one more problem he could do without. There had also been a few murmurs amongst the men that his retribution had been too severe. He could not help feeling he made an error of judgement. Several of the men had liked and respected Yuri, and his team's morale, just before a critically important deal, had been damaged. It made the success of tonight's mission even more essential.

His thoughts were interrupted as the General's craggy, intelligent face appeared on screen. He looked tanned and relaxed as always. Timayev privately wondered just how much he saw of the front line fighting, but there was no doubting his reputation and financial power. The General controlled a 49% stake in his company.

"Good evening Akhmad. I trust everything is in order," he began.

"Yes General, our operatives are ready and in position with the merchandise."

"Good, good. I have been in negotiations with the Somali leader to confirm the logistics. As soon as you make the delivery and they have checked the merchandise, they will make an instantaneous wire transfer to our usual bank account. Do not leave the area until I give you confirmation the money has been received."

"You can count on that General."

"Remember this gang is one of the most volatile groups we have ever dealt with. Most of them are former pirates. They are fearless and brutal, but more importantly they can be reckless and trigger happy if anything goes wrong. They have very little regard for their own lives, never mind others. Your men must be totally focused and disciplined tonight. You know the importance of this deal to our cause and there are a lot of things that can go wrong."

Timayev was getting a little tired of these lectures from the General. He knew his business. He could not hide the annoyance in his voice. "General, you do your job and I will do mine."

General Medov frowned and was silent for a long moment. He sensed a level of disrespect Timayev had not shown before. He would let it pass for now. Tonight was too important, but he never forgot.

The General had done his research on this particular gang and at first he had been reticent about engaging in a deal with them.

Somali drug gangs had only really surfaced in the last few years as the country's ailing infrastructure created opportunities for regional warlords to diversify into other activities such as piracy and drug smuggling. One of the distinctive aspects of these gangs was an arrogance drawn from the fact that they believed themselves to be untouchable, which in most cases was the truth, at least from the disparate and disorganized Somali law enforcement. Indeed, it was sometimes difficult to draw the line, particularly when some of the poorly paid policemen could earn twice their monthly wage in one day with a casual bribe.

Many of the members of Somali drug gangs were also very young, and this in itself increased their volatility. The largest North American Somali community was in Minnesota, and the community had suffered an ever increasing number of drug and gang related killings that, with an inherent distrust of authority amongst the people, yielded few witnesses. Somali gang activity had been increasing more recently in Canadian cities such as Edmonton and Ottawa. With the general failure of the Somali community to integrate successfully into Canadian society, many, fleeing from a background of civil war, had found only poverty and racism in their adopted homeland. This bred deep distrust and resentment, which fuelled the gang culture. Now these gangs had an established presence in Canada and the United States. They had a particular desire for heroin, crack cocaine and various barbiturates, and Timayev's gang had been tapping into their supply chain to fill the order for the last six weeks. The Jamaican deal had been one of those supply routes. It would be a big test for his protégé, the General thought pensively.

Timayev glanced at his watch. They would need to head out soon. The transaction would take place at a location Timayev had used before, in the Kahnawake Mohawk Reserve on the south bank of the St. Lawrence River across from the city. Kahnawake was an Indian reserve of about eight thousand inhabitants. The people had a historical reputation for being fearless iron workers, mainly from the various construction and bridge building projects which had passed through the Kahnawake lands. However, the Reserve had significant problems with alcohol and gambling addiction and it had not been hard to recruit some tough operatives who would be able to secure the warehouse and ensure everything was in place for the transaction. His company had used the Reserve for legitimate shipping of its antiques and art pieces, as storage and subcontracted labour was cheap. He had also used Kahnawake for the other side of the business several times, especially trafficking in girls, so far successfully. He felt these men could be trusted as long as the lure of easy money was available to them.

There was a sheltered cove within the Reserve that held some abandoned warehouses, and it was here the goods had been stockpiled under heavy guard over the last few days. They discussed the final preparations and he undertook to keep Medov informed at all stages of the transaction.

"Who are you going to use for the delivery?" asked Medov finally. He knew the "mule" was always the most exposed person in the deal. "I am using one of my girls, a Bulgarian girl. I have made sure she is compliant."

Medov grinned, showing a pair of even white teeth. "You have always had a weakness for your women Akhmad. I have always found the gentler sex to be unpredictable in these situations."

"General, we have pumped her so high that she will do absolutely anything for the next fix. You need not worry."

"Excellent. Until tonight then." Medov broke the connection and his tanned face faded from the screen.

Timayev breathed a sigh of relief and grabbed his cell phone. He had one more call to make. It was answered on the third ring. The voice at the other end was quiet, hesitant, as if he had been expecting Timayev's call. The Chechen smiled and said almost condescendingly, "You have done well my friend. Keep up the good work and you will be rewarded handsomely, and more importantly your family will stay alive."

CHAPTER 18

As Dan headed out on the long, straight road to Montreal, his thoughts whirled around his brain in a jumbled mass, making it hard to concentrate on the road ahead. It did not help that the route was so tedious but at least traffic was light and he made good progress. What if he had made a stupid mistake? Maybe there was no drug deal at all? Even if there was, how would he locate it? He was working on little more than educated guesswork and a hunch that the deal might happen somewhere in the Kahnawake lands. Even if he was right, why would Marisa even be there? Yuri had suggested that she might be but he could think of no good reason. Probably the most he could hope for was to find out a little more about the gang holding Marisa, but he knew that this mission, if it did produce any leads, could prove highly dangerous. He trusted his surveillance skills and his ability to melt into the background. However, spying on cheating husbands or fraudsters was one thing, staking out a drugs deal between two heavily armed gangs was quite another.

Vasil was up early in the morning to see him off and had again warned him not to go, but Dan was convinced he was right. He had repeated his promise to find Vasil's daughter, and urged him to remain vigilant, to lock the door to the bedsit at all times and stay safe. Privately he knew the paper thin walls and rickety entrance door to his bedsit would provide little protection to anyone determined to break in, but Vasil had promised to be careful. As Dan had left, the diminutive Bulgarian had given him a bear hug, and his eyes glistened with gratitude. It made Dan all the more determined to deliver on his promise.

The old Chevrolet ate up the miles with Dan so lost in his thoughts that he barely remembered the journey. He took a few short breaks and put in several calls to Carl's office, but he was told each time Carl was "out in the field." He left messages but did not receive any call back. He did not expect to, but he was curious as to whether Carl had found out any more information. He did not like going blind, and he also secretly wished Carl would offer the reassurance that his unit would be on patrol and cover his back. It seemed an unlikely possibility and as he crossed the border into Quebec he suddenly felt very exposed.

He crossed the St. Lawrence River at a bridge a long way west of the city and took the road that skirted the southern edge of the river through several small villages huddled by the riverside and later against the vast stretch of Lake Saint-Louis, before entering the Kahnawake Mohawk Reserve. At this point he still did not have a clear idea of what he would do next when he arrived, and after taking a short break to eat he drove along the quiet roads of the Reserve at a leisurely pace, surveying the scenery around him. The road was cracked and broken in places, a legacy of the severe winters suffered by the region, and his Chevrolet creaked and rattled on the potholes. On both sides were scrubby grasslands broken by a line of trees, some of them still skeletal, waiting for the late spring to bloom, and through them on his left he could see the deep blue of the river glistening in the early evening sun. He decided to head toward the main Kahnawake port terminal, if only to have some direction, and continued to drive slowly along the rutted road.

The grass gave way to thicker forest and soon it appeared to press in on him on both sides, so that it was dark enough for headlights despite the blue sky. Then from the gloom he noticed something very curious. In his mirror he spotted a flash of white moving through the trees. He quickly pulled over and observed a small van emerge from the forest on what must have been a dirt track before emerging onto the main road and speeding off in the opposite direction. It looked curiously out of place and with no better plan, Dan decided to investigate.

Dan parked the car in a small turning behind a group of trees a little further up the road, so the car was concealed from passing traffic, and grabbed his backpack. He scurried over to where the van had emerged, looking around furtively in all directions. The only sound was the rustling of the trees in the wind and a distant, shrill tweeting of a group of terns.

There was a narrow dirt track leading off into the forest toward the river. It was not well used, and in places was overgrown so at times the track seemed to disappear aimlessly into the undergrowth. However, Dan was able to follow the telling signs of trampled bush which indicated recent traffic. As he inspected the ground, he heard the whine of another vehicle close by. He quickly darted into the bushes to seek cover and, sweating profusely, crouched low against the ground, squeezing into a small hollow at the base of a large elm tree. Convinced he was out of sight, he watched another white van pass by. This van was smaller and it bounced along the rutted track, its engine labouring. He just caught a glimpse of the driver through the side window of the vehicle, a hard faced man of about forty with cropped marine style blond hair. His face was set in concentration, and even from his position Dan could see the scowl. Not a man to be messed with, but the type he had come across many times as a narcotics officer.

This sighting convinced Dan that maybe, just maybe, he had stumbled onto what he was looking for. His senses were heightened with fear and it took a while for him to emerge from the hollow. He stayed alert, listening hard for the sounds of other vehicles, but it was eerily quiet. Keeping low and a reasonable distance from the track, he wrestled through the undergrowth in the general direction of the van, ready to dive into the thicket at any time. Within a few minutes, the blue expanse of the river widening out into Lake Saint-Louis was visible through the trees. He realized he had been climbing gently uphill, but the track remained on level ground. This gave Dan an elevated view of the surrounding area, and from there he was able to see a clearing cut into the forest set back about a hundred feet from the water's edge, shielded by trees on all sides. However, Dan could see clearly through the thin leaf cover, and he had to stifle an almost audible gasp.

He sunk even lower into the soft ferns and took out his field glasses. They were high magnification and equipped with night vision, which he was certain he would need later. They were an essential part of his surveillance equipment, and with them he could clearly observe the activity from a safe distance. He saw a large clearing surrounded on all sides by trees and foliage that created a natural shield, so the clearing could not be seen from the ground until you almost stumbled into it. Only from the air or from his raised vantage point could the clearing be seen. Within the clearing was a derelict warehouse, its wooden structure decayed and weathered. Part of the corrugated iron roof had fallen in and been hastily patched up, but the frame was generally intact and clearly in use as a storage facility.

There were several vehicles parked to the side of the warehouse, including the van that Dan had seen on the track. A number of men, including the van driver, were coming and going around and inside the warehouse, engaged in what seemed to be urgent, bustling activity. Some wore sunglasses despite the gloom beginning to descend, and others dragged on a cigarette as they went about their business. A small group was engaged in what appeared to be intense conversations punctuated by wild gesticulating. All appeared to be armed, either a small pistol in a holster round their trousers, and others with seriously powerful looking automatic machine-guns slung over their shoulder. All were dressed in combat uniform, and there was a military efficiency to their movements. Dan counted about twelve men in total before several more emerged from inside the building.

One of the men seemed to be directing operations, clearly the leader of the group. Dan used the field glasses to zoom in on him. His frame was smaller than the rest, yet it was sleek and wiry like a coiled snake. Like the rest of the group he was in combat pants, but a short sleeved shirt clung to his square chest like a second skin, and accentuated his tattooed biceps. His relatively short stature accentuated his athletic physique and he held his assault rifle like an old friend as he swaggered arrogantly around the clearing, confidently issuing instructions.

Despite his strong physique, the man seemed to carry an almost scholarly expression, as if a keen intelligence burned behind that focused gaze. He looked like a man who would be ruthless when necessary, but equally was capable of compassion and reason. Dan hoped that would not be put to the test.

As he zoomed in on the leader, a movement caught his eye and he trained the glasses on a Land Cruiser that had just arrived. Another "soldier" got out and opened the passenger door. This soldier had a long black beard and straggly hair protruding from his combat cap, but he was an imposing wall of muscle. He roughly pulled out three girls from the vehicle and hastily escorted them inside the depressing looking warehouse. The girls were turned away from him and Dan cursed, unable to see their faces even with his glasses. They did not struggle but appeared subservient as they were jostled and manhandled, and quickly disappeared inside the building.

There is no doubt I am in the right place, thought Dan. He had stumbled on this place by chance, and it was secluded enough that a person could pass within ten feet of the clearing and still fail to notice it.

Dan made himself comfortable and settled in to the hollow. His job had trained him for long periods of inactivity, to remain patient, yet focused and ready for when things did happen. This was going to be a long night.

CHAPTER 19

As the sun drifted toward the horizon, it cast long shadows, which added to the gloom in the clearing. Despite the deep blue sky overhead, the light was failing quickly, although it was of little concern to Timayev. The bulk of the work was done, and the merchandise had been loaded onto the large pallet in boxes in the warehouse. His team had set up some small arc lamps which would provide sufficient light in the derelict warehouse, although these would not be turned on until much later.

As he watched his men working diligently with the final preparations, Timayev allowed himself a moment of reflection. Carefully stacked on the pallets was a combination of drugs including cocaine, heroin, ecstasy pills, methamphetamines such as crystal meth and even barbiturates that had been assembled to order for the Somali gang. They held a combined street value of over $80 million and he had entrusted Alexi for the security of the consignment over the past few days since its delivery to the warehouse.

He trusted Alexi as his right hand man completely, but it was always just before the actual transaction itself that his nerves began to rattle. All the months of preparation came down to tonight, and there were far too many things that could go wrong. This gang had a fearsome reputation and he had more operatives on site than usual. There would be a total of eighteen men around when the Africans arrived, although they would only see six of them. The others would be positioned at strategic points in and around the building but under cover in the woods, ready to strike at the first sign of trouble. These were Kahnawake Mohawks he had recruited for this deal. In the past they had proved reliable and efficient, with their knowledge of this area a vital asset in his preparations for this deal. They acted as a useful complement to his small core group, all of whom would be based in the warehouse. Most would be armed. Other Mohawks would be stationed further along the track in the woods as lookout to provide advance notice of the arrival of the Somalis.

His reverie was interrupted by the sound of a Land Cruiser which swept into the compound and slammed to a halt next to Timayev. Rahmon was driving and the huge Tajik was hunched over the wheel, his bulk filling the front of the cab. He got out quickly and, fingering his beloved Kalashnikov rifle menacingly, he barked at the passengers to get out. From the vehicle emerged three girls, looking dishevelled and blank faced. They did not resist as Rahmon grabbed at them and pushed them, still shouting and waving his rifle, and ordered them into the warehouse. There was no need for his aggression but the giant Tajik, Timayev reflected, enjoyed inflicting pain on others just for the hell of it, particularly on defenceless women. His intimidating presence ensured the Toronto brothels ran smoothly. The girls rarely caused trouble with the ever constant threat of the volatile giant lurking close by. Most had been on the end of his painful retribution at some point.

The girls were part of his usual strategy, brought in as sweeteners as part of the deal. If the Somalis wanted some fun with them, he would make them available. It was a goodwill gesture and if the men wanted to keep the girls, it was fine. He could always recruit some more. His contacts in the Eastern European region had been useful. However, he would be a little disappointed if they took the girl Marisa. She had proved highly spirited and it had taken a lot to tame her. Despite the fact she had nearly destroyed the Jamaican deal, he felt a grudging respect for her. Although he had given Rahmon permission to punish her appropriately, he had also warned the Tajik to curb his usual brutality, and to do only what was necessary to keep her compliant.

As she shuffled past him, hollow-eyed and passive, hardly even responding to Rahmon's prodding with the rifle, he felt a tiny pang of guilt, but quickly dismissed it. He was running a business, and there was no room for emotion. He could have dumped her on the streets but she was a useful asset, very popular with the clients, despite her cold demeanour. Forcing her into heroin addiction was the most efficient way of keeping her compliant, and it had worked so well she would have a very useful role to play tonight. She would act as the drugs mule, making the actual delivery. The boxes were crated and ready for her to deliver the $80 million pallet to the African gang.

Watching Alexi give the final briefings to his assault team, Timayev reached for his cell phone and called the General. So far, everything was going to plan.

Marisa had slept for most of the long journey from Toronto, although even that did not bring her peace these days. Sleep often brought vivid nightmares from which she would wake screaming and drenched in sweat, her body shaking as it jerked itself out of another drug fuelled trauma. However, even when she was conscious she had little realization of the world around her. The only motivation in her life was the need for another shot, to stop her body shaking and her head feeling it was about to split in two. When they first injected her with heroin, it actually brought her a feeling of pleasure and contentment as she sensed it coursing through her veins, even though she had struggled fiercely as they held her down and pressed the needle hard into her arm. When they had injected her again a few days later, she still protested, but more feebly, as she anticipated that feeling of pleasure again, and she had not been disappointed.

After a couple more injections, she no longer fought them and found herself offering up her arm, her body feverishly craving the rush of pleasure as the poisonous liquid travelled up her arm. But each time the sensation of pleasure had been less, and was rapidly followed by a weakness in her mind and spirit that made her feel so full of despair she no longer had the will to fight her tormentors, and the endless stream of clients seemed to pass by in a blur. Her waking hours became dominated by the need for more heroin, and after a time she vaguely realized she was completely addicted. By then the feeling of pleasure upon injection had gone, and she needed the next fix just to stop the shaking and feeling of utter despair. In one of her few lucid moments, she wondered whether those people who had never been addicted, though appreciating the physical damage to the body, understood the mental deterioration. Her mind was focused on one thing only, and she soon realized that only her captors could provide her with the drugs her body needed. She quickly learned that if she did what they wanted, then she would soon be satisfied.

They had assumed complete control over her body and mind. They knew that if she did not follow their rules, they would withdraw her fix, and it was something she could not risk. She vaguely realized that eventually she would inevitably die from this cruel addiction, but would probably die in any event if she did not receive her fix. She found herself almost past caring, as the drugs propelled her into a dreamlike state where her family, home and friends ceased to have any significance, as if they belonged to another person. Most of her clients did not care about her drug addiction. Some were addicted themselves in any event. However, she knew it must have put off some of the more discerning clients, although Rahmon continued to send a steady stream of men night after night. It did not matter, as she didn't feel anything anyway. When she had looked in the mirror, she hardly recognized the person staring back. The pockmarked arms from too many needles, sallow skin and dark-ringed eyes were those of an old woman, but as she stared in horror at the reflection she felt too weak even to cry. Within ten minutes of seeing herself like this she was visited by her drug friend and begging him to give her a shot as she offered up her shaking arm. He always came and went without saying a word, and usually Marisa would drift off into unconsciousness and her ugly dreams, as the body's craving was satisfied for the moment.

Marisa was rudely awakened by that deep, aggressive tone that had become so familiar. "Get out, now!" Rahmon barked at the girls as they arrived outside a large warehouse in the middle of a forest. Marisa stirred slowly from her broken dreams and Rahmon grabbed her by the arm, his strong fingers pressing painfully against one of the many holes in her arm. Marisa had no idea where they were, but then all of her senses had become blurred anyway. She vaguely recalled something about going to Montreal, and there were two girls with her in the Toyota. One of them was Olivia, her only true friend in the world she now existed in. Olivia had become so much tougher and streetwise than the frightened little girl who journeyed with her on that trip from Newfoundland—when?—It seemed so long ago, almost an eternity of unrelenting misery. It was strange how time passed so slowly when you were suffering and just wanted it to be over. Olivia looked scared now though, and Marisa could not understand why. Rahmon had forbidden the girls to talk on the long, weary journey, but it was a relief to be away from the demoralizing dreariness of the brothel.

She had no idea where they were, but the sun was low in the trees and it would soon be dark. A cold breeze flapped at her scanty clothing and she wrapped her skinny arms around her body in a futile effort to stave off the chill as Rahmon marched them inside the dilapidated warehouse, where they were forced to sit in the corner. The three girls huddled together, taking comfort in one another's presence, with no idea why they were here.

Marisa whispered to Olivia, "I'm so cold."

One of the gang, a rifle slung over his broad shoulders grimaced and moved angrily toward them. "Silence," he rebuked harshly.

Olivia looked at Marisa sadly. Her friend had suffered so much. Marisa had always resisted their tormentors, fought against the terrible deception they had all fallen into. She had always been the one who had shown defiance and a strong will that could not be subjugated, even after a stinging blow from Rahmon. That monster could crush any of the girls with one of his huge bear-like hands, but he often held back because the clients did not like to sleep with a girl who had ugly marks obviously caused by a beating.

If it had not been for Marisa she did not know how she would have survived the terrible isolation of their degrading life. Marisa had helped her manage the anger and frustration, to not let it destroy her but to draw strength from their humiliating ordeal. There were times when she had felt suicidal, but Marisa had counselled her and helped her overcome those feelings. Even in the blackest moments Marisa had been there, sometimes making jokes about their situation, and she had proved popular with the other girls in the brothel, even those who had initially resented her beauty and strong personality.

What had those savages done to her? They had not been able to break her indomitable spirit by force, but when Marisa had jumped overboard from the Jamaican boat, they had decided to punish her by getting her hooked on heroin. She had rapidly spiralled into a shell of her former self. Her eyes were bottomless, as if her very soul had been sucked out from them, and she meekly obeyed her captors like a trained circus animal. The one quality Olivia admired so much about Marisa had been taken from her, and sometimes she felt a flash of anger that Marisa had given up so easily. But then, thought Olivia, how would she have coped? They had not pumped her full of drugs, not yet anyway.

She cowered, drawing close to Marisa as she saw Timayev striding toward them. The cruel Chechen gang leader had the ability to strike fear in the girls just by his presence. Olivia had never seen him hit any of the girls, but then he did not have to. He had plenty of minions to do that for him. The girls knew he held total power over them, and it gave him a certain moody charisma that struck fear into their hearts whenever he visited the brothel. Olivia knew he had been particularly fond of Marisa, and even though the drugs had visibly aged her, she was still attractive. Timayev ignored the other girls and smiled at Marisa. He was carrying a large hypodermic needle, waving it tantalizingly in front of Marisa's face. He pulled her to her feet and led Marisa by the hand to a small office within the large warehouse. It was rapidly growing darker, and soon she heard the growl of a large vehicle like an army truck. Olivia did not know why they had been brought here, but she felt more frightened than ever. She was left in the corner with her other travelling companion, a young Polish girl, Martha, for what seemed ages, lost in her own terrified thoughts. There had been rumours floating around at the house about a deal with a particularly nasty African group, but the girls rarely had the opportunity to speak freely. However, when she saw the door swing wildly open at the far end of the warehouse, Olivia had to suppress a feeling of rising panic as she saw the rumours were true.

Carl reached his office in the heart of old Montreal at about quarter past eight. The office was nearly empty, apart from a few dedicated operatives with nowhere better to go, even on the weekend. Much like himself, he mused with a touch of regret. He checked his email. A few routine messages and one from the chief administrator of the Montreal ERT, the Emergency Response Team. The ERT was a group of highly trained members of the Royal Canadian Mounted Police, capable of employing specialized weapons, equipment, and tactics to resolve high risk situations such as hostage crises, high level surveillance and anti-narcotics operations. The potentially violent and often dynamic nature of these situations required a highly integrated and coordinated tactical response that was beyond the capabilities even of the Montreal Drug Squad.

Carl had worked with the ERT on several occasions, usually on more high profile raids, and he was on first name terms with the chief administrator, a surly veteran named Charles Deegan. He had discussed Dan's call informally with Deegan earlier in the day. Deegan knew of Dan's history.

"Carl," he had said, "Look at the facts. Dan is no longer an official source. He stopped being that when Toronto let him go. He has suggested there may be something going down in Kahnawake, but you agreed there is no corroborating evidence, and no one knows where this alleged deal is going to happen. I cannot requisition a team based on hearsay from, what is not, quite frankly, a credible source."

Carl had to agree with him and despite his investigations during the day, he had found nothing convincing that would persuade Deegan to change his mind. He checked his phone—there was another missed call from Dan. He had noted two earlier calls during the day and had ignored them up to now. There was nothing he could offer Dan and if he wanted to pursue this pointless venture, it was up to him. He had at least indulged him, based on past association, by checking into his claims, but he had to agree with Deegan—Dan was probably not a reliable source.

He read the message from Deegan, which confirmed what he already suspected. Deegan had met with the operations team and they had advised Deegan there was absolutely no chance of sending an Emergency Response Team to Kahnawake tonight. It did not surprise him. He just hoped Dan had taken his advice and not stupidly travelled to Montreal on a wild goose chase. Although Dan had promised not to do so, Carl was not convinced. It was clear from their conversation that Dan strongly believed a deal was taking place, even though he had no way of proving it. Dan was not delusional, he was sure of that. Before his troubles Huberman had been a fine officer. He ought to call Dan as a courtesy. He pulled out his phone and searched for Dan's number. As he did so the phone vibrated, an incoming call. The number was unlisted, a blocked caller ID, but he knew who it was immediately.

As he listened to the caller, his face turned white and he listened intently. At the end of the call he said a perfunctory "thank you" and rang off. With shaking fingers he dialled Dan's number. Jesus, he hoped Dan had taken his advice, but he had to warn him and make sure he was nowhere near Montreal tonight. The call connected but immediately the connection was broken. He tried again but this time his call went directly to Dan's voice-mail. He did not want to leave a message—he wanted to speak to Dan directly. His next call was to Deegan. He knew the administrator would chew his ear off but he needed this favour. Despite Deegan's insistence that a response team would not be mobilized tonight, he now knew there was no choice. It might take some time at eight-thirty on a Friday night, but he prayed it would not be too late.

CHAPTER 20

The evening was drawing in quickly as the sun dipped low, shimmering on the river like dancing fireflies before it gently disappeared below the horizon. Although it was May, there was a bitter chill in the air, and Dan shivered, rustling some of the leaves pressed around him. He began to regret that he had left his Gore-Tex sweater in his trunk. The discomfort from lying in the same position for several hours was making him fidget, and it was not helped by the feeling of dampness and the occasional scurrying of unknown insects over his body. He would have much preferred his usual surveillance posture, sitting in his Chevrolet munching on a burger, but he had to force himself to concentrate.

It was anything but boring. Often his surveillance involved nothing happening for hours at a time. It was certainly not the case here—in the hours he had been observing, the clearing had been a flurry of activity, and he could only guess at the activity inside the building. The leader of the group had been in and out of the warehouse. A few minutes earlier he had taken a call on his cell phone and sent off a number of armed foot soldiers into the forest.

When Dan saw this his heart beat furiously, pounding in his ears, and he sank further down into the hollow. He prayed for it to grow dark quickly, and hoped the sheltered hollow would protect him from view. He surveyed the forest around him with his night vision goggles and stayed alert for any rustling or snapping of twigs close by. No sign of anyone near, but he felt his body stiffen, his muscles as taut as bowstrings. The forest sounds seemed amplified, any small noise a potential threat. Even so, the throaty roar of a trio of military jeeps striding through the narrow forest path drowned the natural cacophony. Despite the forest gloom, the vehicles had no lights on, but Dan tracked them with his goggles until they stopped at the far end of the warehouse.

He trained his glasses on the vehicles. Despite the luminescent green lens, he could clearly distinguish a group of African-Americans step out from the car, guns trained and looking round in all directions as if they were covering each other. They assembled in regimented fashion behind a heavyset man in combat fatigues and wearing a beret. He also sported a fat cigar and sunglasses. Dan smiled to himself. Like a Cuban revolutionary, he thought.

The "Cuban" was greeted by the leader from the other side. They shook hands warily. Not only did both leaders carry their own weapons, but each had several men behind them with guns slung over their shoulder in readiness for any trouble.

Even from where he was positioned, Dan could sense the tension between the two parties. They seemed to circle each other like prize dog fighters about to strike any second, before each party headed inside through separate doors at opposite ends of the building. Dan needed to get a better view. He had managed to take a few snapshots with his camera, but the lighting was now too poor and a flash would be suicidal. He needed to see what was going in inside the warehouse. Could he believe he was even thinking this? There were only a couple of guards patrolling outside the warehouse, and they looked completely bored, each dragging on a cigarette complacently as if there was no chance of action tonight. Even so, it would be a huge risk, not far short of jumping into the lion's den. But he had to know if one of the girls was Marisa, although what good would it be if the gang caught him?

After wrestling with his conscience for a while, he decided to stay put. He might be a coward but at least a safe one. The best he could do was observe and learn what he could. Even if Marisa were here there was little he could do for her. Not without help from Carl and his team. Carl had not rung back. Just as well, considering where he was. In fact he should turn off his cell phone. He reached for it and as he did so it vibrated and began its merry jingle. He nearly jumped out of his skin. With trembling fingers he managed to turn it off. The sound pierced the relative silence like a clarion call.

Dan waited, his heart pounding like a jackhammer. There was no movement, and even the guards down below seemed too self-absorbed to have heard it. Nearly five minutes passed. *I've got away with it,* he decided with huge relief.

He stayed motionless for a little longer, listening intently, but there was nothing to disturb the usual forest sounds. The twilight had fallen quickly and he could barely see in front of him. He trained his night vision glasses on the warehouse, but there had been no activity since the two groups had entered the building. There was little more he could see, short of walking up to the building and peering in through the scratched and dirty windows.

The best thing now would be to call Carl, but he had to make his way to his car first. He had to move quickly because he did not think the gangs would hang around exchanging pleasantries—they would make whatever nefarious deal they had agreed on and move out. There might still be time for Carl's team to get here and apprehend them, but there was nothing he could achieve on his own.

He had begun to stiffen up, having lain prone for so long, and the dampness of the forest ground had permeated his clothes into his skin. He shivered with a sudden chill. He collected his equipment together in his rucksack and got up to make his way down the hill. Dan kept the glasses out as he would need these, although he had a good idea of the direction to follow even in the dark. It would be a relief to get out of there, away from the acute sense of danger he had felt since he had seen what was going on.

He stepped out of the hollow as quietly as possible, and began to make his way down the hill. It was then he felt a chill far worse than a damp forest floor, and he had not seen or heard it coming. It was the icy, harsh chill of cold, hard steel pressed into his neck.

It was a complete standoff, like a bad Western movie the Canadians loved so much, thought Timayev wryly. Not even the Russians were as paranoid in the presence of Chechens. The Somalis had not let their weapons down for a second, and their eight strong contingent had their weapons, mainly semi-automatic machine guns (Russian made, Timayev noted ironically) gripped tightly and poised for action. Other than the "Colonel," they were a rag tag bunch, like a group of street fighters in ill-fitting shirts and baggy trousers, but he was careful not to underestimate them. It was a volatile situation. His own men also had their weapons drawn and it would only take one false move from either party to spark a potential bloodbath.

They had refused Timayev's goodwill offer of the girls with insolent disdain.

"We do not want your filthy whores!" their leader Colonel Asad had spat, chewing on his cigar. Timayev would have liked to strangle him with his bare hands there and then. He doubted whether the self-styled colonel had ever seen military service, and his army fatigues and sharp looking sunglasses was probably just a show.

He reminded himself to stay focused. The deal would soon be completed and he would be considerably richer, and the Chechen cause would carry on with fresh financing for weapons and training. They were so close. He carefully watched the Bulgarian girl haul the pallet full of drugs across the uneven concrete floor toward the African gang at the far end. Although the pallet was on caster wheels, it would be heavy, and she strained hard as she slowly moved it along, neither side inclined to help her. A couple of the Somalis had put their weapons down and one was setting up equipment to test the purity of the merchandise. This was likely to be an exhaustive process as they were intent on checking every single box. He could hardly blame them for their lack of trust—this was not a business in which honesty prevailed. Another was setting up a laptop, ready to make the connection and wire the funds.

The warehouse was silent, but the air bristled with tension, all eyes on Marisa. Next to him Alexi stood impassively, weapon in hand, when his cell phone went off. Timayev gave him a thunderous look, and Alexi spoke quietly into the phone. Alexi gave Timayev a look that he did not like.

"We have an intruder," Alexi whispered to Timayev.

The Somali leader tensed as he saw the Chechen talk into his boss's ear. He did not trust these white people at all, but the merchandise they offered was impossible to obtain in the quantities he needed for his operations.

"What *ees* the problem?" he barked across the warehouse, his voice resonating in the stuffy air.

Timayev spread his hands wide in a placatory gesture. "There is no problem," he assured him. "We seem to have an intruder in the forest. My men will take care of him."

At the mention of an intruder, the Somali gang raised their weapons even higher, safety catches off. Asad waved them down, and his face broke into a wide beam, displaying broken tobacco stained teeth, cigar perched on one side of his mouth. He gave a hearty, booming laugh that surprised everyone, even his own gang of vicious thugs. He took off his glasses for a moment, and his bloodshot eyes were full of mirth.

"Then perhaps we should have a *leettle* sport," he declared.

Timayev nodded gravely, not wishing to antagonize the Colonel. He would have preferred that the intruder be quietly shot and he did not hear about it. This was an unwelcome distraction, but he turned to Alexi. "Have the intruder brought in."

Marisa, hardly aware of what was going on around her, finally reached the Somali gang with her heavy load and two of the men began swiftly unloading the boxes from the pallet and slicing them open with their razor sharp knives. They unceremoniously shoved her away and she staggered back to the relative safety of the Chechen group and flopped down against the wall where Olivia and Martha sat, rigid with fear.

Olivia cradled Marisa's head in her arms. The Bulgarian girl's eyes were wide and bloodshot, and stared past Olivia into space, as if she was invisible. Marisa could not focus and Olivia could tell from those blank eyes and the fresh puncture wound that they had shot her up just before she made the delivery. She was also shivering badly. Olivia allowed her tears to run freely but silently down her cheeks as she gently rocked her best friend, and Martha stroked her hair. Surely Marisa could not take much more of this? They were slowly killing her and Olivia could sense that at any time the next shot could be her last.

Olivia looked up, startled as the door burst open and in rushed two men, holding a third man who was struggling ineffectually against their iron grip. Each man had an arm pinned against his own body so the prisoner had no leverage to break free. With his free hand one of the other men had a small handgun pressed against his throat.

Dan had not seen them coming. They were local Mohawks, and they knew the territory well. They had crept through the wood like silent panthers and pounced on Dan before he was even aware of their presence. They were also incredibly strong, and he could not move his arms, as if they had been pressed into a vice. He still struggled, despite the gun pressed hard and painfully on his Adam's apple, until he was brought into the warehouse.

All eyes turned to him from both sides of the large barn type building. He felt almost naked under their baleful glare, and as he was shoved onto the cold stone floor, he sat still, aware of the several sets of guns now pointing unwaveringly at him. It was clearly an old workshop, as there were several old lathes and other rusting machinery, benches and boxes scattered about. The large warehouse was silent for what seemed like hours but in reality was only seconds. Time seemed to have stood still for Dan and he felt the sweat trickling slowly down his neck.

Then from across the far side of the room, the man he had labelled "the Cuban" dragged on his cigar and broke the silence with a hoarse laughter which seemed to echo around the vaulted ceiling. Dan could not see his eyes behind the large sunglasses, which made the laugh sound even more sinister. His two captors stood menacingly over him, their dark, swarthy features set in a grim expression. He tried to get up but one of them pushed him back with the sole of his heavy hiking boots.

As several of his team continued their work on checking the merchandise, Colonel Asad's other men moved in closer toward Dan. All the guns seemed to be pointed at the intruder now, rather than at each other. It was almost as if the mutual hostility and mistrust had been offset by the appearance of a common foe, a trespasser who had to be dealt with.

Colonel Asad puffed on his cigar. "Is he a friend of yours Mr Timayev?"

Despite his situation, a thought flashed into Dan's mind. The name sounded familiar, and then he remembered. One of the directors of Yuri's company he had checked up on—wasn't he called Timayev? Yes, it was Ak—.

A bruising kick smashed into his ribcage and he keeled over, the breath violently expelled from his lungs. There was a sharp cracking sound. The pain was excruciating and as he clutched his side he wondered vaguely if a rib had been broken. The Chechen leader stood over him, his face a mask but a fierce expression in his eyes. His frustration at this untimely intrusion had been channelled into that kick.

"Does that answer your question Colonel?" he said.

"Well," laughed the Colonel. "That *ees* certainly no way to treat a friend. So who *ees* he?"

The Chechen looked down at Dan, poised and ready to kick again. "Answer the Colonel," he spat. "Who the hell are you?"

Dan cowered on the floor, his body tensing itself against another savage kick, but he stayed silent. One of the Mohawks handed Timayev the prisoner's wallet, which he had relieved him of before they reached the compound. Timayev pulled out Dan's driving licence and casually tossed the wallet aside. As he saw the name he raised his eyebrows in surprise.

"Ah, Mr Dan Huberman. I seem to recall specifically requesting you to stay away from my business affairs, and here you are turning up uninvited to my party. Surely your office closure was a little incentive not to get involved with us. I guess you're a little slow to get the message. Perhaps something a little more direct may persuade you."

Dan tried to stare up at Timayev with as defiant an expression as he could, but Timayev was bending over him like a parent admonishing a child. Dan could not rise anyway as one of the Mohawks was standing on his left leg. His attempt at defiance was futile and Dan was certain his expression betrayed the sick feeling in the pit of his stomach.

Timayev sensed his fear and let out a taunting laugh. He turned to the Somali chief. "Well Colonel Asad, you rejected the pleasures of our girls, even though it was a goodwill gesture. So, as another gesture, I hand Mr Huberman's fate over to your discretion. What should we do with him?"

Colonel Asad broke into another wide grin, and puffed on his cigar. He blew the smoke out in long, lingering circles, clearly enjoying the moment. Dan sensed he was not the first man whose fate rested in this large man's hands, and Dan had no illusions about being shown any clemency. His worst fears were confirmed when Asad pointed at the ceiling.

CHAPTER 21

High in the vaulted ceiling was a huge hook which hung from a pulley system with a strong steel cable. It was not clear what the hook had been used for, but it looked like an over-sized fish hook, and its end looked razor sharp. It could easily impale a human, thought Dan, and it seemed Asad had the same idea.

"Pull the hook down and haul him up. My boys need some target practise."

His gang of mercenaries began waving their guns and whooping in enthusiastic support of the idea.

Timayev was not pleased with the situation. He just wanted to complete the deal and get the money safely into the account and head back to Toronto. This unexpected delay made him nervous. It would be much cleaner to shoot Huberman and get out of here as quickly as possible. If he had found them, who else might know about this deal?

Even so, Asad was calling the shots and he had no choice but to comply. He nodded at Alexi who ordered one of his men to work the pulley. The pulley handle was located to one side of the building and the Chechen soldier found it rusty and stiff from lack of use. Using his considerable strength to force it loose, he pulled it to the middle of the hangar on the steel cable and lowered the hook to the floor with a grinding sound.

The two burly Mohawks who had captured Dan hauled him to his feet as he still rubbed his heavily bruised ribs. They began to pull him toward the hook. His eyes were wide with fright and the gang members from both sides relished his fear as he was dragged relentlessly toward the hook. He tried to struggle, but again the Mohawks were too strong, carrying him with an iron grip that pinned back his arms.

Dan turned to one corner where three girls sat silently shivering. He only had a moment to see them before the Mohawks twisted him round so he had his back to the rusty metal hook, which was swinging gently on the cable. That was all he needed to recognize Marisa. Her image had been virtually imprinted on his brain by Vasil's endless supply of photographs and leaflets which he kept all over the bedsit. She was lying motionless in another girl's arms, and her eyes looked glazed, her skin yellow, her expression lifeless, but he knew it was her.

Dan had seen the look before, a haunted look that his daughter had borne in the days before her death, the drawn skeletal expression of drug abuse. The hook was lowered further on the cable so that it was level with the small of his back. He felt blind panic as he fully comprehended what they meant to do—impale him like a piece of slaughterhouse meat on the hook and winch him up for the Somalis to shoot at him. He struggled even harder but to no avail. The strong arms pinned him like a vice over the huge hook as Alexi positioned it in readiness, ready to plunge it into the small of his back.

He gritted his teeth and closed his eyes ready for the cold steel and the excruciating pain, but then things happened very quickly.

Alexi dropped the hook and turned at the sound of shouting as the door was kicked open. In burst a group of heavily armoured, helmeted soldiers carrying high powered rifles, which they pointed menacingly at the occupants in the building. They fanned out in military style, covering each other's backs in a well drilled formation. They had the element of surprise and they barked urgently and insistently at the group, their voices strained and angry.

"Get down, now! Weapons on the floor! Move it or we will shoot!" several of them screamed, their comrades shouting incoherent commands to add to the noise and confusion. Dan reacted quickly, seizing on the momentary hesitation of his Mohawk captors as they relaxed their grip. He broke free and spun round, delivering a deft karate kick to one of his captors just behind the knee, causing him to collapse in a heap on the floor. His other captor had already dived to the floor, no longer interested in the prisoner, and Dan flung himself down and rolled in the general direction of Marisa and the other girls, who were screaming and cowering in the corner.

The forces were organized into two distinct groups which streamed through the doors as part of their offensive against both gangs separately but simultaneously. Their urgent, resounding cries echoed around the empty warehouse and at first the gangs were too stunned to respond. The Somali gang was completely overwhelmed and outnumbered by the forces that flanked them on several sides. The unit carried a cache of weapons sufficient for a small army and their Kevlar helmets and high technology combat uniform intimidated the African gang. Their discipline collapsed immediately and they quickly surrendered to the unit, throwing their guns to the ground and raising their hands submissively.

"On the floor. NOW!" barked a soldier, his voice even more gruff through his helmet. They meekly complied and hit the floor without a shot being fired. Even the Colonel rolled to the floor, squashing his cigar, his face masked in rage and humiliation. They were quickly handcuffed and frogmarched out of the warehouse.

The far side of the warehouse was a different matter. It erupted in a volley of deafening gunfire as Timayev mobilized his team with military precision. Their surprise at the ambush had been only momentary before his team of battle-hardened veterans quickly grouped into a tight guerrilla-style formation, diving for cover behind any obstruction they could find. The Emergency Response Team's leader, Sergeant Bannister, a twenty-year field operative and strategist was momentarily caught off guard as the small group dispersed behind boxes and old rusted machinery with lightning efficiency. He suddenly found his own men exposed. His men looked to him for the signal to open fire but he held off for two vital seconds, a fatal error of judgement. Even as his own men scrambled for cover, the first volley of sniper fire hit one of Bannister's men in the neck and he dropped like a stone, blood squirting through his fingers as he desperately pressed his gloved hand over the wounded area.

In the panic of the moment, Bannister knew his man had sustained a fatal wound from a shot so precise that he knew it could only have come from a highly trained soldier. His mind working furiously overtime, he considered the next move. They were up against a determined and efficient enemy and a wrong decision now would cost the lives of more of his men, yet whatever the decision, it had to be made quickly.

Their advantage of surprise now gone, Bannister screamed at his squadron to hold positions as they began spraying the area with the rat-a-tat-tat of machine gun fire. He heard one of his men screaming for a medic as he and a colleague bent over their fallen comrade, his body twitching and bloody, and carried him out of the warehouse. Bullets ricocheted off metal surfaces and bounced dangerously around the building, the noise reverberating deafeningly in the hollow acoustics.

Timayev had been in many situations like this. The key thing was to remain alert and focused. He had always been able to detach himself from what was going on around him so the horrendous noise and the frenzied heat of battle seemed to wash over him, as if he were watching the drama unfold on television. This allowed him space to think calmly and analyze the situation dispassionately and strategically. He crouched low, sheltered behind an old metal lathe, reloading his automatic rifle, and even allowed himself the luxury of glancing over at the African camp. He saw them being herded like sheep, handcuffed and beaten, into a waiting armoured truck. So much for their fearsome reputation, he thought contemptuously.

With gunfire raging around him, he assessed the situation. His men had taken out several of the invading force, but he noted with alarm that as the Somali gang had folded so easily, the unit now had additional resources, and a number of armed combatants were moving menacingly round the side of the building to outflank them. If his gang allowed them to do this, they would be surrounded, with no means of escape other than shooting their way through, and they were heavily outnumbered.

He raised his head above the metal surface of the lathe, and instantly a barrage of bullets pinged off the metal inches from his head as he ducked down quickly. He waited for a few seconds and raised his head again so he could see above his cover. He saw an advancing soldier exposed for less than a second, but that was all it needed for him to pump two shots straight into his chest. Although he wore full bulletproof body armour, the impact of the two shots combined flung him backwards and he landed motionless with a crack on the hard stone floor. Timayev knew his armour would likely save him from fatal injury, but he would take no further part in this offensive and would have some major bruising to wake up to.

It was only a temporary respite as two more of the fallen man's team advanced menacingly, darting behind broken furniture and machinery and firing off a flurry of covering shots that whistled above his head. Alexi fired off a couple of rounds in retaliation, and both men ducked just in time, a bullet grazing harmlessly against one of the men's Kevlar helmet.

Out of the corner of his eye he could see Alexi waving at him, toting his machine gun in the other hand. He caught the nod of the head and the glance from those steely blue eyes, but he was already ahead of him. It was a common guerrilla tactic, one which had saved his life more than once in the hostile battlegrounds around Grozny. Although his men were putting up stern resistance, the enemy numbers were too great, and he needed an exit plan. He looked toward the dark corner where the three girls were still cowering, sobbing and clutching at each other in abject terror.

As a couple more soldiers darted menacingly behind cover, intent on taking out the Chechen leader, Alexi let loose a cannon of rapid gunfire that sent the two soldiers scrambling frantically behind an old steel plate, from which the bullets pinged and bounced off like shrapnel. Timayev used the attack to dart from his hiding place and with the speed and intensity of a coiled viper he launched himself across the concrete floor and rolled in front of the girls. As he did so he grabbed Marisa and tried to pull her in front of him to act as a human shield. Despite her condition she realized Timayev's intentions, but the drugs had left her too weak and slow to resist. Despite her frail attempts to beat him off, he easily spun her round so her body blocked his from the savage conflict that raged on. He wrapped his powerful arm around her throat and pulled her forward. She was strangely silent as he forced her into the firing line, grinning inanely.

As he pushed her forward, a crushing blow to his ribs knocked him off balance and sent him sprawling to the floor. Clutching desperately at Marisa as he fell, she also crashed to the cold concrete and rolled away, her momentum forcing him to release his grip. He had not seen it coming and he glanced up quickly and fired a succession of shots in the general direction of his attacker, who had already darted for cover in a blur of movement. Timayev suddenly found himself exposed and watched, as if in slow motion, one of the soldiers raise his gun to fire. His quick reflexes saved him as he scrambled behind more broken machinery, the space where he had been a split second earlier riddled with bullets, blasting away chips of concrete. He was temporarily trapped, and he watched with frustration as he saw his attacker. *Jesus, it was Huberman*, he thought angrily. He could do nothing as he saw him grab Marisa and haul her over one shoulder in a fireman's carry, straining under the weight despite her emaciated frame. Amidst the crackle of gunfire, he ducked low and was met by one of the soldiers who quickly hustled him out of the warehouse door, shouting rapidly into his helmet mouthpiece.

Bannister assessed the situation. It was not looking good. He could not risk more men. They had seized the merchandise and quickly taken out the Somali gang, but the other side had quickly recovered from their initial surprise and he suddenly found that his men were under attack from a well armed and efficient group. His Emergency Response Team was not equipped for a long drawn out street battle. The strategy for his team was always to burst into the hostile area using the element of surprise, take out the enemy with minimum casualties on either side and move out as fast as possible. He now found his men in a siege type situation, an effective stalemate, both sides reduced to taking cover behind anything they could find and firing hasty shots when an enemy suddenly presented itself. He had lost two men and three more had been severely wounded. Even in the heat of battle he thought about the enquiry that would follow—his every move and instruction analyzed and dissected and pointed questions raised from investigators who had never had a crazed terrorist point a Glock or an Uzi in their face. Hell, most of those bureaucrats had not been within a country mile of a siege or hostage situation.

He made his decision. In a strained voice he spoke into his helmet mike. "Pull back, pull back!" he ordered them. His men immediately began to withdraw, stepping back cautiously toward the exit, still looking for targets as they swept the area with their automatic weapons, but the chaos had subsided and only the occasional shot now pierced the air.

Timayev glanced around and saw Alexi orchestrating his team, urging them to hold position. Timayev knew this was a fight they could not win, although as he looked around he saw with relief that despite being heavily outnumbered, none of his men were down, a tribute to their fighting prowess. Only Rahmon had been injured, suffering a deep gash to his shoulder, but the huge Tajik warrior had merely patched it up and continued, as if he had received a playground scrape. Their best hope, he reflected, was to escape with minimum casualties, but more importantly for none of his men to be taken prisoner. Although the assault team was retreating, they still had to get out of there.

He darted over to where Alexi was crouched, waving instructions at his men.

Timayev turned to Alexi. "How do we get out Alexi?" he whispered harshly.

His bodyguard's purple scar seemed to throb vividly across his cheek as he smiled confidently at Timayev. "Don't worry comrade, we will prevail."

No sooner had he uttered this when there was a shriek of splintering wood and two Land Cruisers crashed through the flimsy wooden wall, sending shattered planks of wood flying like shrapnel.

Timayev reacted quickly, flinging himself into one car's open front passenger door which swung wildly as the vehicle spun round in the warehouse, its tyres screeching and smoking. His men followed their lead and dived into the back of the vehicles, even managing to drag the two remaining girls and hoisting them into a car. The cars bounced around, narrowly avoiding the heavy metal machinery that had provided such effective cover and with a sharp angled turn headed back out of the gaping hole they had created, jolting wildly as they careered over the wreckage of the warehouse wall. One of them bumped a heavy metal lathe, throwing its occupants around inside the vehicle, and a soldier spilled out as the vehicle lurched drunkenly. He frantically grabbed at the tow-bar but missed and rolled on the floor. The rear doors were shut on him and the Toyota veered crazily into the dark clearing, barely under control.

Bannister was incandescent with rage. How the hell could his men have allowed this to happen? Clearly they had failed to properly seal the area. There would be time for incriminations later. They had to react quickly.

"Shoot the tyres!" he commanded. His men had raised their rifles in readiness before his command, but they were still too late. It had been a matter of seconds from when the Land Cruisers crashed into the building and when they disappeared in a haze of smoke, before they hurtled off into the night. His men could not get a clear shot at the tyres. They managed only a few desperate shots that punctured the metal at the rear of one vehicle before the duo of Toyotas crashed out into the night, as another ERT unit raced around the side of the building to try and head them off.

The front vehicle, carrying Timayev in the front passenger seat, a still bleeding Rahmon, Alexi and the girls, careened toward a hastily assembled roadblock. Waiting for them, rifles poised, were two soldiers, with another pair racing to join them. The Land Cruiser slammed fast toward them and Timayev thought the Mohawk driver was going to try and mow them down. He ducked instinctively, waiting for a hail of bullets to shatter the front windscreen, but before it came the vehicle almost vaulted into a sharp left turn that sent the occupants tumbling around at the back of the vehicle. The Land Cruiser was suddenly in dark forest, bouncing along with whiplash intensity, the sound of crunching and scraping of metal deafening as the trees and thick bush protested its invasion. Timayev glanced in the wing mirror and saw the other Land Cruiser following closely behind. He could just make out a small track on the ground in the light of the headlights before the driver cut them and the two vehicles plunged blindly at speed into the black forest, engines racing with a throaty hum.

Any second they could hit a rock or be upended by a huge tree, but the vehicles bounded on, the Mohawk driver grim faced in concentration. Timayev had to admire the locals he had recruited. They knew this area like their own backyard and they were fiercely loyal. As branches slapped and scraped against the Land Cruiser, Timayev peered into the darkness but could see nothing, yet the driver raced on, oblivious to the battering sustained by the vehicle, as if an empty highway stretched out on a sunny day.

"This is a back way boss," said the driver, eyes fixed firmly ahead.

Timayev nodded. "Good work," he said simply.

With no pursuit in sight and little chance of being followed down a track that was virtually invisible, Timayev took a deep breath and allowed himself the luxury of reflection. He was not aware of what had happened to his men guarding the warehouse and surrounding forest, but his team inside had escaped virtually unscathed from a police ambush, a tribute to their resilience and fighting skills. Only one man had been sacrificed, Sulim, a strong and ruthless member committed to the cause. He was confident he would not betray his comrades and would stay silent whatever the provocation. The problem of Sulim was for another day.

Of greater concern was the loss of the valuable merchandise that he had spent a king's ransom gathering. This was to be the real breakthrough deal, to finance the rebellion for at least another eighteen months and propel him to multi-millionaire status. He had been working toward this deal for several months and its collapse was hard to take. As the true scale of the failed operation flooded his thoughts, he banged the dashboard with both fists in frustration. The Mohawk driver glanced at him curiously but said nothing. As they continued to race through the virtually invisible track, it became clear they were not being pursued, although Timayev wanted to get away as far as possible in case there was another ambush.

Who the hell had tipped off the drug squad, or whichever armed unit of the police that had attacked them? He was confident of the loyalty of his men. Given the importance of the deal, he had kept most of the details secret from all but his key operatives until that very evening. Only one of his paid informants within the police was aware of any deal, and even he was unaware of the time or place. It was obvious really. Huberman had somehow tracked them here and clearly had called for back up, but how could he have known where the deal was? Yuri had not told him where the deal was taking place and the warehouse in the Kahnawake Reserve was the most nondescript location, known only to a few locals who had never let him down. He made a silent promise to himself that whatever it took, Huberman was a dead man walking.

His cell phone began vibrating in his pocket. He pulled it out and stared at the name lit up on his screen. It was the call he had been dreading. He turned the phone off. It would have to wait.

CHAPTER 22

The journey across the Honoré-Mercier Bridge and into Montreal at night passed by in a blur to Dan. He felt an overwhelming sense of tiredness and did not protest when they placed him in a cell in the police station in the old town. Even the indignity of turning out his pockets, being fingerprinted and having a mug shot, the harsh glare of the flash accentuating his dishevelled state, barely concerned him. The two officers at the station were polite, almost respectful, and even provided him with an extra blanket when they locked him in the cell. Only a faint light glowed from a small barred window at the top of one brick wall.

They had taken Marisa from him and carried her limp body into a small ambulance which had somehow made it into the forest clearing, and he saw two paramedics bending over her in the back of the ambulance before they slammed the doors and drove away. He also saw what looked like a badly injured soldier in the gurney opposite Marisa.

They had bundled him into a squad car and quickly whisked him away, but mercifully he had been spared the handcuffs, opting instead for a burly, grim-faced officer who sat silently watching him throughout the journey. As he lay down in the cell he finally succumbed to exhaustion and drifted into a troubled and restless sleep.

The following morning he was awakened early and released from the cell and allowed to wash. He was then brought to an interrogation room and left waiting for over half an hour. A battered plastic table and chairs provided the only furniture in the pale, dreary room, its bare walls broken only by a large mirror opposite him. He knew exactly what this was for—no doubt they were observing him closely through the one way mirror as he waited for someone to arrive. He stayed as motionless as possible, trying not to portray anxiety, but he knew the tactics all too well. Let them stew for a while and watch their body language. The non-verbal signs were always a good indicator. However, he had a clear conscience. In fact he could not understand why they were keeping him here, and he was considering this when the door opened and in walked Carl. Despite the years since they had last met, he recognized his old colleague instantly. He looked exactly the same, a few more lines and the clumps of pepper hair more accentuated. He was accompanied by a vaguely familiar face with distinguished features and close-cropped, almost white hair. His shiny black suit hung tight on his stocky frame. He had an aura of efficiency. This was a man who had seen a lot of field experience, mused Dan.

Carl extended a hand to Dan. "Thanks for coming in," he smiled.

"Did I have a choice?"

Carl glanced at the other man. "We just needed to make sure you were not in on the operation. Sorry about the accommodation. The best we could do at that time of night." He gestured to the suit. "This is Charles Deegan, the Emergency Response Team chief administrator. You should thank him. It looks like his team saved your ass." Deegan shook Dan's hand vigorously with a strong grip. "Hello Dan," he said simply.

His interrogators both settled in the sparse plastic chairs across the table from Dan.

"Do I need a lawyer?"

"We just need to ask you a few questions. The first one I think is obvious. What the hell do you think you were doing there?"

"I was looking for Marisa."

Carl nodded in affirmation. "Ah yes, the Bulgarian girl."

"How is she Carl?"

The Drug Squad officer exchanged a furtive glance with Deegan. "We can deal with that later. How did you know where the deal was taking place?"

Dan let out an irritated sigh. "Look, why do you think I had any involvement in this other than nearly being hung up on a meat hook? I tipped you off, remember? When I got to Kahnawake I had no idea where the deal was going to happen. Jesus, I didn't even know if it was going to happen anywhere near Montreal. I just had a gut feeling. Call it a private investigator's professional instinct."

Carl leaned forward. "Take me through what happened."

Dan related his experience of the previous night in detail and as he did so Deegan scribbled furiously. When he had finished he sat back and looked expectantly at Carl.

"You are either very foolish or very brave my friend. Maybe both."

"I have a question for you now," said Dan. "As you did not seem too concerned about returning my calls, how did your team find out the deal was happening at that warehouse?"

Carl turned to Deegan, who nodded his assent. "We got a tip off from one of the local Mohawks. He can be unreliable and his leads aren't always accurate, but when I matched your tip against his, I knew we were onto something."

"I saw the African gang being taken away. What happened to the Chechens?"

Again Carl looked uncomfortable and glanced across at Deegan. He would let him answer that one.

Deegan hesitated. "They got away," he mumbled.

"What!" Dan jumped up, sending his rickety plastic chair flying. "You had the place surrounded. How could you let them get away?" He glared furiously at Deegan.

"We got one of them," replied Deegan, as if that was enough justification. "We questioned him earlier although he isn't giving away much. They had inside help and disappeared into the woods. My team scoured the area but as yet we have found no trace of them."

"Dan," chimed in Carl. "You probably don't need me to tell you this but you need to watch yourself. You may be a target. They know about you and right now they are going to be pretty pissed that they just lost eighty million dollars street value of hard drugs. They will be looking for retribution. I suggest you lay low for a time."

Dan picked up his chair and slumped back down into it. He had found Marisa. Her father would be absolutely delighted, but he had seen the tell-tale signs of a heroin addict in her face and body. Her road to recovery would be long and difficult. Even when her body healed, what psychological scars would remain? The mental scars always took longer to recover, he knew from bitter experience, and sometimes they never healed. He needed to see her.

"Am I free to go?"

Carl ran his hand through his close cropped hair. "Of course," he replied, "but watch your back. I can arrange for a security guard to be with you for the next few days if you wish."

The inference to Dan was that after this time he was on his own. These criminals were not going to give up after a few days. They knew what he looked like, where he lived, where he worked. He was a marked man.

"Can you take me to see Marisa?"

"I've already arranged for someone to take you to the hospital."

He suddenly remembered as he felt the keys in his pocket. "Did you find my car?"

Deegan's square chin broke into a curt smile. "Was it the battered old Chevrolet parked up the road? We stripped it and searched it for drugs. We have impounded it for now but I'll tell the boys to put it back together and we'll have it with you in a couple of days."

"A couple of days? How do I get back to Toronto?" Dan protested.

Carl leaned forward. "My advice would be to stay in the city a few days. Spend some time with Marisa in the hospital. Lord knows after what she has been through she is going to need a friend. What better than the guy who saved her life?"

Carl and Deegan stood up. "We will need to question her in detail when she is better but the driver is waiting to take you to the hospital."

Dan stood up and Carl grasped his hand firmly. "It's good to see you after all this time. I'm glad to see you have lost none of your balls, although I think you have become a bit more stupid with old age," he smiled.

Deegan also shook his hand in an iron grip. "Thank you for providing such an important lead." He glanced at Carl. "And good luck," he added ominously.

The Douglas hospital in Verdun, a borough of Montreal set along the St. Lawrence River, was an imposing redbrick building set amid beautiful manicured grounds that sprawled over many acres, a half hour drive from the police station in the old town. The driver said nothing on the way, occasionally glancing in the mirror to stare at his dishevelled passenger. That suited Dan who was deep in his own thoughts. They had whisked him out of the station into the waiting car and he realized he had not washed or eaten that morning. For some reason these trivialities did not matter at the moment.

As he stepped through the bustling foyer to the reception area, the driver hung back at a discreet distance, but Dan could feel him keeping a close watch on him, like a pair of lasers trained on his back.

The stern looking receptionist peered at him coldly over her bifocals, and regarded him suspiciously when he admitted he was not a relative. Her distaste for his appearance was barely contained and she was not pleased his French was limited, as she had to rely on her own imperfect English. She finally relented and directed him toward the intensive care area in the bowels of the building. As he wandered down the long whitewashed corridors, he had a familiar feeling when confronted with hospitals. It was the smell of sanitization, the chemical tinge that seemed to permeate everywhere and which he associated with illness and death. It was like the smell from the mortuary when they had taken him to formally identify Sarah's body.

After following the French signs through a maze of corridors, he realized the hospital specialized in psychiatric cases, including substance abuse. It took him a while to find the ward where Marisa was located. Thankfully his driver had not followed him in and he was ushered to Marisa's bed by a harried looking nurse.

"You can see her but you only have a few minutes. You can talk to her but she has been under sedation and so she will be very groggy. She needs to keep her strength too. She has been through a nasty ordeal and is a long way from getting better."

The nurse ushered him to Marisa's bed, shielded by drawn curtains on all sides, and quickly departed, waving a clipboard, and he took his first proper look at Marisa. She had tubes up her nose and through both arms, hooked up to the electrocardiograph which hummed and beeped in a steady rhythm as it monitored her vital signs. Her eyes had dark rings around them and her skin was a pasty yellow, but even so her features held a hint of budding beauty. She reminded him of Sarah so much that he had to swallow hard against the lump in his throat.

Her eyes fluttered and she stirred slowly, as if awakening from a long slumber.

"Good morning," he said, smiling.

Her dark eyes suddenly snapped open at the sound of his voice and she turned to him, a look of abject fear on her face. She began to struggle weakly against the tubes and Dan noticed for the first time that she had been gently restrained by what looked like masking tape tied around her arms and the bed-rail. Dan looked around to see if any nurses were nearby and suddenly one of them stepped in the room holding a syringe. Dan moved back and the nurse quickly and efficiently swabbed and plunged the needle into Marisa's heavily marked forearm.

Marisa instantly calmed down and lay back and closed her eyes again. Her breathing was deep and regular, and the monitor continued to beep in rhythm, apparently undisturbed by her small outburst.

The nurse responded to Dan's questioning look. "It's methadone, a heroin substitute. We need to administer it several times a day and gradually reduce the dosage." He nodded silently, and she continued talking to fill the awkward silence that followed.

"Coming off a drug like heroin is a traumatic event for the body. We can't just stop it dead, otherwise her body, which is expecting the drug, may violently protest. That can lead to convulsions and seizures. We have to wean her body off the drugs gradually, particularly in the first few days to avoid severe distress. We also have to monitor her closely and carry out tests. Long term heroin use can cause infection of the heart lining and valves, collapsed veins and severe liver damage. She has a tough battle ahead of her during the next week or so, but the early signs look hopeful that she will pull through without any lasting harm."

Dan nodded and murmured, "Thank you for being so honest." The nurse gave a kind, sympathetic smile and left the ward. She probably thought I was her father, mused Dan.

Her eyes opened again, but this time her expression was calmer, and her eyes clearer. She stared at Dan, trying to recognize him, as if he looked vaguely familiar but she could not tell where she had seen him.

"Where am I?" she whispered, her voice hoarse and cracked.

"In hospital. Do you remember me?"

She looked confused. "Where is Rahmon? He gives me my fix."

"Not anymore. You're safe now. We—I rescued you from that gang. They can't hurt you any more."

Her head sunk into the pillows as her memory came flooding back. The months of imprisonment and humiliation, the drugs.

"I remember you now," she said weakly. "You pulled me out of the warehouse." She gave a thin smile. "Thank you."

Dan again had to swallow hard. It could have been his own daughter there if he had reached her in time. "They tell me you are going to get better. You won't need the drugs soon."

Her face creased in anger. "But I need them!" Again she struggled weakly, and Dan looked around, hoping to see the nurse outside the room. She was nowhere around and Marisa grew more agitated as the restraints prevented her from sitting up. The rhythmic beeping of her monitor became faster and Marisa shouted, "Let me out of here! What have you done to me?" Her eyes were wide and full of malice, and Dan stepped back in surprise.

Fortunately another nurse had heard the commotion. She was the ward sister, a squat matronly woman who brushed Dan aside and gently spoke to Marisa, her soothing tone helping to calm the girl. After a few minutes, Marisa flopped back in the bed, closed her eyes and turned her head away from them.

The nurse turned to Dan, her flabby face showing sympathy. "It is best she has some rest now. You know drugs play with people's minds as well as their bodies. Makes them more moody and aggressive, especially when they don't get the drugs they need. We have given her methadone but it isn't the real thing and it will affect her mood. Methadone can have side effects of its own, like nausea and vomiting and sometimes even seizures. We expect a few violent episodes before she is well again." She pointed at the restraints. "A necessary precaution I'm afraid."

She gave a warm smile and gently steered him out of the room. "Come back tomorrow. She should be stronger then and you can talk to her some more. She is still very ill at the moment."

Dan nodded and promised he would return the next day. She was clearly in good hands. He needed to call Vasil and give him the good news. Whatever she had been through, she was at least in the best place for now.

CHAPTER 23

Although the flat was cramped and Vasil had all his belongings neatly ordered around the sofa, he felt comfortable there. There had been no word from Dan as yet and it was now late Saturday afternoon. He had decided to postpone his usual vigil of handing out photocopies of his daughter today. Despite his tenacity and determination to find Marisa, his enthusiasm for the task was waning. He had received no leads and he was beginning to recognize some of the same faces he had given leaflets to. They clearly recognized him as well, because they would shake their heads at his offer of a leaflet and just smile sadly at him. He had even been moved on by the police a couple of times, but he had merely set up around the corner and carried on. It was, however, a dispiriting and lonely task and only Dan's support and boundless optimism had kept him going.

He paced around the tiny flat, thinking about Marisa, and constantly staring at the cell phone Dan had given to him, turning it over in his hands and willing it to ring. He had been tempted to call Dan's number, but his friend had been quite explicit before he left—do not call me, I will reach you, he had said. It took a great effort of will not to call, but he had placed all his trust in Dan. However, Vasil had harboured his own doubts, and felt privately that Dan's mission was unlikely to yield anything. Although he admired and respected the investigator, he thought Dan had rushed into this situation without a proper assessment of the circumstances.

Lost in his thoughts, he nearly dropped the phone when it suddenly began to vibrate and buzz in his hand. With trembling fingers, he pressed the talk button.

"H-hello?"

"Vasil, it's Dan here. I have some good news. We've found Marisa."

Vasil's heart leaped with joy and instantly the tears began streaming down his eyes. "Thank God!" he managed to choke.

"Vasil, I don't want you to get your hopes up too much just yet," he cautioned. "She is in the hospital and is not ready to come home, but she is in good hands."

Vasil's elation quickly evaporated. "What is wrong? I must come to see her."

There was hesitation at the other end. "She is doing fine, trust me. They are just keeping her under observation for a while. She has been through a lot and she is exhausted. I can tell you more when I see you. I am going to stay a day or two here to keep an eye on her and then I will come and fetch you. Be patient, you will see her soon enough. And remember to keep the door locked and don't answer it to anyone."

"But I should be there with her," he protested.

"You will be soon enough. Patience. She is safe."

He rang off and Vasil stared at the phone, feeling simultaneously numb with shock and overwhelmed with joy. Marisa was safe! He let the tears flow freely and flopped onto the sofa bed, hardly daring to contemplate the thought of holding his daughter in his arms again. He had to call his wife and let her know the good news. He had to calm himself first, however. He was trembling with excitement and his face was wet with tears of sheer joy.

His thoughts were interrupted by a small, almost imperceptible creak. Although it was very low, it seemed very close, inside the flat rather than outside. He could not remember if he had unlocked the door that morning. He got up and checked the stained wooden front door. Yes, he must have, the lock was free and the metal link chain was hanging loose. He must be getting old, he thought to himself. He did not remember taking the chain off and he did not usually do so until he was ready to go out. Maybe he was just getting confused in the excitement, he thought.

He spun round quickly as he heard another creak, behind him this time, and there was no doubt it came from inside the flat. He waited silently, still as a statue and hardly daring to breathe, but there was no further sound for several minutes. Probably nothing, he reassured himself. He was getting too jumpy. Then he heard the creak again, very gentle but this time more than one. The gentle creaking continued, and it was getting closer . . . .

Timayev could not avoid the call from General Medov forever but he needed time to collect his thoughts before they spoke. Holed up in a safe house within the Mohawk community, he was confident the immediate trail had gone cold, and they had outrun the authorities for now. However, they would need to remain vigilant, and make good use of the informants on their payroll. He needed to know how much the Drug Squad knew about his group and its activities. Was his gang still as untouchable as it had been in the past? With the help of his paid informants, they had always kept one step ahead of the law, but it was always going to be a precarious existence, one reliant on greed and corruption, on the vicarious trust bought with financial incentives on the one hand and threats of blackmail or worse on the other. He had to admit he had been surprised by the attack, believing the location and his meticulous planning would enable the deal to pass unnoticed.

Away from the immediate pressure of escaping his pursuers, he could analyze the turn of events more objectively, but that had made him only more angry at this severe setback. He had convinced himself Huberman was the key player in this disaster, but could not understand how he knew so much. Perhaps he would tell all just before Timayev killed him.

As soon as the General's face shimmered onto Timayev's laptop screen, Timayev knew it would be a difficult call. Medov's face was contorted in anger, and he did not waste time on pleasantries.

"What the hell went wrong?" he snarled.

Timayev fought to control his own anger. He wanted to lash out at this arrogant warlord, to demand his respect, but he knew he was no longer deserving of that.

"A tip off," he replied meekly.

"A tip off?" mocked the General. "A tip off that has cost us countless millions earmarked for the resistance effort. We were relying on that funding. Our brave men fighting the cause are doing so with the most outdated weapons and hardly any body protection. We had a deal lined up with the Chinese!"

"You don't have to tell me what it's like fighting in the front line with useless equipment General. I've been there."

"Not for a while, Akhmad," taunted Medov. "Perhaps you have forgotten what our troops are going through. Otherwise you would not have screwed up this deal."

Timayev seethed but said nothing. "This is a bad day for the rebel alliance," continued the General. I have spent the last few days making grovelling apologies to our glorious leaders. I have been humiliated. They were relying on me and I was relying on you to deliver. Your credibility has plummeted my friend."

There was little Timayev could say. There was an awkward silence before he responded. "This is a setback but we will get past it-"

"A setback!" screamed the General, his angry face filling the screen. "This is more than a setback. It is a disaster! Are you really a true patriot, committed to the cause? I want the people responsible rooted out and exterminated. Is that clear?"

Timayev was bristling. "Please do not question my patriotism, General," he said coldly. "We have already taken steps to identify and eliminate those responsible. They will be held to account and I promise you I will put this right."

"Don't make promises you can't keep Akhmad," sneered Medov. "You will have to work hard to win back my faith in you." With a final angry frown the General broke the connection.

Dan arrived early at the hospital the following day. He had stayed at a cheap and uncomfortable but obscure hotel near the hospital and had slept fitfully, so he was up well before sunrise. The walk to the hospital was pleasant, a cool late spring day with a gentle breeze, and the air was fresh. As he descended into the bowels of the building, the surgical tinge in the clammy air made him feel slightly nauseous, and when he arrived at Marisa's bedside he flopped lazily into the armchair. The curtains around her bed had been drawn back and she was asleep, breathing peacefully when he arrived.

The equipment monitoring her vital signs was stable and pulsing rhythmically and before he knew it he had drifted off too.

He bolted awake with the sound of shouting and urgent voices, and he felt his arm being gripped firmly and shaken.

"Sir, I am afraid you are going to have to leave," a male intern told him in a polite but firm voice.

The curtains had been drawn again for privacy and he saw Marisa struggling against her restraints and cursing angrily as two nurses tried to calm her down. Her body shook violently and her hair was matted with sweat. A male nurse held Marisa tightly as she thrashed about futilely, and his colleague was preparing a syringe in full view of the screaming girl. Dan thought briefly how insensitive this was before he was led away into a nearby waiting room. He knew the injection was necessary to help her, but she had probably seen similar from her captors when they were about to inject her with heroin.

After about half an hour, the kindly ward sister who had spoken to him the day before came out to talk to him. Her round face had a grave expression.

"She is struggling badly with her addiction. She was pumped so full of heroin it is amazing she survived at all. It reaches a point where the body needs drugs like it needs food and water. It can shut down from drug starvation. We have to withdraw the drugs gradually. Marisa is one of the worst cases I have ever seen. She had a bad night and I was worried at one point we might lose her." The sister sighed wearily. "Her body has been through a lot and she is hopefully over the worst but we have to watch her carefully. I don't think you should see her again today. It is going to be difficult." She touched his hand gently. "Be patient but don't expect too much too soon. She still has a few battles ahead of her." She smiled weakly and quickly departed, leaving Dan standing alone in the waiting room.

Marisa had been drifting in and out of consciousness for the last few days and even when she was awake she was barely lucid. All she could hear were voices around her that seemed muffled, distant, as if they were on the other side of a thick wall. She saw faces peering over her, blurred and indistinct, yet they seemed friendly and concerned. She could not remember exactly where she was but she knew it was not back at that evil house where the ever present threat of violence from the huge monster that ran the brothel loomed like a menacing shadow.

At least Rahmon had given her what she needed. She found herself craving desperately for the heroin, but whoever they were only gave her a little at a time, not nearly enough. Her body protested and she suffered agonizing stomach cramps and such bad nausea that she vomited heavily, her throat like razor blades.

Although the faces that peered over seemed friendly, she was still a prisoner. When her body really needed the heroin, she surprised herself with her own strength as she tore against the bonds that held her arms down, but she could not escape. Her rage boiled over and she heard herself cursing them, as if it were someone else, and her futile struggles left her exhausted and fighting for breath. All the time she suffered the constant throbbing ache of desire for the drug. She knew they gave her something—she could feel it coursing through her veins every so often but it did not give her the rich satisfying feel of the heroin. It felt empty and unfulfilling, a poor substitute for what she really needed.

Her body oscillated between bouts of burning up, as if someone had placed her over a flaming campfire, and freezing, awful chills which sent her into spasms of shivering.

She woke and looked across at the man dozing in the armchair next to her bed. She vaguely remembered him, a man who had helped her. She recalled the terrible warehouse, and then their escape. She tried to talk to him but then her body took over and she heard herself screaming for the drugs again.

Dan left the hospital quite disturbed by what he had seen and heard. Her recovery was clearly going to be difficult as her body weaned itself off the drugs. There was little he could do at the hospital, so he decided to head back to Toronto to collect Vasil and take him to the hospital. He took the metro to the police station and collected his car from the impound lot. There was still a cloak of white powder on the seats and upholstery round the car where the police had taken prints, and it looked like the inside door panels had been wedged open and carelessly replaced. They had clearly stripped the car and hastily reassembled it, but Dan knew better than to protest.

He drove the long, lonely road back to Toronto under heavy, overcast skies that had come rolling in during the morning. Before long the first large drops of rain had begun to splatter the windscreen followed by a steady drizzle, and within twenty minutes the road was slick and visibility limited. He decided to pull over just outside Brockville to call Vasil but there was no answer from the cell phone. He tried several more times but it just rang continuously before clicking off. It was odd as when he had called Vasil before the Bulgarian had answered immediately, even if he was on the road delivering leaflets.

He dismissed it as nothing, but as he continued through the steady rain, squinting through the spray at the tail lights in front, a sense of unease gripped him and his mild anxiety became stronger as he tried several more times while driving, all with no answer. He found himself involuntarily driving faster in his haste to reach downtown Toronto, but as he arrived on the eastern outskirts of town, the traffic was crawling in the Sunday early evening commute. He drummed impatiently on his dashboard as the sluggish traffic eventually brought him east of Finch, past his burnt out office, now boarded up, and to the small side road running past his apartment. He pulled up quickly and bounded up the narrow concrete steps to his tatty door. He did not need the key—he pushed it and it swung open, a bad sign.

Dan had warned Vasil to keep the door locked even when he was in. Dan decided against calling out but stepped gingerly into the apartment, his rigid body pressed against the wall as he moved slowly forward. The apartment was tiny and it did not take long to discover that any intruder had long gone, but as he looked into the tiny lounge he saw a pair of feet sticking out from behind the sofa. His heart beating furiously, Dan dashed over and peered over Vasil's lifeless body. There was little sign of trauma except a small but deep red hole precisely in the middle of his forehead. It was a neat and professional job. Even the pool of sticky crimson blood was in a neat circle around his cranium, and his open eyes stared ahead like glass, his face expressionless.

He probably had not even seen it coming, and it would certainly have been quick, thought Dan, but that was little comfort. The body was cold and there were early signs of rigor mortis, which meant his death had occurred at least four or five hours before. Suddenly overwhelmed with exhaustion, he flopped onto his sofa looking over his friend, and the bitter tears began to flow. He quickly pulled himself together. He had to call Carl. If they could get to Vasil, they could surely find Marisa.

CHAPTER 24

Brad was just returning from a surveillance operation, an unproductive five hours tracking a suspected drug dealer who had done nothing but wander the streets, meet up with a few friends and do his grocery shopping. A complete waste of time, he thought bitterly. It was an essential part of the job, and sometimes this type of discreet espionage did yield results, but it was often more a matter of luck than judgement. He was on the way back to the police station when he received Dan's call.

The voice on the other end was breathless and carried a nervy edge.

"Brad, you have to help me. I've got a dead body in my apartment."

"Christ, Dan, what have you been up to? Who is it?"

"Vasil, Marisa's father. I need you to come over."

Brad stiffened in his seat. The heavy traffic crawled by unnoticed. "Please don't tell me you got involved with this gang? I warned you not to."

"I know I know, you can tell me off later, I need you to take care of this. I have to go to Marisa."

"Where is she?"

"She is in a hospital in Montreal."

"Which one?"

There was a short silence on the other end of the line. "At the Douglas. Does it matter?"

Brad replied quickly, "No, no of course not. But you need to stay put. Call 911 and I will get there as soon as possible. You know the standard procedure. The first on the scene is always the first suspect. Don't do anything hasty. Let them eliminate you from their enquiries first. Do you think she is in danger?"

"I'm certain of it."

"Okay," replied Brad, weaving through an amber light and ignoring the angry blare of a car horn. "I'll make some calls and see if we can get some protection arranged for her. Whatever you do, stay put and be patient. Why the hell did you have to get involved?" he sighed, almost to himself.

Dan ignored the accusation, thanked Brad and hung up.

Brad decided to pull over to make a call. He dialled the number carefully, a number he knew very well but was careful not to place in his contacts folder on his cell. The phone answered on the third ring.

"What do you have for me?" asked the calm, authoritative voice that always made Brad's spine shiver. It was a voice Brad had learned to hate, mainly because of the powerful hold it had over him.

"She's at the Douglas hospital," said Brad simply.

"Thank you my friend. You were right to call me."

Dan spent over an hour answering pointed questions over and again, and finally lost patience when they decided to continue the questions at the local station.

"Am I under arrest?" he said bitterly to the detective assigned to the case, a middle-aged, overweight veteran called D.I. Burnett. The detective ran his hand through his greasy, thinning hair and adjusted his trouser belt, which was under great pressure from his overhanging stomach. His bulk was a legacy of too many long days on the job, grabbing fast food and doughnuts when he had time to eat. When he had started the job thirty years before he had been as thin as a rake.

"No, you are not under arrest, at least not yet, but I strongly suggest you come with us and finish answering my questions so we can eliminate you and find out who really did this."

There were police crawling all over his tiny apartment and a forensics team dressed in white space suits were combing the area immediately around Vasil's body, meticulously searching for any physical clues. They hunched and peered over the figure like he was a museum artefact, not a body which had been a living, breathing person merely hours before. Their almost casual approach made Dan shiver.

The flat was also covered in yellow tape that declared in bold, black letters "Crime Scene—Do Not Cross" which was being ignored by almost every person in the room. A photographer took pictures of Vasil from all angles, his flashbulb bathing the room in an eerie white light.

"In any event," continued Burnett, "Your flat is a crime scene. You can't stay here. You are going to have to get a hotel for a few nights at least. I suggest you get a bag together."

"I already had one packed. I just got back from Montreal when I found Vasil."

"So you say," remarked Burnett, in a disbelieving, almost sarcastic tone.

So for the second time in the last few days, Dan sat in a bleak, windowless police interrogation room answering the same questions repeatedly. He asked Burnett several times to phone Carl, but he either completely ignored him or claimed he could not reach him. Dan doubted he had even tried, and it felt to him that Burnett had already made up his mind about who the killer was. So much for the burden of proof. It seemed Dan had to prove to Burnett that he was *not* the killer. His theory about a Chechen drug gang assassinating Vasil did sound unrealistic, even to himself. Burnett's younger, leaner sidekick sat impassively in the corner taking notes and saying very little, preferring Burnett to lead.

Burnett never really liked private investigators, regarding them as amateurs who sometimes got in the way of proper investigators like himself, but he had to admit Huberman answered the questions directly and honestly. After thirty years of interviewing homicide suspects, he could tell a person's body language to a fine degree. It was always the suspect's involuntary non-verbal signals that were most telling and Huberman clearly believed the truth of what he was saying. Reluctantly, he had no choice but to let him go, having asked the same questions a hundred times in different ways.

"Okay, Mr Huberman, thank you for your time. You are free to go. But don't leave town just yet. We may need to call you in again."

"Thank you," replied Dan with a grimace. Leaving town was exactly what he planned to do, as soon as he got out of here.

By the time he was released from the station it was already dark. There were no spaces available on flights to Montreal at such short notice at this time of the night, so he wasted no time in getting back on the road to Quebec. As he raced along Highway 401 he made good progress in clear conditions and light late evening traffic. After an hour or so, however, the lights from oncoming cars seemed to dazzle and blind him. He realized how tired he was and felt his vehicle swerving slightly more than once as he fought to stay alert. He had to keep on going. Even now it could be too late. He had wasted several hours answering the same inane questions and he felt a little angry at Brad for not having arranged things more smoothly. He had taken Brad's advice and called 911, which he knew was the sensible thing to do, but this had caused him considerable delay, and Brad had been nowhere in sight all the time that overweight prick Burnett had been needling him.

He felt frantic as he raced along and as soon as he was on the open road, his speed began to edge up so he raced well beyond the speed limit. Calm down, he kept telling himself. Getting a ticket for speeding was not going to help his cause and only lead to more delays. He had to keep it steady and be patient, but he slammed his phone in frustration on the dashboard as he connected to Carl's voice-mail for the hundredth time. Leaving a message was risky—he had to speak to Carl directly.

After several hours of intense driving, dazzling lights one second and pitch black the next, he felt his eyelids began to flutter and he opened his window to feel the invigorating rush of cold air roar into the vehicle, snapping him awake. He knew, however, that the shock of cold air could only keep him alert for so long and at the next rest stop he reluctantly pulled over and grabbed a coffee.

His legs were stiff from the five hour drive from Montreal in the morning and he had to ignore the dull ache of sitting in one place for too long. He was glad to walk around and take a break and fill up on gas, but he allowed himself only a few minutes before hitting the road again. Even so, the few minutes of rest had refreshed him and he pressed on with renewed vigour, flying past any vehicle that had the temerity to be in his way.

It was past three o'clock in the morning before Dan crossed into Verdun and reached the imposing classical facade of the Douglas hospital. Its extensive grounds were subtly lit, but there was no sign of movement anywhere around the building. It was deathly quiet, and Dan found the stillness quite eerie.

The reception area was manned only by a security guard who appeared to be immersed in a good book while attempting to watch a number of security camera screens simultaneously, and he did not notice Dan slip by him into the deserted white corridors. The harsh fluorescent lighting was even more intense in the dead of night, and the only sound was the faint buzzing they emitted along the length of the corridor.

It was not exactly visiting time, thought Dan, but he had to see Marisa if only to reassure himself that she was safe. He would sleep in the armchair next to her and in the morning, if she was well enough, he would have some difficult news to break to her. All the corridors looked the same, and even though he had been here less than a day before, he had to follow the signs.

At the far end of the corridor he saw two white-coated individuals carrying clipboards and deep in conversation. They did not appear to have noticed him, but he decided to slip into a side entrance out of sight. No point having to answer awkward questions about why he was here, thought Dan. He waited in the shadows until they passed by, still engaged in lively debate, and continued on to the Psychiatric Ward where Marisa had been placed.

She still had a long battle to regain her health, and he did not relish the thought of having to tell her about her father. Maybe he would wait until she was fully recovered. The ward appeared deserted, and the lights had been turned down low, but he had a strange feeling there was someone else present other than the patients sleeping peacefully in the ward. It was not a sister, but a more furtive presence lurking in the shadows.

He stood completely motionless, his body rigid. Apart from the low melodic hum of the various monitors and electronic equipment, the ward was deathly quiet. He glanced toward Marisa's bed, her curtains fully drawn. However, even in the subdued lighting he could make out a form that darkened her bright, plastic curtains. He tip-toed toward the drawn curtains, anxious not to make a sound, the blood rushing in his ears. There was definitely a ripple behind the curtain, and he moved toward it.

His heart pounding, he reached the curtain and ripped it open. At first he was too shocked to react at what he saw. The figure by Marisa's bed was hunched over her and was carefully administering a syringe in the unconscious girl's forearm just below the crook of the elbow. Even in the split second it took him to register the scene he could see that the figure applied the syringe with considerable skill, but it was not a nurse. The figure was in a charcoal coloured overcoat and a trilby type hat that was pulled low to hide his face. He turned toward Dan, and his dark unshaven features framed by narrow brown eyes held a glint of fear and hostility.

The intruder reacted quickly. He let go of the syringe, which hung loosely from Marisa's arm and swung round with his fists at Dan, who stepped backwards involuntarily, tripped over a chair and fell sprawling on to the hard tiled floor. The intruder took the opportunity to make his escape and he sprinted out of the ward with surprising speed and agility.

Dan picked himself up and glanced at Marisa, her eyes staring glassily at the ceiling, motionless and with a deathly pallor. The electrocardiogram was no longer showing a healthy, rhythmic blip, but a flat line, the machine emitting a desperate whirring. He spotted a red button by the side of her bed and slammed his fist down on it. Immediately a strident alarm began clanging from inside the ward. He ran out after the intruder but he had lost vital seconds. The corridor from the ward was already empty in both directions. The intruder could have gone either way.

Dan was considering which direction to take when out of nowhere a team of doctors in surgical scrubs came running into the ward, pulling a small gurney with strange looking equipment like a small battery pack and a thin tube with two flat hand-held devices. They almost bowled Dan over in their urgency but barely noticed him as they gathered round Marisa's bed. The curtains were shut tightly and Dan could hear the surgical team barking commands at each other as they used the defibrillator to desperately try to restart Marisa's heart.

"Jesus," he heard one of the doctors exclaim. "Someone has given her Pavulon! Forty milligrams of adrenaline. Quick!"

He heard a flurry of activity as he waited outside the curtain. Another doctor shouted "Clear!" followed by the dull thump of the defibrillator, and then another shout of "Clear!" This action was repeated at least five times and then was followed by a harsh guttural cry as Marisa sprang into consciousness. He heard the monitor beep before returning to its rhythmic beat. In the commotion other patients were stirring and as they slowly awoke, they stared at Dan with curious, suspicious eyes. He could sense the doctors relax behind the curtain and the curtains were drawn aside. One of the doctors began wheeling the gurney out and noticed Dan. He was tall and athletic looking, despite his spectacles, and raised himself to his full height as he eyed Dan suspiciously.

"Who the hell are you?" His tone was full of hostility.

"I came to see Marisa," replied Dan lamely.

Scowling, the doctor looked Dan up and down and then spoke to his colleagues, all of whom were now regarding Dan warily. "We had better call Security."

The next morning, Carl and D.I. Burnett sat across the desk in the type of room that was becoming quite familiar to Dan—a police interrogation room. Posted by the door was a uniformed officer on sentry duty as if Dan might attempt to make a break for it.

Dan gave a weak smile but Burnett looked grave. The fact that he had been dragged to Montreal probably did not help his mood, and he had made it clear several times he resented the fact that Huberman had skipped town in defiance of his instructions.

Fortunately, after being manhandled by hospital security and handed to the police to be thrown in yet another jail cell for the rest of the night, his plea for Carl to come was finally listened to.

"Winding up in police cells is becoming a bad habit with you Dan. It would be quite amusing if it wasn't so tragic," said Carl.

Burnett shifted his heavy body in the small plastic chair. His gravelly voice carried an air of threat. "Don't think you are off the hook yet, Mr Huberman."

Dan ignored Burnett and turned to Carl. "I appreciate you coming over Carl," he said.

"While I do not condone your actions in creeping round the hospital in the dead of night, it was lucky you did, because Marisa had been administered,"—he glanced down at his notes—"Pancuronium bromide, or Pavulon as it is known. Apparently it is a muscle relaxant which is also used in lethal injections in the United States. The amount given would have caused Marisa to lapse into a paralytic coma and her heart to fail—she would have been dead within minutes."

"How is Marisa now?"

"She is doing fine. She is a very strong girl and the doctors tell me she has made remarkable progress. Another few days and she should be ready to leave."

"And the intruder?"

"We checked the hospital's security cameras. He can be clearly seen slipping into the building but he was very careful not to show his face. All we saw was a black shape and it's going to be virtually impossible to get a positive ID on this guy. You are the only one who saw his face." Carl sighed and added ominously, "The perpetrator was clearly a professional."

Dan glanced expectantly at Carl who anticipated his question. "Don't worry, this guy is not coming back. We have placed her under armed guard while she is in the hospital, but we can't protect her forever. As soon as she is well enough you should arrange to send her back to Bulgaria. Her father can't help her and whether you like it or not, you're the surrogate."

Burnett leaned forward, breathing heavily. "I want you back in Toronto. I am going to find out who killed Mr Dimitrov and right now you are my only lead so you'd better stick around this time."

"I want that more than anything, but I've answered all your questions a dozen times over."

"I may have some more."

"Alright," sighed Dan. "I will take her back to Toronto. But I want protection, at least until I can get her out of the country." He turned to Carl. "Can you arrange it with Brad?"

"I'll speak to him today." His tone softened. "Dan, when she is well enough you need to tell her about her father."

"I know," replied Dan sadly. "That is going to be the hardest part."

CHAPTER 25

Dan spent the next few days kicking his heels in a cheap motel just north of the Parc Leroux, a few blocks from the hospital. Carl had arranged an armed guard to stand outside his room, and he stood impassively outside his door for hours at a time, a silent sentinel, while Dan remained imprisoned inside, banned from leaving until he received a call from Carl. He did not know whether it was for his protection or to keep an eye on him so he did not do anything stupid.

He spent the time carrying out some more Internet research on the company Rebel Antiquities, but it revealed very little. The company had a website, but it was fairly basic, a few colourful photos of fine antique furniture, nothing of any substance to provide any further clues about the real people behind the company. However, when he keyed in the catchphrase set out on Yuri's business card underneath the name, **победа в крови**, he discovered this was Russian for "Victory in the Blood." Also the symbol of the wolf with the green background was the traditional symbol of Chechen independence. He was beginning to understand.

He also spent a lot of time trying to contact his clients, many of whose numbers were located on his phone. Most had heard about the fire at his office and several expressed their sympathies and promised to re-engage him as soon as he had sorted out his business affairs. However a few were more distant, and did not offer any guarantees. It was clear to Dan that rebuilding his business was going to be a long, hard road, but it could wait for now.

Dan knew Carl's team were making enquiries but they were still hoping to interview Marisa when she was ready. Carl had ensured that Marisa was properly protected. After the last security breach, which had embarrassed the hospital immensely, they took no chances and had a guard posted by her bedside at all times.

After what seemed an eternity, Dan eventually received the call from Carl that Marisa had completed her addiction treatment and was sitting up in bed, taking solid food. He ran the few blocks to the hospital in the early morning sunshine, his guard loping at a discreet distance behind, scanning all directions like a hawk. As he reached her ward, he saw her smiling and talking with a doctor. He suddenly pulled back before she saw him. He had some painful news to tell her and he did not quite know how to approach it. The thoughts of that fateful night when Sarah died seemed to swirl vividly in his brain, as if he were in the moment again, feeling the crushing ache of bereavement.

She turned and saw him and gave a smiling wave. He had to admit she looked really well. The dark circles around her eyes had faded only slightly, but her eyes no longer carried that vacant, dull look. They had character and expression, and it was really the first time he had seen her smile, an attractive grin that carried warmth and humour; which made it all the more difficult for what he had to say.

Dan approached her, smiling, and the doctor left, assuring Marisa that he would sign her discharge papers shortly. Dan settled into the easy chair next to the bed and to his surprise Marisa reached out and wrapped her thin arms around his neck. Dan gently eased out of her embrace, completely taken aback.

"You are looking a thousand times better," observed Dan.

Her eyes still looked tired but seemed to bore into Dan, and they displayed real affection. "That is because of you. How do you say in English—my knight in shining armour!" She gave a girlish giggle, as if a heavy weight had been lifted from her shoulders. Then suddenly her face clouded over and her expression changed. "They did some terrible things to me. I am too ashamed to tell my father." She suddenly began weeping, a plaintive, remorseful cry.

You won't have to. He had to tell her but the words stuck like razor blades in his throat.

He gently comforted her and then with a mighty effort of will he summoned the courage. "Marisa, you have to listen to me carefully. Your father, he was—shot."

She instantly stopped crying and glared at him sharply. "What do you mean, shot? Is he alright?"

"No he isn't."

Marisa cut him off, her tone urgent. "Tell me what happened. Is he badly hurt?"

Dan fidgeted uncomfortably. *God I'm making a mess of this.* He swallowed hard. "I'm afraid he was killed."

Her mouth opened wide in terror but there was only silence. Her whole body seemed to sag and she flopped back in the bed. "Tell me what happened," she choked.

"He was a brave man. He came to Toronto to look for you and he asked me to help. He was staying at my apartment when it was broken into and he was shot a few nights ago. I managed to tell him you were safe before he died. At least he knew that. I believe it was the same gang that held you hostage."

Her face was set like alabaster, and only a single tear betrayed any sense of emotion. It was enough to give Dan an enormous lump in his throat. "Where is he?" she whispered hoarsely. "I want to see him."

"He's in the mortuary in Toronto. He had an autopsy and the Homicide Unit is running some ballistics tests. I can try and arrange for you to see him but perhaps it is better you remember him as he was."

She turned to him, more tears trickling as if a dam was about to burst. "I have to see him."

"I understand Marisa. We also have to tell your mother and we will need to arrange his burial. But most importantly, we need to get your passport organized and get you on a plane back to Bulgaria. You can't stay here. They have already made one attempt on your life and they could try again. They are obviously scared you are going to talk."

Now her face was set in steely determination. "My village has an honourable tradition that has served it well for centuries. If someone does wrong to another, they have to pay back for their wrong in equal kind either to the person wronged or their family. We do not call it revenge. It is more about restoring karma. An eye for an eye. I am not leaving this country until those—" she hesitated, searching for the right English word—"*bastards* who killed my father restore karma."

Dan thought to argue but the look on her face convinced him otherwise. Now was not the time. He wanted to tell her that she didn't know what she was up against but ironically enough she probably knew better than anyone.

"The best way you can restore karma at the moment is to tell the police everything you know. They are gathering evidence against these men and you can help to confirm their identities. They are waiting outside to interview you. Do you feel strong enough? I can ask them to come back if you wish."

She shook her head, wiping away her tears. Beneath her surgical gown he could still see the ugly scars raked into her arms. He hoped for her sake they would fade away eventually and not leave her with a permanent reminder of the abuse she had suffered. She nodded her silent assent and Dan took her hand and squeezed it affectionately. "I'll come back and take you out of here when you are discharged later today. I made a promise to Vasil that if I found you I would protect you. I intend to honour that promise."

She gave a weak smile and he quickly left, his own emotions beginning to falter.

In the waiting room he saw Carl and Deegan, the latter anxious to discover more about the gang who had made such an audacious escape from his team. It was the third member of the party who surprised Dan the most. A familiar face, an old friend, but not one he expected here in Montreal.

His friend's handsome rugged features broke into a broad smile. "Good to see you Dan. I see you have been making a nuisance of yourself so I thought I would come over personally and sort you out!"

"T-Thanks Brad," he stammered.

Dan decided to wait in the intensive care waiting room as the trio interviewed Marisa. He sat ruffling through a lifestyle magazine taken from a nearby coffee table but did not really register the words or pictures. He had been taken aback when Brad turned up, but as he thought about it, he convinced himself it made some sense, as the gang were known to be based in Toronto and therefore on Brad's patch. He could however, have waited until they were back in Toronto where he could interview her at length, but given the possible danger they were in, he probably wanted to get a statement on record before . . . . he did not wish to think about that.

He knew they were in considerable danger, and no doubt Brad had arranged to take over the case and protect them. Dan could not think of a person he trusted more than his old friend to support them. Even so, whether he was being paranoid, he could not say, although given the events of the last few days it was probably wise—he just could not shake off the feeling that something did not appear quite right.

As he sat there lost in his thoughts, he was interrupted by a gentle cough. Standing over him was the tall, swarthy and athletic doctor who had confronted him on the night Marisa was attacked. He stood there expectantly in his pristine white coat. Dan stood up and found himself several inches short of his visitor, thinking he was going to get thrown out of the hospital again.

"I'm Dr. Lemerre," he smiled, offering his hand. The doctor's grip was strong and he carried an air of authority and confidence that suggested he was a senior, well respected figure in the hospital.

"I am sorry about the other night," he said, looking rather embarrassed. "A matter of protocol I am afraid." Dan smiled inwardly as he recalled being frogmarched out of the hospital and delivered to the police who had immediately cuffed and searched him. It had taken a few hours of confusion before it became obvious Dan was not the attempted killer, by which time the real perpetrator had long disappeared.

Dr. Lemerre waved Dan back to his seat and sat in the opposite chair, leaning forward so his knees jutted out awkwardly. He perched his spectacles on the edge of his pointed nose and referred to a folder he was carrying.

"Mr Huberman," he began, his Québécois accent carrying a soothing quality. How many families of patients had he broken bad news to, wondered Dan. He was probably far better at it than he was. "I am fully aware of the circumstances that Marisa came to us. I cannot imagine what she has been through, never mind what happened the other night." He shuddered as he recalled how they had nearly lost her. "Considering everything, her recovery has been nothing short of miraculous, although she has been in excellent hands." He said this without a hint of smugness, clearly proud of his team. Despite their first meeting, Dan found that he instantly liked this affable, friendly doctor.

"However, I must warn you that overcoming addiction, particularly to a drug like heroin, is one of the most difficult challenges a human can face. She was in an advanced addictive state when she arrived and getting clean has put her through a painful and harrowing ordeal. She was exhausted mentally, physically and emotionally, but she is over the worst. She is a survivor, a very strong lady."

He paused, scanning his folder and then looking hard at Dan, his dark eyes boring into him like laser beams. "Surviving addiction is a long term process. We can do no more for her in the hospital, but if she is to be taken into your care you must never give her the chance to take any drugs and you must watch closely for any signs of relapse. Considering her experience, there is also a real chance she could suffer post-traumatic stress disorder. I know about her father, and a shock like that could send any recovering addict spinning out of control. She is extremely vulnerable right now, but I am going to discharge her. Please do not give her the chance to undo the progress she has made here." He continued to study Dan, looking at him over his rims like a dutiful headmaster. "Can I trust you?" he said simply.

Dan felt an overwhelming sense of responsibility, but at the same time flowed a strong determination that he would not let Marisa down like he had his own daughter. He owed that much to Vasil.

"Absolutely," he replied.

CHAPTER 26

Although Dan had strong reservations about returning to Toronto, Brad had convinced him it was the most reasonable option. Although he had no desire to run and hide, travelling back to the city felt a little like entering the enemy's lair, but Brad had repeated his assurances that he would personally take care of their safety and coordinate the investigation of the trafficking gang from Toronto. When they had finished interviewing Marisa and entered the hospital waiting room, Brad had looked ashen faced, clearly troubled by what he had heard. "We will bring these men to justice," he had remarked hoarsely to Dan.

After Marisa had been discharged, Dan had taken her to a steakhouse bar just east of the Pierre Trudeau airport, where she had eaten like a starved hyena, an encouraging sign that her health was returning to normal. She said little during the meal and was happy to let Dan guide her, often lost in her own thoughts.

A large part of the journey in Dan's old Chevy along the straight, tedious route from Quebec was conducted in silence, even when Marisa was not sleeping. The young girl clearly needed her space. She had made an emotional phone call to her mother in Bulgaria, and Dan had heard her anguished wailing and sobbing, the pent up emotions finally unleashed. She had silently handed Dan his cell phone back, her eyes red and blotchy, and her face raw with grief.

As they passed Kingston after several hours monotonous driving on a gloomy late afternoon, he cast a sideways glance at his passenger. Her expression was blank and she stared ahead intently to the horizon, not focused on anything in particular.

"Brad has arranged for us to stay at a safe house just east of the city tonight. In the morning we need to go to the Bulgarian Consulate to arrange a replacement passport for you. He has promised to pull whatever strings he can to get you the passport as quickly as possible, but you may be here for at least another week."

Her tone carried the stubborn edge with which he was rapidly becoming familiar. "I don't care about going home yet. I told you I want to see my father."

Dan sighed. He had discussed this already with her, but her resolve would not be shaken. She had been through enough and Dan feared her fragile mental health would be dealt a further serious blow if she persisted in seeing her father's body. Dan had seen plenty of corpses in his time, and he knew a shooting victim was never a pleasant sight, no matter how much the pathologist cleaned them up. It was often the expression in the eyes that spooked Dan—the sheer terror and shock that were permanently registered in the eyes at the exact instant of death. The haunting eyes, and the mask of death chilled Dan far more than the blood and gore from some brutal slaying, or the innards exposed under the skilled but detached knife of the pathologist.

The guest house was a tall rambling townhouse in a quiet, nondescript backstreet, the type that had very little passing traffic. As Dan pulled up outside the house, he checked the address Brad had given him and confirmed it was the right place. Apart from an old rusted sign marked "vacancies" creaking in the light breeze, there was no other outward sign to suggest that it took paying guests. As he pulled up in the small car park next to a narrow alley at the rear of the building, Dan felt satisfied that this was a good place to remain inconspicuous—several miles east of town, not far from the Scarborough Bluffs, and a chance for Marisa to return to some degree of normality.

The place itself was tatty but clean, and the ancient landlady who showed them to their rooms on the top floor could barely make it up the stairs. She smelt of stale cigarettes, and when she smiled her thin, bloodless lips revealed a row of yellow, cracked teeth. Dan and Marisa exchanged glances, and he detected the merest hint of mischievous humour in her eye. However, when the landlady announced in her croaky voice the two different rooms, Marisa objected and insisted on both of them staying in the same room. The landlady growled and argued she would still need paying for both rooms. Dan quickly placated her and offered to sleep on the floor and Marisa had the double bed.

The landlady quickly departed, muttering to herself, and the smell of tobacco followed her like an invisible cloud. Dan brought up his holdall and her meagre bag of possessions and placed them on the bed. The room was gloomy but functional, the light from the windows struggling through thick net curtains. The ceiling was low and sloping, following the pitched roof of the house. Apart from the bed there was a small dresser, table and chairs and a recessed wardrobe. In the corner was a large old fashioned television sitting precariously on a battered cherry wood cabinet. Marisa immediately reached for the remote and began flicking through the channels on the television, the sound turned high.

"They would not let me watch TV," she declared over the din.

Dan escaped from the noise into the hallway and called Brad to let him know they had arrived safely.

"Excellent," he said in his usual upbeat tone. "We are a little short on resources. I will send someone over tomorrow but just sit tight. No one knows where you are."

They also discussed the arrangements for getting the passport. "It may take a little longer than I thought," explained Brad. "The Bulgarian Consulate is not being too helpful, but to be fair they do not have a lot to go on. The girl has no records in this country."

"Brad, she wants to see her father as well."

"Oh Christ Dan, is that wise after all she's been through? They carried out an autopsy on him you know. He isn't a pretty sight."

"I told her Brad, but this girl sure is stubborn."

"Okay, I will call the mortuary and text you the arrangements." Brad was tight lipped about the investigation into the trafficking gang, but Dan was not surprised.

The night passed relatively peacefully, although at one point in the dead of night he heard Marisa cry out. He quickly got up from the floor and ran to her, but she was still asleep, in the middle of a nightmare, the bed sheets damp with sweat. He gently woke her and she immediately drifted off again, this time calmer, but it was the last sleep he had that night.

The day was chilly and dull, with a stiff breeze blowing off the lake. From his elevated position the sniper could see clearly, a mile or so south, the vast stretch of Lake Ontario, a gentle swell lapping toward the shore. It looked lifeless and uninviting, as it often did on days like these. Although it was nearly the middle of May, it was one of those typical spring days in Toronto where the biting cold of winter had not quite disappeared altogether, and came back to remind one that the warmth of summer was still a few weeks away.

The building he was on was perfectly situated across from the guest house. It was an old architect's office that still had a few occupants, but the fourth floor was abandoned and the sniper had been able to walk up the stairs without encountering anyone. Even better, there was a small set of fire stairs onto the flat roof of the building and the sniper had been able to set up his equipment behind the low parapet so his telescopic sight was positioned to face the window in the guest house.

When the Chechen had approached him, he had initially refused, telling him he was now retired, but the man had made him an offer difficult to turn down. You come highly recommended, he had said. That always made him smile. Hiring assassins was definitely a business where word of mouth referrals worked best. They could hardly advertise in the *Globe and Mail* after all. But he often wondered who talked to who. The best people to talk about the quality of his work were those who no longer had a voice, precisely because he was so good. However, as he set up the tools of his macabre trade, he reminded himself that this would definitely be his last job. No more planning the kill, tracking the target and skulking on rooftops waiting for the right moment. The sumptuous beachfront villa in the Cayman Islands was waiting.

The window was a storey lower and at a slight angle, but good enough for a clean shot. He sealed the fire escape door by fixing a small plank of wood under the handles. He did not wish to be disturbed in the unlikely event anyone came up here. Then he pulled his overcoat tight and sat against the concrete parapet, checking the rifle and its telescopic sight, which peeked over the parapet, were accurately positioned for when the opportunity arose. As usual in his line of work, all he had to do now was wait and watch.

The visit to the Bulgarian Consulate had been as unproductive as Brad had warned, and Dan and Marisa had spent several frustrating hours trying to explain the extraordinary circumstances behind Marisa's emergency passport application. Occasionally Marisa conversed with the consular staffer in Bulgarian. Although Dan could not understand a word of what was said, he could tell from the tone of the conversation and the scowling on both sides of the glass screen that the exchanges were becoming heated. They left with a vague promise from the Consulate official that he would do his best to help them, but his promise did not seem genuine, rather an attempt to get rid of them. "Come back next week," he said airily, as if everything would be solved by then.

At least for Dan the waiting and arguing postponed the grim prospect of visiting the City mortuary. Despite his attempts to persuade her otherwise, she was determined to see her father, and they drove to the mortuary in silence.

The pathologist in residence had been expecting them, and he quickly ushered them through the waiting area into a corridor that was brightly lit with fluorescent tubes, which gave the area a cold, sanitized feel. As they passed into the holding area where the bodies were kept in steel drawers like oversized filing cabinets, the lighting was more subdued. Even so, the large room had an uninviting, metallic feel.

The pathologist moved with quick, rodent-like action and without hesitation pulled out the heavy drawer. The body was covered in a white sheet, and the pathologist quickly checked the label attached to the toe, and nodded grimly to indicate this was Marisa's late father. This time he did hesitate and he looked kindly at Marisa over his round rimmed spectacles.

"Please prepare yourself, Miss Dimitrov. Are you really sure you want to go ahead?"

Dan could see Marisa's eyes already glazed with tears, but she gave a weak affirmative nod. The pathologist gently pulled away the white sheet and Marisa gave an audible gasp and buried her head in Dan's chest, looking away, before turning back to the body and studying it carefully with an almost detached interest.

Dan had seen lots of bodies lying like a slab of meat on a mortuary table like this, or on some occasions lying in the street during his time as a drug squad officer, but somehow never got used to the macabre feeling of observing a corpse close up. He always felt this irrational fear that the corpse would rise up and wander zombie-like toward him like some trashy B-movie, but it was even harder when you knew the victim. Vasil had become a friend and a sense of guilt nagged at him as he recalled how he had advised Vasil to stay in the flat. He needed to make amends by helping Marisa.

Fortunately they had done a professional job of cleaning him up. There were no blood marks, although the raw wound in the middle of his head was purple and blotchy, and there was a ragged scar circling his forehead where they had performed a cranial autopsy. The stitches still looked fresh, but thankfully Marisa did not seem to notice. The body looked shrunken and withered, a cruel parody of the strong man he once was. This was inevitable no matter how effective the cold storage, and often made the body unrecognizable. As he began to turn away, Dan caught sight of the eyes. He wanted to avoid looking at them. It was always the trauma in the eyes that spooked him, and he quickly tried to banish the image burned into his brain.

Marisa continued to silently gaze at Vasil before she nodded to the pathologist that she was finished. With a grim but sympathetic expression, he respectfully laid the sheet over the corpse and pushed the drawer back, crossing himself as he did so.

"Catholic," he said simply in answer to Dan's questioning look. "Good to believe in this line of work." He gave a weak smile and pushed his glasses up his nose nervously.

"Thank you doctor," choked Dan. He guided Marisa out of the room and steered her quickly out of the building. Only when she felt the chilly fresh air as they walked to his car did her emotions finally emerge in a torrent of sobbing. Again she sought sanctuary in Dan's chest, and all he could do was pat her back awkwardly. He could not tell her it was going to be alright. It never would be again.

CHAPTER 27

Marisa arrived back at the room emotionally exhausted and she slumped on the bed like a limp rag doll, her eyes still red from the bitter grief-stricken tears. Dan kept his distance, allowing her some space which he was certain she needed. There would be plenty of time for her to grieve her father, and there would be funeral arrangements to be taken care of. He had not discussed with Marisa yet whether the body should be flown back to Bulgaria, although it was not an immediate issue as the pathologist had suggested they might wish to undertake further forensic testing as part of the ongoing investigation.

Dan stepped outside into the hallway and went to get some water from the kitchen. It felt like it had been a long day, but it was still only four o'clock. He trudged down the narrow stairs and as he did so he tried to call Brad on his cell. There was no answer. Where was the guard Brad had promised? It was taking a long time, although he was not unduly worried. He felt comforted that Brad was taking charge of the investigation, and this place was so quiet and inconspicuous he felt no immediate danger, although both Carl and Brad had stressed that they were likely to remain a target. The sooner Timayev's gang were apprehended the better, but they were clearly a professional unit and had continued their operations under the noses of the police for a long time, if the formation of the company was anything to go by.

How could anyone escape scrutiny for so long without being stopped? They were either so intimidating that the drug squad did not have the resources to fight them in what would effectively be a turf war, or they had infiltrated the police, or maybe both. He had not heard of this gang before and he had not had a chance to speak to Brad at length about just how much he knew of them.

Maybe they had kept a low profile up to now, engaging in small time racketeering and running their squalid brothels, but the events in Montreal had changed all that.

He reflected on this as he sauntered back up the stairs with the jug of water and gently opened the door. Marisa had got up from the bed and was standing at the window, peering out into the dull sky.

"I brought you some water."

She said nothing and continued to stare out of the window.

"Marisa?" he called more firmly. She turned toward him, bending slightly and moving away from the window when it came. The window shattered, glass flying inwards with a high pitched crack. There was a whoosh as a speeding bullet grazed Marisa's hairline and smashed a small hole in the opposite wall, the plaster crumbling into dust. It was instantly followed by two more rapid shots, both of which passed within millimetres of Marisa's body and cannoned into the wall. Despite the shock, she reacted quickly and was already on the floor cowering behind the bed when another volley exploded into the wall behind her.

Dan also hit the floor, the jug thrown aside and its contents spreading over the threadbare carpet.

"Marisa," he screamed urgently, "Crawl over to me, quickly." He reached a desperate hand out to her but she was across the room and it seemed a marathon distance with the sniper fire. She began to crawl but she was too slow and another volley erupted on the floor by her head. She screamed, panic stricken, but managed to edge forward further until Dan could grab her and dragged her like a sack of potatoes so she was shielded out of sight from the window. Another shot buried itself in the carpet, splintering the floor underneath just inches from Dan's foot. They scurried out through the door into the hallway.

On the building opposite, the sniper cursed his momentary hesitation. He had the girl in his cross-hairs and had waited a vital split second to position the shot in the middle of her forehead, always the cleanest shot. But just as he pulled the trigger she had turned and the shot whizzed by her face, and he could see from the flurry of activity that she had not been hit. He fired several more volleys, more in fury, and the shots did not carry the lethal accuracy he usually applied. He had waited for hours for a clean hit and had blown it. Perhaps, as he had reflected earlier in the long wait on the roof, he was getting too old, and should have stayed in retirement. He no longer seemed to possess the exceptional levels of concentration and cold lethal accuracy required in this profession. Killing was an art, and even a small dip in performance was enough to turn a clean kill into a messy affair. He quickly packed up his equipment and holstered his small Glock semi-automatic pistol. Unfortunately this was going to be one of those messy affairs.

The shooting had stopped as they threw themselves breathlessly into the hallway. Dan looked around wildly, considering his options. They had to get out of the building and fast. The break in shooting was surely only a temporary respite, a chance for the shooter to reload. Leaving the front of the building was not an option. Their room faced the front, where the shots had come from. Marisa was shaking but she stayed silent.

"Stay with me Marisa," he urged her. "Do exactly as I say." He wanted to reassure her that they would get out alive, but he could not be so sure. It was not clear how many assailants there were.

Dan and Marisa lay there, breathing heavily and assessing their options. They had to somehow reach his car and get away as quickly as possible, but there was always the chance they would be waiting by his car. How long had they been watched? He was convinced he would have noticed had they been followed at any time during the day. An elderly couple came out in the hallway to see what the commotion was and saw Marisa and Dan crouched on the floor. He waved them back frantically, and wide-eyed and frightened, they retreated back into the safety of their room, slamming the door.

After a minute which felt like an eternity, Dan stood up and flattened himself against the wall and motioned for Marisa to do the same. They quickly slid along the wall to the rear window where the rusting steel outer stairs of the fire escape creaked in the breeze. He forced open the large window. It was stiff and unyielding. Heaving with effort, he managed to force it open and they both stepped out onto the stairs, crouching low and looking around anxiously for movement. They had to move quickly as they were exposed on the stairs, a sitting target for their attacker. Keeping low, they headed down as fast as possible, their feet clanging on the metal steps.

They were at the back of the building, facing the deserted alleyway, loaded with dumpsters and garbage strewn across the narrow path. It looked deserted from their high elevation, but Dan was only too aware that any of those garbage receptacles could hide a sniper. They had no choice but to head for his car, which was parked at the end of the alley about one hundred feet away from the bottom of the fire escape.

They fled quickly down the four stories to the ground but it felt like a long way down, as he mentally braced himself for another volley of gunfire. Fortunately, despite being exposed on the fire escape, none came and they hit the ground running, Dan looking all ways and pulling Marisa by the hand as they sprinted for the car. They were going to make it, he thought with an irrational feeling of elation. Only fifty feet to the car and they would get away.

Then a dark, menacing shadow appeared between them and the car. The figure had a small pistol aimed directly at them and moved forward silently but purposefully, the weapon steady and unwavering. Dan looked around wildly. The alley was narrow and despite the dumpsters offered very little in the way of cover. Even worse, the alley at the far end was enclosed by a large wire fence. A dead end. The sniper lay between them and the only escape route.

The sniper was striding toward them fast and whatever decision Dan made had to be quick. They backed away, neither of them taking their eyes off the weapon. For a fleeting moment, Dan wondered whether there was any chance of negotiation, but one look into the cold, dead eyes of their assailant ruled out any such thoughts. They had nothing to negotiate with, and even if they did, this was a ruthless, hired killer. They were not human to him, just another pay cheque.

They backed into a doorway of the terraced house adjoining their guest house, and Dan frantically tried the door. It was locked and solid, no chance of breaking through. He banged on it with his fists in frustration but the thick wooden door stood resolute. Meanwhile the sniper was moving toward them. The pistol was aimed and ready, the safety catch off.

The hunted pair quickly moved out of the doorway and with no place to go, cowered in the next alcove. The sniper was now within comfortable shooting distance, and Dan could see the smile break out on his sallow face as he measured them up, no doubt deciding who to shoot first. There was another door in this alcove, but if this one was locked they were as good as dead. With all his might Dan crashed against the door shoulder first, but this door also stayed firm. Less than twenty yards away, their would-be killer smiled even more broadly, sensing that their last escape route had betrayed them. He raised the gun to take aim, and took one last look around him. The sniper did not want any witnesses. Maybe the hit would not be so messy after all. An effective silencer and one clean shot to the brain for each of them, and a quick exit.

Dan rubbed his sore shoulder, his panic rising as he looked into the barrel of the gun. Marisa said nothing but began tugging and pulling at the door handle, which miraculously began to turn with a heavy squeak. They forced open the door and rushed in just as the sniper, realizing what had happened, fired off a desperate shot that splintered the wooden door frame where Dan's head had been a split second earlier. Marisa saw the smile disappear from the sniper's face and allowed herself a moment of satisfaction as they stumbled in the dark. The way ahead was gloomy, and despite the dull light of the day, it took a little time for their eyes to adjust. They found a stairwell heading down and quickly ran down it into a dark, damp smelling basement. It was almost pitch black, with no windows even at the top, but it provided the perfect cover for them to hide. Within seconds the sniper had followed them in and he prowled around the basement like a panther, alert and ready to spring for the kill. Hiding behind an old grandfather clock in the corner, hardly daring to breathe, they watched his figure, a shadow deeper black than his surroundings, moving stealthily round the basement. He would find them, there was no doubt.

Dan could feel his own heart beating furiously and Marisa next to him, breathing in small gasps. Fortunately the low hum of an electricity junction box concealed their sounds, but Dan knew he had to act soon. He saw the black shape move toward them, hesitantly at first but then with greater purpose. Had they been seen? He could not wait to find out. He launched himself from behind the clock and aimed a deft karate chop to the middle of the torso. He was aiming for the kidneys but in the darkness could not be sure where he had hit, but the shape went down with a hoarse grunt and he heard the clatter of the gun being dropped on the concrete floor. The black shape quickly recovered, however, and Dan sensed that he saw the gun and was about to pick it up.

"Run!" he shouted at Marisa, and they both bounded up the stairs and rushed out of the door into the daylight, feeling a momentary disorientation as their eyes adjusted. They locked hands and bounded toward his car. With his free hand he fumbled for the keys and opened the lock with his remote, still forty yards from the car. He looked around and saw the gunman come bursting out from the doorway, sprinting after them, his gun raised. A shot whizzed past Dan's ear and punctured the metal chassis of his old Chevrolet. They quickly got in and Dan pushed Marisa, her tearful eyes full of fear, so her head was below the dashboard on the passenger side.

"Stay down!" he warned her, his hands shaking as he turned the key. The engine turned over but the ignition did not catch. He looked up. The sniper was almost on him, this time a crazed, angry expression contorting his features. Again Dan felt the momentary panic of being cornered, no escape, but then the engine roared to life, and the car lurched forward and slammed into the sniper. He rolled over the bonnet of the car, the gun clattering out of his grasp, but managed to hang onto the wing mirror and haul himself back onto the front of the car with both hands. He tried desperately to hang on, his face purple with rage, inches from Dan's and separated only by the windscreen. With surprising strength, the gunman held on with his right hand and began to reach into his jacket with his left.

Dan shot forward and the sniper spun round crazily like a spinning top on the bonnet, using both hands to hold on. His extra gun slipped out of his pocket and bounced on the metal but with lightning agility the sniper managed to grab it. Dan had no choice. He slammed his foot on the accelerator and raced down the alleyway toward the wire fence at the end, knocking bags of garbage and other detritus out of the way.

The sniper hung on grimly, but a look of fear clouded his face as he realized what Dan was about to do. Just before the car went hurtling into the fence, Dan slammed on the brakes as hard as he could. The car skidded and they were thrown forward. Marisa had put her seat belt on but Dan almost hurtled through the glass. On the other side of the screen, however, the momentum of the sudden stop sent the sniper flying through the air and he crashed heavily against the fence, limbs flailing, and slumped motionless on the dirty ground. Dan recovered quickly and reversed the car down the alleyway. He spun round, tires screeching and flew down the road as far away from the guest house as possible.

CHAPTER 28

Olivia lay rigid on the grubby bedclothes in the tatty room which had been her home and workplace since her arrival in Canada. Her face was a mask, calm and serene on the outside, but hiding the turmoil that lay within. She dared not move. Next to her, breathing heavily but still awake, the wiry, intimidating bulk of the Chechen leader slouched lazily next to her. The stale smell of his sweat mixed with the dank odours that hung around the room like a toxic cloud.

When he was on top of her, his weight and strength almost crushed her tiny frame, and she found herself fighting for breath as he thrust awkwardly on top. His technique often bordered on the brutal, but today there seemed an extra edge, a raw pent-up aggression as if he was releasing all his frustrations on her frail torso. He was fully aware he hurt her, but that was clearly of no concern to him. She could not have felt worse if he had used her as a punch bag to alleviate his stress. At least that way she would not suffer the inevitable mental anguish that flooded her mind after each session with the barbaric Chechen. Olivia had never realized the act could be used to convey so much anger and hostility, but now she understood more clearly those times as a small girl, cowering in her tiny box room, listening to the cries of her mother through the paper thin walls as her drunken father forced himself upon her. Then she had felt only confusion, a sense that her mother was in pain, yet an unknown fear holding her back from rushing to comfort her. Only as she grew older did she understand the disease that afflicted her father and made him do such terrible things. Alcoholism was an insidious disease that wrecked the senses, to the extent that the afflicted person had absolutely no concept of the pain they caused others, usually those closest to them.

As an only child, she had felt a huge sense of guilt at making the decision to leave her broken home, but they were poor and faced an uncertain future. Her father was beyond redemption, and her mother beyond rescue. Surprisingly, however, she had felt, almost unconsciously, a simmering resentment and contempt for her mother, that she had been too weak to break free from her degrading situation and allowed herself to be punished for so many years. Olivia had watched her suffering and decided to flee before it was too late for her. She thought of her mother often, rarely of her father, and the one shred of comfort Olivia derived from her present circumstances was that she did not know where Olivia was now. It would kill her more surely than the slow agonizing decline of living with an alcoholic husband.

Her only true friend in this desperate existence had now left her, and she missed Marisa terribly. Of course she was happy she had escaped. She had paid the price for defiance, and would surely have died if they had continued to pump her full of drugs as they had done. Olivia prayed regularly that Marisa had survived. She had no way of knowing, but Marisa was strong and resourceful. That was the one attribute Olivia admired about Marisa. She had been like a big sister to her, and despite the one year difference in their ages there was a gulf in maturity. Marisa had continually urged Olivia not to give up hope, never to lose spirit, because that would be the ultimate defeat. They could try and control our bodies but never our minds, she had said fiercely many times.

But now she was gone, and while Olivia's existence had been just about bearable, she now felt more alone than ever, even more than as the little girl hiding from the pitiful submission of her mother behind the bedroom door. Marisa had always been the Chechen's favourite, probably because of her undoubted spirit, but since she had gone he had turned his unwelcome attentions to Olivia, almost as if to punish Marisa's best friend. Every time he laid next to her, sated, her body stiffened with a mixture of disgust and fear. His brooding presence was enough to instil fear in any of the girls, because of the power he held, and there was even more reason to fear lately. Since the Montreal fiasco, his mood swings had become more pronounced, bordering on the psychotic at times.

Timayev's cell phone rang, beeping tremulously, and much to her relief, the Chechen got up. She was hoping he would leave but instead he paced around the room like a caged animal, a tiny vein on his hard forehead just below his cropped hair throbbing rhythmically. The man spoke in his native language, which Olivia faintly recognized as being from the Dagestan region, although she understood very little of what he said. It was the hard scowl and his agitated movement that indicated he was receiving bad news. He turned and glared at her and then turned away, raising his voice and speaking with a strained urgency. Suddenly he shouted in English, and his explosion of anger startled her.

"I want them dead, you hear me!" he snarled, his face now tinted red with rage. "Bring the mole to me!"

He slammed his cell phone against the wall and it hit with a metallic crunch but miraculously stayed in one piece and clattered across the dirty wooden floor. He turned toward her, eyes blazing, and a tiny smile formed on his thin, bloodless lips. She stifled a sob as his hard fingers began probing her naked body.

In the rush to escape they had left most of their meagre possessions behind, and Marisa agreed with Dan it was too dangerous to go back. Fortunately Dan always carried on him his two most important possessions, his wallet and cell phone. Dan just kept driving as Marisa sobbed, her chest heaving, fighting to control her panic. Grim faced, Dan said nothing and concentrated on the traffic, driving aimlessly, alert for any signs of being followed. After a while Marisa became more composed and Dan turned to her. He could see the tears streaked across her soft features and he offered a weak but reassuring smile. She just looked at him with frightened, desperate eyes.

"We need to get out of the city, get away where we can't be traced."

"They found us before," she protested. "They are going to kill us!" This brought a fresh wave of sobbing.

"Come on Marisa," he chided her. "You're tougher than that. We are both targets but I'm here to protect you."

The words sounded hollow even as he said them but Marisa just stared ahead, her lip still quivering.

"Where are we going?"

That was a good question. It had taken Dan nearly an hour to calm down and think rationally, and in the slow traffic they found themselves on the northern outskirts of the city. He glanced over his shoulder at the skyscrapers of the business district, dwarfed by the arrow-like CN tower, glinting in the weak evening sunshine.

"We're heading north. I don't know exactly where yet. We need to hide out for a few days and think about what to do next. But first I need to stop off and get some cash before we go too far. We need shelter and food, and a few more clothes. We need to pay cash. I can't risk using my card and giving away our location. They traced us before. I have no idea how. Who knows what they are capable of? Better to be safe."

Marisa nodded meekly, now more composed.

He rubbed his stubbly chin thoughtfully. "Can't do much about the car, but if I hire one it could be just as dangerous. A hire car always attracts attention. Less conspicuous in an old car, and I don't think they know what I drive. I hid it well when I went to Montreal."

Dan pulled off the road to a small, ramshackle service station with a teller machine. Dan withdrew some cash and filled up the car with gas. He looked around surreptitiously as he did so and Marisa waited anxiously for him to get back to the car. He got in quickly and pulled over to a piece of waste ground at the side of the station.

"I have a bone to pick with someone," he said, almost to himself. He took out his cell phone and dialled Brad's number.

Marisa sat back silently and closed her eyes. Dan glanced over at her. She looked tired and drawn, Dan observed, and this day was far from over. He waited impatiently, drumming his fingers on the dashboard, and then Brad answered.

"Hey buddy, what's up?" His usual upbeat tone only served to irritate Dan.

"I'll tell you what's up, *buddy*," he sneered, his tone full of sarcasm. "We were nearly killed from a sniper attack and there was no sign of your armed guard. Where the hell was our protection?"

There was a long pause at the other end of the line. "Jesus, Dan, I'm sorry. I tried my best to get someone to you quickly. Are you still at the safe house?"

Dan could feel his voice rising. "No we are not at the damn safe house. It wasn't very safe. We are on the road."

"Just tell me your exact location and I will get someone out to you immediately, I promise."

Dan hesitated. "I can't do that Brad. Let's just say we are heading out of the city for a few days to let things calm down. I need to get my head together and Marisa needs to be safe. We can't rely on anyone but ourselves."

"You can rely on me, Dan. Just tell me where you are."

"No I can't!" he yelled into the phone. Marisa's eyes snapped open and she looked oddly at Dan. He spoke more calmly. "We've been friends a long time so you will have to trust my judgement. Marisa has had two attempts on her life since she escaped and despite her evidence you are no nearer to catching them. The bloody Emergency Response Team had them in their hands and let them slip away. They murdered Marisa's Dad for Christ's sake? When are you going to bring these savages in?"

"Dan we have some good leads. We are working on everything we have but you know the nature of these gangs. You have to cut them off at the head, take the leader down. We are still trying to track them down but they have proved elusive."

"Well until you do we are off the grid. I will call you in a few days."

Before Brad could reply Dan broke the connection and turned off his cell phone. He needed some time to consider their options, to hide out and make themselves invisible for the time being. He was not sure if he had done the right thing refusing Brad's offer of protection, and he only had a vague idea of where he was heading, except to get lost in the Canadian wilderness for a short time.

He turned to Marisa. "Do you fancy camping?" he smiled.

Dan fired up the ignition and smoothly slipped into the early evening traffic and joined Highway 400 heading north out of the city.

CHAPTER 29

As they left the city, a vast expanse of forest stretched out before them, and the long straight road ran like an arrow into the lush green wilderness until it was lost from sight. They stopped off at an outdoor store and Dan bought some camping gear, a small tent, sleeping bags, a camping stove bag and some freeze-dried provisions. He also bought a small camping knife, bug spray and a fishing rod.

The cashier glanced at them oddly, not just because the man insisted on paying in cash. They made an odd camping couple, he thought. The girl was half his age at least. They did not look like father and daughter, but who was he to judge? She was a pretty girl and good luck to him.

They were soon on their way. Traffic on the highway was light and Dan fell into a relaxed rhythm of driving while Marisa curled up on the passenger seat next to him and drifted off to sleep. The northern sky ahead had darkened considerably and a few black clouds scudded across the horizon, and it felt like he was driving into an unknown abyss. Although summer was not too far away it was still quite chilly, especially at night. He recalled there was an old abandoned tumbledown cottage near Dorset on the Lake of Bays. It had belonged to an old barrister friend who had always been too busy to renovate it, although it had been several years since he had been there or spoken to his friend. It might have been sold and repaired by now but he would take the chance. At least it offered some form of shelter. Even checking into a motel seemed risky at present. They had to stay anonymous and the Canadian wilderness offered a good prospect of that. If the cottage was still available they could use it as a base and keep their camping equipment there for a few days.

He pulled off the highway north of Lake Simcoe and onto the narrow Highway 11. The darkness descended abruptly like a curtain and the road was almost deserted, other than the odd vehicle driving south, its glaring headlights illuminating the inside of the car. Marisa's eyes fluttered in the sudden bright light and Dan shielded his eyes from the dazzle. He was more paranoid, however, when he saw a car speed up behind him and he would slow down and let it pass, all the time watching it intently.

Presently a light rain began to fall and the headlights picked out the scurrying of a rabbit or a raccoon caught in the glare, its glassy eyes staring into the car before it darted away.

Visibility was reduced in the rain and Dan felt an overwhelming tiredness as he squinted for signs in the dark to find his way. It had been a long day and he forced himself to stay alert, rolling down the window a touch to let the cool, moist air rush in. Marisa stirred but did not wake up. She needed the rest. It had been another traumatic day for her. It wasn't every day you saw your father laid out on a stone cold metal slab and then get shot at by a crazed sniper.

The route was fairly simple, but the road curved and bent around sharp corners, and he had to drive cautiously, especially when he was skirting the silent black mass of a lake. He had heard many times of people taking a bend too fast and plunging into the icy black waters of one of the many lakes in these parts. Most of the lakes here were deep and freezing cold all year round. They would suck a car and its occupants under very quickly with little chance of escape.

With a sigh of relief he soon came to the lights of Dorset, and crossed the small single-track bridge in the middle of town where the river opened out into the vast lake. The houses were well lit, but there was little activity outside. However, as he turned off the main street heading out of town, his lights played on an old man walking a large Alsatian. The dog jumped up angrily as he passed by, barking furiously while his owner pulled on the lead. The owner glared at him as balefully as the dog, as if strangers, even those passing through, were not welcome at this hour.

He remembered the cottage was about two miles further up along the lake shore on this road, but he had to be careful not to miss the turning. Although the rain had begun to ease and his wipers screeched on dry glass before he turned them off, it was still oppressively dark as the trees began to close in, creating an eerie canopy. He went slowly and the road rose up a small hill before curving round and falling gently down toward the lake, and to his relief he found the muddy track easily.

The track was rutted and as he bumped along, Marisa jolted awake and she gave a small cry. She took in the darkness and felt an irrational moment of panic before she realized Dan was still driving.

"Where are we?"

"Well, if I can find the place, this is our home for the night."

"Here?" she said with obvious disdain.

"Yes, here. We are going to set up camp. Give you a taste of the great Canadian outdoors."

"I would prefer a taste of the great Canadian indoors. Preferably with a roaring log fire."

"I can certainly do a fire."

He saw the black shape of the cottage silhouetted against the sky, which was now clear and full of stars. "Stay here, I am just going to investigate."

She turned and grabbed his arm, her eyes full of alarm. "Please Dan. Don't leave me in the car." Thoughts came flooding back of the last time she was in the forest at night just before they were picked up in the dog van on the journey to Toronto.

He gently removed her arm. "Marisa, I will be less than a minute. Just stay in the car. There's no one around."

She bit her lip. "Okay, but be quick."

He grabbed a small but powerful flashlight from the glove compartment and skirted the building. He was pleased to see it was still deserted but remarkably intact considering the ravages of the Canadian winters. The decaying front door was already open and he stepped inside, waving his flashlight around the bare concrete walls. The kitchen still had a rusty old stove, the gas main long disconnected, but there was a rickety wooden table. In the lounge there was a beaten up old sofa, and the fireplace still had some logs. There was the sign of an old raccoon nest as well, and the threadbare carpet was ripped and scratched.

He waved to Marisa and hurried back to the car.

She reluctantly followed him into the cottage and rolled her nose in disgust as she surveyed the wrecked cottage.

"It's not exactly the Hilton, I know, but it will do for now and it is off the beaten track. There are even logs in the fire. It's as if someone was expecting us."

"Don't say that."

"If we get a fire going we can make this a real home—our little hideout."

They both unloaded the car and laid the mattresses on the lounge floor, Dan kicking away the remains of the raccoon nest. Dan got the fire going, and the welcoming flames brought a warmth and vitality to the room that lifted their spirits. He took out the camping stove and, groping in his bag of food supplies, found some freeze dried sausages and a tin of beans. He cooked them on the stove and placed them in their mess tins, and she wolfed the food down hungrily with bottled water.

Dan inspected the two bedrooms upstairs. The first one was empty and he heard a rattling noise from the other. As he stepped in gingerly, he saw it came from a open window with a broken latch that was tapping gently against the rotted frame in the cool breeze. He secured it tightly and went downstairs. He left the fire burning steadily and they both climbed into their individual sleeping bags fully clothed.

"Tomorrow we will go into Dorset and get some more supplies," he promised.

They talked for a time, and Marisa became visibly more relaxed. He told her a few stories about the methods he used to catch adulterers for his client, usually a jealous wife. "Those jobs were always the best," he smiled. She laughed at his tall stories, and her tired eyes sparkled in the firelight. It was the first time he had seen Marisa smiling and relaxed. It was a good start to her healing process—one step at a time.

She soon fell asleep again, her breathing heavy and rhythmic, and he fought to stay awake, listening for every sound. There was only the gentle rustle of the wind and the occasional squawk of a heron on the water, and within minutes he began dozing and drifted away into a deep, exhausted sleep.

CHAPTER 30

Timayev sat back in his black leather easy chair and surveyed the sun dipping below the Toronto cityscape, bathing the towers of the business district in a soft ochre glow before it dipped below the horizon. The penthouse lounge, with its high curved windows offering a stunning view of the town, often served as a venue for the company's board meetings, and his rich walnut desk doubled as a boardroom table. A waitress, a plump Latvian girl rescued from one of his several "pleasure houses," as he liked to call them, served the assembled group cocktails and beers before Timayev dismissed her with a casual wave.

The informality and relaxed buzz of conversation from the six men in the room hid the fact that their organization was in crisis. As the men chatted amiably, Timayev peered out of the window. Somewhere out there in the city Huberman and the girl Marisa were still alive when they had no right to be, and it bothered him.

He noisily cleared his throat and the general hubbub of conversation died to a murmur. In accordance with the custom at these operational meetings, Akhmad spoke and the others listened until they were invited to present their report.

"Gentlemen welcome, welcome, let's get down to business. I had to report today to General Medov regarding the two fugitives. His intelligence sources advised him they are still on the run. The sniper we hired failed badly and I will see to it that he retires permanently after this botched job. General Medov is not happy. He is a major stakeholder and supporter of our business, and without his support we have no credibility with the rebel factions in Chechnya. He has threatened to cut off our funding and if he does we will never be able to finance another deal like Kahnawake. We have to find these two and bring their heads on a platter to the General. Only then will he be satisfied."

He turned to Alexi. "What is the status comrade?"

Alexi leaned forward on the heavy polished desk and clasped his meaty hands together. "We brought in the mole. He is not certain where they were headed but is confident they drove north out of the city. The mole can track any payments Huberman makes with his credit cards but so far only a large cash withdrawal has been traced back to a teller machine in the North York area."

"Do you think he is loyal to us?" asked Akhmad.

"As if his life depended on it," affirmed Alexi with a malicious smile. "We will find them."

"We have to do it quick. Medov is getting impatient."

The rest of the meeting was taken up with reports on the usual business operations. The legitimate import and export business of fine art and antique furniture remained profitable. His manager Farooq, a scholarly looking Ossetian with a degree in fine art and a passion for the trade, presented his report with his usual enthusiasm, but Timayev barely heard him. Farooq ran the business well, and though he recognized the business was used as a vehicle for the group's more nefarious activities, he preferred not to get involved on that side. He was happy to turn a blind eye when the products were used to smuggle drugs. It was amazing how much could be stashed into secret compartments, in say, an antique writing table. In any event, Timayev preferred it that way.

Timayev thanked Farooq and the manager sat back and cleaned his glasses before he was politely ushered out. Timayev ran his business on a need to know basis, and the mild-mannered art dealer had no further business there.

Alexi was next, reporting on the local drugs trade, where the group still had a stranglehold on a large part of the local supply chain in Toronto. It was a constant turf war; rival gangs were always trying to encroach on each other's territory. Timayev's gang had been more successful than most, having established a fearsome reputation over several years of dealing with interlopers. However, the grapevine spread quickly in this industry, and news of the Montreal fiasco had reached the street, resulting in some gangs becoming bolder and trying to encroach on their territory. Also, suppliers had been less keen to deal with them, expecting that Timayev would soon be arrested following the Montreal drugs bust. Those who continued to deal had raised their prices, eroding profit margins just when he needed to boost finances. Alexi painted a grim picture, and it did not help Timayev's mood.

Serge was more positive on the trafficking side. Their network of Eastern European suppliers was working well, and all the houses were run in a disciplined, authoritarian manner. With the giant and unpredictable Tajik Rahmon overlooking the operation of the three Toronto brothels, each with eight occupants, the girls rarely stepped out of line. There had been plans for further expansion in Montreal using the properties they had there, but these plans had been put into serious jeopardy by recent events, even if they did not directly affect that part of the business. He suspected a couple of the properties were under police surveillance, and they had moved a number of girls to different locations outside the city as a contingency. He was confident that if they raided the properties now, the police would not find anything to link them back to Timayev. The clan leader was anxious to avoid Montreal for a while. Serge had proved to be a good hands-on manager on the trafficking side. He enjoyed visiting St. John's to transport the girls personally, although even this remote route into the country was becoming more hazardous, under more scrutiny now than in the past.

Times were not good for his organization. Even before the Montreal fiasco, he had made a huge strategic error in liquidating Yuri. It had badly affected morale, as the medic had been a popular figure, and even Timayev found himself missing his cool and professional advice. The man had a conscience, which was not an asset in this dirty business, but he had been a useful ally.

Timayev got up and turned to the window, hands clasped behind his back.

"Thank you, gentlemen, that's all." He continued to peer out at the darkening sky as they filtered out. These were indeed difficult times.

CHAPTER 31

The following morning emerged as a beautiful fresh day, the blue canvas sky marked only by a few clouds occasionally drifting lazily across the sun. The air was warm despite a cooling breeze off the lake, and Dan made some coffee on the camping stove as Marisa stripped to her underwear and dived into the lake, before screaming in shock and quickly running out.

"It's f-freezing," she gasped. As she ran out she mumbled to herself, "I should have known better." She had been in the water in Newfoundland and dived into the icy Lake Ontario when she had tried to escape. Those times seemed a distant and unpleasant memory. It seemed every lake in Canada was icy cold.

Dan threw her an old towel from the trunk of the car and she quickly got dressed. After coffee they packed their camping gear in the trunk and headed back along the narrow, winding road into Dorset. The area was much more inviting in the morning sun, which glinted through the canopy of trees enveloping the road. They stopped in a small parking area on the edge of the woods opposite the tiny parade of shops. The hills that loomed over Dorset were turning green, although they were still mottled by brown patches, and the place had an air of tranquillity as the locals gently went about their business. They even found time to offer a friendly good morning to the two strangers who stepped out of the beaten Chevy, and Dan grinned back. No sign of the cantankerous old man and his ferocious dog, he mused.

They bought some more food in the well stocked general store that looked like a relic from the old gold rush days, its painted white timber front gleaming in the sun. Dan also hovered over the glass shelves selling cameras. He picked up a few and inspected them and opted for a small black Nikon. He turned it over in his hands, inspecting it carefully, and gave a satisfied nod. "A good price and allows for twenty minutes of video footage. Just what we need."

"Is this really a good time to go around taking pictures like a vacation?" asked Marisa, a little sarcastically.

"A perfectly good time," Dan retorted. "We might as well enjoy ourselves while we are here."

They put the provisions in the trunk, which was now nearly full, and set off on the quiet road out of town north-east toward the Algonquin National Park. Their route was lined by hemlock and pine trees that seemed to crowd and press in on the road. As they reached the boundary of the park the forest became denser and they had to slow down as the road became more rutted, still recovering from the rigours of the harsh winter.

Marisa looked around her in wonderment at the vivid shades of greens and browns illuminated in the bright sunlight. "This is more beautiful than the Pirin foothills back home!" she exclaimed.

After another forty-five minutes driving at a leisurely pace through the main corridor skirted by spectacular hardwood forest, they soon reached the huge wooden and glass structure of the Algonquin visitor centre. They spent a pleasant hour learning about the history and ecology of the park, and Marisa particularly enjoyed the lifelike dioramas showing moose, black bears and beavers in their natural habitat. The stuffed animals seemed to stare at her with their unflinching glassy eyes, and she almost expected them to start moving, as if awakening from a long sleep. They headed out onto the rear balcony, which reminded Dan of an over-sized barbecue deck, hanging over the terrain like a precipice. However, it offered a sweeping vista of the park to the north, line upon line of trees stretching to the horizon, broken only by the occasional steely blue of a distant lake.

"Let's get lost," declared Dan. He packed an old backpack with food and handed Marisa the bug spray. They followed one of the many walking trails into the interior of the park and she was glad of the spray. As she began to perspire in the light humidity, she seemed to attract an unwelcome swarm of midges, and she could also hear the soft buzz of a mosquito repelled from its attack by the spray. Dan was less bothered by the insects, and tramped forward through the undergrowth confidently, occasionally slapping one hand on the other to squash a tiny blackfly that was after his blood. Dan explained the blackflies were a particular nuisance as they could cause a wound completely disproportionate to their tiny size, because they tore the flesh rather than pierced it, and also because they injected an anti-coagulant that made the blood flow copiously. Rather like sharks attracted by blood in the water, the blackflies would swarm at the first sniff of blood and could quickly make life very miserable for a hiker. After that sobering advice, Marisa sprayed herself again and was vigilant not to allow any blackfly past her chemical armour. The insects were a little troublesome because of the recent rains. There was a fresh, damp feel to the air, and the plants glistened with dewdrops.

The trail underneath was slightly muddy, and Marisa was acutely aware her casual pumps were completely unsuitable for the walk. She had nothing else, no possessions except those she was wearing. No wonder the girls Akhmad kicked onto the streets when they no longer attracted customers found it hard to survive. They were exploited in the brothel and exploited on the cruel streets, when they were destitute and desperate. She had heard some chilling stories in the house about the fate of several girls who had been chucked onto the streets. She shook her head to dispel the morbid thoughts of life in the house. She was still weak from her ordeal, mentally and physically, and was grieving for her father, but she felt safe in Dan's company, and right now she was in a beautiful place.

The riot of colour was quite staggering, a sea of blues and greens interspersed with some vivid pinks, the latter from the rose pogonia orchids that seemed to rise through the tall grass and shrubs, reaching out for the sunlight.

At times on their walk, Marisa felt like she was walking on a plush carpet, especially near a stream or lake, although she did not care for the slightly acidic smell. At other times they wandered into deep, dark forest which blotted out the sun, the trees bent over the narrow path like sentinels, rustling gently in the breeze. The variety of trees was fascinating, ranging from thick conifers like balsam fir, cedar, hemlock and various pines. Further on they encountered silver and red maple trees. Dan pulled off a leaf and showed Marisa the distinctive shape, one that even Marisa recognized from the flags that seemed to hang from almost every public building. He was very attentive and patient. Marisa had the impression that if Dan was on his own he would go marching off into the bush at a brisk pace in an effort to cover as much ground as possible, but he hung back for her and took pains to explain the beautiful sights around them. At one time, she heard the distant baying of some feral creature. Dan explained it was probably a pack of wolves, and he laughed loudly at the look on Marisa's face.

"Don't worry," he assured her, still laughing. "They won't eat us, and there's no full moon tonight!"

They took a break for lunch near a small tinkling stream that glistened in the sun, and Dan filled a water bottle. The water was pure and clear, and Marisa found it highly refreshing, especially as the day had grown steadily warmer. She laid back in the soft grass and looked up at the blue skies, complemented by a few puffy white clouds that did little to dispel the gentle warmth. Even the skies were active, a small flock of jays darting by, and a Merlin falcon swooping majestically, wings outstretched and gliding effortlessly from one treetop to another.

After lunch the terrain climbed steadily higher, and the ground more rugged. Marisa felt as though she had walked for miles, and although her feet were a little sore, she felt curiously energized. Dan referred to the small guide he had picked up from the visitor centre and showed her the route they had taken. Her legs began to ache and she had to stop a few times, still feeling the lingering weakness but eager not to disappoint Dan. As she got hotter, the flies and mosquitoes seemed to converge, and she swatted them away angrily. A further burst of bug spray and a cooling swig of water provided much needed relief and she pressed on. They skirted a huge granite outcrop and as they turned a corner and reached the summit, they found themselves perched on a ridge overlooking a deep blue lake surrounded on all sides by a vast expanse of greenery. In the distance a lone canoeist threaded slowly across the middle of the lake, and the whole vast expanse before her was a scene of great serenity.

She sat down, knees pressed against her chest and took in the view.

She returned Dan's expectant look. "Yes, yes," she sighed. "It was worth the effort."

As they tramped back down the trail, the sun had dropped lower but Marisa was still perspiring freely and fighting off the marauding swarms of midges and blackflies, swatting at them aimlessly and topping up her bug spray. She also found she had to concentrate more on her footing going down than up, and it was a relief to arrive on level ground. The dense forest they soon arrived at was cool and fragrant.

"We are heading back to the visitor centre now," announced Dan, striding purposefully ahead of her.

Marisa nodded her approval with great relief. Her feet were sore, and the insects were a problem. Her legs felt shaky as they protested against too much exercise, and she was beginning to feel really hungry. Yet despite the discomfort, she felt a curious sense of peace in the vast beauty of the wilderness around her. To be able to stand and look out across a vast expanse, stretching for miles and miles to the distant horizon, was something she had not done since she had stood on the summit of one of the foothills in the Pirin mountains back home. She had done that far too infrequently, failing to appreciate the true beauty close to her home. After spending several months imprisoned in the house, staring at the insipid, peeling walls of the bare room, being out in the open was a wonderful sensation. Even feeling the warmth of the sun on her cheek, and the cooling breeze running through her hair was pleasurable. It was easy to imagine her horrific drug-fuelled nightmares belonged to a different person, someone she wanted to forget she had ever known.

Marisa found herself thinking of her father, and a profound and deep sense of loss pressed down on her. She had talked to Dan about her guilt over his death. If only she had not deserted the family to seek a better life in Canada, he would not have risked everything to search for her, and would still be alive today. Her family already faced an uncertain future, and without her father that future now looked bleak. Dan had tried to lift her spirits, and in a curious way it appeared to work. She found herself accepting the logic of what he said—how she could never have predicted the events that led her to this moment. He assured her Vasil was one of the bravest and most resilient people he had ever met. No greater love could be shown by a parent than that demonstrated by her father. He had risked everything to come to a foreign country and had worked tirelessly to track her down, never giving up hope. Dan told her that in the short time he had known Vasil they had become firm friends. Though his life had taken a sudden and dramatic twist since he had met Vasil, Dan assured her of his strong sense of responsibility to protect Marisa on behalf of her father.

In her own mind, Dan had already assumed the role of father figure, and she found herself accepting his natural tendency to take the lead, so she happily followed his direction. She felt a sense of security in doing so. He had already saved her life several times, and considering what was out there she knew how vulnerable she would be on her own.

"If we could turn back the clock," declared Dan, "I would be the first to put the hands in reverse."

That revelation had led him to talk about his own daughter, and as he did so she understood better his desire to protect her, and felt a wave of compassion toward him.

For Dan himself, it was an opportunity to talk about his daughter in a way he had not done for a very long time. He found Marisa a willing listener, and even as he talked he still found the emotions were quite raw. Perhaps it was harder because Marisa was not much older than his daughter when Sarah died, and she too had suffered from the scourge of drugs. Marisa had survived, and he found himself desperate to make sure that she stayed alive, whatever the cost. He had failed with his own daughter, and he had to live with that knowledge every day of his life. But now he had been given the opportunity to make some form of amends. Though it would never bring Sarah back, he was determined not to make the same mistake with Marisa. When he looked in her eyes he could almost delude himself she was Sarah. He found himself having to tear his eyes away. They were very alike both in physical stature, and in their strong-minded, stubborn personalities. He felt a close connection with Marisa, and he told himself he would not fail a second time.

As they talked openly on the final stretch of their hike, both baring their soul in some way, Marisa slipped her hand in his. He smiled to himself as he remembered the feeling of his daughter's soft hands that he used to hold tightly, feeling the same sense of responsibility for her protection. His resolve was firm. Failure to protect Marisa was not an option.

It was still bright when they arrived back in Dorset. They stopped to buy some spare clothes and he watched Marisa move happily through the small racks of outdoor wear, picking out items and holding them to her for size. She would occasionally wave a shirt at Dan and he would nod his head approvingly, and then she would change her mind and put it back. She was certainly an independent girl, observed Dan. Whatever decision she made, whether choosing clothes or otherwise, would be hers alone. She was not easily influenced. She eventually opted for an oversize lumberjack shirt and a pair of denim pants.

They carried on back to the tumbledown cottage and laid out their sleeping bags. Dan built the fire while Marisa set up the camping stove and made coffee. They sat on the battered sofa and sipped their coffee and Dan played around with his new camera, checking the settings. Outside the sun was lower in the sky and the light was diminishing.

"Alright Marisa, we have twenty minutes of video time on this camera. We ought to start filming." They went outside and Marisa sat on a small, flat rock, gathering her thoughts. The lake, a gentle swell drifting lazily to the shore, offered a scenic backdrop as Dan positioned the camera. He carefully placed the camera on the tripod so it was level with Marisa's upper body and her face was in the middle of the lens. When he was satisfied he motioned to her.

"Are you ready?"

She nodded silently and took a deep breath. They had discussed what she should say but as she saw Dan press the record button, she suddenly found herself speechless. Where would she start? She looked helplessly at Dan, waving his hands frantically to urge her on. She began with her visit to the Bulgarian recruiter, making sure she cited names and dates as much as she remembered, as Dan had coached her. She found within a minute she was in full flow and told her story fluently and eloquently, only stopping occasionally when her emotions got the better of her. She talked about how Timayev hated smoking, considering it an unhealthy, dirty habit, yet he was happy to let the clients smoke in their cramped, airless rooms if they wished to. He also let the men smoke as long as they did not do it around him, and most of them did, coming from a region where it was so prevalent. He was quite happy for the girls to suffer the effects of passive smoking. He had no consideration for the health of the girls at all. He was casual about the clients using protection and was unconcerned about the devastating effects of any of the girls contracting hepatitis or any other sexually transmitted infection. She related a few stories she had heard where he had thrown girls who had become so afflicted onto the streets with no money or medical care. To him the girls were not human lives, but expendable commodities which could be easily replaced. After all, his view was that there was an endless supply out there.

This would make compelling evidence to a jury, thought Dan. She came across as a credible and influential witness. He hoped it would not be necessary to use it, but it was useful insurance. When she came to the part about her father's murder, she looked as if she would break down totally, but she composed herself and continued on. The hard drive had only seconds to run when she finished her story and Dan switched off the camera.

He nodded to her admiringly. "That was incredibly brave."

She had described her experience inside the house and everything she knew about Timayev and his group. Although there were many things she did not know, including the exact location of the brothel, there was enough to make a strong case against Timayev and his seedy gang if and when it came to trial.

They spent the following day in Dorset, first visiting the huge fire tower at the top of the largest hill overlooking the town. Their feet clanged noisily on the metal steps as they climbed the tower, and as they moved higher they were soon above the trees. The whole open aspect of the tower made it feel like they were floating above the ground. The steps were slatted and if Marisa looked through the gap in the stairs, she could see the ground far below, and it gave her a knot in her stomach. A group of giggling Chinese schoolchildren came bounding past them, pushing through exuberantly and running up the stairs, peering over the edge as they reached each platform.

Marisa followed Dan with renewed purpose. If these eight year-olds can do it, so can I, she thought. However, as she neared the top, she could not help looking down between the slats, especially as the last flight of steps was positioned outside the main structure. It seemed to hang at the edge so there was nothing under her feet but the step and a huge drop to the trees below, and the tower seemed to sway lazily in the wind. She was relieved to reach the enclosed platform at the top and enjoy the stunning view of the Lake of Bays from what felt like firm ground, although the platform still seemed to creak and sway in the stiff breeze several hundred feet up.

Dan turned to her, smoothing his ruffled hair. "I'm impressed," he said. "You made it to the top. Not everyone does."

She looked around. The Chinese group had been and gone and only a few middle-aged tourists shared the platform. "I can't deny I will be glad to reach solid ground. I think I have earned a coffee."

Dan laughed and grabbing her hand they quickly descended and after a quick lunch, drove back into the village. They stepped into the small Internet café on the high street and ordered two hours of access time. Dan settled in front of the PC and Marisa pulled up a chair next to him.

"First things first." He signed into his hotmail account and then took the small SD card from the camera and copied the file with the video to a draft email. He emailed the file to himself and then sat back, pensive. Should he send the file to Brad? He instantly dismissed his doubts. Brad had been his loyal friend for years. Even so, he hesitated before clicking the 'send' button. Brad was in charge of the investigation. He needed to see this more than anyone, he told himself.

Dan also sent the file to a third recipient. He checked the email address from his contact list. It had been a long time since they had last been in contact and he hoped the address was still current. He sent a short covering message.

"Who are you sending the file to?" asked Marisa curiously.

"An old friend, the same one who owns the old cottage. He's a barrister who helped me after Sarah died. Other than Brad, he's the only person I can think of. Just a form of insurance." He sent the file and removed the SD card.

"From what you have told me about Timayev, he must have a bit of a history. Let's get down to business and see what we can find out about this bastard."

They spent the next few hours in intensive research on the Internet. Dan had previously checked out Timayev's company, but it had yielded very little. With the information Marisa had about Timayev, it was possible to draw a clearer picture of the man and his group behind the trafficking and drugs ring. He typed in various searches, starting with "Chechen War." This provided a detailed history of the insurgency and its brutal repression by Soviet armed forces.

"They constantly talked about the guerrilla resistance and Timayev often boasted about the financing they provided for the rebel factions, and how the Chechen people would eventually drive the Russian barbarians from their land," said Marisa.

Further research revealed that Timayev was mentioned in a few articles on the war, as an "influential" rebel fighter, but his exact status was unclear. Indeed, one posting suggested he and another soldier were wanted by the Russian authorities for the murder of two Russian soldiers at a manned border post on the Dagestan frontier. Dan clicked to some images and in one he found a picture that made Marisa exclaim aloud. Although the picture was a little grainy it was unmistakable. Her blood ran cold as she recognized Timayev in full battle uniform. In each hand he held a severed head, no doubt of the Russian soldiers, the dead eyes upturned and the mouths turned down in some grisly parody of a theatrical tragedy mask. He gripped them by the hair as if he were about to toss them like bowling balls, and his smile carried a hint of triumph at his prized trophies. Dan printed the shocking image and placed it in a plastic cover along with other documents he was collecting.

Marisa had revealed that Timayev often boasted about the empire he ran after just five years in the country. Dan typed in various Google searches and was able to access Timayev's immigration records. It was surprising just how much information could be found on the Internet, despite Canada's strict privacy laws. It seemed no law could guard against the vast free flow of information that the Internet represented, on any subject. Whatever information a government or any other body sought to suppress, the Web always found ways to circumvent it. So it was that Dan accessed Timayev's fast-track application for refugee status, on the basis that Timayev would be persecuted, tortured and probably killed if he was repatriated to Chechnya. Instead, thought Dan ruefully, the government had decreed his entry into Canada on humanitarian grounds after a strong argument from his lawyer. However, they had failed to track him afterwards. To the outside world, he was a respectable businessman, someone who had built a thriving import and export business, one of the success stories of Canada's tolerant immigration policy. His nefarious activities had clearly not come to the attention of the authorities.

As far as Dan could tell, he did not have a criminal record in Canada, although he found one newspaper report from a time shortly after his arrival that named him amongst a number of people who had been prosecuted but acquitted on drug possession charges. A later report mentioned in passing a charge of supplying Class A drugs, but again Dan could find no record of any conviction. However, he came across an interesting article in the Toronto Sun from two years before which suggested the underground drug trade was heavily influenced by Chechen militia, drawing comparisons with Kosovans and Jamaican "Yardies" in London. There was also a subtle reference to corrupt practises, which the article suggested was partly the reason for the lack of convictions and clampdown against these gangs.

The last article set Dan wondering. Just how far had these gangs infiltrated the authorities? When Dan had worked for the Drug Squad he heard rumours of it, but it was never out in the open and nothing could be proved. He had never heard of the Chechen militia taking a stranglehold during his time in the force. It was always the Hell's Angels or Asian groups such as offshoots from the Triads. However, it was concerning that, despite everything, Brad's team had made little progress on the case, at least as far as he knew. Maybe the file he had sent to Brad of Marisa's testimony and the information he had collected might help, even if the latter was merely circumstantial evidence.

Dan felt it would be useful to gain some insight into the motivation behind the group's activities, and he learned much about the Chechen War, which, though officially over, still continued as a low level war of attrition. Both countries had their own mafia, organized crime groups that controlled large drug cartels in their respective regions, and both had their own fundamentalist beliefs, at the opposite end of the religious spectrum. In fact, there were reported rumours that even the Taliban and Al Qaeda had procured the services of the Chechen mafia, (known as the Obshina, meaning "the community") in the past. They certainly shared similar aspirations, a fundamentalist Islamic movement fighting off the infidel Russian invaders.

The conflict itself was marked by a staggering level of brutality and human rights violations that often targeted civilians on both sides, punctuated by rebel terrorist attacks on Russian civilians that drew widespread international condemnation. The war had lasted many years and resulted in hundreds of thousands of casualties, mainly civilian. It was a war which was marked heavily by suicide attacks and selected assassinations on military and high profile political leaders. The capital Grozny was almost completely obliterated when the Russians laid siege in the early part of the war and there were enough abuses such as arbitrary arrest, extortion, torture and murder to keep the European Court of Human Rights and the War Crimes Tribunal busy for the next few decades. A nasty, vicious war, Dan concluded, but it explained a lot about the type of people they were up against.

He printed the last of the documents and placed them in his folder. Marisa had been quietly observing as he carried out the research.

"Let's go," she urged him. "I can't stand to see any more of this."

Dan nodded silently. He knew exactly what she meant.

Timayev was alone in his condo poring over his company's latest quarterly figures when his cell phone vibrated and the text came through. He fished it out of his pocket and reviewed the message. It said simply, "Check your email. You might want to see this."

The Chechen scratched his stubbly beard in surprise and clicked onto his email. The message was blank but contained a windows media video file. He instigated his firewall protocols to check the file was not a virus. Cyber attacks were a real problem in this business. When the computer had scanned the file as clean, he opened it and a familiar face appeared on screen. For an instant he was taken aback but allowed himself a wry smile as he settled back to enjoy the show.

CHAPTER 32

Dan slept fitfully and every so often he would wake up with a start. He would look around wildly to see Marisa in a deep slumber in her sleeping bag in the other corner. He would relax and then doze off again for a time before waking again. The noises at night seemed amplified and distorted, but they were not out of the ordinary—the gentle roll of the lake's swell lapping against the water's edge, the cadenced warble of one of the park's nocturnal birds. Even so, his mind was irritatingly active, a flurry of jumbled, disconnected thoughts, all centred on his research findings on the Chechen gang leader. They could not stay here forever—his cash was running out and it would be dangerous to use a nearby teller machine in case it alerted them to their location.

They were short of options. They could only run and hide for so long, trying to cover their tracks, but to do so required money and with his business effectively shut down, he had already eaten deep into his modest savings. Brad had let him down with the guard, and it had almost cost his and Marisa's life, but he could not think of anything better. They needed to deliver their findings and trust Brad to protect them until Timayev and his clan were off the streets. He resolved to call Brad in the morning before he dozed off again into another dream-filled, restless slumber.

Dan was woken by a diffuse light filtering in through the broken windows, and the soft patter of rain on the roof. He stretched and clambered out of his sleeping bag and looked outside. The rain was drizzling steadily, and the whole sky was an unbroken ashen blanket. Even the trees seemed to have lost their colour. The water was seeping through every crevasse and crack in the ceiling and the plasterboard walls, running in rivulets down the walls until it began pooling on the floor.

He gently coaxed Marisa awake and after a few dazed seconds, she sensed the cold and wet, and quickly got dressed.

They packed up their mattresses and bedding and Dan ran out to the car, stuffing them in the trunk.

He ran back, his hair already slick from the teeming rain. "I think it's time to go back anyway."

Marisa stared at him, perplexed. "Back where?"

Dan saw the tension in her face. "We need to get back to Toronto, to see Brad. We can't go running and hiding indefinitely. I have a business I need to resurrect and we are running out of cash. If I use the local teller machines it might attract some unwelcome attention. We needed to get out of town for a few days to ease the pressure but it will not solve anything longer term. We need to sort your passport and Brad can help keep us safe."

"He did a lousy job last time," Marisa retorted.

Dan could not dispute her assertion. Whatever the reasons behind Brad's prevarication, it had nearly been fatal to them, and he could understand Marisa's reticence at relying on him again. But Brad was an old friend and he trusted him deeply. Indeed, what other choice did he have?

He picked up his folder. "I need to get this to Brad. This information might help in rooting Timayev out. At least it's worth a try."

"But if we go back to the city they will find us. Surely out here we are safe?" protested Marisa.

"There are plenty of ways to get lost in the city. Trust me Marisa. I have to call Brad."

He turned away, partly to avoid her frightened expression, and wandered upstairs to look at the rain as he dialled Brad's number.

Marisa watched him trudge up the stairs. She felt a gnawing sense of fear, but she could not pinpoint it, just a vague feeling that something was not quite right. When Dan's friend Brad had interviewed her at the hospital in Montreal with the two other officers, he had said very little, but noted everything she said very carefully. She occasionally caught him staring fixedly at her while the other two talked. It had made her feel uncomfortable, but she could hardly read too much into it. Dan had assured her Brad was a consummate professional and had every faith he would locate Timayev, and with Marisa's testimony, bring him to justice. Dan's blind faith in Brad was a little worrying. She did not share his view, but then she had only met Brad once, and she was not the most intuitive of people. She cursed herself for her naivety with the recruiter in Sandanski. She continued gathering her gear together until it was in a small pile.

Minutes later Dan emerged down the stairs, looking purposeful. "I've spoken to Brad. He is sending someone to collect us. They should be with us in a few hours."

"He said that last time."

"He feels terrible about that. He's not going to let it happen again. I've known Brad for a long time. He's not that careless. As you pointed out we are out of the city. No one can find us here unless we want them to. Let's just sit tight for a few hours and soon we will be under police protection. Brad assures me they are making good progress in the investigation."

"Have they made any arrests?" said Marisa, her tone challenging.

"Well no, not yet —"

"Then Akhmad's people are still out there and we are targets."

"Just because they have not made any arrests yet doesn't mean anything. The police have to build strong evidence they can confront them with before hauling them in for questioning. It's complicated with these narcotics gangs. They know the law, know how to play the system. If the police are going to bring them in, they have to make sure the charges stick. These gangs are slippery and elusive. They have contacts and work underground. I remember my time in the Drug Squad, we relied heavily on anonymous tips, but often it was too late. By the time we got there, the gang was long gone and whatever deal they were making had been completed. They have to move carefully and hopefully outmanoeuvre them. It's like a game of chess."

Marisa breathed a long sigh. "Dan, I think we should be careful. I don't want to go back to Toronto but if we have to we should be protected. I think we should hide until Brad's man comes for us."

Dan gave a dismissive wave of his hand. "Nonsense," he said. "We are perfectly safe here. You are being paranoid. In any event, I am not going anywhere in this rain."

"Please Dan. Maybe I am being paranoid but I have a right to be. I can't explain why, but I don't think we should be here when Brad's man comes. Maybe we can, how do you say—check him out first."

"Okay, if it makes you happy we'll stake him out. I'm sure it won't be necessary."

"Thank you Dan." She smiled and briefly touched his arm, sending an electric jolt through him as he immediately thought of his daughter.

Dan moved the car down a nearby track so it was sheltered behind a clump of trees away from the main road. The wheels skidded on the wet, muddy trail, the rain still drizzling steadily, and the tyre tracks on the ground were impossible to conceal. He wasn't too bothered as he felt it was a pointless exercise anyhow, but Marisa was tangibly nervous. They had agreed to stake out the cottage from the nearby woods and once they were assured of his identity, Dan would present himself to the officer. Surely an unnecessary formality, he thought, but Marisa had seemed comforted by the suggestion. Mercifully the rain became more intermittent, but the small copse they stood behind was damp and chilly. The clouds refused to part, and it remained a dull and dreary day. After a while, they heard the sound of an engine, which idled for a few minutes at the top of the lane, before it was turned off. They could not see the vehicle but within a few minutes they saw a uniformed figure moving stealthily down the lane toward the cottage, trying to keep within the shadows.

Marisa and Dan watched him closely, hardly daring to breathe, although he was a good thirty yards from them. He circled the cottage, moving carefully, evaluating and calculating, before he went inside. Just before he did however, he drew the gun from his holster. Marisa stifled a gasp and Dan continued peering, full of concern. He was in the cottage for several minutes before he emerged, gun still in hand.

Although he was in uniform, it was ill fitting, almost bursting out of his broad frame. He had a mean, hard expression that suggested to Dan he would not greet them warmly. Was this really Brad's envoy come to protect them? He had his suspicions, and they were compounded when the figure pulled out his cell phone. Still afraid to breathe, Marisa and Dan listened carefully. Despite the gentle rustling of the trees, he was so close his voice was audible.

"They are not here," he said simply.

He listened and nodded as if taking instructions.

"I will keep looking. *They won't get away this time.*"

Dan and Marisa glanced fearfully at each other, their worst suspicions confirmed. They kept as still as statues. Marisa's legs felt wobbly, but she did not move.

The figure peered around and for a fleeting second he seemed to stare right at them. Dan's heart leapt in his chest and he swallowed hard. He was convinced they had been discovered as the figure continued to stare balefully at the clump of trees, but then he turned away and began heading up the lane toward his vehicle. Not until they had heard the car roar off into the distance did they venture out of their hiding spot.

"We have to get going now," Dan urged Marisa. They trudged out of the copse and down the track where the car was concealed, constantly keeping a watchful eye on the road in case the officer came back. They had not seen his vehicle but Dan suspected it was not a police car.

"Where the hell is Brad's guy," asked Dan, almost to himself. "We can't wait for him."

Marisa turned angrily to Dan. "Maybe he was Brad's guy!"

Dan pulled the branches away and threw them aside to reveal his battered old Chevrolet. They got in the car and Dan rubbed his chin thoughtfully. The bristles were hard and scratchy after three days without shaving. "I can't believe that. Someone intercepted our call. I guess it was Timayev's welcoming committee."

"I'm scared Dan. Where do we go from here?"

He started the engine and the car struggled up the track, its wheels slipping as it struggled to gain traction on the wet, muddy earth. They reached the main road and Dan looked both ways. The way was clear and he took a right, anxious to put some distance between them and the cottage. He had no clear idea of what to do next. His original thought had been to get back to Toronto and sit it out with Brad's protection, and in the absence of any alternative he followed the road southwest toward the town of Bracebridge.

He refused to contemplate the troublesome suspicions that kept popping into his head. Jesus, was Marisa right about Brad? Was he too blind to see it? He shook his head to dispel the thought. No, there had to be a better reason. Brad was his closest friend. However, he decided not to call Brad until they had reached a safe distance from the cottage and could find a pay-phone. This latest incident left Dan deeply concerned. If Timayev's gang had intercepted his call or were being tipped off, they would need to keep moving to stay one step ahead. He glanced over at Marisa. She sat up straight in the seat, lips pursed and her body rigid with tension.

Dan stiffened as a car raced up behind them. It followed closely for several miles. Dan glanced in his rear view mirror. A bunch of youths, laughing and boisterous, occupied the Ford Explorer, no doubt coming back from a camping vacation. He pulled over and waved them on and they roared off around a bend in the road.

The rain had stopped now but the roads were shiny and slick. The thick clouds pressed down and the threat of more rain lingered. A car travelling in the opposite direction seemed to slow down as it passed, and its single occupant appeared to gaze fixedly at them as they passed by. Was that him? It was impossible to tell his features in the poor light as the cars passed by at speed, but Dan could not escape the feeling of paranoia. He watched the car recede into the distance until, just before he lost sight of it, the driver pulled to the side of the road. Marisa sat quietly in front—she had not noticed the vehicle pull over and Dan said nothing, but instinctively he drove faster. He continued for another half hour before he began to relax—they were not being followed.

They passed through the pretty town of Bracebridge, stopping for gas, using the last of his cash. He would have to use his debit card again very soon. He had avoided doing so as a precaution but somehow they had still tracked him. He could not understand how, but he decided to take a different route back to Toronto as a precaution, taking the highway to the east of the vast Lake Simcoe and onto some smaller roads crossing north of the city.

They had passed the immense, murky lake shimmering in the light breeze and continued south on a narrow regional road when a large diesel truck, spouting black fumes from the long funnel at the side of the cab, appeared in the distance. The rain had started to fall again in a steady, miserable drizzle, and even the farm buildings and rolling hills at the side of the road lacked colour in the subdued light.

Dan glanced in his mirror. The truck was growing larger in the mirror, and seemed to take up the whole width of the road.

He let out an exasperated sigh and turned to Marisa. "Can you believe some truck drivers flying along on a road like this? They should stick to the highways."

He sped up a little but the truck was still making ground on them. Dan had never really liked the trucks which flew along Canada's highways. Some of his school friends had been obsessed with them but he did not care for the way they looked—with their large front grilles and piercing headlights they always reminded Dan of some angry beast.

Marisa glanced in the wing mirror, and saw the truck, still moving closer, its tinted black windows above the enormous grille adding to its intimidating image. "Let it pass."

"It's okay," he replied casually. "I'll just step on the gas. He won't get any closer."

Marisa's voice was faltering. "I think we should pull over, let him go past."

Dan glanced in the mirror again. The truck was gaining ground. "No, no don't worry. I'll just go faster. There's hardly room for him to pass us anyhow."

He pressed lightly on the accelerator and the car jolted as he ran over a small pothole. He cursed to himself. These side roads were never well maintained, especially after the winter. The truck loomed large in his mirror and had more than matched his increase in speed, its funnel angrily spewing black smoke. It moved closer and closer until the enormous grille seemed to fill his rear view mirror. Those memories of an angry beast came flooding back to Dan. Marisa peered intently at the wing mirror, and she gripped her armrest tightly until her knuckles were white.

"Perhaps you're right," Dan said. The truck was now looming over them like some giant brute. He gently applied the brakes, careful not to slow down too sharply as the truck was now so close it would never stop in time. These behemoths had a long braking distance and the guy had probably been driving for the last twelve hours straight, he reflected. He indicated to pull over and carefully veered over to the right toward the gravelled side of the road to allow room for the truck to pass. He had to be cautious as the roadside was lined with ditches at regular intervals.

The truck let out a long, booming blast of its horn and flashed its lights, but it made no attempt to pass. It stayed right behind the Chevy, and crept up even closer behind so Dan was certain it would bump the car.

"What the hell is this guy doing?" shouted Dan. He opened his window and waved frantically out to signal for the truck to pass. As he did so the roar of the truck was amplified, adding to its menacing presence, but still it refused to overtake. Dan moved further to the side to allow the truck more room, his tyres skidding on the wet gravel. He had to fight to keep a straight line, but now there was plenty of room for the monster to get by. What was the driver's problem?

The truck let out another long, raucous blast of the horn, and continued to bear down threateningly on the Chevy. Dan was frantically looking for a place to turn off but the road was straight and the ditches made it impossible to pull over safely. Then came the inevitable bump, gentle but noisy and Marisa screamed in surprise. Dan immediately went faster, even though half the car was driving over wet gravel, and he gripped the steering hard, his knuckles white, trying to keep the car in a straight line. The car skidded and he had to fight to steer back onto the road, narrowly avoiding a ditch. He over-steered and the car veered onto the other side of the road. He managed to gain control but he was immediately jolted by another bone crunching thump from the rear. The force made Marisa's head snap back and she let out a choked scream. Dan tried to accelerate away, but the powerful truck matched him easily for speed, and followed it with another shunt. It felt and sounded like the back of the car had been torn away, such was the tortured screech of tearing metal. Dan looked back for a split second—the interior at the rear was still intact but he did not want to imagine the damage to his outside bumper. The snarling grille filled the back window and still the truck ploughed relentlessly on.

The next grinding bump shattered the rear windscreen, shards of glass showering inwards and Marisa spun round, terrified. "Faster, faster!" she pleaded.

The force of the shunt sent the car careening to the side of the road and Dan just managed to avoid slamming into a steep ditch by steering hard to his left. The truck took the opportunity to accelerate forward so that it ran parallel with the Chevy. The horn blared again, rising above the roar of the hammering pistons. Dan's heart was thumping so furiously it threatened to burst out of his chest. Only his window separated him from the huge silver wheel revolving just inches away from the car. Marisa was crying and rubbing the wrenched muscles in her neck. He looked ahead. A car appeared travelling in the opposite direction. There was no room for all three of the vehicles to pass by simultaneously, but undeterred, the truck ploughed on. The driver, sensing this, waited until the last moment before realizing the truck was not going to move from the middle of the road. The driver gave a long but useless hoot of his horn and spun off the road, scraping against a clump of thorn bushes before finally coming to rest.

The two vehicles were now travelling side by side at over ninety kilometres an hour, a high speed for this type of road even in normal conditions. As he glanced sideways, the wheel moved in closer, and there was a growl of rending metal.

"He's going to force us off the road!" screamed Marisa. Adrenaline pumping, Dan tried to steer away from the side, but it was no use. The huge eighteen-wheeler could swat the Chevy effortlessly, and the driver's side door was screeching against the wheel. The car was being drawn inexorably toward the side of the road. He no longer had full control over the vehicle. The road curved slightly and as they rounded the bend like two stock car racers pitted in a deadly duel, Marisa grabbed his arm and pointed ahead with a shaking finger.

Then he saw it. Set back only three feet from the road, a huge, thick oak tree stood there like an impregnable fortress, solid and impassive. It was less than three hundred metres away and the truck had forced them into a collision course with the tree. He was totally boxed in and at the speed he was travelling he had about eight seconds before impact. He slammed on the brakes but another shove from the truck sent them hurtling out of control. The car spun crazily toward the tree. The roar of the truck, the Chevy's racing engine and Marisa's terrified screams all suddenly became muted, as if he was hearing them through a thick wall. His mind seemed to blot out everything but the tree ahead as he fought to regain control, but it was too late. He saw Marisa, with remarkable composure, clipping her seat belt off and hurling herself out of the car. She rolled crazily on the gravel. The last thought he had was a vague hope that if she survived she would not suffer too much, before the tree seemed to rush up at him with a sickening thud, and everything went black.

CHAPTER 33

When the truck was several miles down the road, it pulled off onto a dusty concession track which ran off into a small outlying group of hills. The truck was nearly as wide as the rutted track, which bounced and jolted and blew up a huge storm of dust. After another mile the truck pulled over, and was met by a Land Cruiser. Serge steered the truck to the side, and he and Alexi jumped out of the cab.

"What about the truck driver?" asked Serge.

Locked in a tiny cabinet in the back of the cab, and bound hand and foot, the driver struggled in the cramped, claustrophobic conditions. His attackers had stuffed a black sack over his head and taped his mouth. He could hear the wheezing of his own breath and the heaviness of his chest. His body had been forced into an unnatural position and was starting to stiffen.

He had not even seen them coming. They were hiding in the back of the cab when he got in after a short break on the road. They quickly overpowered him and stuffed him, bound and blind in the cabinet. He did not even see their faces and they said very little, and even that was muffled. He felt the truck grind to a halt and then he felt the cabinet being opened. He was able to lurch out onto the floor of the cab, and he sensed one of his attackers pause above him. His tormentor ripped the tape painfully across his mouth and then was gone. He heard a vehicle drive away. He was still incapacitated but at least he could breathe properly.

The pair climbed into the back of the Toyota which sped up the track onto the main tarmac road. There was very little traffic and the Land Cruiser headed inconspicuously toward Toronto.

In the back Alexi spoke quietly on his cell phone. "Yes, we hit them hard. I don't think they would have survived the impact." He listened for a moment. "No, no, I am almost certain they are dead. There is no doubt. They hit the tree head on!"

Alexi clicked off and Serge turned to him. "Do you really think they are dead? Maybe we should have gone back to make sure."

Alexi shook his head. "No time to do that. We had to get out of there, make it clean, like an accident, at least for now. I hope we finished them off but we can't be certain—but it is what Akhmad wanted to hear."

Serge glanced at his comrade curiously. He hoped Alexi was right. Surely they could not have survived the impact. If they did, then he and Alexi would have some explaining to do.

It had taken Frank Carroll a long time to track down Dan's number. He had not heard from his friend for several years, not since shortly after his daughter's death, which had left his friend a broken man. He had given Dan plenty of legal advice at the time, particularly when he faced suspension after beating up a street punk. He knew Dan had rehabilitated himself and ran a reasonably successful private investigation agency. He felt a tinge of guilt as he reflected on his old friend. He should have called him maybe once or twice in those intervening years, even just to see how he was coping, but Frank had been so busy with his own caseload, and there never seemed to be an opportune time, until he had genuinely lost contact.

It was a poor excuse, of course, and in his heart he knew it. His guilt magnified when, during his enquiries to find out Dan's number, he had heard about the fire at his office. He had to admit he was intrigued by the email he had received from Dan. It carried a short, concise message asking him to hold the file "in case anything happens to us."

The file in question was dynamite, an emotional testimony by a young, attractive Eastern European girl detailing the horrors of her kidnapping and sexual slavery at the hands of a Chechen clan. During his long career as a barrister in the public attorney's office, he had considerable exposure to various shady, underground gangs, often powerful and influential enough to swing juries and witnesses, or worse still, to make bribes or threats to ensure they never reached a courtroom in the first place. He had seen corruption and the abuse of power at so many levels in government agencies that he had long ceased to be angered by it. As he had got older and more experienced he had become more accepting of the "system," knowing it would never change. Instead, he tried to use it to his own advantage where he could. However, it still hurt when a criminal was let loose on a legal technicality or some other spurious reason, free to commit more crimes as if they were bulletproof.

He had heard about the Chechen clan, now one of the most feared groups on the Toronto "circuit," but he was not aware they had been involved in human trafficking. It saddened but did not surprise him. Increasingly over the years, one of the safest metropolitan areas in North America was becoming a battleground for ethnic groups flouting the law and corrupting the youth with drugs and guns. They acted as if they were immune from the law, and it sometimes seemed to Frank that they were, when another carefully planned prosecution collapsed.

The Chechen clan he knew were extremely well organized and run more like a legitimate business than many of the smaller gangs. They existed ostensibly to support the Chechen cause, but clearly their protests about human rights abuses by the Russians did not prevent them committing their own. The footage was highly convincing. The girl was articulate and credible, and her testimony would provide strong evidence if the matter ever went to trial.

He had replied to Dan's email asking him to get in contact, but he had not received a reply, so he managed to find his cell phone number. It rang and rang, but there was no answer. He was curious to find out more about the girl and kept trying. He checked his sources to make sure the number was correct. He had made no mistake, but the result was the same. No answer.

Brad was at his desk when he received the phone call. After the caller had hung up, he just stared at the phone in disbelief before he got up and walked silently to the bathroom. He stumbled in and checked no-one else was in there and went to a cubicle, locking it behind him. Totally alone, he could not suppress the deep well of emotion that erupted inside him and he slammed the cubicle door with his fists in frustration, before collapsing into heavy, grief stricken sobs. He sat there with his head in his hands, unable to stem the flow of salty tears. He suspected this day would come since Dan had got involved with the Chechens, but the caller had been so blasé, so matter of fact about the death of his long time friend. It had been inevitable, yet like a runaway train he had been powerless to stop it. There were too many forces involved, and the events of the last few days had narrowed his choices until he was completely bereft of free will. The mind had a way of rationalizing and justifying one's actions, and he could explain to himself that what he had done was the only logical choice. However much he could try and convince himself, however, it did not prevent the overwhelming surge of guilt that washed over him like a tidal wave.

Marisa's whole body felt like it was on fire. Her skin was an ugly mass of grazes where she had scraped along the unforgiving gravel and hurtled headlong into a deep ditch. She also had an ugly laceration along the length of her left leg, her jeans torn and flapping open to reveal the gaping, bloody wound. She fought the urge to vomit and lay there gagging. She was weak from the pain and shock, and when she tried to move it felt like she was being stabbed by a thousand knives. She was not sure if she had been unconscious, and if so for how long. It was deathly quiet, the only sound the nearby trees rustling in the light breeze. The rain had stopped and the sun was threatening to break through. The truck had zoomed off. They probably had not seen her jump out as she was on their blind side and luckily the ditch she fell in had hidden her from view. They likely assumed that both of them were in the car when it slammed into the tree.

God! What about Dan? With a great effort of will, she hoisted herself out of the ditch, her body protesting vigorously. She clenched her teeth in agony, and dragged herself out of the ditch, collapsing onto the ground exhausted. She lay there breathing heavily for a time before she mustered enough energy to stand up. The pain was almost intolerable. Marisa limped over to the wrecked car, her left leg dragging uselessly behind her.

The front end of the car had crumpled inward like a concertina, and the passenger door was still hanging open where she had dived out, although it hung at an acute angle, the hinges partly ripped away. The car was tilted at a strange angle where the front wheels had spun up against the tree but it was clear from the position of the car that it had not hit the tree head on. There was a hiss of escaping steam from the ruined engine. Marisa hobbled over to the car as fast as her one useful leg would allow, and looked inside the front. There were shards of broken glass over the dashboard and seats where the windscreen had shattered on impact, and sprawled across both seats was the prone form of her companion. He had a deep gash to his forehead, and the blood was trickling lazily onto the passenger seat where his head had come to rest. The seat was stained crimson and it was slowly spreading. The front end of the car had been pushed in on the driver's side, and it looked as if his legs were trapped, so that his body was inclined at an unnatural angle. There were no other outward signs of injury, but he felt cold to the touch. She pulled her hand away in horror, but then noticed the merest flicker of his lips. She brought her ear close to his mouth. He was breathing, just. It was shallow and laboured, but it was regular. She felt for a pulse. It was also weak but rhythmic. He was hanging on, just, but he was losing blood from the head wound. It wasn't gushing out, but the dark patch on the seat indicated he had already lost a significant amount.

Her immediate priority was to stem the blood loss. Forgetting her own pain for a moment, she ripped a piece of his shirt and fashioned a makeshift tourniquet, and carefully lifted his head, wrapping the thin material several times around it. The cloth immediately began to darken but she tied it as tightly as possible, and it held firm. With a supreme effort of will, she managed to push his body upright, her injured leg shooting with pain as she did so. He was now positioned in the driving seat, his head against the backrest but lolling to one side.

She had to summon help quickly. She looked around. There was very little traffic on the road and the nearest farmhouse was about a mile away in the hazy distance. It would take her the best part of an hour to drag herself to the house. She sensed that Dan did not have that much time. She needed to find his phone. He always kept it on him but where? She hauled herself forward so she perched with one knee on the passenger seat, her useless leg hanging limply behind her, and began gently feeling around his jacket pocket. She did not have to search long. The phone began chiming and vibrating and she pulled it out. The number was unfamiliar and she pondered for a second before answering.

"Hello?"

The voice at the other end hesitated, slightly taken aback. "You're the girl in the video aren't you?"

"Who is this?"

The voice was easy, relaxed and conversational. "This is Frank Carroll. Dan sent me the file. Don't worry, I don't bite, at least only in person. Is he there?"

Marisa's voice was tinged with panic. "He's dying. I need help."

Frank's easy tone turned immediately serious. "Tell me what happened and where you are, quickly. I will get someone out to you."

"We were forced off the road by a huge truck and crashed into a tree. Dan is out cold but he is still breathing. He has a big wound to his head and it won't stop bleeding." She looked at the temporary tourniquet—it had already turned completely crimson.

"Marisa, tell me exactly where you are."

"I don't know," she cried in anguish.

"Marisa, stay with me okay? Tell me exactly what you see."

"It's just trees and fields and a house up the road. Nothing special." She looked up and down the road. "Wait, there's a sign up ahead. I can't see it from here. I need to get to it."

She howled through clenched teeth as she pulled herself out of the car and hobbled onto the road toward the sign.

"Are you hurt too?" asked Frank, his voice full of concern.

"I'm okay." As she hobbled toward the sign a car zoomed past. The lone woman driver stared curiously at the bedraggled, bloodstained figure on the side of the road and decided not to stop. Marisa was now close enough to read the sign.

"The sign says 'Blackwater 10 kilometres'," she recited. "We were travelling into Toronto."

Frank was already looking at his map and quickly found Blackwater. They had clearly travelled east of Lake Simcoe, taking a more circuitous and less busy route south into Toronto. Only Dan would know why.

"Marisa, listen carefully. Stay with Dan and keep pressure on the wound and keep his head upright. I am going to call 911 and get a paramedic to you as soon as I can. Be brave. Dan is depending on you."

"Okay," replied Marisa tearfully and rang off. Her teeth gritted in pain, she hobbled back as quickly as possible to the car. She hauled herself into the passenger seat again, wincing from the pain. Dan's breathing was still shallow, but he was hanging on. She ripped another piece of his shirt and carefully placed it over the old blood soaked tourniquet, pulling it tight around his head, trying not to think of the ugly gaping wound underneath. He barely stirred as she did so. A sharp, stabbing pain forced her to turn her attention to her own leg. The blood was trickling out and she could see white muscle tissue amongst the sea of red. Fighting her feelings of nausea she dressed her own wound, choking with the pain as she ripped her own shirt and wrapped it several times around her leg, pulling the dressing tight. She sat back in the seat, the pain coming in waves, and she closed her eyes and prayed. As she began to drift into an exhausted sleep, she was roused by a blaring siren. She looked out to the road to see an emergency medical services van racing up the road, and she began to cry with relief.

The emergency medical van pulled up by the side of the car and two paramedics in fluorescent yellow jackets jumped out. They worked fluently and efficiently, talking quietly to each other as they examined the unconscious driver. Marisa stepped back and watched them. The nearest paramedic, a youthful looking Indian man with cropped black hair, turned to her and offered a sympathetic smile.

"We'll see to that in a minute," he said, pointing to her leg, which was now throbbing with pain.

Working as an efficient partnership, they firstly checked his airway and breathing. It was still shallow but regular. They also took his heart rate and the youthful medic gave a concerned frown. "His heart rate is weak. We have to get him into the van."

His colleague, an attractive but tough looking girl who, Marisa thought, did not look much older than her, tugged gently at his legs. There did not seem to be any obvious trauma to his lower body, but his foot was caught in the footwell, where the front of the car had been pushed inwards. "Ranjit, we can't move him. We need help."

The woman muttered quietly into her radio as Ranjit gently placed a head brace around Dan's prone form and lightly straightened his body so he sat fully upright. He ran his hand along his back. No obvious sign of spinal injury. He then turned to Marisa and treated her leg, removing the clumsy tourniquet that Marisa had fashioned. He swabbed the wound and wrapped a large bandage around her thigh, and cleaned the numerous cuts and grazes with iodine. She winced in pain as he did so.

"Don't worry," he reassured her. "The cuts are superficial. You were lucky you bounced. Not even a fracture. The leg will take a bit longer to heal. There is some deep soft tissue damage. We will need to stitch you up and put you on a course of antibiotics when we reach the hospital. You will need to rest up for a few days—no putting weight on that leg or it will swell up like a balloon."

He gave another reassuring smile that Marisa found quite disarming, despite her pain. "You're a brave girl. Takes a lot of courage to jump out of a speeding car, even one which is just about to slam into a tree."

"Is Dan going to be okay?" she asked, her voice trembling.

"Thanks to you, we got here in time. We need to get him to the hospital as soon as possible to do a brain scan. He may need surgery. It's too early to tell. We need to get him out of the car and quick."

As if on cue, a fire truck and police car arrived together. The police officers sealed off the road while their passenger, dressed in civilian clothes, took photographs of the incident from every possible angle. A fireman jumped out and his colleague handed him an over-sized wire cutter. The woman paramedic guided him to the driver's side. He stared in and gave an understanding nod.

"We'll have him out in no time," he said confidently. He leaned down into the footwell and began snipping at the twisted metal as if he were cutting out paper shapes. Very soon he had cut away a large chunk of metal, and he gently raised Dan's foot so it was free of the obstruction. "Okay, let's get him out of here."

Between them they were able to guide Dan's limp body onto a stretcher, being careful to keep his back straight and avoid any sudden movements. It was a laborious process lifting him out of the car. They had to move him slowly and gently, until they could place him on the stretcher, but they were skilled and patient. As they loaded him into the back of the emergency services van, one of the police officers approached Marisa.

"Miss, I will need a statement from you, but it can wait till the hospital. I will follow the van back there. It looks like you had a lucky escape."

Marisa nodded silently and was helped into the back of the van by the woman paramedic who introduced herself as Jane. She watched Dan silently as Ranjit drove the van to the hospital, lights blazing, but mercifully no siren, and Jane closely monitored Dan's vital signs. Marisa did not like the grim look on her face as she checked his pulse.

CHAPTER 34

This time it was Marisa's turn to keep a bedside vigil for Dan. They had rushed him into the emergency ward at Sunnybrook Health Sciences Centre, and had prepped him for surgery, but the brain scan showed only bruising to the cranial area. He had not suffered a fractured skull, and his brain activity registered as normal. He was however in a state of deep shock, and although he had not been diagnosed as being in a comatose state, he was expected to remain unconscious for at least another twelve hours. However, his heart rate had recovered to a nearly normal function.

As she sat by his bedside in her wheelchair peering at the monitors, another visitor entered. Marisa looked up and saw a short professorial looking man in his late fifties with a scruffy beard turning white at the edges and thick spectacles. The open collar on his shirt was far too large and stuck out over his Pringle sweater, lending him a slightly comic look, particularly with his unkempt salt and pepper hair. He gave a broad, friendly smile and she recognized his voice instantly.

"Marisa I believe. You two have been hard to track down." He extended his hand. "Frank Carroll. How is the old boy doing? I gather he is going to pull through."

Marisa gently shook his hand. His grip was firm, locking and squeezing her own small hands tightly.

"Yes, the doctors say he is going to be okay. No permanent damage. They tell me we have both been very lucky. It doesn't feel like it."

"That's good to hear." He pointed to Marisa's leg, wrapped tightly in a heavy bandage that showed a tiny spot of red. "How are you bearing up?" He studied her closely. Her face had numerous superficial grazes and she had several dressings around her chin and upper neck. The dressing gown she wore was short sleeved and he could see lacerations on both forearms.

"I've had better days. You wouldn't believe it but they cleaned me up. Treating the cuts hurt like hell but they said I should be out of the wheelchair in a day or so. I will be on crutches for about a week though. I lost count of the number of stitches they put in my leg. They gave me antibiotics, horrible big pills and they taste foul."

Frank smiled kindly and pulled up a chair alongside her. "You're alive, that's the main thing." He paused and took a conspiratorial glance either side of him, and leaned toward Marisa. "It might be better if you and Dan were dead, at least as far as the outside world was concerned."

Marisa stared at him, confused. "What do you mean?"

Frank looked at her intently. "I made some enquiries. I know Brad Miller, who is in charge of the investigation into your gang, also received the video. I talked to him this morning. He seemed pretty happy to hear you two were alive. I got the impression he thought you had died in the crash. Anyway, he agreed the best way forward is to report that you had in fact been killed. This way the gang will think the job has been done. They won't come after you again. It gives you a little breathing space to recover until the police can bring these guys down.

"Brad is keen on the idea but he has insisted you and Dan stay close by and that means staying in Toronto. I offered to put you both up at my place, and he agreed. I owe it to Dan—I wasn't there when he really needed me and this is a way of making up for that. What do you say?"

Marisa paused and ran a hand through her long auburn hair. "What if they find us? I don't want to stay in Toronto."

"They won't find you because they won't be looking for you. We put out the media reports and they think the job is done. I understand Dan caused them a lot of trouble in Montreal. They will tick you both off their wanted list and move on to planning the next deal. You will be history for them. You will be safe at my house."

Marisa was still sceptical. "That's what Dan said to my father. And they still found him." The sudden memory of her father caused tears to well up in her eyes.

"They won't find you," Frank reassured her. "We put the media reports out now and they will never know. It really is the best way."

Marisa considered for a moment, staring at Dan. He looked serene, only the huge bandage enveloping the top of his head hinting at the trauma he had recently suffered.

"Will they buy it?"

"Why shouldn't they?" He gave a short laugh. "When do the press ever lie?"

The female newscaster adopted a suitably sombre tone when she reported on the local City TV the devastating news that a local private investigator Dan Huberman and his "girlfriend," who police were still trying to identify, had succumbed to their injuries following the tragic accident in the Blackwater area a few days before. She reported that firefighters had to free them from their vehicle after it appeared they had swerved to avoid what turned out to be a stolen diesel truck and struck a large oak tree. Police had interviewed the truck driver who claimed he had been attacked from behind and locked away in his cab. He had therefore seen nothing of the incident and it appeared there were no other witnesses on the remote country road. Although police were looking for two assailants, they currently had no firm leads.

The report carried a still photo of the crash before turning back to the newscaster, her serious expression matching her tone. She suddenly broke into a beaming smile as she introduced the weatherman and engaged in some playful banter with him, the terrible crash already forgotten.

Marisa smiled to herself as she watched the television in the large, deserted waiting room. Frank had left earlier in the day, and it was now late in the evening. She had promised to call Frank when Dan woke up. She was tired and it was a real effort getting about in a wheelchair. She had not realized how difficult it was, even in the supportive environment of a hospital. She could not imagine taking to the streets in this bulky contraption. She continued watching the television, thinking she would need to head back toward her own ward soon. The doctors had suggested that she stay overnight for observation, but it seemed likely she would be discharged by the morning. The leg was still painful and she could feel the stitches pulling if she moved her leg too sharply.

A nurse peered round the door. "Ms Dimitrov. You can come in. Mr Huberman is waking up." She strode over to her wheelchair and guided her to Dan's private room. A doctor was already bent over Dan, taking off a blood pressure armband and then checking his pulse. She could see him stirring and his eyelids fluttered open and he gave an exhausted sigh.

"Where am I?" he said groggily. Marisa stared down at him, grinning broadly. "You're dead," she replied.

It was not very often Olivia was allowed to watch the television. Rahmon and his crew kept the girls under tight control, and part of that control was to effectively isolate them from the rest of the world. It was another method to subjugate them. However, for some strange reason he had assembled all the girls in the tatty old lounge that served as the reception room for their detestable visitors, and turned on the local news. They sat there silently, still confused, as Rahmon's brooding, intimidating presence lurked behind them.

The girls rarely spoke when he was around. His mere presence was enough to force them into a fearful silence. Too often they had been on the end of one of his beatings, sometimes just a slap across the face but other times a lot worse. The most frightening thing, Olivia reflected, was the pleasure he clearly received from inflicting pain. He rarely hit out in anger. He did so for his own pleasure, and to punish the girls. After all, she thought bitterly, he came from a culture where the women were not just treated as second class citizens, but fell below a man's livestock in the pecking order. She shuddered to think what he would be capable of when he was angry. Thankfully she had never antagonized him, although she'd heard the chilling screams behind closed doors of other girls who had.

He seemed to be in good humour today, if that were possible for such a man. They continued to watch the local news, mystified as to why they were there, but no-one dared to ask the huge Tajik. Toward the end of the news, a report of an accident to the north east of the city on a remote road near the village of Blackwater caught their attention. Rahmon turned the volume up with the remote control and the scene switched to a still photo of a crumpled car.

They watched in confused silence as the newscaster described the horror of a stolen eighteen-wheeler truck having forced the occupants of the car to swerve and collide head on into a huge oak tree. They named the private investigator but police were still trying to identify his girlfriend, although updated reports suggested she was a Bulgarian national. The name of the PI was familiar—they had heard both Rahmon and Akhmad, when he visited, cursing him loudly. However, it was when the newscaster referred to the Bulgarian that Rahmon threw his head back and broke out into a cruel, taunting laughter.

At this point most of the girls realized the awful truth. They had all known Marisa, and most had admired her strong, defiant spirit. A few of the girls began to sob quietly and several others just looked down at the floor, as if to hide their wounded emotions from view. Olivia was too stunned to react. Rahmon was still laughing, and she bit her lip in fury, watching him with a mixture of fear and hatred. She wanted to drive a red hot poker through his mouth to shut him up, but she knew with deep frustration she would never get the chance. His huge, powerful, malevolent frame terrified the girls so much they dared not even contemplate striking out. Maybe if he was asleep, she pondered resentfully. Only Marisa had stood up to him. She could not bring herself to believe that her friend, someone she had admired and looked up to, was now dead.

Rahmon sat back and addressed the girls. "This is what happens if you try to escape. We will find you and hunt you down. You belong to Akhmad. If any of you are thinking about getting out of here, just remember that. We will find you." His voice carried an ominous tone, and he let out another guttural laugh.

Strangely Olivia felt very little, just an overwhelming well of emptiness as if her body had lost all its strength. She knew the tears would come later but now she was numb. However, when Timayev came around that evening, she could hold back no longer. Her body froze as his hard, sweaty hands touched her. She pulled away and oblivious to the consequences, delivered a stinging blow across his cheek. It was more symbolic as he barely flinched, but his eyes narrowed in surprise. He did nothing, but fixed her with an icy, malevolent stare.

"You killed her, you monster!" she shouted, the tears suddenly beginning to flow. She bravely attempted another strike but this time Timayev, shocked at her temerity the first time, was ready. With lightning sharp reflexes, he grabbed her right arm and twisted it until she howled in agony, and then with the back of his other hand, he swatted her effortlessly across the room. She landed in a heap on the dusty wooden floor, crying in misery and pain, clutching her bleeding nose. He stood up off the bed, and angrily buttoned his shirt. Something deep inside him, however, felt a sense of pity for this wretched, vulnerable girl. He had lost his appetite for sex, but decided he would not instruct Rahmon to punish her further.

"Just make sure you are not next!" he spat at her, grabbing his jacket and slamming the door hard as he left.

CHAPTER 35

Frank's house was a comfortable three storey redbrick house in the St. Andrews area of the city. It was built in the 1950s and sat on a generous plot of land. The extensive garden was well kept and shielded by tall hemlock trees. As Marisa looked out of the window of his study, she could see their thin branches swaying gently in the light breeze.

She turned and continued practising her walk on the crutches.

"Not on the wooden floor!" Frank protested.

Dan just smiled at them. He was still feeling weak and confined to a wheelchair for the next few days at least. His left foot was now in a cast. He had sustained a hairline fracture when it was caught in the impact. He also had extensive bruising to his ribs and at present his upper abdomen was a dark shade of violet. Considering everything, he was lucky to have escaped more severe injury. He touched his bandaged head cautiously. His head still throbbed and it felt about to burst, but the painkillers were working well. It had been several days since he and Marisa were discharged from hospital, and so far they had not ventured from the sanctuary of Frank's home. Frank had wisely suggested they stay indoors for a few days just to let the media coverage die down. No one, apart from Carl and Brad and their investigation team knew where they were. He and Marisa were effectively dead to the world.

They had just finished a delightful *Calabacita* Spanish steak prepared by Frank's Latin housekeeper, and now relaxed in the study with after dinner drinks. Dan had declined Frank's offer of a large port. The doctors had banned him from alcohol for the foreseeable future. Marisa had also opted for a more sensible fruit juice, so Frank relaxed in his padded leather armchair swilling the purple liquid around his glass.

"There is some good material here," he said, referring to the stack of documents Dan had printed from the Internet.

Dan nodded. At least they had recovered most of their few possessions even if his old Chevy was a write-off.

"It's very interesting, particularly the part about the Chechen war, but much of this is going to be difficult to put forward as evidence. I think the International Criminal Court would be interested in his activities during the war, although they are quite busy with a few African dictators for the time being."

"Well I'm not hiding out here forever while I wait and hope for the police to get him and his gang off the streets. Not that I don't appreciate your hospitality Frank," said Dan.

Marisa gave up on the crutches and flopped onto a sofa and sipped her drink. "So what do we do now?"

"I know someone who would be very interested in this material," said Frank, rubbing his beard thoughtfully.

"Who?" asked Dan, suddenly interested.

"No, no, it's a preposterous idea. Forget it."

Dan looked as if he was about to get up from his wheelchair despite his foot. "Frank, you can't just say that and not tell us who. What are you thinking?"

"No, really it doesn't matter."

"Let us be the judge of that. Don't hold out on us Frank."

Frank gave a heavy sigh. "I was just wondering if the Russians would be interested."

"What Russians?" asked Dan. Marisa sat up and was listening intently.

"The Russian Mafia. A small but well organized branch that engage mainly in extortion, drug running and money laundering." He paused. "Particularly money laundering—they are exceptionally good at that side of the operation. So good in fact that we have never been able to bring a successful prosecution against them."

He peered over his half moon reading glasses at Marisa. "Did you know, my dear, that the Canadian banking system is one of the most secretive in the world? The banks are not required to tell the police about suspicious transactions and our anti-money laundering legislation is woefully inadequate."

"I didn't know there was a Russian mob in Toronto," exclaimed Dan.

Frank turned back to Dan. "Not many people do. They manage to stay under the radar most of the time and stick to a small area. Like I say, their main business is money laundering and they don't need a "patch" to do this. My guess is they have clients worldwide. They have a reputation and they have the technology."

"So why would they be interested in these?" he asked, pointing at the stack of documents.

"I happen to know the head of this little band of mercenaries served as an officer in the Russian army during the Chechen War before he found a more lucrative career. His name is Boris Volkov and he is very patriotic. I don't think he would take too kindly to images of the heads of one his comrades being proudly displayed by Chechen guerrillas. Especially if he knew the killer was operating in this city."

"Are you saying that the Russian mafia don't even know about the Chechen clan?"

"Why would they? They operate in different areas and specialize in different lines of business. From Marisa's testimony the Chechens deal more in human trafficking and large scale drug deals. The Russians are the money laundering specialists and it is unlikely their paths would ever cross. Remember this is a big city. Even if they were aware of each other's presence they would have no reason to be in conflict. These guys are businessmen, not zealots. They like to keep a low profile. They would not draw attention to themselves by engaging in vendettas against other groups unless their business interests were threatened."

Frank paused and sipped at his port. "Although it is a volatile balance. It only needs one spark to light a flame."

"So what are you proposing Frank?"

Frank shifted uncomfortably. "I was thinking that you go to see them. But forget it Dan, it's too dangerous. These guys are not to be messed with. They would slice you up and stuff you in a dumpster if you looked at them the wrong way."

"Frank, I've been nearly strung up and used for target practise, shot at by some deranged assassin and slammed into a tree because of Akhmad. I am not sitting here waiting for his gang to finish us off. They might actually succeed next time."

"Surely the Drug Squad has enough on him by now, particularly after Montreal. Why haven't they made any arrests yet?" pondered Frank.

"Good question Frank. I'm losing faith and I like your idea."

Dan scratched at his chin. "Dan it would be very risky. Who knows what it could lead to? Think about it carefully."

Dan looked at Marisa and she gave him a supportive look. "I've thought about it. I think I should go and see them."

"Yes," said Marisa. They still have Olivia and more of my friends. We have to do something."

Frank raised his hands in a defensive gesture. "Okay, okay, I hear you."

"Can you get us an introduction?"

"No guarantees. It will mean pulling some strings and treading carefully. I have some contacts in the underworld that I can call some favours from. Goes with the territory. Even so, if the prosecutor's office found out I was trying to make contact with the Russian Mafioso I would probably end up sitting on the opposite side of the courtroom. I wish I hadn't suggested it."

"Too late now, Frank," smiled Dan. Do what you can and get us in."

Dan sat back in his wheelchair. Despite his throbbing head, he was starting to feel better already.

CHAPTER 36

It was over a week later before Frank advised his guests he had sealed a meeting with Boris Volkov. In that time Dan and Marisa had both been recuperating slowly but progressively. They were both suffering from cabin fever, Marisa the more so as it reminded her so much of her confinement in Rahmon's house. Frank had urged them not to leave the house or to answer any calls. However, they could not resist spending a little time in Frank's beautiful garden, especially in the early June sunshine, where the azaleas were in full bloom and released a pleasing aroma. When they admitted to Frank that they had ventured out into the garden, he was not too pleased, even though the garden was well shielded by the hemlock trees. He said nothing, just raised his eyebrows in disapproval.

In the evening, after they had eaten and the housekeeper had left for the day, they retired to the study, where Frank cradled his obligatory glass of port. Marisa was now off crutches, but she was still limping slightly, and if she moved her leg in a certain direction, she could feel the skin pulling, as if it was about to rip apart, even though the stitching had dissolved. She winced and sat down next to Dan, who had graduated from the wheelchair to crutches, although his left foot remained in a cast, probably for another week. As they were unofficially dead, a trip to the hospital to have the cast removed would be risky at present.

Frank looked troubled. He swilled the port around in his glass pensively. "I spoke to Brad today. He was very coy about the investigation. He said they were still gathering evidence and hoped to be in a position to issue arrest warrants fairly soon. When I pressed him to be more specific he politely told me to back off, that he could not really talk about an ongoing investigation, especially to a prosecutor. I can understand that, but Brad is not a person to stick to the rules so rigidly, so I was a little surprised. He was very interested in you guys, wondered how you were doing and wanting to make sure you were both still staying with me."

Dan sighed. "So nothing new on the investigation. This is so frustrating."

"Dan you know how these operations work, they have to get the timing right, gather the evidence meticulously, get the warrants in place. I can't tell you how many times I have had evidence contested as being inadmissible because of the way it was gathered. Let them do their job. I am sure they are pretty close."

"Not close enough for my liking. Any news on the Russian front?"

Frank paused, scratching at his beard nervously. "I have managed to secure you a meeting."

Dan's face brightened. "That's great news. Why the look?"

"They insist on Marisa going too."

"No way," said Dan, shaking his head. "It's too dangerous."

Marisa interjected, her voice betraying her irritation. "Don't I get a say in this?"

"Marisa, you've been through enough already. You don't have to go."

"I'm afraid she does," Frank responded. "They made it a condition of the meeting that Marisa comes. No Marisa, no meeting. It was not open to negotiation."

"Then perhaps we should call it off," replied Dan.

Frank looked incredulous. "Dan, do you realize what I went through to secure this meeting? It is not like a visit to the dentist. You don't just cancel on a man like Volkov. You have to go through with the meeting or we risk making an enemy of someone we don't want to be enemies with. He is a powerful man and if he gets angry we will know about it."

Marisa chimed in, looking hard at Dan. "I would want to go even if Volkov did not insist. We are in this together Dan. I am not afraid."

Frank smiled at Marisa. The girl really has spirit, he thought admiringly. Since he had met her he had been impressed by her strength of character and determination, all the more so having seen her video account of how she had suffered at the hands of the Chechen gang. It could get nasty, but there seemed little point in trying to dissuade Marisa from going, even if there was a choice.

Evidently Dan arrived at the same conclusion. He gave a deep sigh. "I will never forgive myself if anything happens to you," he said to Marisa.

"You sound just like my Papa . . . . *did,*" she said, abruptly correcting herself.

Dan gave an embarrassed laugh and turned to Frank. "So when do we get the honour of meeting Volkov?"

Frank stared hard at Dan. "Tonight."

Frank had warned them that they were on their own, no back up, especially not from the police. As Dan limped along on crutches with Marisa toward the meeting place, he certainly felt alone. And exposed. It was late and this area of Leslie Street, in the east of the city, was not a place for the casual wanderer after dark. It was not as if he could make a quick getaway or use his karate. In his current state, he was an easy target for the hordes of ghouls that haunted the streets peddling women, drugs or worse still, looking for tourists or other naïve visitors to relieve them of their valuables. The residents never wandered the streets at night. They were not that foolish. What made it worse was, with Marisa accompanying him, they made an odd couple, and could hardly remain inconspicuous. His only comfort was that they looked like such obvious targets any potential attacker might be deterred from approaching them in the belief such an appealing target was obviously a police sting. Indeed, as they reached the rendezvous point, the most they had received was a few catcalls, taunts such as "cripple" and "spastic" yelled from across the street by a group of drunken lads who collapsed into laughter as he hobbled by.

He checked his watch. It was five minutes to eleven, and they had reached the alleyway at the back of the Russian restaurant where Volkov resided and which was, according to Frank, the hub of his operations. They had been instructed to wait at the end of the alley until eleven o'clock, where they would be met by Volkov's chef. As he peered down the alley, all he could see were murky shadows moving amongst the dumpsters, homeless people looking for a few scraps and anonymity in the darkness. These alleys had a way of closing out all light even in the daytime. At this time of night, the street lamps were unable to penetrate the blackness. The night seemed to envelop you, and an attacker could be on you before you even became aware of their presence.

"Keep close and stay alert," he whispered to Marisa.

She nodded and squeezed his arm lightly. Then out of the shadows emerged a large, rotund man in a tall chef's hat, brandishing a huge meat cleaver. He waved it around, as if he was ready to bring it down on any unsuspecting fool who got in his way. He spotted Dan and Marisa and halted, looking furtively around him before he beckoned them to follow with a flourish of his cleaver.

Dan shrugged his shoulders and turned to Marisa. "Here goes. No turning back now."

They followed the chef through a narrow back door that led through the kitchens and into the main restaurant area. The restaurant had just closed, and the lights had been set low for the evening. He led them up a narrow flight of stairs, pausing impatiently at the top as Dan struggled to negotiate the stairs with his crutches, supported by Marisa.

"Come, come quickly," said the chef, in a thick Russian accent, still brandishing his cleaver. He led them into a narrow landing and he paused outside a door at the far end. He knocked at the door, politely, almost reverently. He gently called out, "*Hozyain*, the people are here."

There was silence, and then a voice from within called. "Good, good, bring them in."

The chef gently opened the door and ushered them in, and he quickly left. Dan hobbled in first. The room was a small office with a desk and computer and a shelf stacked with files dominating one corner. In the other corner two men, both dressed in identical black leather jackets and black roll-neck sweaters, were playing cards under a low-hanging but dim ceiling light. The whole room was poorly lit and had a gloomy feel to it. The two men looked up as Dan and Marisa entered, but it was the man who stood vigorously in front of Dan that grabbed his attention.

Boris Volkov was younger than he had imagined. Barely thirty, he had a craggy face with hollow, angular cheeks. His hair was slicked back and tied in a long ponytail which reached down to his shoulders. His eyes were dark like a Mediterranean that contrasted with his pale skin. They carried an inner intelligence and depth that Dan found unsettling. He wore a short sleeved open neck shirt on his tall, athletic frame, and sported a number of tattoos on his muscular arms, and even on his chest extending to just beneath his chin.

Dan reached out to offer his hand, balancing on one crutch, but Volkov just stared at him with those intense, deep eyes. At the same time, the two card players finished their game and marched toward Dan and Marisa purposefully, carrying expressions of barely disguised hostility. Both of them filled out their jackets squarely and they each stood in front of Dan and Marisa as if to shield their boss. They stood far too close and each was shorter than his respective visitor, but considerably wider. With mean expressions and a nod from their boss, they began to roughly frisk the visitors. Marisa objected as the bodyguard's chubby fingers probed her body, especially when his baleful expression creased into a sly smile. She pushed him away and almost instinctively he reached into his inner jacket pocket, surprised and enraged at her temerity.

At last Volkov spoke. "*Ostanovka, ostanovka,*" he said, admonishing him to stop. "Calm down, Vladimir my friend. You are offending our guests." His accent was deep Georgian tinged with a hint of Canadian which suggested he had been here some time.

He turned to his 'guests' and smiled. "Forgive my comrade. He is very protective but you must let us check you are not wired." Dan turned to Marisa and gave a short nod. Reluctantly she allowed Vladimir to continue his body search, the stubby fingers prodding even more harshly at her clothing. Dan submitted meekly to his body search, and satisfied, the men retired into the shadows, sitting on a sofa by the wall and studying them closely.

Volkov pointed at two hard wooden chairs. "Sit, please."

Dan and Marisa sat down on the chairs. They were very uncomfortable, and as Volkov continued to stand, they had to look up to him. He clearly had the psychological advantage. This was his home territory and he wanted to make sure these two strangers knew it.

"Your friends have gone to considerable lengths to secure a meeting with me. I do not take kindly to being sought out, or to strangers on my turf. You should understand that, in my line of business, a little paranoia is a healthy thing. It enables me to stay in business a little longer." He paused. His tone changed abruptly and his face hardened. "So why are you here?"

Dan and Marisa glanced at each other. They had rehearsed what they were going to say earlier in the day.

"The Chechens. Akhmad Timayev and his clan," said Dan.

"Yes the Chechens. Barbarians on the battlefield. I fought many battles with them when serving in our glorious army. These savages do not follow the usual rules of warfare. They will sacrifice their women and children for the cause and they are suicide bombers, the most cowardly scum." He uttered the last sentence with obvious distaste.

"Did you know they are on your doorstep?"

"I have heard of Timayev and his clan. Of course we despise them as Chechens, but they have not interfered with our business. They have a different field to us." He clicked his fingers and one of his bodyguards poured him a vodka in a crystal glass. He held the glass up to the dim light and regarded the clear liquid admiringly. "Finest Stolichnaya vodka from the Kaliningrad region. Do you know how difficult it was to get this imported into Canada? A land of bureaucracy but also a land of opportunity. I have been in this country for several years and business is good. The Family is good. We look after our own. We have no reason to cause trouble when it does not serve our purpose."

"Not even if the Chechens are plotting against you?" said Dan. He could feel Marisa's eyes boring into him.

Volkov's eyes narrowed and he fixed Dan with a hard stare. "Who the hell are you and what is your interest in this?"

Dan saw the two bodyguards stirring uneasily. One of them was reaching for his inside jacket pocket.

"You had better talk fast comrade," said Volkov menacingly. "I do not like what I am hearing. What is to say I don't cut your throats now and be done. I heard you were dead anyway."

Vladimir stepped forward and produced a long switchblade which he flicked open to reveal a silver blade with a serrated edge glinting in the poor light. He held it in front of his face and waved it in the air across his neck with an ugly grin. Dan tensed, ready to defend himself, although, he thought ruefully, his karate skills were severely restricted with a club foot. To his relief the bodyguard did not move closer, but turned the blade in his hand, as if he was ready to pounce at his master's instruction.

Dan wanted to argue that his and Marisa's death would not go unnoticed but decided not to challenge Volkov. Instead he looked up into the tall Russian's eyes. "I have come with information of value to you. I have no other agenda."

"So why would you help me?"

"Because I think you can help me?"

Volkov paused. "I don't do deals with strangers without checking them out first. Your representatives were desperate for me to meet with you so I have to confess I am curious." He turned to Marisa and smiled. His eyes looked her up and down, appraising her. Marisa had seen that leering look before on so many of her clients, and instantly felt a loathing for this Russian mobster. She wisely said nothing and sat impassively. She had agreed with Dan that he would do the talking and she would only talk if asked a direct question.

"So hear what I have to say."

Volkov turned back to Dan and his tone was suddenly more friendly. "I am being a poor host." He turned to the other bodyguard. "Grigory, fix our two guests a drink."

Grigory shot his master a downcast look. He clearly felt himself above the role of a waiter but did not object. He got up and fixed two glasses of vodka from the drinks cabinet and placed them on the table. Volkov offered them to Dan and Marisa. Dan took his but Marisa shook her head.

"Please, please, take it," he admonished her, an edge of steel to his voice. "It is an offence in my country to refuse a man's hospitality. It is good vodka."

Marisa hesitated and looked at Dan for support. He gave her a subtle nod and she took the drink. "That's better," smiled Volkov. "Now comrade, you talk and keep me interested." He pointed at the glass in Dan's hand and laughed. "Perhaps the vodka will make you talk faster, eh?"

Dan sipped at his vodka, its acrid taste burning his throat. He did not know what to make of this volatile Russian. He appeared to act like a long lost friend one minute and a formidable enemy the next. He didn't know if they would leave as new allies or whether they would end up sleeping with the rats in a dumpster.

As Volkov listened, pacing the room, Dan briefly told the tale of how he had found and rescued Marisa in Montreal, when the Chechen clan's drug deal went badly wrong, and why they now had a contract out on them.

Volkov eventually sat down, his bristling energy unnerving Dan. "Yes, they are savages. But why should I care if they have a contract out on you?" He turned again to Marisa with a leering look. "Although it would be sad in some ways."

"I don't expect you to care about us, but I am sure you care about your operation. We understand that Timayev's clan is looking to expand its activities in Toronto, particularly after their failure in Montreal. They lost a lot of money and they are desperate to find other ways of earning it back. What better way than to muscle in on a rival's operations? That is how Timayev has grown his business in the past."

Volkov stared at Dan intently, his steely gaze boring into him. He stood in front of Dan and, rather curiously, pulled up both trouser legs above his knees. He pointed to the broad, red star tattooed on each knee. "Do you see these stars? They mean that no member of the Family will bow down or kneel before anyone." He tapped his chest. "My name, Boris, stands for warrior in my country. We will crush the Chechens before they even get close to our operation." His voice was tinged with anger.

"Then now would be a good time to crush them. A pre-emptive strike if you like. They have been weakened by the Montreal raid and the police are closing in on them. Take them out and their business is yours."

Volkov looked again at Marisa. "We don't want their filthy business, as long as they stay out of ours. These savages sicken me. The Chechens give the Soviets a bad name."

"And is what you do any better? You might not be involved in human trafficking but is extortion and money laundering any better? They hurt people as much you know, you just don't see the suffering first hand."

In one swift action Volkov grabbed Dan's neck and squeezed his Adam's apple. Dan fought for breath, struggling against Volkov's vice-like grip. Volkov's two comrades had also closed in and stood menacingly over Dan, ready to pounce on their master's signal.

"I do not have to justify myself to you. It is what it is. May I remind you comrade of where you are? This is not the time or place for you to moralize or to criticize the Family."

Just when Dan thought he was going to pass out, the Russian let go and Dan lurched forward in his chair, wheezing and rubbing his neck. God, he is strong, he thought.

Volkov waved his bodyguards back to their seats but they remained staring intently at Dan, poised for action.

He turned to Marisa with an icy stare. "Tell me what they did to you." Marisa hesitated but then haltingly described how the clan had deceived her into coming to Canada and how she ended up working in one of their brothels. The two bodyguards sat back and smiled to themselves, enjoying the description of her terrible ordeal, particularly when she described how they had injected her with heroin. Tearfully, she also described how they had shot her father. When she had finished Volkov merely muttered "Savages," and sipped at his vodka.

Dan, still rubbing his neck, said, "Do you recall the Moscow metro bombing, when the Chechen separatists vowed to take the war to the cities of Russia? Well they have taken their war to the cities of Canada as well. I think Timayev's group financed the operation through their apparently legitimate front company registered here in Ontario. They have been using drug operations and proceeds from their trafficking business to finance the Chechen rebels, and I am certain a number of terrorist attacks in Russia can be linked back to their financial support. Have a look at this."

Dan reached into his jacket pocket and produced an envelope which he threw onto the nearby table. Volkov, clearly curious, picked up the envelope and emptied its contents on the table and began leafing through the various pieces of paper.

Dan continued. "In there you will find out more about the type of man Timayev is. And this is only what is in the public domain. God knows what else he is capable of, but look at this." He reached forward and picked up one of the printed photographs. It was the gruesome picture of Timayev in full combat uniform grasping in each hand by the hair the heads of two unfortunate Russian soldiers.

Volkov stared at the picture, as if transfixed, and Dan watched his expression change from casual interest to a mask of controlled fury. "I know the picture is grainy, but it is unmistakable. The soldier is Timayev. This was taken during the Chechen War. These men would have been comrades of yours, men who stood side by side fighting the guerrillas with you, watching your back and you watching theirs. Timayev is a born murderer. He is not just fighting for a cause. He's a psychopath who loves killing. Just look at his face. That could have been you and now he wants your business."

Despite the pressure of the situation, Marisa looked at Dan admiringly. He sounded very persuasive. The photograph was their trump card and Dan had played it well.

Volkov threw down the photograph but said nothing.

"Please help us," said Marisa pleadingly. She stared at Volkov, who said nothing but looked deeply troubled.

"It's them or you," said Dan, sensing his advantage.

"Whatever you think Mr Huberman, we do not wish to draw attention to ourselves. Fighting a turf war with these savages will not serve our cause. It will be bad for business."

"It will be worse for business if you allow them to overrun you."

"I will talk to the Family, see what must be done. As for you, maybe we should shoot the messenger."

"You're not going to do that."

"Why not?"

"Because as you said, you don't wish to draw attention to yourselves. Killing us would bring the whole Toronto police force on your back. It would be even worse for business than doing nothing about the Chechens."

"Which is why you are still alive," retorted Volkov. He slumped down into a low armchair set against the wall. "Comrades. Please show our guests out."

He turned to Dan and Marisa. "Thank you for the information. This meeting never happened. We will decide how to deal with the Chechens in our own way but if you talk to anyone about this meeting . . . ." His voice trailed off, not needing to complete the threat. "We will be watching you closely. We will make contact again only if we need to. Good night."

As they were dispatched unceremoniously into the chilly night air, the bodyguard throwing Dan's crutches after him, they paused in the dark alley.

Lurking in the shadows behind a pair of dumpsters, the operative watched the pair leave. He was glad to leave the stench of rotting fish and the squeal of rodents running around unseen in the dark. Occasionally he would feel something soft brush against his foot and he would kick it away. He darted athletically out of the alley and watched them leave from a safe distance, the man hobbling on his crutches, the girl supporting him. They hailed a yellow cab and the man awkwardly climbed in, followed by the girl. The cab weaved seamlessly into the light midnight traffic and was soon out of sight.

The operative dialled his cell phone and waited for the familiar voice to reply.

"You were right boss. They went to see the Russians."

The voice on the other line was a little angry, but sounded more perplexed. "What the hell are they playing at, meeting up with the Russian Mafiosi? Does Huberman have a death wish? Christ, he is going to stir up some serious trouble for himself and for us. This could get ugly."

"What do you suggest now?"

"It's midnight. I suggest you go home and I am going to sleep on it. Wait . . ." the voice on the line trailed off. "There is a way we could turn this to our advantage. Let the Russians do our job for us."

The operative stared at his phone. "Boss, what the hell are you talking about?" he said in an irritated voice.

"Nothing," came the reply. "Get some sleep, we'll talk about it in the morning."

CHAPTER 37

It had taken a lot of persuasion to get Carl's superiors to agree to the move to Toronto for this case. There was plenty of work in Montreal, that was certain, but he had lobbied hard to become the lead investigator in the case against Timayev. It had seemed to upset Brad, who viewed it as his case, but this was no time to be squabbling over petty internal politics. They both knew Carl had more experience, and the gang's Montreal connection had swung it in his favour. They had discovered that Timayev's company, which appeared totally legitimate and survived close scrutiny, did, however, have some off balance sheet property located in Montreal. They had the addresses, but locating the Toronto properties had so far been more elusive. The company itself held only one property, a small industrial unit based near Buttonville Airport in the north of the city, which was the registered office and principal place of business for the import and export company. There was nothing registered in Timayev's name at the Ontario Land Registry either. His Toronto properties were off the grid.

Despite Marisa's video testimony describing the house, they had been unable to pinpoint the exact location yet, although they now had a clue as to the general area within about four streets, and he was considering house to house searches. The biggest problem was coordinating the raids. Although they knew the addresses of the Montreal properties, it was premature to raid them now. He needed to locate the Toronto properties and apply for a search warrant that would enable them to enter the houses simultaneously and arrest as many of the gang members as possible without them tipping off their cohorts elsewhere. Meanwhile they kept the Montreal properties under surveillance, although Carl suspected the gang probably had other properties in Montreal that they did not know about. There had been some activity, usually older men accompanying young girls in and out of the house, but no evidence of any overt drug activity.

Though Carl did not believe that the geographic scope of the gang's activities were far ranging, it was the sheer financial scale of his drug activities that alarmed him. The drug haul from the Montreal bust was one of the biggest in Quebec police history, yet Timayev was conducting his operations clandestinely under the noses of the police. On the face of it Timayev appeared an honest businessman who owned a legitimate antiques business, paid his taxes on time and even made modest donations to charity. If he held any anti-Russian views, they were well hidden. It was only the tenacity of a private investigator who had given them the tip on the deal in Kahnawake. If not, they would once again have been chasing shadows. These guys were good. He had suspected all along that they had received inside help, and now at least he knew it. What really concerned him was where the help was coming from, but he would deal with that later. For now, let the double agent do his work and hopefully he would make a mistake that would lead them straight to Timayev's door.

He and Brad stood outside the interview room, watching the interview with the gang member they had captured in Montreal with mounting frustration. In another concession that had involved a lot of arm twisting, the Montreal police had allowed Carl to have him transported back to Toronto where he remained on remand in an isolated cell. If they were hoping he would crack, they were sorely disappointed. He had said absolutely nothing, except to give his name. Even that was probably false, as they had checked immigration records and found no trace of him. They had taken his fingerprints and saliva swabs but they did not match up with any records on the National DNA Bank. The Bank was part of the Royal Canadian Mounted Police's Forensic Sciences and Identification Services, which held a vast number of genetic data for convicted criminals, but not for this guy. He was clean and had apparently appeared from nowhere. When they had picked him up he had no identification documents on his person. He had no past or present, yet he was their only tangible link to the clan.

He had interrogated the Somali drug gang, particularly the Colonel in Montreal, and while he had been willing to sell his grandmother if it would help make a deal, the fact was they did not know much. The ends had been closed off effectively. All the Somalis knew was they were dealing with a General from overseas, they believed from one of the disputed Russian territories, but could offer little more. As long as the delivery agents arrived with the consignment on time and in the right quantities, their identity was of little interest to the Somalis. They did not need to know too much. The other gang members had even less knowledge. They reported to and were paid by the Colonel, and that was enough to follow his instructions. Most of them were young men in their twenties who had little knowledge of the inner workings of the drug trade in which they made their living. They were little more than trained thugs, in it to feed their families, but also for the excitement and escape from hopeless, repressed lives. They were not the disciplined, fearless unit they had portrayed themselves to be.

Still, he pondered, they had Marisa's testimony, and the Somalis had been helpful too, but they needed someone from the inside. The prisoner was incredibly disciplined, showing absolutely no emotion or expression as two of the unit's veteran interrogators threw rapid-fire questions at him, shouted, cursed and made threats, all to no avail. He remained silent, almost as still as a statue, as if he had fallen into some meditative trance. Only his eyes gave him away. They shone with a burning hatred, occasionally flicking a baleful glance at his tormentors. The accused had not asked for a lawyer, yet seated next to him was a balding weasel-like counsel, who was as animated as the interrogators and responded to each question by standing up indignantly and shouting, "My client does not have to answer that!" or similar. Around this maelstrom the prisoner sat calmly, oblivious to the whole circus. Carl snorted in frustration. It was their last chance with him before he was arraigned to appear in court on charges of drug trafficking and attempted murder of a police officer the next morning. The lead interrogator oscillated between aggressive threats of a long spell in prison, to an impassioned promise that he would do whatever he could to cut a deal for him if he talked now. It was all to no avail. The gang member stayed resolutely silent.

Only when one of the interrogators, almost nose to nose with the hard-faced prisoner, taunted him that his friends had deserted him, leaving him to rot in a maximum security prison, did his mouth twitch. He quickly restored his mask, but Carl had seen it, and so had the interrogators. Maybe, thought Carl, he was a casualty of this war on the streets, although they had not completely abandoned him. He had a very irritating lawyer, and someone must have sent him. The lawyer knew well enough he was within his rights not to reveal his client, but maybe they could apply some pressure on him.

The other concern for Carl was the investigation into the murder of the headless man found in Lake Ontario. Fingerprint analysis had identified him as Yuri Umarov, a Chechen in his thirties who had lived in Canada for five years, the same length of time as Timayev, and who had been a director of the import and export company. He may have been the victim of a turf war between rival drug gangs, but Carl was not convinced. The police were no nearer solving the crime since they had identified the unfortunate victim, whose head had never been found, but Carl had a hunch the murder was closely linked to the Dimitrov homicide, suggesting that the gang had purged one of their own. It was not uncommon in these types of organizations for gang members falling out of favour for whatever reason suddenly disappearing without trace. Getting to Timayev was key, but they still needed proof to make the charges stick.

At least an opportunity had presented itself last night, one that he had not yet shared with anyone, least of all Brad. He had spent a restless night in his lonely hotel room tossing and turning, thinking through the implications of his plan, one which was highly risky. If it did not come off, it could cost him his career. Carl had never shied away from taking chances, but this was a bigger gamble than he had ever taken. However, as he weighed it up, he decided it would be better to take the chance rather than allow this investigation, which had run into a series of blind alleys as they struggled to gather cogent evidence, to run on aimlessly. He rubbed his stubbly cheeks and glanced sideways at Brad. He was convinced he was taking the right action, but he would need a little bit of inside help from some trusted colleagues.

Sitting in his comfortable apartment above the restaurant working his way through a small bottle of his favoured Stolichnaya vodka, Volkov had to admit to himself that he was troubled by recent events. The meeting with the private investigator and the Bulgarian girl the previous evening had aroused his curiosity and he had made some enquiries. His underground contacts had verified a lot of what they had said, although there was no evidence the Chechen group was planning to attack his operation. In fact, the clan's own operations were under threat as their Montreal disaster was well documented in the grapevine of the criminal underworld, and other operatives had become more courageous. Sensing the weakness of the Chechen gang, it appeared that several smaller operatives were trying to challenge the dominant position the fierce Chechens held in the local drugs trade, and also in people trafficking.

He personally found the trafficking quite abhorrent. Marisa's story disturbed him, and his network of contacts had confirmed that Timayev's group ran a lucrative and well established business here and in Montreal. He had also been appalled by the images of Timayev proudly holding the heads of the Russian soldiers. He had fought alongside many brave soldiers in the Chechen wars and he knew the rebels never took prisoners. If you were unfortunate enough to be captured by the Chechens, your life expectancy was brutally short.

Then he had received an anonymous email sent from a proxy server that rendered it impossible to trace back to the original sender. As he read it, Volkov wondered if he was being set up. A Chechen gang member who had been arrested in the raid in Kahnawake was being transported to the courts in the morning, and the email suggested that security would be so poor it would be an easy job to break him out and take him hostage. He would be a key element in gathering vital information about the Chechen gang. Volkov doubted the Chechen would willingly yield any incriminating information, but his more brutal comrades were highly experienced in interrogation techniques.

The email suggested that it was an opportunity to make a first strike and gain the element of surprise. As reluctant as he was to engage in any hostilities, Volkov knew well enough the basic rule of war. If conflict was inevitable, it was best to strike first when the enemy was least expecting it. Downing his vodka, yet his mind still sharp, he had considered the problem for several hours and decided to take advantage of the opportunity offered.

"Lights out!" came the belligerent call from the prison officer who ran his truncheon along the bars with a metallic grating noise, his usual routine at nine-thirty in the evening. Sulim always clenched his teeth when he heard the sound. The officer must have known how irritating it was to him and his fellow prisoners because he appeared to take great pleasure in doing it.

He stretched out on the cold steel bed, and as lights were extinguished with a series of sharp clicks throughout the prison, the only illumination remaining came from the faint moonlight that seeped through the bars on the tiny alcove set high up on the wall out of his reach. At least his cramped cell was on the outer walls, where some fresh air was able to circulate. Many of the cells in this maze like structure were set deeper into the innards of the building and unfortunate inmates of these cells only saw or felt any natural light or clean air for about fifteen minutes of each day.

There were certain small privileges to being on remand rather than a convicted prisoner. However, Sulim was under no illusion that with the serious charges weighed against him, and with the idiot of a lawyer representing him, it would not be long before he would be residing in a maximum security cell where the air was fetid. At least for now he had his own cell, a modern clinical box with maddeningly white walls and a steel bed and toilet. Everything was sealed down, there were no sharp edges, nothing to pick up and use as a weapon. They were clearly designed to ensure that inmates were not tempted to harm themselves or anyone else, even though the whitewashed walls were enough to make you believe you were in an asylum. They had not given him a straitjacket yet, but they had provided him with a cleanly pressed bright orange jumpsuit in preparation for the hearing tomorrow. They had insisted he wear it. "Might as well go in there looking your best in the circumstances," the prison guard had chuckled tauntingly.

He laid back on the threadbare mattress, which hardly provided any cushion against the hard steel fold-out bed, and thought about his preliminary hearing tomorrow. This was his second court appearance. The first had been a bail hearing in Montreal. He had not expected to make bail and he was not surprised at the outcome. The charges were just too serious. His wheedling lawyer, clearly uncomfortable in the cell with Sulim and reluctant to sit on the bed next to him, had stood near the sealed door and explained the hearing. He had said that this appearance was to review the disclosure of the evidence and to summarize the prosecution's case against him. He had continued to insist there was nothing to worry about, he was certain the evidence the police had was not enough to secure a conviction. However the lawyer had been wrong about everything else. He was worse than useless and Sulim would have liked to have snapped his scrawny neck in the cell when no-one was looking.

Sulim felt faintly resentful that all his boss on the outside could muster was this pathetic lawyer. There had been no contact, no messages from Akhmad, even through the lawyer. Maybe this was tactical, but he could not help feeling a sense of abandonment. He knew the discipline of military strategy well enough. There were always going to be casualties and the war had to be fought by those still able to fight it. Maybe he was a casualty of war and though they might have held a minute's silence for him, he would have been quickly forgotten. He had been faithful to his training and stayed silent, incriminating neither himself nor his comrades. The police had learned nothing from him about the clan, yet it was highly likely he would be convicted at trial, especially with this weak lawyer defending him. What then?

He did not envisage too many social visits from the clan as he languished in prison. He thought for a second about whether he should consider a deal, but instantly dismissed such a perverse thought, feeling vaguely appalled with himself. However, the persistent, subconscious feeling would not go away, no matter how hard he tried to force it out of his mind. Even as he drifted off into a troubled sleep, his mind kept revolving around the same suggestion.

CHAPTER 38

At six-thirty the following morning, a plastic tray was delivered through the small slot in the wall just above the floor next to Sulim's cell. It contained the usual slop of food, a pasty porridge-like gruel, with a plastic spoon and a plastic jug of water. No knives or forks were allowed here, not even for the half cooked pasta they occasionally served. Even plastic cutlery could be used as a weapon. Spoons were safer. Even a Chechen soldier would find it hard to fashion an effective weapon from the brittle plate and spoon. Although the porridge was thick and tasteless, Sulim hastily finished it off and gulped down the water. There was never enough for a man of his stature, a solid wall of muscle six feet three tall, and hunger gnawed at his abdomen as it had done constantly in his time behind bars.

A soldier learned hardship, he told himself, but even he found the slow insidious starvation hard to bear. The nagging suggestion from last night resurfaced, but mercifully his thoughts were distracted by the click of a key turning in his lock. In came three burly prison guards, two of whom carried an assortment of weapons, including a long truncheon and pepper spray. The two armed guards fanned out, alert and tense, ready to spring into action. The third guard, an older officer with the poise and confidence that came from having carried out the drill thousands of times before, addressed the Chechen.

"Good morning Sulim, I think you know the drill by now. Face the far wall and put your hands behind your back as far as they will go."

Maintaining his vow of silence, Sulim said nothing but compliantly faced the wall, his hands behind him. The middle guard expertly snapped a pair of handcuffs around his wrists and the two armed guards visibly relaxed. One of the guards spun him round and steered him out of the cell. Flanked by a guard holding his elbow on either side, the third guard who had handcuffed him out in front, Sulim marched through the soulless, harshly lit corridors. He kept his posture upright and proud, his face betraying no emotion, but it was purely for appearances. He did not wish to display any weakness or vulnerability, but he wondered who the show was for. The guards were wary of him, and were careful to make sure he was handcuffed at all times when they were close to him. However, they were not intimidated or concerned by his demeanour. They did their job efficiently and were not interested if he refused to talk. It just added to his self-imposed sense of isolation and abandonment.

They passed through several sets of barred steel doors before emerging into the courtyard at the rear of the prison. Sulim blinked rapidly in the strong sunlight and instinctively went to cover his eyes, the resistance from his handcuffs reminding him of his situation. It had been a while since he had been in direct sunlight, and, eyes closed, he paused to feel the warmth on his face. The pleasure was quickly extinguished as he was bundled into the back of an armoured police van with no windows, only a tiny grille which reluctantly let in a few shafts of light. It was uncomfortable with the handcuffs, but the officers moved in alongside him and held him steady, watching him carefully. The head guard turned to him.

"Big day today then Sulim," he said mockingly.

Sulim maintained his silence, staring resolutely at the floor. He was due to meet his idiotic solicitor in the court house for a briefing prior to the hearing, where he understood the prosecution would make its initial presentation of evidence to secure justification for the trial. He was not interested in the legal machinery, but he had no choice other than go through the motions. The confident head of the trio decided to get into the front cab next to the driver. The court van moved off, rocking the three men in the back of the van. Sulim heard the muffled roar of traffic, and the van lurched awkwardly along the road toward City Hall, where the criminal court was situated. Then without warning the van braked harshly, almost sending the men flying against the rear door. Sulim fought to steady himself, not easy with his hands tied, and one of the guards pulled him upright. He noticed the look they exchanged between them and he became aware that the traffic noise had stopped.

Sulim heard the sound of men shouting, distorted through the thick steel frame of the van, followed by a strident banging on the outside of the van. Before the guards could react, the back door of the van was flung open and in jumped two stocky men in black ski masks, waving Kalashnikov rifles at the two guards, who were too stunned to react. Another two stood outside the van, weapons poised and ready. Sulim's heart leaped with joy. Akhmad had not let him down after all. This was a rescue mission. However, his euphoria lasted barely a second before he realized the awful truth when the first gunman spoke. Despite being muffled by the ski mask, the accent was unmistakable. It was not Chechen, but central Russian, the type of accent commonly found in Moscow.

"Get down on the floor, now!" the Russian screamed at the guards. "Take out your weapons slowly and toss them over here." The two guards had no choice but to comply. Outnumbered, and with a machine gun inches from their face, the safety trigger off, they were in no position to try any heroics. They meekly dropped to the dirty floor of the van and released their weapons. Sulim noted with disgust that they did not even have guns, just Tasers and a pepper spray. The Russian kicked the weapons contemptuously away and then turned toward Sulim. The Chechen could only see his eyes, and they were dark and full of hostility. One of the other gunmen pulled out a small cloth sack and handed it to his comrade, who placed it over Sulim's head. Blinded and disoriented, he began to shout in protest, but was answered by a short, sharp stab in the back from the butt of one of the rifles.

"Shut up or next time it is the head," threatened the Russian.

Sulim stayed silent and he was dragged and manhandled out of the van and frogmarched into the back of what felt like a big car, a Range Rover or similar. He could not tell, the blindness making him feel vulnerable, and he was forced to admit to himself, a little afraid. His wrists were sore from the handcuffs and his arms and back ached from being placed in an unnatural posture for too long. There was more shouting and a short burst of gunfire before one of the men jumped into the passenger seat and the vehicle screeched away. It had taken barely a minute for the Russians to ambush the van and kidnap Sulim and the police had virtually sat back and let it happen. He closed his eyes, not that it made any difference to the blackness, and broke out into a cold sweat.

"What the hell are they shooting at!" shouted Carl in panic. He shot up out of his chair, scanning the camera feed, but the sound was off screen. The camera was a highly sophisticated pinhole device with audio that they had carefully concealed as a button on Sulim's jumpsuit. Carl's heart was in his mouth, fearing the worst. He had risked a great deal with this carefully orchestrated operation, but the one variable they could not account for was the reaction of the Russians to this open invitation. The guards had been well briefed and had shown a lot of courage in agreeing to this unusual move. If any of them were killed or even injured he would find it hard to live with, and he would almost certainly be in the Commissioner's office the next morning handing in his badge.

Sitting in this small mobile command centre at the back of a van disguised as a local floral delivery vehicle, surrounded by banks of equipment, Carl's two surveillance operatives worked frantically over their controls. Sulim's pinhole camera was shaking all over the place and they could see that he had been hauled out of the van. There was a lot of aggressive shouting from the Russians, but the picture spun round to the outside of the van.

"It's okay," said one of the operatives. "They have just shot out the tyres."

Carl sunk back in his chair, relieved. "Thank God," he sighed. The camera was working well and the audio quality was excellent. They had acquired a number of these cameras, cleverly disguised as an ordinary shirt button, from the Canadian Security Intelligence Service, and they were already proving useful in the field. Some of the conversation was in Russian but they could translate it later. The computerized recording equipment in their little control centre was picking up everything. His operatives, both wearing small headphones, listened carefully and watched the screens closely.

They could picture the scene from Sulim's perspective as he was manhandled into the back of a large Range Rover and driven away. They could not see the number plate of the car but it did not matter. Carl had posted a few of his colleagues on nearby roofs and they were filming the kidnap with long range cameras.

When it was clear the car had left the scene, Carl said to one of the operatives, a gawky looking communications engineer with thick glasses, "Get the driver on the line. I need to confirm there are no casualties."

"Yes sir," said the engineer obediently.

The driver's voice filled the command centre. "Everything is good here. No injuries, just a few bruised egos and a few flat tyres."

"Good work Officer Simons," smiled Carl. "I will make sure they get the best medical treatment for their egos in the bar tonight!"

The operation had so far been a success and now it was a question of tracking the Russians. He hoped that they could record any conversations as long as possible with the camera. Carl was certain that Sulim would talk to the Russians. He was confident they would be far more persuasive than his interrogation team were allowed to be. He had taken a huge risk based on that belief but so far it had worked out. He just hoped to God they did not kill him.

CHAPTER 39

"I can't believe I'm hearing this! You have really messed up comrade!" Timayev could barely contain the fury in his voice. As he looked out from his huge apartment window he barely noticed the sweeping vista of the Toronto skyline sparkling in the low light of the setting sun. His mind was focused on the news he had just received.

The voice on the other end of the line tried to adopt a conciliatory tone, clearly intimidated by Timayev's anger. The caller knew well enough that Timayev's fury was not to be taken lightly. "Akhmad, don't worry, we can sort this out."

"How the hell do we do that?"

"I-I don't know. But I'm working on it."

"You have failed me comrade," snarled Timayev menacingly. "I took your advice to wait a week or so before taking out Huberman and that whore, and now I hear they have gone to see the Russians."

The voice on the line faltered, its nervousness evident. "There's more I need to tell you Akhmad," he began.

"Go on," said Timayev, his voice a slow ominous drawl. The caller recognized the tone. He had heard it many times before, a tone of controlled anger but carrying a very real threat.

"Sulim was kidnapped by the Russians on his way to a court appearance this morning. They overpowered the prison officers and drove him away. No-one knows where and I am not being told anything. I only found out an hour ago. I think they suspect. This can't go on Akhmad," the voice said pleadingly.

Timayev listened silently for a moment as the voice on the line trailed off, and then he exploded with rage, spewing a range of profanities before he was able to compose himself. He had been trained to stay calm in the most stressful situations, and the ability to think coldly and rationally while chaos reigned all around had been a valuable attribute, on the battlefield and more recently in Montreal. Yet lately he had found his emotions becoming more powerful, clouding his thinking. It was getting harder to think objectively. Even his bodyguard and most trusted confidante, Alexi, had kept a discreet distance as his temperament had become more volatile with each new setback. His business fortunes and his reputation amongst the rebel forces had taken a huge hit since Montreal, and the private investigator had proved to be a thorn in his side.

"Bring in Huberman and the girl now!" he screamed down the phone. "I don't care how you do it, but deliver them to me!" He slammed the phone against the wall. In a calmer moment he'd had the foresight to put it in a rubber case after the last time, and the phone bounced harmlessly along the floor. He flexed his powerful hands. It had been some time since he had killed a man with his bare hands, but tonight he felt like he might just do it again.

It had been a long day and it was nearly midnight. Carl took a deep sigh and chewed on his half eaten pizza, the smell of artichokes pervading the small enclosed listening station. The small pinhole camera had long since reached its capacity but the audio device was still working well. The Russians had not killed Sulim yet. Carl had taken a gamble on that assumption. From his experience of Russian operations in Montreal, they were not fools. He refused to believe Volkov would compromise himself by taking such drastic action. The ease with which they took Sulim must have made them suspicious but for now at least they had played along. Unfortunately Sulim had not. He had maintained his silence under fierce pressure from the Russians. Carl had doggedly monitored every curse and threat, and a few beatings, and he had to confess to a grudging respect for the Chechen. He had taken it all over the last sixteen hours and still not caved in, and Carl was growing impatient.

His two communications operatives from the morning had been relieved by night shift operatives and Carl was feeling tired. Another fifteen minutes and he was out of here. They would have to call him for any developments. He took off his headphones, his ears sore from listening, and stretched out almost horizontally in his chair, chewing his pizza and staring at the ceiling.

Frustrated by the inactivity, his thoughts wandering, Carl stole a furtive glance at one of his new colleagues, a fresh-faced communications graduate in her early twenties, new to the force and full of enthusiasm. Great legs, he mused vacantly, quite apart from her flowing black hair. He was just about to go places he should not go with her in his mind when she turned to him, her soft features set in a frown. For a split second he thought she had read his mind and he bolted upright in his chair, nearly sending the pizza box flying.

"Sir, you need to hear this," she said.

"Yes of course," he said sheepishly. He pulled on his headphones and clicked his fingers at the other operative to start the digital feed to the headphones. He listened carefully, trying to picture the scene in some dark, damp basement where they had been holding Sulim for many hours. It seemed he was not the only one losing patience. Volkov's distinctive voice spoke loudly and in stereo in Carl's ears.

"I have had enough of this. The man is no use to me. Shoot him but make sure he suffers before he dies."

Carl felt a surge of panic. It looked like his plan was about to go horribly wrong. Volkov had not issued a threat to Sulim, but a direct order to his men, who had been trying to prise information out of the Chechen clan member most of the day. He could imagine Sulim, bound, bruised and bloody, still refusing to talk like a good soldier. Maybe Carl had signed his death warrant.

There was little he could do but listen. The accusations and finger pointing would come later when the police's internal Special Investigations Unit were making their pointed enquiries. God, if this ever became public. There was a heavy silence for what seemed nearly a minute and Carl cursed the fact that they no longer had the camera. Then something extraordinary happened.

"Please, please don't kill me. I'll tell you everything!" The heavily clipped accent of the Chechen resounded in his headphones. Dan glanced at his operatives, to make sure they were getting all this. Sulim sounded desperately scared. At last he was ready to talk. Maybe he had left it too late. His heart sank when he heard Volkov respond in a stern, dismissive voice. "You had your chance, comrade. Did you think your people would find and rescue you? Believe me, they are not even looking. You are already dead to them."

There was more silence, and then came the Chechen's voice, his self control completely broken down, ready to reveal anything to stay alive. "Please, please!" he pleaded. No response. Then the Chechen's chilling screams reverberated in Carl's headphones. He grimaced and put his head in his hands.

It was just after midnight when Dan, unable to sleep, grabbed a coffee and took it up to his room. The thing he loved about this area was that, unlike his own apartment, which always had groups of youths shouting outside at all hours, this neighbourhood became deathly quiet from about eleven o'clock onwards. Not a soul stirred after that time, so when he heard a car door slam he looked out the window with a hint of curiosity. He was taken aback and confused to see Brad striding purposefully toward the door by the light of the Victorian style lamppost which lit Frank's small front garden. The difficult meeting with the Russians had been the night before last, and yesterday he had received a call from Carl who had been rather irate at first. He had berated him harshly for taking matters into his own hands by seeing the Russians.

"For a start, you blew the story!" he scolded Dan. "Do you know how fast news travels in these circles? Before you know it the Chechen clan will find out and they will realize you are still walking and breathing. They'll come looking to finish you off. When they find out you have been in collusion with the Russians . . . that risks a bloodbath on the streets of Toronto. Seeing Volkov was the height of irresponsibility. What the hell were you thinking? It's lucky they didn't blow your head off before the Chechens. How do you expect us to protect you?"

He had ranted a little more when Dan interrupted him.

"How do you know we went to see the Russians?"

Carl paused awkwardly. "Never you mind. It is our job to know," he had said, his anger dissipating. "For Christ's sake just don't tell Brad; that is if he doesn't know already."

Dan had asked him why not, but Carl had been insistent and refused to elaborate. He had also suggested any communication should be directly with Carl and not to talk to Brad. He was in charge of this investigation. Dan had shrugged his shoulders and agreed. They must have fallen out, he had thought vaguely.

Yet here was Brad at the house at this late hour, and as Dan peeked unseen from an upstairs window, he could tell in Brad's expression, even by the soft glow of the lamp, that something was badly wrong.

Brad rang the doorbell stridently and Frank, who was reading up on a pending case in his study, peeped through his spy hole and answered the door.

"Hi Brad," he said, the surprise evident in his voice. "I thought we had an agreement?"

"What do you mean?" replied Brad.

"For the police not to come here."

"Oh. Things have changed. Can I come in?"

"Of course. Is everything aright?"

"There's been a change of plan. Where are they?"

"Upstairs sleeping I guess. What's this about?" There was a note of concern in Frank's voice.

"Can you get them now please?" It was more of an order than a request from Brad. Frank could tell the police officer was on edge, moving on the balls of his feet, like a cat ready to pounce. He had seen the same stress and tension in witnesses many times during cross-examination over the years. It was usually because they were intimidated by the whole experience of appearing in court, but occasionally it was because they were lying.

Before Frank could react, Dan was coming down the stairs. The nurse from the hospital had visited and removed his cast only the day before and he had given up the crutches immediately after. However, he still walked gingerly, almost hopping down the stairs, fearful of putting too much weight on his foot. Marisa, disturbed by the sounds of voices, had also dressed quickly and joined them. They moved out of the wide lobby into the drawing room. As they did so, Dan glanced at Brad. He looked tired and drawn, as if he had not slept in a week, and his normally upbeat and sing-song voice had a serious tone.

"There has been a change of plan. We have to get you out of here. You've stirred up a hornet's nest by going to the Russians. Timayev's clan found out and we think they are on their way even now to eliminate you. We could only keep you secret for so long, even if you hadn't done such a stupid thing." He fingered his small handgun strapped in its holster. "We have to go now, quickly."

"But Brad—" protested Dan.

"There is no time to argue. We have to go now!" The urgency in Brad's voice cut off any thoughts of further protest.

"Okay, okay," said Dan, placatingly. We just need to get a few things together."

"You won't need them . . . I-I mean we will send them on. Come on there's not much time."

Frank glanced at Brad curiously. His face was drained and lined with worry and his hasty, jerky movements betrayed his obvious agitation. But it was his Freudian slip, unnoticed by the others, that finally convinced him.

They were hurrying to leave when Frank stood in the doorway, blocking their exit. Although Brad towered over him, he did not move.

"What the hell are you doing Frank? Get out of my way," urged Brad, moving toward him.

Frank ignored Brad and turned to Dan and Marisa. "I don't think you should go," he said quietly but firmly.

Brad now stood over Frank, his tired, red eyes boring into Frank's face. "Have you lost your mind Frank? We have to go now. The clan is on their way. We need to get them to a safe house. Please Frank, move out of the way."

Dan looked at Brad hovering over Frank. He guessed it was only out of respect for the distinguished prosecutor that Brad did not shove him out of the way.

However, Frank did not budge. He looked up at Brad, sensing panic in the officer's face. "I think you may be the one losing your mind. Has Carl authorized this?"

Brad's eyes flashed with anger and he moved his face threateningly close to Frank's. "Listen to me, you stubborn old fool. I don't need to get Carl's authorization. I can make my own decisions."

Dan stepped in, trying to calm the situation. "Frank, don't worry. We'll go with Brad. It was only a matter of time before they traced us here. You need to get out too. I doubt they will be pleased to see you either. I'll call you. We'll be fine."

Frank still refused to move. "Dan, I'm telling you something is wrong."

Brad finally lost his patience and in one swift movement he whipped out his solid Glock pistol and struck a heavy blow to Frank's forehead. The litigator let out a stifled cry and slumped in the lobby, blood trickling from an ugly gash onto the carpet.

Dan stared at Brad in horror. "What are you doing?" he said lamely, too stunned to fully comprehend the incident he had just witnessed.

Brad's face was set like alabaster. He wiped some residual blood off the barrel of his gun and rolled it in his hands. "We have to go."

"Are you crazy?" Dan's fury was rising as the shock of Brad's action abated. "We can't just leave him here like this."

Brad glared hard at Dan. His expression was hostile, the eyes narrowed. Dan could sense that he was under extreme duress. His jaw twitched and then he did something else that took Dan by surprise. He stepped back a few paces and pointed his handgun directly at Dan's head, but far enough so both he and Marisa were covered.

"Yes, we can," he said simply.

Dan had seen the stance. The officers in the Drug Squad had extensive training in the use of hand weapons. Dan could not even think about trying to evade Brad. His friend would have a bullet in him and he would be dead before he even hit the floor. In any event, he was too disoriented and confused to act. Instinctively Dan and Marisa both raised their hands.

"Let's get going. We don't have much time."

"Brad, what the hell-"

"Shut up!" shouted Brad. His strident demand left no room for argument. He stepped aside, his weapon trained closely on them, both arms straight and gripping the gun tightly, legs slightly apart for balance. He nodded toward the doorway and Dan and Marisa stepped out gingerly into the chilly night air. Dan was still limping and had no chance of escape. What had got into his friend?

Marisa clung to Dan for support. She had always been wary of Brad ever since the interview in the Montreal hospital, although she could not articulate exactly why. Maybe it was the odd questions he had asked, or the way he had looked at her in the hospital. She had tried to explain her misgivings to Dan but he dismissed them completely, even refusing to consider him in that way after the intruder at Frank's old cottage. Brad was a trusted friend, someone he owed a great deal to, and who had helped him when he was at his lowest ebb. As Brad waved his gun at them, marshalling them out into the cool, deserted street, she glanced at Dan. He wore a bemused expression as he limped along, but of more concern to Marisa was the look of fear on his face. Since she had escaped from the clutches of the Chechen gang he had been her protector, saving her life on more than one occasion, almost like a surrogate father to replace the one she had lost. He had shown courage and resilience in protecting her, and she regarded him as almost fearless. Now that bravado was gone, and it gave her a good reason to feel very scared.

Brad herded them along the sidewalk, holding his gun discreetly but still pointed unwaveringly at his prisoners, trying to avoid any attention. He need not have worried, as no one had ventured out into the night. They walked slowly toward the road junction at the end of the street. Parked discreetly in the shadows, away from the light of any street lamp, the large Mercedes was parked, its engine idling lightly. They said they would be there, but as the trio moved toward the car, still unseen, Brad hesitated, grappling with his inner conflict. What was he about to do? Christ, could he ever live with himself after this? He breathed heavily, trying to force himself not to hyperventilate. Maybe, just maybe, if they cut and run now, this nightmare would be over. But of course, it never could be.

His decision was instantly made for him. The rear car door opened. They had seen them. It was too late now. No turning back, even if he had a choice.

Dan swallowed hard with a mixture of surprise and fear when he saw the figure step confidently out of the car and move toward them with an arrogant swagger. For the merest split second he thought about making a dash for it, but his injured foot would not get him far, quite apart from his concern for Marisa. In any event, he realized he could not gamble on the fact that his friend would not shoot him. He cursed himself for blindly refusing to see the signs about Brad that now seemed so obvious. He could no longer predict anything Brad was going to do as he stood there, the gun steady and poised.

CHAPTER 40

The screams continued to reverberate through Carl's headphones, and any second he expected them to be cut cruelly short as the Russians finished him off. When the screams finally subsided, the Chechen was still alive, panting heavily and sobbing.

"Please, tell me what you want!" he beseeched his tormentors, all pretence of the strong, resolute soldier obliterated. Carl continued to listen helplessly, still unsure of whether the Russians would spare him. Whatever they were doing to him, and he preferred not to know, it was effective. He was ready to sing like a canary. He heard Volkov's intimidating voice.

"Yes I know you will comrade, unless you want more of the same."

The threats continued and there were a few more stifled yells as they continued to knock him around, but Sulim began talking fast and within the space of a few minutes he had given enough information to seriously compromise Timayev's operation. Carl broke out into a broad grin. This was the breakthrough they were looking for. However this turned out, Carl did not rate Sulim's life expectancy very highly, he mused silently. The clan member helpfully described what he knew of Timayev's drug empire and its scope within the Toronto area, as well as events leading up to the Montreal deal, although it was clear he did not have the inside knowledge of a major rank in the clan. He mentioned a link to the Chechen rebel forces fighting against the Russians in their homeland, although he was unable to supply details, imploring that Timayev kept his men in the dark on many parts of the operation. He did confirm, however, that the clan provided some form of financing to the rebel forces.

The Russians pressured him in their own unique way, but even under great duress he could not reveal things he did not know. Timayev had clearly been careful in keeping sensitive information confidential, even from trusted employees. Perhaps, Carl reflected, in case of situations such as these. There was a lot of information to process here, but not much in the way of hard, concrete facts. The ideal situation, if Sulim survived the Russians, would be for him to act as a witness for the prosecution and then disappear. Carl was convinced there was enough here for him to apply for the necessary search warrants and finally move in on the gang. The question now was tracking down Timayev, but surely it would only be a matter of time.

His description of the trafficking in girls was meticulous. It was apparent Sulim had been heavily involved in this side of the operation, and the scale and extent of the activity stunned Carl. Although they believed the clan itself was relatively small, Timayev appeared to have a range of contacts, mainly in Eastern Europe and in the former Soviet bloc countries, which appeared to produce a regular supply of naive girls who thought they were coming to Canada for a new and exciting life, only to be sold into sexual slavery. Sulim revealed that the profits from this side of the business were often used to finance the purchase of narcotics for the street market.

Carl felt outraged by what he had heard about the human trafficking. These girls had to be rescued. They had sat back too long, waiting for the right moment. So when Sulim revealed the locations of the four Toronto brothels, he made his decision.

"Amanda, get Judge Irwin on the line, quickly!" he ordered her.

"But sir, it's past midnight."

"What are you, the speaking clock? I know the time. I need him now!" He said it with sarcastic humour but she just gave him an incensed scowl and turned away. He had blown it with those great legs, not that he ever stood a chance anyway. Even so, he thought, maybe it was turning into a good night.

Superior Court Judge Elijah Irwin was finding it hard to sleep, the day's cases running through his mind as it often did, and his wife, hairnet and all, snoring loudly beside him. He thought vacantly, as he often did, about trading her in for a younger model, as some of the other judges had done with their erstwhile wives. The judges were powerful enough and power always attracted attention. Maybe his secretary would come around again when the wife was out of town on one of her charity functions. He was just drifting off with this pleasant thought when he was startled by the strident ringing of the telephone on his bedside cabinet. His wife snorted and shifted position before she settled back into her rhythmic snoring routine. He reached over and grabbed the phone and said in a surly voice, "Yes?"

"Judge Irwin, this is Detective Carl Rodriguez from the Montreal police. I'm in Toronto working on the Timayev case."

"Yes I recall, Detective. Do you know what time it is?" said the judge, trying to sound as indignant as possible.

"I sure do sir." Carl felt like adding sarcastically that the criminals did not keep office hours, but thought better of it. "I'm sorry to call so late but I need an urgent search warrant."

"Now?" replied Judge Irwin, his irritation palpable. "Can't this wait until morning?"

"I think it may be too late sir. We need to act quickly and move on several premises."

"On what grounds?"

"We suspect the houses concerned are being used for the purposes of prostitution and we have reason to believe there are a number of girls there being held against their will."

"What evidence do you have?"

"Listen to this recording sir." As Carl spoke he waved frantically to his communications technician. "I am going to play you a recording of one of the gang members speaking tonight."

"And just how did you come by this recording?"

"We, uh—wire tapped him sir."

"Did you now?" said the judge in a condescending tone. "I certainly hope you had a legitimate reason for doing so, one that will stand up in court."

"I think we have sir," replied Carl not altogether confidently. He would worry about that later. "Please listen."

Carl's technician played the recording and Judge Irwin listened carefully, while Amanda continued to monitor Sulim's interrogation.

The recording lasted no more than five minutes, but when it had finished, Judge Irwin was more accommodating. "Alright Detective, let's go with this. I'm sure you know the procedure. Email me your affidavit and I will sign and send it back. That's if I can get the damn scanner to work. You realize I don't have my secretary with me at half past midnight you know?" he added sarcastically.

That's not what I heard, Carl smiled to himself. "No sir, thank you. I will get on it right away."

Judge Irwin put the phone down and let out a deep heavy sigh. He put on his dressing gown and headed toward his office to boot up his computer. Clearly he wasn't going to get any sleep for the next few hours.

"Good work mister tech guy," said Carl, his mind blank as he tried to remember his name. It had already been a long night but he had the feeling it had only just started.

"Just call me genius, sir. That'll do," the technician replied smugly.

Carl gave a weak smile and turned to Amanda. "I need the Chief Administrator of the Emergency Task Force in Montreal, Charles Deegan, on the line right away. And yes I know what time it is."

Amanda said nothing and tapped furiously at her computer to bring up Deegan's contact details. It took barely thirty seconds before the line was ringing and a sleepy voice came on the line. "Deegan here."

"Charles, it's Carl in Toronto."

The voice brightened. "Hey Carl. How's it going down there?"

"You mean you haven't read the reports? Not too well until we had a bit of . . eh . . good luck. I am getting a search warrant organized through Judge Irwin in the Superior Court. We need a coordinated response team for four properties. I need you to liaise with your counterpart in the Toronto office. I need them organized and ready in the next hour. I figured it would be better coming from you than me, what with you being golf buddies and all."

Deegan paused. "We've only played golf the once. You're not asking for much are you? Four properties and ready in the next hour? That's a tall order, Officer Rodriguez."

Carl grimaced. Deegan always used his official title when he wanted to show his disapproval. "I'm relying on you Charles. We have a breakthrough."

"That's good to hear. You know I will do anything to nail these criminals. Facing Cameron and De Souza's widows was one of the hardest things I've ever done. I'll talk to the Chief immediately and set this up. I'll call you back."

"Thank you Charles." Carl sat back and watched Amanda, still listening intently to the scene in some hidden basement. It had now gone quiet. It appeared the Russians had left Sulim alone for now. They could still hear his heavy, laboured breathing. He had to admire the sensitivity of the microphone on the shirt button. The camera may have expired but the microphone caught everything, and projected it in stereo so it echoed around the cramped control centre. No doubt he was still heavily bound, and very much a prisoner, and this was only a temporary reprieve. Already, however, he had proved immensely valuable.

Carl tapped his password into the laptop and stretched his fingers. Right, he said to himself, now for the affidavit. He thought about where to start and found himself struggling, but as he began to type, the events came flooding back and his fingers struggled to keep up with the barrage of thoughts and events he recalled. He had to get everything down and he would then re-order it to make more sense. It was, after all, a legal document, but he did not have much time.

CHAPTER 41

The interior of the Mercedes was surprisingly spacious, adapted so the passengers could sit in a square similar to the back of a London taxicab. A large ugly grill separated the back from the unseen driver. As Timayev watched, smiling, Dan and Marisa were quickly herded into the back by two of his brutish thugs who sat down beside them, almost squashing them. Marisa looked up and recognized the heavy purple scar on the man's left cheek. She resisted the urge to spit in Alexi's face, particularly when he gave her the leering grin she had despised so much during the traumatic journey from St. John's. Alexi's cohort sat back unobtrusively but she also recognized the dark swarthy features of Hanif "the believer" and touched her neck unconsciously as she recalled the way he had subdued her in the alley.

Timayev and Brad followed them in, gun still in hand. Dan noticed Brad's hand shaking gently as he continued to point the Glock at his former friend, as if waiting for an order from the Chechen gang leader. Timayev paused for a few moments, enjoying the scene, and then he gently pushed the gun downwards.

"That won't be necessary," he said calmly. I think we have them covered."

Alexi and his companion, who Dan recognized from Montreal, grunted approvingly. Brad looked utterly embarrassed and stared out of the window. The car moved off smoothly but the windows were tinted almost black and it was hard to see out into the night. Brad could feel Dan's icy gaze boring into him and he would have offered anything to be as far away from him as possible. God, what had he done? It was all over now anyway. He felt terrible about whacking Frank on his own doorstep, but as soon as the old litigator regained his senses, he would alert Carl, and Brad's betrayal would be common knowledge. In any event, his career in the force was over. It was amazing he had maintained the deception for so long, but then who would have suspected him?

He had never felt so ashamed of what he had done as he did at that moment. He desperately wanted to explain to his friend how he had been entangled in the web of deceit Timayev had woven, lured in with hordes of cash and the promise of more if he just turned a blind eye or gave a tip off every now and then. The money had certainly helped to supplement his police salary, fairly meagre considering the work and the danger they were exposed to day after day. But once he was in, it proved impossible to get out. They knew everything about him and soon the incentives were replaced by threats of retribution. They had placed him in an impossible situation—bring in Dan and Marisa or his family would be exterminated. Brad knew Timayev was serious in his threat and he was forced into an impossible conflict of betraying his friend or allowing his beloved family to be butchered by these terrorists. The choice had taken little thought, but that did not ease his conscience.

Timayev broke the heavy silence. He turned to his prisoners and smiled broadly, showing his recently acquired gold tooth. His movements were agitated and his expression held a glint of mania. His tired eyes and unshaven features suggested he had not slept for days. When he spoke his voice carried an edge. "You never know who you can trust these days. I had the same trouble with Yuri. He should not have spoken to you. I understand the police are still looking for his head. Very unfortunate, because he was one of my most capable employees. You just never know."

Brad interjected. "I'm really sorry Dan. They have Laura and the children. I had no choice."

Dan stared at him, his voice full of contempt. "Save it Brad. There's always a choice. How can you live with yourself?"

Brad said nothing and lapsed into a sullen silence, staring out of the window.

"I have to compliment you both on your ability to stay alive," continued Timayev. "As a former soldier I know all about struggling to survive against the odds. You two seem to have nine lives, but your run of luck is about to come to an end. Very sad, because Marisa you are looking really well, though I am sure you will be happy to join your father."

Marisa exploded in anger and launched herself toward him, wanting to claw his eyes out. Hanif, sitting next to her, anticipated her move and hauled her back with ease, pushing her like a limp rag doll into her seat. Timayev barely flinched.

"You murdering animal!" she yelled. "You killed my father. He was innocent! He had nothing to do with this."

"Innocence is subjective Marisa. If your father had not come to Canada looking for you he would not have found Mr Huberman here, and Mr Huberman would not have caused the trouble he did. But I agree, he had the best intentions. If it is any comfort, we had come to eliminate *him*." He crooked a finger at Dan. "Your father was in the wrong place at the wrong time."

Marisa glared at him, her eyes full of hatred and rage. Hanif held a strong arm over her chest to prevent her trying any more wild lunges. She struggled to push it away but he held it there firmly and effortlessly, smiling as he did so and pushing harder against her so she felt the air being forced out of her lungs. She ceased struggling and he relaxed slightly, but did not take his arm away.

"So what do you propose to do with us now?" asked Dan, almost certain of the answer.

Timayev looked at him closely, his eyes narrowed, full of hostility. As he moved closer, Dan could perceive the gang leader's fragile temperament. He looked as if he would lash out at any time. "You, Mr Huberman, have caused me a lot of trouble. I warned you to stay away, gave you every incentive not to interfere in matters of no concern to you. Anything that happens to you tonight you have brought on yourself."

"I had to interfere. I'm a private investigator, it's my job."

Timayev stared at Dan, his manic expression unnerving. "Your job is done, comrade, and your payment comes tonight. I owe you a slow and agonizing death. It's long overdue."

Brad groaned inwardly and turned to Timayev with a timid expression. "Akhmad, I don't need to be here now. I did what you asked—I delivered them to you."

Timayev's tone betrayed his annoyance at the interruption. "Yes you did."

Brad, a hint of hope in his voice, said, "I held up my part of the deal. Is my family safe?"

"Of course they are safe. You should know me better than that. They were merely collateral. You honoured our deal. You are free of me." He gave the merest hint of a nod to Alexi.

Brad, not noticing this, gave a hopeful smile. "So I'm free to go?" His smile turned to a look of panic-stricken horror as he saw Alexi whip out his gun and point it directly at Brad. Hanif edged forward, arm still draped across Marisa, but also watching Dan closely in case he was foolish enough to intervene. However, Dan also edged back in his seat, fearful for Brad but mesmerized by the gun. Surely the Chechen bodyguard would not shoot Brad here in the confined space of a speeding car?

As if to read his thoughts Timayev whispered something incomprehensible through the grille separating the driver and the car began gently slowing down. It was hard to see through the windows exactly where they were, but Dan judged from the speed of the car they were on a highway. Brad must have guessed their intentions because with his quick reflexes he grabbed the small handgun and tried to twist it out of Alexi's hands.

Alexi was momentarily surprised but he too reacted quickly and held onto the gun. Both men now had a strong grip on the weapon but Alexi's hand was curled around the trigger and Brad had the barrel, pushing it away with the surprising strength of a desperate man. Marisa screamed and curled into a ball as the two men struggled, grunting and heaving, their bodies pushing against each other like two rams locking horns. The frenzied struggling went on for barely fifteen seconds, but felt to Dan like a slow motion movie as the thoughts of the gun going off any second raced through his head. Suddenly Brad tired, even in his fight for survival unable to match the raw strength of the larger man, and Alexi prised his grip off the barrel. In doing so, the gun fell to the floor with a metallic rattle. Brad reached down to grab it but with his attention no longer focused on Alexi, the Chechen quickly grabbed him by the neck and slammed him so hard against the door that it flew open. Although the Mercedes was gradually slowing down it was still travelling at considerable speed and it veered crazily as the driver fought control. Brad was now hanging half out of the door but grabbed at one of the passenger handles on the interior ceiling and hung on grimly. With another quiet word from Timayev the driver, now having regained control, began to speed up again and Brad did not have a strong grip. Most of the weight of his body was hanging outside the car and he desperately tried to haul himself back in. He pulled hard, the cold rushing wind tearing at his hair, but Alexi was too strong.

He kicked hard against Brad's chest and Brad gasped as his breath was violently expelled from his lungs. He felt like his chest was collapsing and felt his grip loosen, but somehow he managed to stay in the car. However in that instant Alexi retrieved the gun bouncing around at his feet and levelled it directly at Brad's temple at point blank range.

As if in slow motion, Dan saw Alexi take aim and begin to squeeze the trigger, while seeing the look of sheer terror on Brad's face, his eyes wide and mouth agape ready to scream. Without thinking Dan pushed past a startled Hanif and lunged at Alexi's outstretched arm, which held the gun poised and ready. He pushed the arm away just as the gun went off with an ear splitting bang that left everyone in the car deaf for several minutes. The bullet avoided Brad's head but lodged deep in his left shoulder. He let out an agonized cry and his left hand, still gripping the passenger handle, twitched and lost its grip. He tumbled out of the car and rolled along the freeway and was instantly hit with a dull thump by a car speeding behind that could not swerve in time to avoid him. Timayev saw through the still swinging car door the vehicle that had hit Brad screech to a halt a few hundred yards from where Brad's twitching figure lay, pushed to the hard shoulder. Timayev waved the driver on as Alexi reached out and grabbed the handle and slammed the door shut.

Carl had finished writing the affidavit in less than fifteen minutes. It was disorganized and rambling, and certainly would not win any plaudits for coherency, but it set out the salient points. He whipped it out of the printer and signed it and handed it to Amanda. "Witness please," he said brusquely, hardly noticing her legs now, so focused was he on getting the document to Judge Irwin. She scanned it quickly, made one correction, signed and handed it back. He put it through the scanner and e-mailed the scanned file to the Judge and then he waited, pacing the tiny command room impatiently. Things were still quiet in the basement, and even Sulim's heavy breathing had slowed to a more relaxed rhythm. They heard the occasional scraping, like wood on concrete. He was probably trying to escape from his bonds, and dragging the chair as he did so, Carl surmised.

It seemed an age before his laptop beeped to indicate receipt of an email, although it had been little more than ten minutes. He quickly scanned the email. It was from Judge Irwin but there was no text, just an attachment. He clicked on the attachment and when he saw the Judge's signed search warrant authorization, he clenched his fists and uttered a triumphant "Yes!"

Amanda took the cue and within seconds Deegan was back on the line.

"Charles, we are good to go. How's it going?"

"I've spoken to the Chief and he was pissed about getting out of bed, but didn't waste any time. They should have four emergency response teams assembled within the next half hour. Forward me the search warrant. He won't move without it. Got his fingers burnt a few years back. Do you know if Timayev will be at one of the properties? We've got to cut off the head to kill the beast."

"I can't say for sure. We don't have a search warrant on his apartment yet. He may still be in hiding."

Deegan drew a heavy sigh. "It would be best if he was there. Let's hope the evidence we find at the houses will lead us to him. We don't want him to slip away again."

"We're getting closer to him, Charles. Thanks again."

Deegan rang off and Carl quickly forwarded on the email with the scanned search warrant to Deegan's address. He leaned back in his chair, hands behind his back and allowed himself a satisfied smile. Everything was falling into place.

His moment of relaxation ended abruptly when his cell phone buzzed into life and he pulled it out of his jacket pocket. He frowned when he saw the caller, mainly because after the events of the last few days, it was so unexpected. Why was Brad calling him?

CHAPTER 42

The pain was excruciating and Brad could not move his legs. They lay there, a limp, bloody mess, blood seeping on the dirty gravel and concrete of the hard shoulder, sharp, splintered bone protruding out from the shin area of his right leg, which was twisted at an unnatural angle. Strangely, there was no pain from this hideous looking injury, but his legs were completely unresponsive. He knew instantly he was paralysed, although not fully, as his upper body was still functioning and was the source of his agony. When he had fallen out of the car he had tumbled at high speed on the road and been struck a glancing blow by another car which had pushed him onto the hard shoulder. Miraculously however, his head had not been struck and he had not lost consciousness. The only trauma his head had received was a number of deep lacerations when he rolled at high speed after falling out of the car.

He knew he was critically injured, however. He could almost feel the life seeping out of him, as the blood dripped steadily from his leg wound. It was his left shoulder, though, that caused him the greatest pain. The shot had been so close it felt like a red hot poker had been forced into his shoulder blade and left there as it seared the flesh. The open wound was also shedding blood steadily. He gritted his teeth and he knew that any moment he would pass out from the pain. He heard the high pitched siren of an ambulance in the distance, but he knew it was too late. The car that hit him had stopped but it was just two lads and when they saw the extent of his injuries they must have panicked and driven off. At least they had called for help.

He had always imagined his death would be as an old man dying guilt-free in his sleep, but the physical pain was matched by the anguish he felt over his actions. Maybe there was time for one small reparation, but he had to be quick as he could feel the overwhelming exhaustion enveloping him, urging him to sleep.

With an effort of will, he used his good arm to reach inside his jacket pocket and take out his cell phone. The small phone was battered but in its leather case it appeared to have survived intact. Desperately trying to focus through the blur of pain, he located Carl's number and pressed to connect with his bloodstained thumb.

As the phone rang for what seemed an age, Brad could taste blood in his mouth, and his breath came in short gasps.

"Hello Brad." There was no mistaking the surprise in Carl's voice.

"C-Carl, p-please l-listen." His whole body felt as if it was due to shut down any second. He fought the urge to close his eyes. He had to get the message to Carl before it was too late. "Timayev has Dan and Marisa. They are taking them to the c-company's industrial unit west of Buttonville Airport. Y-You have to get there quickly." Brad paused, wheezing heavily, the sour taste of the blood in his mouth growing stronger.

Carl let out an audible gasp. "Man, you sound rough. Where the hell are you?" Carl put his cell on speaker-phone and frantically waved at Amanda as they spoke. She tapped away furiously to retrieve the address from the investigation's database.

"It doesn't matter now. I-I'm sorry Carl. I was their inside man."

Carl paused briefly. "I know Brad."

"You do?" The pain and the exhaustion were closing in. His vision was becoming blurred, as if he was looking at the world through a long tunnel.

"We always wondered why Timayev seemed to be one step ahead of us, even after Kahnawake. I began to suspect you a few days ago but I couldn't be certain so I kept you on the team hoping you would lead us to them."

"W-What have I done?" The anguish in his voice was not just from the pain.

"You did the right thing telling me. We are onto it. You need to come in to help us. I'll arrange a driver to pick you up. You sound like you are already on the road." Carl could hear the occasional roar of a car as it thundered by, and in the distance the low sound of an ambulance siren.

"N-No I can't come in, it's too late." As the blood drained from his body, he had a new sensation, a tingling in his fingers and toes that spread rapidly to his hands and feet until it turned to a numb feeling, as if they were being slowly turned into blocks of ice. And he felt cold. God he was so cold now.

"Carl. They threatened Laura and the kids. P-Please don't let him harm them. You will protect them won't you?" He closed his eyes, his breath now in short, shallow gasps. The sound of the emergency vehicles was closer, more strident.

"Brad," responded Carl, "You need to tell me where you are so we can bring you in. There's still a chance you can stop this. I will vouch for you in court. I'll tell them how you were coerced with threats to your family. Whatever happens, I promise on my life I will do everything I can to protect them. How much time do we have?"

There was only the wailing siren and background noise at the other end. "Brad, Brad, answer me!" yelled Carl into the phone.

But it was too late. The urge to drift away, to escape the pain and the guilt was too much. Brad did not even hear Carl's impassioned promise. The phone had already dropped out of his lifeless hand.

"Deegan here."

"Charles, it's Carl, we have a new problem. Timayev isn't going to be at any of the houses."

"How do you know?"

"Because he's on his way to the company's offices near Buttonville Airport. And he has Dan and Marisa."

"Deegan let out a deep sigh. "Jesus how did that happen? I thought you had them in a safe house?"

Carl thought about that briefly. He knew he had messed up. He should have moved Dan and Marisa out of Frank's house as soon as he suspected Brad's betrayal. He did not have the resources in his team to guard them day and night, and there was no obvious alternative available. He had never considered Timayev, in hiding as he was, would make such an audacious kidnap attempt, even though Brad must have told him Dan and Marisa were still alive. Christ, he had not even mentioned it to Frank! He could try and justify to himself that he had not done so until he could be certain Brad was their man, especially considering Brad's distinguished service, the last man Carl would have expected. The fact remained however, he had made a fatal error of judgement, one which had caused his key witnesses to be at the mercy of the Chechen gang leader.

"Let's talk about that later please. I need you to get another team together and fast. We don't have much time."

Deegan's irritation was palpable. "For God's sake Carl, the Chief Administrator has just called me to say they are on their way. These guys are fast, but getting another team together is going to be difficult. Even four was a stretch. We are hoping we don't encounter too much resistance at the houses. The team is spreading itself too thin, especially if it's going to take on this gang again. I don't want to be responsible for another Kahnawake."

"How many men can we pull in?" Carl glanced at his watch. It was nearly one o'clock in the morning. He suddenly felt extremely tired.

"I don't know. I will find out but at this time of night it won't be many. Not enough to take on Timayev's gang while the other teams are working the other targets."

Carl's shoulders sagged. He expected as much. They would never get to Dan and Marisa on time, but he couldn't just leave them to the mercy of that barbarian. He recalled the photographs he had seen of the headless corpse of Yuri Umarov. Timayev did not take kindly to betrayal, and he had a score to settle with them both in different ways. He glanced at Amanda, her back turned to him, those shapely legs tucked out of sight under the desk. After getting Deegan on the line for Carl she had returned to her listening brief, but for the last hour or so there had been very little activity since Sulim had spilt his guts. Maybe the Russians had everything they needed from him, or maybe they would finish off their interrogation shortly. He watched her listening intently, totally focused and professional. Then the idea came to him.

"There is another way," he ventured to Deegan.

"Another way?" Deegan questioned, his irritation still evident.

"We could ask the Russians to help."

Carl could almost picture Deegan fall off his chair. "Are you crazy? It could turn into a civil war. It's far too volatile. We don't know how the Russians would react."

"What's the alternative Charles? We can't let them escape us again. We can bring them down this time . . and I won't give up on Dan and Marisa. They're too valuable."

Deegan reflected for a long moment, while Carl waited hopefully. Even Amanda and the tech guy were watching him closely now. "It's madness, Carl, we can't take the risk."

"Charles, this is our one chance! We have to take it!" Carl felt his voice rising.

Another pause from Deegan. "How do we make contact with the Russians?"

"Does that mean you agree?"

"No, it means I am crazy even considering it. We hardly have many options do we?"

"Charles, we need to decide quickly. You give me the green light and I am sure we can get to Volkov quickly. Just say the word."

"I need to speak to the Ontario Chief. He will probably snap my head off. It's his call."

"Then speak to him quickly Charles, please. It might already be too late."

Deegan again adopted an irritated tone. "Carl, let's be clear on one thing. If this goes badly wrong, it will be your neck on the chopping block."

"Understood Charles. I always wanted to be a traffic cop on Mont-Royal and de l'Esplanade."

"Good. Then we understand each other. Stand by."

Carl stared at his phone wondering. He had already taken plenty of risks over the last few days. He could see his fifteen years in the Drug Squad crashing down in flames. What the hell? Maybe it was time for a change. There was a job to be done and he could not wait.

"Amanda, can you make contact with Volkov?"

Amanda gave him an odd look, but did not question him. "You're the boss," she sighed.

Since Olivia had tried to attack Akhmad, the gang leader had shown little interest in sleeping with her, which suited the young Macedonian girl just fine. However she had been punished for her indiscretion. Rahmon had taken great delight in striking her several times with the bamboo cane he sometimes used on the girls, and starving her for three days. All the time she was expected to service the clients in the usual manner, but she had toughened herself to the cruelty and hardship. She even tried to convince herself she had grown stronger from it. What was harder to overcome was the sense of gloom and despondency that had settled over her since hearing about Marisa's demise. Every day she thought about the Bulgarian girl and how she had stood up to these monsters.

As she lay in bed trying to send her thoughts elsewhere as an overweight, slovenly businessman in red polka dot boxer shorts began pawing at her, she reflected on the irony of finding the only true friend she had ever had in such an evil place as this. Her reverie was interrupted by an incessant thumping deep in the bowels of the large Victorian house.

The balding, corpulent businessman paused as the sound of stomping feet and distant, raised voices grew louder. He turned to Olivia with a leery grin which turned to a frown as the sound of a general commotion grew closer. Annoyed at the interruption he got out of the bed and, still in his tatty boxers, softly ambled to the door to find out what was going on.

He heard the rush of feet outside the door fractions of a second before it suddenly burst open and in stormed three men in helmets and combat uniforms. The businessman was knocked backwards and collapsed to the floor in a fleshy heap. Instantly one of the men jumped on him and pinned his arms down with his knees. He deftly turned him over so that his double chins rested on the threadbare carpet. Despite the fat man's vigorous protests, the combat officer pulled his chubby arms together behind his back and expertly snapped a pair of steel handcuffs over his wrists.

"Do you realize who I am?" the man protested. "How dare you treat me this way!"

The officer leaned over so his head was close to the businessman's perspiring face still resting on the floor. Even through the helmet his expression was clearly one of contempt. "I don't care who you are—not until I book you for procuring the services of a minor for prostitution. But I am sure your wife would want to know where you've been tonight. She is going to find out anyway."

The man's pale face turned as red as his shorts and spittle drooled onto the dirty carpet. "Y-You wouldn't," he stammered. "Would you?"

"Just try me," retorted the officer. He hauled the man to his feet and pushed him out into the landing, to be surrounded by other combat officers and still wearing only his boxers, his dignity completely destroyed. "Read him his rights and get him outta here," the officer instructed his colleague. "Bloody pervert."

Olivia watched this scene unfold with a mixture of bewilderment and amusement at her client's humiliation. Curiously, despite the fact so many men had seen her naked over the last few months, she felt a touch of embarrassment and pulled the thin bedclothes over her body.

One of the officers took off his helmet and looked at her kindly. He found a large blanket in the wardrobe next to the bed and draped it round her. As he gently coaxed her out of the room he muttered reassuringly, "Don't worry miss, it's all over now."

He guided her gently down the stairs as other officers milled around them. The whole house was a hubbub of frenzied activity. Some officers were leading away other clients, most of them partly naked, no attempt made by the officers to protect their dignity. The girls, by contrast, were guided gently but firmly out of the house into waiting police cars, flashing blue and red lights turning the quiet street into a scene like downtown Vegas.

The officer spoke quietly and with compassion. "We are going to take you to the hospital to get checked out but we will need to take statements. There's a lot you need to tell us about the people who did this to you. Is there anyone you would like me to call?"

Olivia just shook her head. There was no-one to call. She did not really have any friends and her family was a lost cause.

As she stepped through the front door into the small front garden of the huge Victorian house, she shivered with the cold, despite the blanket. Behind her she heard a volley of shouting and the sounds of a scuffle. She looked back into the doorway and saw Rahmon screaming curses, a combination of English and his native Tajik tongue, and he was waving a large carved ceremonial sword he had sometimes threatened the girls with. He slashed it through the air at the three officers surrounding him and they had to smartly dodge the heavy sword to avoid being decapitated. However, the officers moved in, waiting for their opportunity.

As the arc of the swing headed toward the ground, the first officer rushed in and kicked his legs away just below the knees. As he fell heavily the second officer grabbed the heavy sword and pulled it away from Rahmon who had eased his grip to break his fall. As the huge Tajik rolled awkwardly the third officer pounced on him and delivered a stunning blow from his Taser to his chest, a burst of electric blue light illuminating his face. The huge Tajik jerked and thrashed about and the officer delivered another charge for good measure. The thrashing died to a twitch and a final moan before Rahmon lay on the floor motionless, like a wild animal taken down by big game hunters.

She watched the drama unfold, like some of the other girls, and as they watched him fall, several of them gave a muted cheer. However, as she looked back at the house for the last time, a huge surge of emotion began coursing through her, and unable to hold back any longer, she broke into an uncontrollable flood of tears.

CHAPTER 43

The driver, having regained control of the vehicle, continued to speed away at Timayev's urging. Alexi took the butt of the gun and whipped it across Dan's face. Although it was small, it was solid and Dan recoiled from the sharp, stinging blow. He felt blood dripping from the bridge of his nose, but he was relieved to feel it was not broken. His first instinct was to go for the powerfully built Chechen, but Hanif held him back and glowered menacingly at him.

"Don't even think about it," Hanif warned him, clearly hoping he would.

Marisa glared at Timayev, her eyes full of hatred. She said nothing but Timayev returned the stare and she quickly backed down. There was a wild look in his eyes that she had not seen before, a look of animal rage, as if he was possessed and no longer in control of his senses. Whatever cruelties he had inflicted on her and the other girls, he had done so calmly and unemotionally, always in control. The facade of intellectual detachment was gone. The Chechen gang leader was out for blood.

Timayev turned his baleful gaze to Dan. "Now, where was I? Oh yes I remember, I was telling you about how you were going to suffer a slow and agonizing death. We have everything prepared for you both."

"Give it up Timayev, the police are onto you. It's only a matter of time before they track you down. Let us go and you might save yourself a lot of trouble." Even as Dan spoke the words, he knew they rang hollow, even to himself.

Timayev let out a throaty, contemptuous laugh. "Do you expect me to throw myself at the mercy of the police? I bought them, they work for me."

"I think you just terminated your top inside employee."

"There will be more to follow his lead. Greed is infectious in the police force. Maybe it's because I make more in one day than they earn in a year."

"Not any more. Your operation is in decline. Your days as a drug baron are numbered."

Dan observed a slight twitch and a reddening of the cheeks, as if he had struck a nerve. There was a long silence and when Timayev spoke again his voice was thick with suppressed anger. "What happens to my operation will cease to be your concern after tonight. You will not be around to see it."

Dan felt the blood dripping down lazily from the gash on his nose, and he wiped it away with the back of his hand. Hanif and Alexi were watching him like hawks, ready to pounce at the slightest sign of aggression from the private investigator. Marisa was wedged in between them and could hardly move against their solid weight.

Timayev turned to her again with a piercing stare, those deep grey eyes she remembered so well hard and unflinching. Marisa felt a chill run down her spine. Despite her earlier outburst, she was calmer, and remained fearful of him. When she had been imprisoned in the house, the girls had been conditioned, almost brainwashed, into regarding him with utter fear and respect. He had such an intimidating presence that many of the girls felt physically sick when he was around, so scared were they of him. He cultivated this image carefully, and it was so convincing that even now, despite her futile lunge at him, the sight of him so close set her pulse racing and beads of sweat began to form around her brow.

"I am very disappointed with you Marisa. You were one of my best girls. Some of my clients have been asking after you. I think you made a good impression. You always left them wanting more," he taunted. "I thought maybe I would share you around the men before we killed you, but it just wouldn't be efficient. We have work to do. I'll spare you that at least."

Marisa resisted the impulse to spit at him, the old fears holding her back.

"Where are you taking us?" interrupted Dan.

"I am taking you to my company building. You'll have the honour of a starring role in our propaganda video."

Alexi and Hanif both gave a short, scornful laugh. Dan glanced at Marisa. She looked scared.

Timayev continued. "Not only did you almost single-handedly destroy the single biggest deal we had ever undertaken, preventing the placement of much needed funds to our army's fight for freedom for our great nation, but you went to see the Russians." He paused for emphasis. "Our sworn enemy the Russians.' He spat out the last word with contempt. "Even our mutual friend Mr Miller had no idea why you went to see Volkov and his petty band of criminals."

"That's rich, coming from you, the biggest criminal in this city," shot back Dan.

Alexi, with a nasty snarl, raised his gun threateningly as if to strike Dan again, but Timayev shook his head at his bodyguard. "Leave it Alexi, he'll soon show some respect when he's begging for mercy."

Marisa tried to peer out of the windows but they were too heavily tinted. All she could see were the blurred, opaque lights of street lamps and the passing of other cars. It was impossible to tell where they were, only that they were moving fast.

Timayev turned back to Dan and pointed an accusing finger. "You Mr Huberman are officially an enemy of the State of Chechnya, and you must be punished."

"So put me on trial."

"You are already on trial. I am the judge, jury and executioner. You are guilty of treason against our great nation, and it is my patriotic duty to see that justice is done.' His eyes burned with a fervour Dan found deeply unsettling. "There is only one way to deal with infidel like you,' continued Timayev. I believe the word you use is immolation."

Marisa, listening intently, did not understand and looked at Dan questioningly. She saw his face freeze with fear.

"Jesus, you're going to burn us alive," he gasped.

"Of course, it is an established and long practised ritual in the Islamic world. Everything is set up to film your execution. We even have special fireproof microphones to record your screams. We plan to distribute the video on the Internet worldwide and send it to the global media. I am sure Al-Jazeera would be interested in receiving a copy. You and Marisa will become sacrifices in the fight for Chechen glory and we will strike fear in the hearts of our enemies! You will be immortalized!" Timayev was in full flow now, talking as much to himself as to anyone else in the cramped confines of the Mercedes. His expression was of wide-eyed triumph, as if he were already visualizing the fear his infamous video would spread amongst his enemies.

"You've lost your mind!" cried Dan.

"On the contrary, I have never been so sure of my actions. You should be honoured that I am personally overseeing your execution. Even Yuri did not get that level of attention. But considering the crimes you have committed, nothing will give me greater pleasure to watch you burn. It's a form of execution that has been used since Roman Times, well before the witch hunts of medieval Europe. Death by fire is probably the most agonizing and horrible death it is possible for humans to suffer, which is why the threat of it acted as such a useful deterrent. Did you know that properly applied so different parts of the body burn progressively, it can take victims up to two hours to finally die? Fortunately for you we don't have that long. Even so, it is far more interesting to watch than a bullet to the brain."

Marisa had heard enough. Although she felt the car slowing down, it was still moving fast. Even so, she lurched for the door in a futile attempt to escape. Hanif easily overpowered her and slammed her back in her seat. He grabbed a lock of her auburn hair and yanked her head back, and his other hand grabbed her just below the chin, his thumb and index finger squeezing tight on her jaw.

"It'll be a shame to let that pretty face melt like candle wax. Can't we take her one more time Akhmad?"

"Maybe, if we have time," replied Timayev. "We could film that too. Purely for our own entertainment, of course."

"You really are savages," spat Dan.

Timayev's eyes were cold and hard as steel. "You underestimate us Huberman. Savages by their very nature don't know what they are doing. We, on the other hand, know exactly what we are doing. We are in a war, and you are a casualty of that war. But unlike the millions who die in wars around the world every year, your death will not go unnoticed. You will be famous, at least for a while. You might even go viral."

The Mercedes slowed down further and they could feel the car making a turn into a driveway and down a ramp.

The Chechen prisoner was still tied up in the restaurant basement. He could stay there and rot for all Volkov cared. Once his interrogation team got at him, the gang member had talked freely and openly about Timayev's operations. However, despite his comrade's persuasive techniques, the prisoner had not been able to provide any really useful up to date information. Maybe he had been in custody too long, and his comrades had clearly abandoned him, but he was unable to provide any information that would support the private investigator's claim Timayev's clan was preparing to break the tacit, unspoken pact that neither party would interfere with the other.

Maybe he should have used the same interrogation tactics on Huberman and the girl, then the truth would have been revealed.

Even so, Volkov was uncomfortable. Sitting in the darkened lounge sipping vodka, he pondered the situation. Clearly the prisoner knew nothing. The information he had given about Timayev's business operations was helpful but limited. He clearly had been kept out of the strategic management of the clan and had only limited knowledge of its activities. His main expertise, which he was happy to talk about, was on the human trafficking side, and this only served to support Volkov's utter contempt for Timayev and his gang. However, he still could not be sure if the Chechens planned to attack his operation. A pre-emptive strike might still be necessary, but he had to consider this drastic action very carefully. An error in judgement could be disastrous. In the few years he had been in Canada, Volkov's operations had survived and prospered by virtue of the Russian taking a low profile, conservative approach, avoiding any activities that could draw attention to the Family's activities in Toronto. Launching an apparently unprovoked attack on the Chechen gang would be completely contrary to the strategy that had served them so well.

He needed more information, to talk further to his underground contacts and check if Huberman's claims were true. Everything he had said about the Montreal drug bust had checked out but so far none of his sources had confirmed any attack on the Russians. Occasionally his sources proved unreliable and he did not want to make a mistake on this. He needed more information to make a decision, but he had to do it quickly.

As he got up to head toward the basement to supervise a further interrogation session, his Blackberry beeped and vibrated. He reached inside his jacket and peered at the device. The numbers glowing back at him in the gloom were unrecognizable. He frowned. Only a select few had his direct cell number, and this number was unfamiliar.

"Who is this?" he said, his voice cold and hard.

"This is Carl Rodriguez of the Montreal Drug Squad. I am working here in Toronto."

Volkov paused, unsure of how to react. How the hell did he get this number? Did he have an inside man in Volkov's gang? No, surely not—they were all thoroughly vetted and clean. "What do you want?" His voice betrayed his hostility.

"I want to make a proposal to you."

Volkov paused again. He had to tread carefully. "What proposal?"

"We know you have the Chechen held prisoner."

Volkov took a deep breath. He should have known. No use denying it. A simple case of entrapment, but he had a feeling it was not quite so simple. "You practically handed him to us."

"Kidnapping, false imprisonment, assault, these are serious charges."

"Are you trying to threaten me?"

"No Boris, I am just setting out the facts. Like I said, I have a proposal for you, but there isn't much time."

Volkov sat back and relaxed, sipping at his vodka. "I thought the police might be behind it and I was even more certain when we saw the ease with which we collected him. So I am guessing you did not deliver him to us merely so you could lay some outrageous accusations on us. It will not stick, comrade. We have access to better lawyers than you. So tell me about this proposal of yours?"

"I need you to help us liquidate Timayev's operation."

"How?"

"The Drug Squad is planning to make a raid on their office. We need your team to help in the assault—tonight."

Volkov nearly choked on his vodka. "You are asking us to help you with your dirty work. Allow me to reflect a moment on the irony of such a request, comrade. What if I refuse?"

"Then I guess we will have to test just how good your lawyers really are."

"I am not looking for trouble, Detective, but I find your request extraordinary, and quite impossible. I run a restaurant and my activities are generally peaceful. I do not have the inclination to engage in a futile civil war."

Back in the cramped operations van, Carl paused and considered his options. It was a long shot, and a risky one to ask for Volkov's help, and as he had feared, the Russian was not in a mood to cooperate.

"Let me be straight with you Boris. Timayev's clan are holding two people who are very important to us. I believe you know them."

"Who?"

"Dan Huberman the private investigator and Marisa Dimitrov, the Bulgarian girl."

Volkov gave a short laugh. "Should I know them?"

"Of course you do Boris. They visited you the other night."

Volkov hesitated, taken aback. "I guess your spies are everywhere Detective. But why should I help them? They came to me stirring up trouble, suggesting the Chechens are just about to attack us.

I have not found anything to suggest any truth in this, and our mutual friend Sulim knows nothing. Whatever the Chechens do to them is of no concern to me. It will probably save me the trouble."

"We need your help Boris. You have my word that any charges relating to Sulim's abduction will be quietly dropped—as long as you don't harm him."

"First you threaten me and now you are pleading with me Detective. It suggests to me that you are not in a very strong bargaining position."

"I'm offering you a clean slate. We won't hassle you."

"I will consider your offer very carefully Detective. I will consult with my Family and you will have my answer in the morning."

There was an edge to Carl's voice that betrayed his tension. "The morning is too late. I need to know now."

Then I'm afraid, Detective Rodriguez, the answer is no."

Carl banged the desk in frustration. His pizza had given him indigestion. The call to Volkov had not gone well. It would be hard to pin anything on Volkov because inevitably there would be an investigation into how the Russian Mafia had found out about Sulim being moved to the court when prisoner movement was usually highly confidential. Even worse, it would be difficult to explain why it had been so easy for the gang to abduct Sulim. He had called in a few favours and twisted a few arms to engineer Sulim's capture, and he had hoped to use it as a bargaining tool with Volkov. Jesus, the Special Investigations Unit would have a field day if they investigated this one and he was under no illusions it would be his ass hung out to dry. If this blew up then the accusing fingers would be pointing in only one direction.

He had misjudged the Mafia boss. Despite his young age and relative inexperience as a crime lord, he had not been intimidated by Carl's threats. He was far too shrewd. He was well aware that Carl had placed himself in a vulnerable position by delivering up Sulim.

The tech guy and Amanda glanced at him sympathetically. He was running short of options. He stuck his head in his hands and pulled anxiously at his short hair, as if trying to dislodge it from his head. He felt very old and tired. Why the hell hadn't he pulled Dan and Marisa out of Frank's house immediately when he discovered Brad's betrayal, he reflected ruefully. There would be time for inquests later. They had to reach Dan and Marisa before it was too late, but they were going to have to do it without the Russians.

His phone began to vibrate again and he recognized Deegan's number.

"Hi Charles."

"Carl, how did it go with Volkov?"

"Not too good. He is refusing to play along with us. We are going to have to go it alone."

"Damn. I have some more bad news for you. There's been some trouble at one of the houses and the Chief has pulled in back up. Apparently the occupants did not want to give up their girls without a fight. Guns fired on both sides. No word on casualties, but it means we're on our own, at least for now."

"Jesus, you mean we have no task force support at all?"

"Not until they have sealed off the four houses and put the situation to bed; which could take some time."

"Charles, they have Dan and Marisa. God only knows if they are even still alive. We can't go in there without the task force. Timayev's men are trained guerrilla fighters. You know their level of firepower from Montreal. If I send in ordinary policemen with limited weapons training they will be lambs to the slaughter. We have Timayev in our grasp but I need an elite force!"

Deegan's tone was sympathetic. "If it's any help Carl, I have an open line with the Chief and he will keep me informed of developments. As soon as we have men available they will be redeployed. I can't say any more than that."

Dan kneaded his temples. "Let me speak to him!"

"No Carl," cautioned Deegan. "You asked me to be the liaison and I agreed. I'm on your side but we have to be patient, keep a cool head. I'll keep you posted."

Deegan rang off and Dan stared at his phone. He felt his stomach acids rising, and not just with the pizza. This could not get any worse.

Amanda turned to him, a concerned look on her face. "Sir, there is activity coming through." She put the audio feed on speaker and once again the sounds coming from the secret transmitter in Volkov's basement transmitted loud and clear. The unmistakable heavy accent of Boris Volkov filled the tiny capsule.

"You've had your chance, now it really is time to put you out of your misery!"

Once again the Chechen's chilling screams reverberated around the van.

CHAPTER 44

The driver reached up and pressed a control attached to the sun visor and the wide steel door to the underground parking lot rolled up and open. The car lurched down the ramp and screeched to a halt. The driver stepped out and held the door open for Timayev to get out. Alexi followed Timayev out of the car and then waved at Dan and Marisa to get out, his gun trained unwaveringly at Dan's temple. Hanif pushed them out and stood behind them, his menacing bulk looming over them, ready to pounce if they tried to make a break for it.

They found themselves inside a cavernous but empty and dimly lit underground parking lot. Dan knew that any attempt to escape was futile. Even if he wrestled out of their grasp and ran off as fast as his damaged foot would allow, he was certain Alexi would prove to be a more than capable marksman. He would be dead before he hit the floor. In any event, he would not leave Marisa. He looked around. It was out of the question.

The driver got back in and the Mercedes spun around, and with a light screech of tyres it stormed back up the ramp and disappeared into the cool night. Timayev directed the party toward a small door set inconspicuously in the corner, a battered old entrance set within dull, oil streaked walls. Their footsteps echoed and Alexi's barking at his prisoners reverberated in the enhanced acoustics of the empty space, bouncing off the thick, stubby pillars.

"Get a move on," Alexi snarled, as Hanif manhandled the pair, pushing them forward, trying to catch up with Timayev, who was striding purposefully toward the door. He swung open the heavy door and held it open until Alexi caught up and took over. Leaning his considerable bulk against the open door, he motioned with his gun and Dan and Marisa stepped through into a narrow, badly lit stairwell, closely followed by Hanif. Alexi stepped through and the door, clearly a fire door with its high tension metal springs, slowly swung shut with a dull clang.

Dan was expecting to go up the stairs, but Timayev led them down, where it was even more gloomy, the only light coming from a small glass lamp set in the wall. There was a rancid smell of decay, a close, musty smell that permeated the walls. They descended a further three floors, the claustrophobic gloom enveloping them as they continued further underground. It was a relief when they stopped and entered through another heavy fire door, this time into a poorly lit but wide corridor with piping and ducts lining the walls and ceiling. The walls glistened with dampness and somewhere from within came the gentle but incessant drip, drip of water. The decay in the stairwell was replaced by the suffocating smell of dampness that seemed to catch in one's throat and linger on the chest.

Timayev led them down the corridor until they reached a solid steel door with a combination lock to open. However, Timayev merely rapped on the door three times with exaggerated slowness, paused for five seconds and then repeated the action. There was no sound from behind the steel door, and only the gentle drip of the water broke the still air. Then there was a clicking sound, followed by the sound of locks being drawn back, and the door swung lazily open.

Filling the doorway was another of Timayev's compatriots, someone Marisa vaguely recalled from visits to the house. He was small but wiry and his completely bald head was framed with a blasting of pockmarks that made his head and face look heavily cratered. He had a broad black moustache that was so precisely cut it looked as though he had drawn it on. His ruddy face broke into a broad smile when he saw Timayev.

"Welcome sir," he grinned. "Everything is ready."

He stepped aside and allowed the group to enter. "Watch your step," he instructed everyone helpfully. There was a small lip at the base of the door which made the door frame resemble a submarine hatch. Marisa stumbled and Dan steadied her as they were marched in.

They entered into a vast hangar-like area with a ceiling at least twelve feet high which gave it an exaggerated feeling of space. Dan would not have guessed that such a large area, about half the size of a soccer pitch, would have existed underground. It looked like it had been used in the past as a storage area. Lining one end were a number of high metal storage racks built on a large platform with caster wheels for easy transport.

The area, without the benefit of natural light, looked gloomy and depressing. However, in the middle of the area a number of people were milling around, bathed in the intense glow of small but powerful arc lights rigged up on rolling stands. Dan also noticed a video camera set on a tripod, and as several of the men moved around he saw through the gap that the camera was aimed directly at two wooden chairs. Hanif pushed and prodded Dan and Marisa toward the chairs. The assembled group moved aside. He counted eleven men in the group, several of them heavily armed with assault rifles and a battery of ammunition slung over their shoulder, wearing berets like modern day Che Guevara's. Dan could not conceive of any reason why they would need such heavy weaponry down here in the bowels of the building. They would never be found here, and with that realization a cold chill of fear ran through him. It was unlikely anyone apart from Timayev's gang even knew this place existed.

The men looked at them with a mixture of contempt and expectancy, some of them with thin, cruel smiles on their faces, as if in anticipation of what was about to happen. Several of them had the deranged look of zealots in their eyes, similar to the look he had seen in Timayev. The only common element to their expressions was one of hostility. Dan and Marisa had no friends here.

There was a gentle "whoosh" as an air conditioner started up, blowing gently from the several air ducts and ventilation shafts set in the wall near the ceiling.

Hanif jostled and pushed the pair into the wooden seats where Dan and Marisa found themselves surrounded. Two members of the clan raised their heavy weapons and trained them directly at the prisoners. A third had a handgun and, clearly enjoying himself, pointed it at them. He pursed his lips and made a "boom" sound and laughed like a hyena. The men were in good spirits and ready for some entertainment.

Timayev, his eyes still wild, moved to the centre of the group and talked loudly to make himself heard. "Comrades, comrades, thank you." He made a gesture with his palms outstretched and facing down to ask for silence. The excited chatter gradually died down and as Timayev continued, his voice was amplified in the vaulted acoustics. He moved forward to what appeared to be an improvised lectern and rested on it. He stood slightly to the right and in front of Dan and Marisa so they could see him clearly as he began his speech.

"Comrades, our brothers in Chechnya continue the struggle to liberate our people from the infidel. They have endured great hardship and we share their pain. We have had many trials and setbacks, but the events in Kahnawake were the most damaging. We were unable to supply desperately needed funds to our soldiers, funds that could have helped turn the war in our favour. However, we have learned never to give up the fight and we will recover and grow strong again.

"The fight for liberation is not just in the battlegrounds and streets of Grozny. We live in the digital age, the era of mass communication where we can get our message across to millions in minutes. The role of propaganda and public opinion is as important as the number of dead Russians. We can send a message to our supporters, but more importantly we can deliver a message to our enemies, the infidel, those who would subjugate our people. We will strike fear in their hearts when they see how we deal with the enemies of our great country and our great faith."

He raised his arms toward the ceiling as if in worship. "Tonight we burn the infidel in the name of Allah!" he cried, his voice echoing around the vast arena. The men cheered and raised their weapons in the air. One of them even let off a deafening volley of shots that pinged around the metal piping on the ceiling near one of the walls.

After this show of euphoria, the men quickly assembled into their respective roles, demonstrating their usual military efficiency. Most of them arranged their machine guns on shoulder straps and moved toward the several entrances set in the walls. There was also a hatch set in the ceiling at one end and below it a metal rung ladder set in the far wall. One of the soldiers stood at the bottom of the ladder, ready to pick off any unwelcome guests trying to get in through the hatch.

The chance of anyone finding them in this subterranean hole was bleak and the probability of escaping virtually zero. Yet they were taking no chances, thought Dan, his heart sinking. He was beginning to feel like a condemned man. A small group stayed around the area where Dan and Marisa sat, still closely supervised, gun barrels barely six inches from their faces. Timayev spoke with a tall, bespectacled operative who was making adjustments to the video camera on the tripod. He pointed it directly at Dan and Marisa and peered through the lens as Timayev whispered to him, and then gave a satisfied nod. The two men standing over Dan and Marisa both pulled on balaclavas and stood behind chairs. Hanif pulled from a storage box a large Chechen flag and unfurled it and placed it to one side on its stand, slightly to the right of the prisoners. The cameraman checked his lens and gave an affirmative nod to confirm the flag was in the viewfinder. He also produced a large board that was filled with the long flowing words from the Arabic alphabet. Alexi and Hanif also pulled on balaclavas so four of them stood behind Dan and Marisa. They had the air and the look of executioners. He glanced to one side. Marisa was trembling and starting to cry.

He reached over and gave her hand a reassuring squeeze but Alexi, now brandishing an AK-47 assault rifle swung it toward him, motioning for him to take his hand away. The tears were streaming down her face but she made no sound. The cameraman handed Timayev a sheet of paper. He scanned it briefly and handed it to Dan.

"Get on your knees and read this," he ordered Dan sternly. As he said this, the cameramen adjusted his lens and Dan heard the faint whirring of the camera beginning to record.

Dan scanned the paper as the camera rolled. "I'm not reading this utter crap!" he cried indignantly, throwing the paper dismissively on the floor.

He did not see the blow coming. This time it was Hanif who delivered the strike from his own assault rifle on the side of Dan's head with such force that it momentarily felt like his skull had collapsed inwards. He fell off the chair and collapsed on the hard concrete floor, groaning in pain. His vision was blurred for a full minute before the pain began to subside. He gingerly hauled himself up using his chair as support, but Hanif stood over him, his air of menace accentuated by the mask. "Stay there on your knees," he commanded.

Dan did not protest. He did not relish the idea of another blow like that. Like the crack to his nose from Alexi, this one had drawn more blood and he felt weak as it began to drip through his hair. It felt like he had a crater in his head. It was throbbing so much his head felt as if it was being squeezed in a vice.

The cameraman was still recording. "Don't worry," he said to Timayev. "We can edit what we need."

Timayev tossed the piece of paper at Dan. "Don't try anything stupid again," he growled. His voice rose. "Now read it!"

Dan picked up the paper and in a deadpan emotionless voice began to read the carefully prepared script.

"My name is Dan Huberman. I am a traitor to the glorious cause of the struggle for liberation of the great nation Chechnya. I understand that as an infidel and an enemy of the state I must be punished. I am a spy and an agent for the Russian invaders and I freely admit I have been collaborating with them in the attempted overthrow of the great Chechen rebellion."

He hesitated, frowning over the next few sentences. Alexi swiftly raised his gun from behind Dan and pressed the barrel against the back of his head. Dan felt the cold metal pressing into his already aching skull.

"For this," he continued, "I will burn to death today and I will burn in Jahannam for the rest of eternity. I accept my punishment and accept that it is justified for the greater glory of Islam. Death to all infidel and long live the glorious nation of Chechnya."

He finished and heard the camera click off. Dan gingerly lifted himself back into the chair. He winced as he put pressure on his bad foot. His whole body was aching and his mind was racing with a thousand thoughts, none of them pleasant. Were these barbarians really going to burn them? His heart was pounding and he found he was sweating profusely at the possibility.

"Now the girl," said Timayev, his voice flat. Hanif grabbed her by her long flowing hair and used it to pull her to her knees. She cried out and protested but did not resist. Three of the masked gang members crowded round her, their weapons pointed at her head, and the remaining gunman fixed it firmly on Dan. When she was on her knees, Timayev handed her a sheet and she scanned it. The camera whirred into life and Alexi prodded her back with his gun barrel, prompting her to begin.

Her voice was cracked and choked with sobs, but they stood around her like statues until she had finished. "My name is Marisa Dimitrov and I am a whore and a slut. I have slept with many Russian soldiers and they have shared their secrets with me. I have plotted with them to kill many glorious Chechen people and to support the Russians' illegal and oppressive fight against them. I accept that I must be punished and—" she swallowed hard and fought to control her shaking voice—"and I submit myself to the truthful and merciful justice of the glorious nation of Chechnya by the sacrifice of death by burning. I repent all my sins and long live Allah." She threw down the paper and burst into an uncontrollable flood of tears. Dan wanted to rush to comfort her, but it was impossible, and her sorrow only prompted twisted grins from her tormentors.

When she had finished the tall cameraman adjusted his glasses and gave a sign of approval to Timayev. He gave a sarcastic clap. "Bravo, good performance. You will soon have your fifteen minutes of fame and more. In fact I think for a few days at least you will be the most recognizable faces on the planet."

Alexi and the rest of the gunmen pulled off their balaclavas. "Do we want to tie them together?" he said, sweeping a thick muscular hand though his short blond hair.

"No, no I want to see them thrash around. It will have more impact."

Alexi grinned, a cruel, twisted smile. He lowered his weapon and ambled to a storage rack by one wall and quickly returned, carrying a heavy looking jerry can which he handled with ease. He placed it alongside Timayev. Dan could smell the unmistakable fumes of petroleum. Timayev unscrewed the jerry can and lifted it to an area away from the camera, and then poured a tiny pool on the floor. Keeping the jerry can angled so only a small amount flowed out, he walked over to Dan and Marisa in their chairs, so that when he put the large can down, there was a line of petroleum on the hard concrete floor about thirty feet long ending in a pool at Dan and Marisa's feet. He put the jerry can down and wiped his hand with a small rag one of the gang members passed to him. He gave a short, almost imperceptible nod to Alexi and Hanif. The man they called "the believer" was incredibly strong, and as he moved around behind the back of Dan, he curled a forearm around his throat so Dan could barely even struggle as the breath was knocked out of him. Hanif was not strangling him, but his grip was solid and left no room for struggle. His hands tried to prise the iron grip free, but they barely registered on the burly Chechen.

Accompanied by Timayev's cruel, manic laugh, Alexi picked up the jerry can and sloshed half of its contents all over Dan's body. Hanif suddenly let go and then as he did so Alexi threw the liquid at Dan's face. He gasped and coughed as he tasted the acrid, nauseating taste that seemed to permeate his tongue and slide down his throat. He closed his eyes just in time but even his hair was drenched in the clinging liquid. Marisa realized she was next and without even thinking made a bolt from the chair. The two other gunmen anticipated her move. One of them easily held her and dumped her back in the chair, his face grim, challenging her to try again as he pointed his assault rifle directly at her temple.

Without hesitating Alexi moved astride her and emptied the rest of the jerry can all over Marisa like a refreshing bucket of water on a hot day.

Timayev gave another manic laugh. Everything was in place. Even the guards posted at the entrances to the building had relaxed and began to move in from their assigned points. Hardly anyone knew this place existed. Posting guards at the entrance was a conservative but hardly necessary precaution. They would not be disturbed now and the men wanted to see this. Let them move in for a better view, he thought. They have earned this. He smiled to himself. It was show time.

CHAPTER 45

It had been a snap decision but one Carl had made easily. He could no longer sit back in the communications van and listen as the world collapsed around him. His career was on the line, yes, but right now he was more concerned with Dan and Marisa. The fact that they were in Timayev's clutches was partly his fault and he did not know if he could live with himself if they came to harm. He felt a deep personal animosity toward Timayev that far exceeded the bounds of the professional distaste he felt for the criminals and lowlife he regularly met in his job. This gangster had turned a fine officer into a traitor and now Brad was dead, his reputation and memory sullied by tonight's events.

He had quickly commandeered a team of eight officers from the York Regional Police Service, although he had to wake a very grumpy Chief to do it. Although each officer had firearms training and were licensed to use their weapons, only two of them had used their tactical skills in live situations. This was no time to be fastidious, and the group had assembled for duty quickly and efficiently. Within half an hour of his original call Carl and the team were racing up the highway toward Buttonville Airport. It was past two in the morning and there was very little traffic, and he had instructed his small convoy not to go blaring with sirens. He had moved quickly, unable to listen any further to the Chechen prisoner being tortured and inevitably to be killed by the Russians. He would have to answer for that to the Special Investigations Unit in due course, and he would be found wanting. But as the police van and the lead car rushed through the still night toward the company's small industrial unit in the business park west of Buttonville, he had received a call from Amanda that surprised him greatly. It appeared the Russians had not followed through on their threat to kill Sulim.

They had taken him out of the basement, but unfortunately the audio feed had failed shortly after. There was nothing to indicate the Russians had discovered it on Sulim's jumpsuit, and it suggested Sulim might still be alive.

He felt a small twinge of encouragement, but even so he had no idea what he would find at the company's premises. As the dark expanse of Buttonville airport opened up on the right as they looked, the small convoy exited the highway and followed the road as it curved left into the sprawling industrial area to the west. The three cars slowed down and moved cautiously along the dark, twisting road. Although it was badly lit, Carl instructed the drivers of the three cars to kill their headlights and the small procession slowed even further as the drivers struggled to follow the line of the road. Carl squinted at the large white boards on the roadside showing directions to the unit numbers. He could just make them out in the gloom, and only then because they had their own small light attached. They were on the correct street, but the road meandered around the length of the park, and they continued carefully for another three quarters of a mile before Carl saw the number.

"There it is," he pointed out to the to the officer in charge, a swarthy Mexican called Sanchez whose shaved head showed under his peaked cap and his angular face sported an immaculately groomed goatee. Despite the gloom, Sanchez was still wearing his mirror sunglasses, but he nodded in recognition as Carl stared at his own distorted reflection. Carl hoped they would not affect his aim, if it came to it. After the Montreal battle, it was almost certain the team would need to use their weapons. Carl did not realistically expect the Chechen gang to surrender without a fight. In fact he had no idea how large the reception committee would be. His small unit might be heavily outnumbered, but it was the best he could do in the time available. So, despite his desire to get to Dan and Marisa as quickly as possible, if it wasn't already too late, they had to proceed slowly and cautiously, hoping for some element of surprise.

The front of the unit, flanked by a small car park, showed no signs of activity, but several cars were parked in the bays adjacent to the building, including a Toyota Land Cruiser. There were no lights on in the building. Their reception committee was clearly not going to make itself known, thought Carl. It was critical to stay alert. It could be a trap.

Officer Sanchez took off his sunglasses and his tired, brown eyes peered intently at Carl. "Just so we get one thing straight, Detective. I am in charge of the tactical side of this operation. If we have to use our weapons, I decide when and how. You can handle the negotiations, although I guess from your earlier briefing there will be little scope for that. So I want you to stay in the background. Is that clear?"

Carl let out an exasperated sigh but nodded his assent. Carl pondered whether Sanchez had been the type of kid who would storm off with his ball if the other team scored a goal. Always wanting to call the shots. Tonight it was okay. He was just grateful Sanchez had been able to muster this team together, inexperienced as they were, at such short notice. His main concern was getting Dan and Marisa out alive. Snaring Timayev would be a bonus, although on reflection it was probably critical to the success of the mission.

They parked up and the team filtered quietly out of the vehicles and gathered around Sanchez, listening intently as he quietly set out his strategy for entering the building. Carl stood at the back, observing the team, fully focused on their mission. All the officers sported coiled earpieces and each checked them scrupulously and gave Sanchez a thumbs-up sign. Communication was always vital in situations like this, especially when conducting a search which inevitably involved the officers splitting up. As Sanchez issued final orders to his team and they quietly began to move out, checking their weapons and adjusting their Kevlar vests, he glanced again at the building, standing like a dark, silent sentinel in the dead of night, and wondered with concern whether Brad had got it wrong? Surely his former compatriot would not have deceived him right at the very end. He had nothing to gain by doing so. Carl was convinced Brad was telling the truth. He would stake his reputation on it, although after tonight that might not be worth much. He had not expected the clan to meet them with guns blazing, but it did not look promising.

The small group fanned out and cautiously headed toward the dark building. Sanchez walked just behind them, his head darting each way, dark features alert and brow furrowed in concentration. Carl stepped in next to him and Sanchez gave him a stern disapproving look.

"Where do you think you're going, Detective?" he asked casually.

"I am right by you on this. I owe it to my friends in there."

Sanchez put his glasses on again but it did not hide his scowl. "I told you to stay in the background."

"I'm the negotiator right? I need to be where the action is. Don't worry, I know how to use this," he said, fingering his small but powerful Italian Beretta handgun.

Sanchez hesitated but finally relented. "Just make sure you don't interfere with our tactics. You know I can't be responsible for your safety. You're on your own in there."

"Fine, I can handle that. Let's find these bastards quickly."

Sanchez touched his earpiece, listening intently. "Doesn't seem likely. My men have been round the perimeter of the building and it is completely empty. All entrances into the building locked and shuttered. No sign of any activity."

Even through the sunglasses Carl could interpret his accusatory expression. "Maybe your man got it wrong," he suggested, a slight hint of contempt in his voice. Carl was really starting to dislike Sanchez, but he had to admit the officer might be correct.

After several minutes the group reassembled from their respective points around the building. They all reported a complete lack of activity, the building silent and dark on all sides. Even a sweep of the upper floors with infra-red binoculars revealed nothing. If anyone was in the building, they were keeping themselves well hidden.

Sanchez turned to Carl and, glasses off, once again peered intently at the detective. Carl grimaced at the accusing look those tired eyes gave him, as if to say why the hell have you brought us out here at this hour on a wild goose chase? "Well, Detective?" he said simply.

Carl paused, not sure how to react. Before he did so, however, one of the officers piped up. "There is a parking lot under the building. A small side road to the rear leads to a ramp and a garage door. We could probably get into the building through there. We just need to disable the lock."

Carl glanced at Sanchez hopefully and the team leader shrugged his broad shoulders. "Okay," he said casually. "We are here anyway. Nothing to lose. But stay alert team," he warned.

The team spread out again, this time in a tighter formation when they reached the ramp heading down to the garage door. One of the officers took out a small handgun from his holster and screwed a long black silencer onto the barrel. He looked at Sanchez, who gave an affirmative nod. The officer carefully aimed the gun at the sensor panel located on the top of a thin concrete pole about four feet high. There was a sharp "plink" as the officer shot the sensor out, its glass casing shattering into a thousand pieces. The men grabbed the bottom rail of the heavy steel door, and straining with effort, heaved it upward until it moved freely on its runners and was fully open. Inside, the parking lot was empty and poorly lit, but a small, tatty fire door set back in a small alcove was visible at the far end. With no other obvious entry or exit, the team had no choice but to head toward the door. They did so cautiously, using the concrete pillars as temporary sanctuary in the unlikely event of a surprise attack.

There was a sudden metallic scratching sound from the pipe work running along the ceiling and several officers trained their guns on the source of the sound in a coordinated, fluid motion. There was a flash of black and out of the shadows a raccoon scurried nervously across their path and hurriedly retreated into another recess. Carl saw the officers visibly relax and as they moved nearer the door, they appeared more at ease, almost complacent. Carl sensed they believed their leader's assertion that he was mistaken; he himself was not as convinced as he had been.

However, one of the officers noted something on the ground and knelt down beside it. He took off the glove on his right hand

and began rubbing the ground vigorously with his fingers before inspecting and sniffing them. He glanced back at his colleagues.

"Fresh rubber, still carrying a faint amount of heat. These tracks are new, probably less than an hour old. Someone's been here tonight." Sanchez nodded but said nothing. It was hopeful but not conclusive, thought Carl. In fact, he reflected with a sudden twinge of fear, they may have just missed them and now they could be taking their hostages anywhere. His mild twinge of panic was instantly dispelled when another officer examined a ventilation shaft set in the wall about ten feet from the door. Smoke curled lazily from the ventilation shaft and drifted aimlessly into the heavy, turgid air of the parking lot. "They are still here," he declared confidently.

CHAPTER 46

Sanchez gathered the men together for a further team briefing. They all checked their weapons in readiness to head down the stairwell. It was unclear exactly where the gang was, but it was apparent from the way the smoke drifted gently upwards through the ventilation shaft that they were several floors down in the bowels of the building. Sanchez warned his team that they would need to take full advantage of the element of surprise. His concern was they did not know which floor the gang was located on, and the only entry point in was likely to be through the narrow door from the stairwell. It could make his men sitting targets if they did not disperse quickly enough. It was a dangerous manoeuvre but they had no choice.

The men listened carefully as he laid out his strategy for entering the chamber. They would have to try each floor and adopt the same approach—assume that the gang would be there and ready to fire on his men. The first few seconds would be vital. They would need to clear the door area and spread out immediately, and hope the element of surprise would buy them enough time to adopt an attacking position.

"Okay, team, you know what you have to do. We need to be a coordinated unit. Is everyone ready?" said Sanchez. There was a chorus of "Aye sir" and a final check of weapons and adjustment of Kevlar vests, before the team began moving toward the stairwell. As they did so, Carl detected a hint of nervousness on some of the men's faces, young guys who probably had families, maybe a young wife who was lying sleepless in their bed waiting and hoping her husband would make it back home in the morning. He had seen it so many times before. Jesus, he had been there himself a long time ago, before his wife could no longer stand the stress of wondering if he would survive every day and packed her bags. At least they had had no children, he reflected ruefully. Leaving behind a bereaved child was the biggest fear faced by any officer in the force.

They all looked grim and focused, but the quiet, still air was suddenly shattered by the sound of a car engine gunning down the ramp, followed by several others. As the cars screeched down the ramp and took a sharp left turn, the headlights arced around and shone directly at them, blinding the group with their intense beam. There was little time to react before the cars were on them, evenly spaced in a wide semicircle so the men were surrounded. The cars braked hard and stopped barely thirty feet from the group. The officers raised their weapons and trained them on the cars, waiting for a signal from Sanchez. Suddenly they found themselves in the middle of a bizarre stand-off. The car engines were switched off but the blinding lights stayed on, and through the tinted windows it was impossible to see if there was any activity. The whole strange confrontation lasted barely a minute, but for the officers, and for Carl, squinting against the blinding light, it felt as if time stood still. Sanchez watched the cars like a hawk, waiting for some sign of activity, his own gun armed and ready.

One of the car doors flashed open, and Carl heard the click from the officers' weapons as they disengaged the safety catches, poised and ready to fire. The atmosphere was electric, ready to explode like a powder keg. A man staggered out of the car, as if he had been pushed, and he stumbled and fell to the floor, his hands raised in supplication as he saw the weapons pointed resolutely at him. Carl recognized the cowering figure instantly, someone he was convinced would be dead by now. He didn't even wait for Sanchez.

"Hold your fire!" he shouted in desperation.

Marisa was crying hard, spluttering and choking as the bitter liquid ran down her face onto her lips, her tears stinging her cheeks. Dan felt the rigid, helpless fear of a condemned man, but even worse, he knew he could no longer help Marisa. Right until the last minute he had been convinced the gang would not follow through with such a barbarous act of utter depravity, that even Timayev was not capable of this level of cruelty. He now realized he had misjudged the clan leader. Any hint of humanity he possessed would surely be extinguished as surely as their own lives in a hideous death that was now only seconds away.

Timayev stood back behind the camera, to where the pool of petroleum had been emptied, the liquid running in a lethal line directly underneath the chairs of the two prisoners. He was careful not to tread on the thin, golden liquid, but pulled out a lighter and flicked the flame open. He had merely to drop the lighter to his feet and the flame would shoot across like an arrow to Dan and Marisa and engulf them in flames. Their captors sensed that now was the time and stepped back slightly, fierce grins on their faces. The camera whirred and clicked, capturing the prisoners' final moments for history.

The cameraman panned the camera round on his tripod and took a shot of Timayev holding up the lighter like an Olympic flame in his right hand. "What I do now I do for the glory of the Chechen Republic and for the fight against the infidel." Then, like an executioner in an American death row jail, he said slowly and deliberately to them, "Do you have any last words?"

The camera panned back to the prisoners to capture their final agonized moments. Dan was just about to launch into a tirade condemning these savages when the camera suddenly stopped whirring and the cameraman slapped it in frustration. He adjusted his spectacles and examined the camera but it would not restart.

"Damn," he cursed, and turned to Timayev. "Sorry boss, the camera battery has died. I'll need a few minutes to replace it."

Timayev gave the cameramen a fierce, withering look. "You fool." He put the lighter away, still glaring balefully at his operative for having stolen his moment. The sense of excitement that charged the air fizzled out somewhat and several of the men returned to their posts by the entry points into the chamber for a smoke, careful to stay a safe distance from the middle of the room, which stank like a refinery.

Sanchez gave Carl a furious stare but he reinforced the command with a wave of the hand in a gesture to stand down. The men relaxed slightly but held their weapons close, waiting expectantly. The man, realizing with relief he was not about to be riddled with bullets, summoned the courage to stand up and he looked hard at Carl. Although the weapons remained fixed on him, his expression was one of great relief.

Carl broke out into a broad smile. "Nice to see you again Sulim."

Before he could answer another figure stepped out from the car. The officers shuffled nervously and, still looking for guidance from Sanchez that was not forthcoming, kept their weapons poised and ready. Volkov ignored them, taking off his sunglasses and confidently striding forward in front of Sulim. Carl moved forward and offered his hand. The Russian paused and regarded him curiously, his dark eyes studying and evaluating Carl. His thin lips curled upwards and he moved forward and took Carl's hand.

"Detective Rodriguez, I assume," he said in his deep Georgian accent.

"I'm glad to see you Boris, but why are you here?"

"Well, Detective I couldn't sleep and it sounded like you really need my help."

"You got that right. We think they are in there but I'm certain if we try an assault we could find ourselves outnumbered. What can you offer me?"

Volkov's smile twitched a little. "More to the point, what can you offer me?" he retorted.

Carl considered the matter for a few seconds. "A complete amnesty in regard to our mutual friend Sulim. We won't press any charges."

"And?"

"Don't push your luck Boris. Kidnapping, false imprisonment and torture are serious charges. Take what I'm offering."

It was Volkov's turn to consider carefully. As he paused, several bodyguards, some nearly as wide as they were tall and all dressed smartly in suits, heaved themselves out of other cars in the party and regarded the police group with barely disguised hostility, as if they were to enter a pact with the devil.

"Agreed," he mused, almost to himself. Sulim scowled angrily at him, especially when Volkov grabbed him by the arm and hauled him forward, pushing him roughly in Carl's direction. "He's all yours. He wasn't very useful anyway."

"Good," replied Carl. "If you are coming in with us, a few ground rules. We enter first and you do not fire without our express permission or if you are in lethal danger. This is not a vigilante mission. Our plan is to minimize casualties. Is that clear?"

"Clear."

Sanchez was apoplectic with rage. "I'm in charge here," he blurted out. His rage quickly abated in the awkward silence that followed. His men looked at him expectantly but Volkov merely gave him a contemptuous, unpleasant stare. Sanchez, embarrassed, visibly shrank back.

Carl broke the heavy silence. "How many are you?"

"There are fourteen of us, all armed and ready. Just say the word," responded Volkov. Without even looking back, he raised his right arm in a silent gesture and his cadre stepped out of the cars, several adjusting their weapons and striding over purposefully to their boss.

Carl smiled inwardly as he regarded them. Most of these Mafioso operatives' sported intricate tattoos visible over the edges of their combat clothes, reaching up as high as their necks and down as far as their wrists. They looked a fearsome group, with a swagger and purpose that suggested they were ready for action. His only concern was they might prove a renegade, trigger happy bunch. They were superior to the small police unit in both numbers and size, and a glance at Sanchez revealed the officer's surprise mixed with a hint of fear at the brutal looking group. Carl decided to rescue Sanchez.

"Excellent. By my reckoning our combined numbers should easily outnumber the Chechen clan. However, Officer Sanchez here is in charge of the tactical side of the operation and we need to follow his instructions."

The Russian force was unconvinced, but their leader assented with a nod and all eyes turned to Sanchez. His authority restored, he grew in stature as he addressed the assembled force with his plan. He suggested they use Sulim as the stooge to gain entry through the main door into the chamber, and they would also gain access through the ventilation shaft openings in a coordinated effort to quickly surround the gang. Only when all the men were positioned and ready in the shafts would they proceed, so that entry into the chamber would be simultaneous from all access points.

Carl was impressed by Sanchez's briefing and even the Russians nodded in affirmation, before Sanchez, with new found confidence, loudly announced, "Okay, let's do it."

The group moved purposefully through the doors and down the stairwell. Several pairs of men, each consisting of a police officer and a Russian operative, in keeping with Sanchez's orders, found the metal grilles for the ventilation shaft embedded into the wall. They easily removed the grilles and hoisted themselves up into the shaft and inched their way forward. Sulim reluctantly revealed to them that the chamber was three floors down, and it would be easy to tell when they had reached the chamber as the stairwell opened out into a wide corridor outside the vast room. When all the men were positioned behind the grilles in the chamber, they would give a pre-arranged signal so they could jump out into the chamber at the same time as the main group, led by Sulim, stormed the doorway, in a coordinated surprise attack.

Sanchez knew the attack force in the shafts were vulnerable but it was the only way to gain access to the chamber, and he hoped the element of surprise would confuse the enemy for the vital few seconds needed to surround them. The other concern was how far he could trust the Russians to follow the script. He had no authority over them, and while they were prepared to follow his lead at the moment, how could he trust them once the attack occurred? Jesus, siding with the criminals was not in the manual. If this all went horribly wrong, he would make sure the truth came out and point the finger at the damned detective. This was all his fault.

CHAPTER 47

Farid had not even been born in Chechnya and none of his family had perished as a result of the Russian incursions into the Republic. He had been born in Azerbaijan in a relatively peaceful village by the Caspian Sea. He shared little of the zealotry and idealism practised by most of the men in Timayev's clan, and although he regarded the Russian military with a mixture of fear and disdain, he had nothing against Russian people generally, most of whom came from poor peasant families just like himself. In many ways he was little more than a hired hand, and his lack of passion for the cause had effectively excluded him from the inner sanctum. He was the grunt who stood guard while the real decisions were made by the true patriots. At least it was a job, and a better life than the one endured in his home country.

He had seen the prisoners dragged in and had been instructed to stand guard outside. There he stood in the wide but dirty hallway leading to the concrete stairwell, the only light coming from a weak light bulb hanging precariously from a frayed cord. Hardly anyone knew this place existed, so far below ground as it was, and it was nearly three o'clock in the morning. He slouched back against the wall. It was typical he had been sent out here where there was nothing to guard against rather than to enjoy the party like the rest in the chamber. He was tempted to pull out his Camel cigarettes and light up, but he had been categorically instructed by Alexi to stay alert and not smoke down here.

He slouched against the chipped drywall, the boredom and the late hour making him drowsy, and he allowed his eyelids to droop for just a few seconds. When he opened them he was startled to see the familiar figure of Sulim striding purposefully toward him. The vision of him was too sharp to be a dream. He straightened up and broke into a broad grin at seeing his old comrade.

"Hey Sulim. Man you look rough. Did they bust you out at last?"

Sulim returned the grin but said nothing and continued to stride directly at Farid. As Sulim's arm shot up, Farid realized his intentions too late. He had no time raise his weapon or even to react to Sulim's lightning speed as he chopped his former compatriot in the neck. The guard let out a stifled moan and hit the floor in a crumpled heap.

Sulim bent over and checked Farid. The guard was completely unconscious, his face frozen in an expression of utter surprise. He quickly looked around. The corridor ran off in each direction, skirting the large chamber, until it trailed off into the gloom. There did not appear to be any more guards around the perimeter, even though the metal double doors ahead were clearly the main entrance to the chamber. No doubt his old boss was not expecting any visitors. Sulim gave a short wave and out of the shadows from the stairwell the assault team emerged, guns cocked and ready. Sanchez was at the front of the group, but Volkov stood right next to him and moved menacingly toward Sulim. He pressed his gun against the Chechen's jaw and locked eyes with him.

"Good work, Sulim. Keep this up and you may just live to see the sunrise. Now when we give the signal you can make your grand entrance and we'll be right behind you. Remember, comrade, any tricks and you won't even see the bullet."

Sulim nodded in assent. His brutal treatment at the hands of the Russians earlier had endowed him with a healthy fear of the Russian Mafia and Volkov in particular. His body still throbbed with pain and the scars would take years to heal, but the water boarding had been the worst. Sulim had nearly drowned in a boating accident as a child and the Russians had brought the pain and desperation flooding back. He was ready to comply.

Sanchez cocked his head to one side and spoke quietly into his Bluetooth unit for several minutes, glancing at his watch as he did so. He then turned to the assembled group. "Gentlemen, we are positioned and ready to go. I have instructed our teams in the ventilation shafts to attack in . . ." He glanced at his watch again. "Precisely two minutes and fifteen seconds from now."

A murmur arose from the assault team and they carried out a final check of their weapons. Carl stood at the rear, his own Beretta holstered at Sanchez's insistence. He felt naked going into a situation like this even if he was at the back of the firing line. He fingered it nervously as the two minutes ticked by slowly in the dank air, heavy with tension. No one even dared breathe. All eyes were on the set of double doors in front of them, focused and ready, as Sulim worked the combination lock.

The girl was still wailing even as his comrade tried to fix the camera, the sense of anticipation now somewhat deflated. The clan member stationed by one of the ventilation shafts listened to her and shook his head in contempt. He wished she would just shut up. The sooner they burned her the better. He knew his comrade on the camera would be punished by Timayev when this was over. Allowing the camera to break down at such a moment was negligent and sloppy, and Timayev did not tolerate such lapses of discipline. He was glad he was not behind the camera. He took a long drag on his cigarette and happened to glance up at the ventilation shaft just as it exploded outwards and out slid a bulky figure in heavy jackboots, brandishing a semi-automatic weapon. The figure landed deftly on the floor like a gymnast and the clan member had little time to react before the figure swiped his forehead hard with the heavy metal gun. Just before he slipped into blackness, he saw a second figure shoot out of the shaft like a torpedo.

At all four ventilation shafts running down into the chamber, the same scene occurred simultaneously. The men guarding the narrow grilles were tired and complacent, not contemplating in their wildest dreams they would be interrupted in this remote chamber, especially at this late hour. They were easily taken out and within a few seconds there were two armed intruders at each of the four corners of the large chamber.

Synchronized with the surprise attacks from the ventilation shafts, the main assault team led by a reluctant Sulim burst through the wide double doors into the main chamber and immediately total chaos ensued. The men inside the chamber scrambled for their weapons, and seeing Sulim flanked by a number of armed black figures in full combat gear, they hesitated momentarily. It provided just enough time for the assault team to surge forward and assume an attack formation, so only the men at the front did not have cover, but they were low to the ground and difficult targets. The trio of police officers at the front, equipped with riot shields, fired off a volley of shots at the ceiling. It sounded like crashing thunder in the enclosed space, and the metallic *ping* of the bullets bouncing off the walls echoed around the chamber.

Despite the noise and confusion, Sanchez spoke through a tiny amplifier which distorted his voice to that of a robot, but also projected it above the noise and chaos.

"You are surrounded. Put down your weapons and surrender or you *will* be shot," his voice boomed and reverberated around the chamber. Hanif, seeing Russian infidel, his face contorted with outrage at the intrusion, was the first to react. He hoisted his assault rifle to his shoulder and aimed at the police chief. Before he could pull the trigger, he staggered backwards and his eyes rolled upwards. A red spot the size of a coin appeared directly in the middle of his forehead and spread rapidly outward.

Undeterred, one of the gunmen who stood over Dan and Marisa fired at Sulim just as he dived for cover. The gunman's curse of "You traitorous dog!" was barely heard in the mêlée but the shot met its target and Sulim let out a howl of agony as he rolled onto the floor clutching his left shoulder. He pressed his hand over the searing wound, and the blood began seeping slowly through. As he did so, his would-be killer was silenced by a fatal shot to the back of the head from a police marksman closing in along with the other pairs entering through the ventilation shafts. He staggered forward and sent the video camera and its tripod clattering to the hard stone floor under the weight of his lifeless body.

The Chechen gang held their weapons poised but they had no cover and it was clear as they glanced around that they were both outnumbered and outflanked. They had enough combat experience to know when an attack would be suicidal.

"I said lay down your weapons," Sanchez's amplified voice boomed. "You will be shot."

The Chechen gang, now only eight strong, failed to comply, but neither did they raise their weapons. They looked to Alexi for guidance but his face was set like alabaster, completely devoid of expression. Timayev, however, was far more animated. His expression was a mask of impotent fury. His own weapon remained holstered and his gang took this as a sign of surrender. Several of them dropped their weapons to the floor. The odds were stacked against them and their attackers had clearly shown their intention to kill if necessary. With a scowl of defeat, several more threw their weapons on the floor and raised their hands in surrender. The noise quickly abated as the shooting stopped. Sensing the moment, Marisa leaped out of her chair and ran toward the advancing group. A couple of the Russian group pointed their weapons at her, but with a harsh *"Niet!"* Volkov ordered them to stand down. They sheepishly pointed them back at the Chechens. Crying with relief, Marisa fell into Carl's broad arms and the detective, standing close to the wall at the rear of the group, wrapped his arms around her. He breathed in and spluttered at the acrid fumes of petroleum that enveloped her. As Marisa pressed close to the detective, she felt the bulk of the handgun in its holster push against her hip. In that instant, her decision was made. She nodded imperceptibly to herself. It had to be done.

Dan, seeing Marisa dart out of her chair, also stood up to follow but finding it difficult to put weight on his bad foot, was much slower. As he rose, a solid, muscular arm curled itself around his neck and he suddenly felt cold steel press sharply against his throat. He felt his windpipe being compressed and the lack of oxygen made him feel weak and dizzy. He desperately pulled at the strong arm pressed like a vice around his neck, but he was too weak and the knife cut into him, drawing blood. He felt himself being dragged backwards and into a standing position. Dan tried to shout but his voice would not come. The grip on his throat was too tight and he only managed a strangled croak.

Timayev's clan were seasoned veterans in the battlefield and they knew when a situation was hopeless. Although Timayev had continually implored them to fight to the death for the glory of Chechnya, their instinct for survival was ultimately more powerful. Having seen two comrades fall in quick succession, they allowed the police officers, backed up by the Mafioso still waving their guns threateningly, to snap handcuffs on them and force them to sit against one wall as a dishevelled, defeated group, guarded by two officers.

Timayev, however, was in no mood for surrender. He backed away, dragging a gasping Dan with him and looked around him, his eyes wild and head darting from side to side.

Several men who had entered through the ventilation shaft were on his blind side. "Move them away where I can see them!" he shouted.

Sanchez and Volkov both nodded at their respective men and, guns trained on Timayev, they edged into his line of vision so the Chechen leader had no-one behind him and was not vulnerable to a shot in the back. He was ready for a tense stand off. His left arm still gripping Dan's throat like a boa constrictor, he deftly moved his faithful German combat knife around with his fingers so that it hovered directly over Dan's carotid artery. One slash and Dan would have no chance. The pressure on the artery was such that any rupture would certainly cause him to bleed to death. With his right arm he quickly fished into his pocket and replaced the knife with a lighter which he held up for his audience to see.

"Any sudden moves and Huberman becomes a fireball," he snarled grimly. "Now back off!" His voice echoed in the large chamber as he yelled at the group.

The chamber went suddenly quiet. Apart from the officers guarding the prisoners, all eyes and guns were trained solely on Timayev and his hostage. Sanchez waved at his men and they backed away just a half step. Volkov ordered his men to retreat and moved back himself so Sanchez headed the group. Let the police deal with the hostage negotiations, he thought. This was not his war.

Carl gently let go of Marisa, relieved to turn away from the strong odour of petroleum and moved forward alongside Sanchez. The stuffy air of the underground chamber was electric with tension.

Carl broke the heavy silence. "Let him go Timayev. It's over."

"This is far from over. I said back off!" He flicked the lid of the lighter open and held it in front of him for all to see, a theatrical gesture but effective. Carl spread his hands in a placating gesture, his hands nowhere near the weapon holstered on his hip.

"All right, all right, whatever you say. Don't make it worse for yourself Akhmad. Your empire is finished. We've released all the girls from your sleazy brothels here and in Montreal, and your drug supply lines have dried up. Your reputation took somewhat of a battering after Kahnawake. But it's not too late to do a deal."

Timayev stared at him, his face taut with anger. "How the hell do you know where my girls are?" He continued to hold Dan in an iron grip as his prisoner gagged, faint from lack of oxygen. Christ, he's like a bull, thought Dan vaguely, as if his rage and bitterness had served to increase his strength.

"Because I told them."

His left shoulder now wrapped in a blood stained tourniquet, Sulim stepped forward, gritting his teeth against the burning pain.

Timayev loosened his hold on his hostage just slightly, although Dan could still feel the restriction to his windpipe, a slow strangulation. He stared at Sulim questioningly. "Sulim. I thought you were in jail?"

Sulim scowled at his former boss. "Yes, and you would have left me to rot there forever. After the loyalty I showed you. I kept quiet and all you sent me was a cheap and useless lawyer to spy on me."

"You were a prisoner of war. You knew the risks and you broke our vow!" spat Timayev.

"I only talked after the clan had abandoned me. We always looked after our own on the battlefield," replied Sulim, clutching his blood-stained arm and wincing in pain.

"Not when they're already dead!" countered Timayev.

"Is that how you saw me? Dead and useless to you? Then I am glad I told them everything even if they had to torture me to get it!"

Timayev hesitated, his guard down just for a split second. Then his face hardened again. "You are a traitor to the cause and you will suffer for it!"

Alexi pushed forward, his muscular but manacled hands pushing past the officer who arrested him. "Akhmad, I told you we should have tried to get Sulim out. Give it up. It's over." The officer grabbed Alexi and hauled his solid frame back against the wall.

"Shut up!" screamed Timayev, his face contorted in anger. "Traitorous dogs! You are all dead men. You will burn in hell like the infidel!" Timayev pressed hard on Dan's neck and he felt his windpipe being compressed further. Dan gagged and fought hard to stop choking on his own bile, his head throbbing and his vision blurring. Several officers and a few Russians had their guns trained on the pair, and one of them took a cautious step forward as Timayev became more agitated. Despite his raw anger and apparent insanity, he was still shrewd and aware enough to use Dan as a shield, his soldier training kicking in instinctively. He was not in the least bit intimidated by the weapons pointing at him. He quickly scanned the area around him. There was no one out of his peripheral vision. They could not get a clean shot. He was safe.

Timayev talked directly into Dan's ear, his teeth gritted. "We could have been set up but for you Huberman. The money from the Montreal deal could have financed our guerrillas for years. I would have had the freedom of Grozny and you screwed it up for me. He flicked the lid of the lighter open again and Dan could feel the heat of the tiny flame on his skin. Timayev only had to move it an inch closer to his face and Dan would erupt into a fireball.

Carl took a hesitant step forward, his hands still spread out, palms raised. "It seems like your comrades have left you. Listen to them Akhmad. We can still do a deal."

Timayev's face was red with anger and indecision and Carl could sense him wavering. Timayev was volatile. He had to get Dan away from him or there was a real risk that Timayev would carry out his threat to set Dan alight in one last act of defiance. Already several of Sanchez's men were scanning the area for fire extinguishers, and Carl had no idea how to stop the Chechen leader.

"I don't do deals with infidel. Get away or Huberman is a dead man." Timayev reached into his pocket and took out his faithful German knife which he pressed deep into Dan's neck for emphasis and Carl took a couple of paces back. As he did so a figure brushed heavily against him and strode confidently forward to face the Chechen leader and his hostage. Carl caught the whiff of petroleum and frowned in confusion at Marisa. Even Timayev looked at her strangely, not quite comprehending. She said nothing but the fierce intent on her face was evident. Then everything happened quickly, although Carl would later recall everything as if he had observed it all in slow motion.

Even the police and the Russian Mafia were caught out as they observed her move forward, too surprised to jump in and apprehend her until she faced Timayev and her hostage just twenty feet away. With one fluid movement, as if she had done it all her life, she raised her right arm, quickly followed by her left, so that both hands were wrapped around the small Beretta handgun in a firm, protected grip. The chamber resounded with a single explosive shot. Dan would later recall feeling the bullet whistle past his ear and scrape his earlobe before the pressure around his throat eased. As Timayev was using Dan as a shield, there was only the most narrow gap to strike, but the shot had the precision of a sniper rifle and Timayev merely grunted in shock as he fell backwards, blood pumping out from the hole set like a bull's-eye in the middle of his forehead. He was already dead before his body hit the floor like a sack, his glazed, lifeless eyes still wide with shock.

She did not resist as one of the officers rushed forward to grab her. He snatched the gun out of her hands and roughly pushed them behind her back and snapped on a pair of handcuffs. Her face was set like stone, clearly in shock. "That's for my father," she said simply.

There was a deep sense of disbelief around the area. Alexi, Serge and the rest of the gang stared impassively at their fallen comrade, the blood slowly pooling around his head, before they were led up the stairs into a waiting police van. Carl walked over to the body and, knowing it was a pointless gesture, checked Timayev's pulse. Nothing. He glanced at Sanchez who immediately whispered into his communications mike. As he bent over he could not feel the reassuring weight of his handgun. He frantically felt the holster just above his waist. It was empty and the realization dawned on him. "Oh hell," he whispered to himself.

The officer who had apprehended Marisa began to gently steer her toward the exit. "Go easy on her," Sanchez instructed the officer. "It's been a long night." The officer gave a sympathetic nod. "I will sir."

Dan, holding a cloth supplied by an officer to his neck, turned to Marisa. "You never told me you were so handy with a gun," he said.

Her face was streaked with tears and oil but she gave a faint smile. "I'm not," she said. "It's the first time I ever used one."

As Marisa was led away, Dan gingerly felt his ear, which was burning from the hot graze of the bullet. At least his head was still in one piece.

As a trio of officers began heaving Timayev and his other dead comrades into heavy black body bags, an officer approached Carl, holding his Beretta.

The officer stroked his jaw. "Sorry, Detective I can't release the gun to you. We will probably need to use it for evidence."

"Understood." How the hell had she stolen his gun from under his nose without him even noticing? And her shot was precision. He had a grudging respect for the Bulgarian girl who had been through so much. She clearly had some hidden talents.

The early morning peace was shattered by a procession of police cars and vans, lights flashing and sirens blaring. They parked in front of the building by the ramp leading to the underground car park. The police were quickly followed by a trio of paramedic vans, whose occupants quickly stepped out and were ushered into the underground car park and down the dingy steps carrying their medical bags. The prisoners were escorted up and swiftly herded into the back of two armoured police vans, only a small windowless grill providing any ventilation. When they were all secured, an officer rapped the rear door twice with his fist on each vehicle and they sped away.

Marisa, her hands still cuffed, was gently led up the stairs and the ramp. She filled her lungs with the freshness of the cool morning air. Toward the east she saw a faint orange glow in the sky as the first fingers of dawn began to creep over the horizon. It had been a long night. She felt no pleasure at having avenged her father and her own suffering. Instead she just felt hollow, an emptiness that pervaded her whole body, as if someone had given her an injection to numb her emotions. Who ever said revenge was sweet? It did not feel like it to her.

Carl trudged up the steps into the cool, breezy air. He saw Marisa being led away. "Take the damn cuffs off her," he shouted harshly at the officer holding Marisa by the crook of her elbow. "Can't you see she needs medical attention?" The officer sheepishly nodded and cut her free. Marisa rubbed her wrists sorely and a female officer draped a blanket over her and gently steered her toward a paramedic van.

Dan staggered up into the fresh early morning air, filling his lungs with deep draughts. The air tasted sweet after the stale, suffocating stench in the underground hangar, and the choking fumes of the petroleum all over his body. He had ripped off his shirt and a towel was draped over his shoulders. A small dressing had been applied to his neck where Timayev had cut it. His nose and left eye were also badly swollen and he pressed a cold flannel over them. Blood was matted in his hair around the wound he had received to the head. He spotted Carl amongst the flurry of activity and flashing lights and hobbled over.

"Looks like the cavalry arrived just in time," said Dan with a weak smile.

Carl looked him over and frowned in concern. "Jeez, man, you look beaten up. We need to get you to a hospital."

Dan gave a dismissive wave. "I'll survive, but I want to see Marisa."

"No problem, she's in the paramedic van over there," he said, pointing at the small emblazoned vehicle, lights still flashing. Carl paused, his dark face carrying a grave expression. "Do you think he really would have burned you and Marisa alive?"

Dan touched the dressing on his neck. "Without a doubt," he replied. "You've seen his record. The guy is—*was*—a war criminal. He would not have given it a second thought. We were going to play a starring role in his propaganda masterpiece. The camera was ready. You guys were just in time."

"Thanks to Brad."

"Brad?" replied Dan, his face creasing in confusion.

"It was Brad that led us to the gang."

Dan hesitated, not wanting to know the answer. "Is he . . . . still alive?"

Carl did not have to say anything. His expression, eyes turned to the floor, said it all. "God rest his soul," Carl replied simply, placing a gentle hand on Dan's shoulder.

Dan said nothing. He had not expected any different. It was never likely he could have survived being thrown out of the car at that speed, but even so he felt a turmoil of emotion. Finally he said, "I don't understand. How did he lead you to us?"

"He called me just before he died. Told me where you were headed. One final act of redemption. I really hope it counts in his favour." Carl crossed himself.

They paused, oblivious to the buzz of activity around them, lost in reflection. Despite recent events, they both had reason to grieve for their friend. Finally Carl said, "You should get in the van with Marisa. You both need the hospital. Hurry before it goes. Dan nodded silently and hobbled over to the van where one of the paramedics in his fluorescent yellow jacket, gently guided Dan into the back.

As Carl watched him, a strong hand rested heavily on his shoulder. He turned and faced Volkov, whose craggy features broke into a wide smile. "A successful night, Detective," he began. "Only three dead." Carl was not sure if Volkov was mocking him but he did not like his tone and the Russian's smug expression.

"I may have offered you an amnesty this time, but don't think you're off the hook, Boris. We'll be watching you closely. Kidnap, false imprisonment, assault, as I mentioned before. Add to that torture, attempted murder. One day the prosecutor's office will have a field day on you and your Mafia Family."

Volkov gave a dismissive laugh and held his wrists together as if inviting Carl to handcuff him. That irritated Carl even more. "Come on Detective, you are surely not serious. If it wasn't for my "Family" you would still be trying to figure out how to get to the Chechens and you would be sweeping up Huberman and the girl's remains in an urn. I think you owe me a debt of gratitude rather than threatening me."

"Tell that to Sulim."

"A necessary formality I am afraid. At least he is still alive. I seem to remember a proposal you made to us only a few hours ago. We came through for you when you needed us."

"I wonder how much of it was self interest?" replied Carl. "You saw an opportunity to take the gang down legitimately and you took it."

Volkov's mocking smile disappeared and his expression turned steely. "It doesn't matter what our motivations were, Detective. I put my men at risk and we fought shoulder to shoulder with the police. You would still be down there counting your dead but for my Family." His hostile expression burrowed into Carl, challenging him to refute that. Carl had to concede Volkov was right, although he would never admit it to the Mafia boss.

Volkov's arrogant smile returned. "So, Detective, I am curious to know why it was so easy to get to Sulim? It was like—how do you say it here?—taking candy from a baby. And on your watch too."

Carl said nothing. He peered at the flashing lights and the bustling activity, now starting to wind down. Volkov's squad were preparing to leave and the pathology team was loading the body bags off a gurney for transporting to the mortuary, no doubt for an autopsy. Thank God none of those bags was a police officer this time, he reflected with relief. Behind one of the remaining vehicles, Carl could see Sanchez debriefing his team. They had done well, no major injuries sustained. Two of his men had shot dead Chechen gang members with a precision and ruthlessness in the heat of battle that usually came only after many years of training. At the time they had not hesitated, their actions instinctive, ingrained into their brain and their muscles. It was fortunate they were so efficient, as their police chief would have been the first casualty. Not bad for an assault team hastily assembled in the middle of the night.

Even so, it had to be remembered his marksmen had shot dead two human beings. Whatever the circumstances and the necessity for doing so, they had to live with that fact. Carl had seen it before. Inevitably the guy who pulled the trigger would need counselling, to help him understand it had been the right thing to do at the time, the only logical course of action. The mind played tricks in these situations. Even though the marksmen himself knew this, it sometimes did not stop him being haunted by his conscience. In carefree moments with a young family, the vision of the man he shot would suddenly return. He had heard reports where the officers, racked by guilt, never picked up a gun again. He hoped the two men who had used their weapons tonight would remain mentally strong, especially when the Special Investigations Unit came along asking awkward questions, which they inevitably would. Their swift actions had prevented a potential catastrophe.

Volkov clicked his fingers to get Carl's attention. "Detective, I am guessing by your silence that it was not totally accidental. He peered intensely at Carl, who did not return his gaze. I am guessing maybe you sent me the email, yes?"

Carl stayed silent under Volkov's intense gaze until the Russian mobster broke into a hearty laugh. "I thought so," he said playfully. "No wonder it was so easy to get Sulim out. Your police guards did not exactly go beyond the call of duty to save Sulim."

"He was wired. We heard everything you did to him."

Volkov's expression turned serious. "I guessed you might. We were never intending to kill him, whatever you heard. I would strongly suggest that your recording of our little bit of fun tonight stays firmly locked away. I have no doubt our lawyers would be crawling all over this one, claiming entrapment. I really don't think you would come out of it too well. It would be a sad way to end such a noble career."

Carl stayed silent, gazing into the distance at the faint glow of the dawn in the east, shafts of amber light spreading slowly out over the rooftops of the industrial units. A new day was breaking, and he felt frail with exhaustion.

Volkov's tone brightened again. "Come, come we should not talk of such things. Tonight we should celebrate a successful mission. The Family is always pleased to help on the side of law and order if we are needed. You are welcome to share a vodka with me at my restaurant anytime Detective," he smiled.

Carl's tone was sour. "I'll get back to you on that."

CHAPTER 48

Frank's housekeeper had found him slumped in the hallway, the front door still open, creaking lazily in the light early morning breeze. He was still unconscious and she saw with horror the dark, sticky liquid staining the carpet around his head. She babbled to herself furiously in Spanish, but composed herself enough to run to the phone and call 911. She spoke rapidly in her native language and it took the operator a short time, with the help of a colleague, to decipher her panic-stricken call for help, gently cajoling her to calm down.

Eventually he got the address from her and dispatched a paramedic immediately to the house. He asked her to stay on the line and with great patience he was able to instruct her to check his airway, and ascertain that the prone figure was breathing shallowly.

It took just three minutes for the paramedics to arrive and come storming through the door. They checked him over thoroughly as the housekeeper looked on, crossing herself and trying not to cry. The lead paramedic looked up from his examination and nodded reassuringly at his female colleague. "He's going to be alright," he said. "A nasty head wound though. We'll take him in for observation."

He turned to the maid. "What's his name?"

She stared at him, not quite understanding, and mumbled unintelligibly.

The female paramedic, dark haired with coffee coloured skin, smiled and said in fluent Spanish, *"Cuál es su nombre?"*

"Frank Carroll," she replied in her thick Latin accent.

The paramedic expertly dressed his head wound, and gently tried to revive Frank, waving a flashlight around his eyes. Frank slowly came around, mumbling incoherently, eyelids fluttering.

"Frank," said the paramedic loudly. "Can you hear me? You don't have to speak. Move your hand so I know you heard me." Frank slowly flexed his fingers back and forth and moaned as he began to regain consciousness. It was then he winced in agony, a sharp dagger-like pain shooting through his brain.

"Frank," continued the paramedic, still speaking loudly at his patient. "I need you to sit up for me if you can." Frank nodded and as he became more alert, he tentatively touched his throbbing head. With the help of the two paramedics, he rose heavily to a sitting position and was gently hoisted to his feet by them. They slowly guided him into the back of the van. The female paramedic got in the back with him and the paramedic van drove off, its lights flashing, leaving Frank's maid looking worried and trying not to burst into tears.

Although it had been just over a month, it felt like years since Dan had lived in his tiny flat. The place had never been comfortable to start with, but now it felt cold and unwelcoming. Although the police had long ago finished their forensics tests, the bloodstained, threadbare carpet was still there as a reminder of what had happened. There was an atmosphere of death in the turgid air, and Dan doubted whether he could bear to stay overnight in the flat, never mind live in it again. He touched his bandaged head, still sore from the beating he had received, and the sense of claustrophobia as he entered the flat made his headache even worse.

It was no good, he decided. He would have to find somewhere else to stay. He peered at the pile of manila files in the corner and reflected ruefully on his business. It was going to be difficult to revive it. Although a lot of information was still on his home computer sitting in the corner and hopefully intact, he had lost most of the physical files and all of the information on his office computer which had been destroyed in the fire. His office was a burnt out shell and his clients had stopped calling, chasing up their cases, after about two weeks. While he had been absent without leave, they would no doubt have grown tired of chasing him and signed up with a competitor. Unemployed and soon to be homeless, he did not feel like he had achieved a major victory. But at least Marisa was safe.

The doctors had released him from the hospital earlier in the day, but had kept Marisa in for observation. Although she had not sustained any major physical injury, they were particularly concerned about her fragile mental state. Also, while she was not technically under arrest, she had committed a homicide and the police were duty bound to investigate. He had stayed with her for a time but she had said little and made it obvious she wanted to be alone, so Dan had decided to head back to his flat and get some rest.

As he surveyed the flat, however, he knew he did not wish to be there any longer than necessary. He gathered a small case with his essential belongings and headed for a hotel.

Carl's temporary office in the Toronto narcotics division made him feel distinctly uncomfortable, but he had no choice. It was vacant, for obvious reasons. His superiors had ordered him to stay in Toronto for at least the next ten days and probably longer as he cleared up the case and got to the bottom of Timayev's operations. The former clan leader's two main cohorts, his former bodyguard Alexi and his key trafficking operative, Serge, had been highly cooperative, no longer seeing any reason to protect someone who was already dead, and angling for a plea deal that might secure them reduced jail time if they collaborated with the police. Even so, Carl suspected not even Timayev's most senior operatives had been fully informed about the extent of his empire. It was starting to unravel but there was still a lot of work to do.

The first order of business when he had settled into his new office was to take down Brad's certificates and the photos of his family. He placed them carefully into a sturdy cardboard box and would present them to Brad's family very soon. It was not going to be easy, he reflected ruefully.

He was working through one of the statements provided by Serge when there was a knock at the door, and in walked Dan.

Carl stood up and shook Dan's hand firmly. "Hey man, they let anyone into police premises these days," he joked. Carl pointed anxiously at Dan's still bandaged head. "How is the old cranium? Still in one piece?"

"Just about," replied Dan. It feels like they patched it together with some rusty old staples they had lying about." In truth Dan had needed about fifteen stitches from the blow he had received from Hanif.

"Healthcare cutbacks, my friend. Good to see you up and about."

"Yeah, I've just checked into a hotel nearby. Couldn't stand the thought of being in my flat again."

"I don't blame you man, after what happened." They both fell silent for a while, out of unspoken respect for Marisa's father.

"You know I have the Special Investigations Unit crawling all over my ass," added Carl. "There's a rumour going around that I might have had something to do with Sulim's kidnap by the Russian Mafia."

"When I was in the Drug Squad a lot of rumours turned out to be true," said Dan casually.

Carl was silent for a minute before he answered. "No comment," he replied sourly.

Dan nodded knowingly and tapped his nose. "I also recall that sometimes you do what you have to do."

Dan paused expectantly. "Any news on Marisa? Is she likely to face prosecution? That poor girl has been through enough already."

"I have spoken to the Crown Attorney's office and they are still analyzing the facts, but off the record they have suggested it would be difficult to make a prosecution stick. Given the circumstances it would be the most unpopular prosecution they ever undertook, a political hot potato. I think we are fairly safe on this one."

Dan looked relieved. "Thank God."

"Although I am going to get some heat because it was my gun."

"You'll survive. You should be a hero. You've managed to break up one of the most ruthless and powerful drug gangs in Ontario, one which is funding terrorists abroad."

Carl gave an ironic smile. "I wish it were as simple as that. Too many politics in the force. Once I have cleared up this investigation I am taking off to a warm, deserted beach somewhere, if the SIU don't get their claws into me first."

"Which reminds me. There is one part of the investigation I can help you with."

"I think you've already done your part, Dan. You don't need to put yourself in the firing line again."

"I don't intend to." He pulled out his crumpled old diary from his jacket pocket and flicked through the pages. "I just need to make a phone call."

Georgi Kakov, his huge frame squeezed into a small office chair groaning under his bulk, leered across at the pretty blond girl in the short skirt smiling amiably at him. Her English was quite good, and clients liked that. He could tell she was from a poor family just by her clothes, and that was even better. The promise of a wonderful new life as an au pair in North America was usually too good to resist. This one was barely seventeen and grinned from ear to ear as he explained he had a family on his books which was looking for exactly her type. She hardly noticed him as he watched her ample chest rise and fall as she gasped in excitement. Serge would love this one, he thought to himself.

"Okay, Ivana, I just have a few papers for you to sign and within a few days you will be on your way to the bright lights of Canada. Congratulations!"

The girl squealed in delight as she hastily scribbled her name on the paper in case he somehow changed his mind about offering her such an amazing opportunity. As she turned to go it took all Georgi's willpower not to squeeze her butt with his thick, sweaty palm. He was paid well, but sometimes it would be great to test the goods, he reflected ruefully.

She was just about to open the door to leave when she toppled backwards as the door burst inwards. Five heavily armed figures clad all in black, helmets on and visors down, stormed into the office and pushed past her. She screamed and pressed herself against the wall. One of the figures waved his gun at her, pointing to the door. Taking the hint, she ran out, whimpering with panic.

"What the . . . ?" began Georgi indignantly.

One of the figures rushed at him and with incredible strength, heaved Georgi's heavy body over his desk so he slammed his face on the rustic wooden surface, sending a wire basket flying, the papers fluttering messily on the floor. They were shouting crazily, creating an intimidating racket that scared the hell out of the obese recruiter. Another of the intruders came to the aid of his colleague and between them they wrenched his arms together behind his back and snapped on a pair of steel handcuffs. Georgi squealed in pain as he felt the muscles of his arms being stretched further than they had in years, and he was convinced at least one of his arms would break.

"For God's sake . . ." he cried desperately, tears welling up and running down his pudgy face.

"Shut up, you pervert," one of the officers cut him off tersely. "You're going down." He motioned to one of the other men, who had a rifle pointed closely at Georgi's temple. "You are under arrest for human trafficking in contravention of the Combating Trafficking in Human Beings Act 2003. Anything you do say will be used in evidence against you in the Supreme Court of Law. Do you understand?" The officer yanked on the handcuffs for effect and Georgi cried out as a sharp bolt of pain shot through both arms.

"Yes, yes," he struggled breathlessly.

Two officers hauled him upright and frogmarched him out of the door. The lead officer turned to his colleague. "Read him his rights," he said.

Frank was getting bored in the hospital. He had lots of work waiting for him at home, briefs to read and cases to prepare for, but the doctors had insisted he take a complete rest for the next couple of days. He had to admit his head still felt fuzzy, as if his brain had been enveloped in a dense fog, and it was hard to focus. His brain was lacking its usual sharpness and so he had to content himself with reading some idiotic celebrity magazines from the mobile hospital library that travelled the wards. His housekeeper had brought some clothes for him and when she had visited and seen he was fine, she burst out into rapid-fire Spanish and hugged him tightly. He was touched by her gesture, if a little embarrassed, but it made him realize she was the only woman who had come to see him. Maybe he worked too hard. It was a sobering thought that if he had perished at the hands of the rogue police officer, he had absolutely no one to leave his house and his beautiful art collection to. There had been plenty of women in the past, but he had always been too busy to commit. An incident like this made one re-evaluate one's life. Maybe it wasn't too late to still find a dream woman to share his life with. He settled back and flicked through the pages of an old *Hello!* magazine with their pictures of idyllic couples in beautiful mansions. Yes, he decided. Less work and more play.

He touched the injured area gently and winced with pain. Even through the thick bandaging he could feel the tightness of the skin where they had stitched his head together. Brad had certainly hit him with force and he had been knocked out cold. Getting to the hospital had been a blur, as if he was drunk and seeing himself though the eyes of another, but a good night's sleep had helped, even if the fog was there. The nurses had informed him that Dan and Marisa were fine but had firmly denied any more requests for information until the doctor had examined him. He had no choice but to wait, although even the magazine lost its interest as he cogitated over recent events, which were still a mystery to him.

He had closed the curtains around his bed for privacy from the skeletal old man in the opposite bed gawking like a bird at him, his gummy mouth moving constantly but remaining silent. There was a tap on the metal railing. It must be the doctor. "Come," he said.

It was not the doctor, but a much more welcome face. "Dan, good to see you. How are you? You look like crap!"

"I should be asking you the same question. You're the one in the hospital bed," replied Dan, grinning broadly.

"I heard about your ordeal. I'm glad you're still alive."

"It was a close thing but you were right after all—the Russians came through. How's the head?" Dan touched his own still bandaged head, and they both laughed. "I guess we look like a pair of middle aged old mummies," said Frank jovially. "Maybe we can count each other's stitches when I am out of hospital. Where are you staying at the moment?"

Dan hesitated, pausing for thought. "I am staying at a hotel. I couldn't face going back to the flat."

Frank sat up sharply and winced as the skin on his cranium pulled at the stitches. "Well then that's settled. You come and stay with me again."

"I couldn't possibly Frank. You have been kind enough to me already. And look at the trouble it caused you."

Frank waved his hand dismissively. "Nonsense, nonsense, I insist. In any case, I'm not sure it wasn't the other way round. Remember it was me who sent you after the Russians. Perhaps Brad would have left you alone if you hadn't gone. By the way, I am really sorry about Brad. Whatever turned him, I know you two were great friends."

Dan nodded silently.

Frank continued, "There is one thing I have learned lying here having far too much time to think. My old house is far too big for me to be rattling around it on my own. I need a woman's touch, Dan, and I don't mean a mad Latin housekeeper. However, for the moment you will do and I will not hear otherwise. What about Marisa?"

"Thanks Frank. I'll take up your offer. As for Marisa, we are going to try and get her home to Bulgaria as soon as possible, but it may take a week or so."

"Then she stays with me too until she's ready." He gave a broad smile, excited at the prospect of sharing his house once again. "You didn't bring me any bloody flowers!" he admonished Dan.

CHAPTER 49

It was a gloomy, drizzly day and it matched their moods. Dan and Marisa huddled together under a large golfing umbrella, the persistent patter of rain beating against the top as they stared down at the small plaque commemorating a life cut too short. They stood in the grounds of the crematorium not far from Frank's house in the St. Andrews area, their emotions still raw from the short service and the cremation they had attended less than an hour before. It had been surprisingly well attended, considering that Vasil Dimitrov had known hardly anyone during his short time in Canada. Marisa really appreciated the fact that Detective Rodriguez and several other members of the police force who had worked on her case and her father's murder had come out to pay their respects.

She had delivered a short eulogy but her voice was choked and she found it hard to say the words. Dan had gallantly stepped in when she was faltering, but she got through it. They were now waiting for the ashes to be delivered to them in a small urn which she would take back to Bulgaria and arrange for a proper funeral attended by her family.

It had been a week since Dan had left hospital. His stitches had been removed and his black eye and swollen face had just about returned to normal. Even his leg felt better and he had attempted a light jog twice around the street where Frank's house stood. He was starting to feel human again, he reflected with relief.

Marisa, however, had only been out three days. The doctors had been highly concerned about her mental state and had kept her under close observation for signs of post-traumatic stress disorder. She had also undergone a program of psychiatric counselling, which the doctors were anxious she should continue after she left hospital. However, Marisa had been insistent on returning to Bulgaria to be with her family, and Dan had been trying to arrange local counselling for her, so far without success.

Marisa walked away, her face bloated with tears, and wandered off toward a small copse in the middle of the peaceful, expansive grounds. She threaded her way aimlessly past a number of ornate carved tombstones and statues commemorating loved ones passed on. Some of them looked fresh and new. This was the recently extended part of the crematorium grounds. The old part was at the back of the building, the tombstones and commemorative plaques weathered and beaten with age, the inscriptions barely recognizable; the bereaved that tended the resting place of the deceased long since passed on themselves.

Dan caught up with her, reached into his jacket pocket and handed Marisa a small manila envelope. She wiped her eyes and took it, regarding it curiously.

"What is it?"

"Open it and have a look. I managed to pull some strings though Carl. He was able to call in an old favour at Citizenship and Immigration Canada. They managed to push it through with the Bulgarian Consulate." She pulled the small Bulgarian passport from the envelope and looked inside. It had a recent photo of her and was stamped as having been issued just the day before. "You're free to go back whenever you need to. But I am worried about you Marisa. Are you sure you won't stay longer?"

Marisa hesitated, her face fixed in a pensive expression that was now quite familiar to him. She then closed her eyes and shook her head. Once she had made up her mind that was it. He knew her well enough by now. There was no stopping her.

"I need to see my family and give my father a proper funeral," she said. "I owe him that."

Dan placed a protective arm around her shoulders. "Don't ever blame yourself Marisa. This could not have been helped. You have given him justice so let him rest in peace. You need to find peace as well."

Marisa looked up earnestly at Dan. Through the runny mascara, her eyes were hollow, like glass. "Peace?" she said indignantly. "Can

I ever find peace after what happened to me? Can a person ever regain their humanity after they have been raped, beaten, abused and spat on night after night?"

Dan could not answer. He just squeezed her shoulder more tightly and she lapsed into silence. He feared for her when she went back to Bulgaria. In spite of everything she had been through, there was often a perception in Eastern European countries, especially in the small villages, that somehow they had brought it on themselves, that they were to blame, had brought shame upon the village. He had heard of stories where girls had escaped the miserable existence as victims of trafficking with great courage and fortitude, only to face hostility and narrow-minded prejudice when they returned home, often from family and former friends. This was something he would work to address in his new role.

"I've been offered a new job," he ventured, "and I need a good personal assistant. Are you interested?" She smiled, but it was a weak smile, given only to humour him.

"What is your new job?"

Head of Operations at the Human Trafficking National Coordination Centre run by the Mounties. I'll be based mainly in Ottawa. I feel like everything we went through was for a purpose. Maybe I can make a difference, especially with you at my side. "Tell me you will think about it."

"You'll make a difference with or without me. Dan, I have to go home, to be with my family."

They ambled out of the wooded area into open ground and saw two figures leave the main building and walk purposefully in their direction. "You can always come back to Canada when you have seen your family."

Marisa gave an ironic laugh. "I can't see my mother letting me out of her sight for the next six months, never mind going back to Canada again! Thank you for the offer. And thanks for this." She tapped the envelope containing her new passport. Once she received her father's ashes, she would head back to Bulgaria as soon as possible. She still found it hard to shake off the nightmares, and maybe leaving Canada would help her to find some element of closure. The counsellors had been kind and understanding, but their words had little impact. No one could really understand what she had been through unless they too had experienced it.

The two figures were closer now and definitely heading for them. Dan recognized Carl's dark, broad figure, dwarfing the tiny blond girl walking next to him. Marisa peered closely and then gasped in surprise and put her hand to her mouth. At the same time the diminutive figure broke into a broad grin and sprinted toward Marisa. The taller girl held out her arms and the two girls hugged each other firmly, tears rolling down their cheeks.

"Olivia. I thought I would never see you again."

Olivia's voice was faltering, and the tears flowed freely. "They told me in the house you were dead. I never knew until I got out."

The two girls linked arms and walked off chatting excitedly, oblivious to the two men.

"Thanks Carl," said Dan.

"My pleasure. I gather you are off to Ottawa soon. When do you start?"

"Once I clear things up here in Toronto."

Carl smiled. "You're looking better. Not so . . . eh . . . beaten up. Good luck in the new job, man. I'll be watching progress from Montreal. We won't be so far from each other so we should meet up every now and then."

"Definitely."

They shook hands and Carl walked briskly off. Dan watched him go. The detective was under enormous pressure at the moment as the investigation continued. As far as Dan was concerned, he should be the hero, but as Carl had rightly mentioned, and he knew only too well, it did not always work like that in the politics of the police force.

CHAPTER 50

The head of the Royal Canadian Mounted Police in Ottawa was a tall, smooth and well groomed figure, an eloquent public speaker, more like a senior civil servant than a police officer, despite the decorated uniform. Dan barely heard him as he spoke to the assembled mass of high ranking public servants, journalists and invited figures from the business community. It was a highly distinguished group which filled the large semi-circular conference hall at the Chateau Laurier, a beautiful, stately old hotel close to Parliament Hill. Dan was concentrating on his own speech, and he was up next. He scanned his notes for what seemed like the hundredth time. He knew the contents so well that the notes were really only a crutch in case he suddenly lost his way. He had researched his speech diligently, and the more he discovered about the issue of global human trafficking, the more passionate he felt about his new role.

He reached down and rubbed his right ankle. The damn thing seemed to throb when he was nervous, like a rheumatoid arthritis sufferer sensing rain. He knew his words would be printed and replayed to him, might even define his initial three year term in the role. He had to get this right. However, in a curious way, he was anxious to get up there on the podium, to spread his message across this influential group of luminaries, so they too would be aware of what he knew, maybe even to share in his passion. This was more like a mission to him than just a job, but he knew if he was going to make a difference, he needed the support of the movers and shakers in this city and in the rest of Canada. He would be taking his message on the road, that was certain. He lost himself in thoughts of preaching to massed audiences across the country, when the soothing baritone of the RCMP head jerked him back to the present as he mentioned his name.

"I want you all to join me in welcoming Mr Huberman to the podium, in his new role as the Head of Operations at the Human Trafficking National Coordination Centre. Ladies and gentlemen, distinguished guests, Dan Huberman." The speaker waved his right arm in Dan's general direction, his silver hair glinting in the harsh overhead lights. Dan rose from his chair to the side of the stage and ambled to the podium to a round of encouraging applause. He placed his notes on the heavy wooden lectern, coughed gently and pulled the microphone a little closer. The lights dipped a little, and he looked out over the crowd, waiting for the applause to die to a ripple. A few camera flashes went off and the room faded to silence. He let out another nervous cough and glanced over his notes.

"Ladies and gentlemen, distinguished guests," he began, scanning the audience. "It has been a wonderful evening and I am honoured to be in the presence of such dignified citizens of this great land of Canada, a country born from conflict but developed as a model of democracy, where freedom of speech, freedom of choice, freedom to pursue opportunities are all part of our constitution, our culture and our heritage. We pride ourselves that we are the bastions of democracy, of tolerance, of how different races and cultures can integrate and live in peace. We are indeed a proud nation, a shining example to the rest of the democratic world."

He took a deep breath. "Yet within our borders and our cities there is another culture, an underground culture invisible to the untrained eye, one that goes unnoticed by most people getting on with their busy lives, rather like the rats in the sewer we hardly ever see or even think about. It is a culture of slavery and of exploitation, a cancer eating at the roots of our civilized, democratic way of life. The cancer is human trafficking in all of its forms. I want to make one thing clear. This is not just about sexual exploitation, although I have to admit that this is one of the most base and degrading forms of trafficking. Humans can be trafficked for a variety of purposes and by different types of people.

"I want to dispel a few myths here today. The first is that human trafficking happens to poor people or people with no education. This is simply not true. Although poverty is one of the biggest risk factors, anyone can become a victim of human trafficking. In fact, some victims are university educated or professional working people who have become ensnared. Let's forget the stereotypes. Many we find are Canadian women. This heinous crime has no respect for a person's status or background. It could happen to any of us, to our friends or to our neighbours. It could even happen to our own sons and daughters."

He looked around and paused for effect. A few murmurs broke the general silence as the audience considered this.

"Let me tell you about a case we are working on. A professional middle class couple, with an eighteen year-old daughter in her freshman year at university, a popular, intelligent and hard working girl who went for a night out with friends where they ended up at a strange club. Her drinks are spiked and she passes out. She wakes up six hours later to find she is squeezed into a crate with three other girls on a cargo flight bound for an old airstrip in the heart of Mexico, to be sold to one of the Tijuana drug lords as his personal concubine. The parents did not discover her whereabouts for six agonizing weeks. She had simply disappeared. Can you imagine what she went through, and how her parents suffered?

"For a story like this, there are hundreds, no, thousands of others, all involving an innocent human being abducted and abused. In fact the number worldwide has been estimated at over two and a half million people annually, and counting. It is an industry worth approximately $40-50 billion a year globally, more than the GDP of many small countries. Other than drugs and arms, it is the most lucrative illegal trade on the planet. Yet the cost in human misery is immeasurable—broken lives, broken families. Millions of people whose lives are destroyed in the pursuit of profit, greed or sheer power. It is one of the greatest crimes against humanity. The impact on these people and on their families is almost too great to imagine. If this was a disease we would be making great efforts and employing vast resources to find a cure.

"Let's not deceive ourselves that this is a problem confined to the Asian or third world countries. It is happening under our very noses. The United States is one of the key global hubs for human trafficking and we, here in Canada, are not blameless either. Several thousand people are trafficked to Canada for sexual exploitation and other purposes every year. At least twice as many pass through Canada on the way to the United States. Our research suggests the number spiked during the Vancouver Olympics in 2010 as the demand for prostitutes increased. Of course, while there is always a demand there will always be a supply.

"Yet, despite these numbers, Canada is not doing enough in law enforcement. Back in 2002 the federal government brought in a specific offence against human trafficking in the Immigration and Refugee Protection Act. The offence provides for very severe penalties—up to $1 million in fines and imprisonment for up to life. In 2005 we passed Bill C-49 as an amendment to the Criminal Code to create a new offence of trafficking in persons. There are numerous other offences in the Criminal Code related to trafficking, such as kidnapping, extortion, forcible confinement, living off the earnings of prostitution to name a few. We have the legal infrastructure. Yet the shameful fact is that only a handful of criminals have ever been convicted of human trafficking. Most operate unseen and with impunity. The potential rewards are great and the risk, because of our complacency, is low. Unlike drugs, a woman can be sold again and again. Canada has been falling behind for a long time in the fight against human trafficking and I intend to make sure we catch up and take a leading position in this global fight.

"Let me get into the mind of a person who deals in trafficking. What drives them to do this? Are they just plain evil? Unfortunately it is way more complex than that and until we understand how these people think it is very difficult to be anything other than reactive. The psychologists tell us to think like a criminal to catch a criminal—we have to think more like them. Part of my plan will be to bring in reformed traffickers who have served their time in society, much like the hackers who become IT security consultants. We have to understand the role of organized crime in the trafficking of individuals, how it interacts with the drugs trade, how we can share information between agencies both inside and outside Canada to prevent trafficking before it occurs.

"Let me dispel another myth, that human trafficking must involve violence and confinement. Yes, it often does but it can also be more subtle. It can involve deceit, psychological manipulation and threats of violence. Several cases we have encountered involve girls who had ample opportunity to run away, but they did not do so, for fear their families would be targeted and suffer as a result, or because they did not wish to go back.

"Another fiction is that most victims of human trafficking want to go back to their own country or home town. This is simply not true. The vast majority of victims do not return home for fear they will be ostracized by their community when they return home. It is a very real and valid fear. Many are treated as if they have brought shame on their family or their village, as if it was in some way their fault; that they brought it on themselves. Many could not cope with that and committed suicide, others drifted into crime or became institutionalized through severe depression. The lasting impact even after they have escaped remains like a festering scar. Until recently, Canada would treat victims of trafficking as illegal immigrants—we would detain, interrogate and deport them. We are an international embarrassment. Our mission here at the Centre is twofold—we need to bring the perpetrators to justice, but we also need to support those who have been freed from trafficking but now face an uncertain future, rejected by family and friends. As if they have not suffered enough trauma already."

Once again he paused and scanned the audience. There was total silence, and all eyes seemed to be transfixed on him. Was he really getting through?

"I am not going to hide the fact we have a mission that is almost impossible. Are we fighting an unwinnable war against an unseen enemy? The answer is inevitably, yes, but it is still a war worth fighting. While we can continue to win individual battles and save lives, or impose justice on these criminals, it will always be worth fighting. But, ladies and gentlemen, we need your support. We need to be able to identify children and adults at risk, we need to seek intelligence and work more closely with the immigration authorities, and national and international policing authorities. We need to be able to train our officers to identify trafficking victims—they do not have a sign on them and they sometimes will not tell you. We need to be able to provide protection and support to victims—safe accommodation, medical and psychological help, counselling, legal assistance and education.

"We also need to raise public awareness of the scale of the problem. Most of you here today probably think it is a problem a long way from our shores, happening to distant unknown people of no interest to us. I can't criticize you for that. I was the same before I became embroiled in a trafficking case in my previous life as a private investigator. I can assure you it is on our doorstep and it is happening all around us. We have to stop burying our heads in the sand and take action now.

"Our positioning at the Centre is to provide a focal point for human trafficking law enforcement efforts and investigations across Canada. We need to protect victims by developing partnerships with domestic and international agencies and with organizations outside government, to share information and intelligence to allow us to prioritize operations and be more proactive in investigating abuses. Every day a person is held against their will is another day of trauma and abuse. We need the resources to obtain reliable intelligence quickly, and when we have that information, the resources and the authority to act quickly. I aim to set up a hotline telephone service and a social media site which will enable people to provide confidential information where they suspect a person is being trafficked. Without the public providing us with this type of information, we are limited in what we can do. We aim to create human trafficking videos and campaigns to educate people in recognizing victims, and get support for the work we do. We need public support if we are to survive and grow.

"One of the most important roles we will provide is the support of victims after they have suffered this trauma. As I mentioned, Canada is woefully inadequate in this respect. At a time when these vulnerable people, having suffered so greatly, need our help the most, we as a nation are turning our back on them. I want to support these people and help them get back their lives, but we need trained counsellors and crisis support and we need the resources to have these people on hand. What does it matter that they may be Eastern European or Asian or African or whatever? We are a diverse country made up of every race and creed, and we pride ourselves on our cosmopolitan culture. These people are human beings and as I said before, human trafficking is a crime against humanity, whatever their race."

Dan took a deep breath and glanced around the vast circular chamber. The silence still prevailed but several members of the audience were shifting uncomfortably. He looked down at his notes and realized that he had wandered off his carefully prepared script. He felt like one of those evangelist ministers on the religious channels spouting their fire and brimstone speeches. Maybe he was preaching too much. It was time to wrap it up.

"Ladies and gentlemen and distinguished guests, thank you for this opportunity to talk about my work. You can probably guess I have a real passion for this, but I want you to share my concern. Like cancer, this scourge can strike anywhere, anytime. It does not respect wealth, education or background. It is truly an affront to civilized society, and we owe it to ourselves and this great nation that we are so proud to be part of, that we fight this scourge and ensure justice is done. Thank you."

Dan gathered his papers from the lectern and shuffled them together. A polite ripple of applause emanated from the front row and then spread rapidly down the aisles until it reached a crescendo of thunderous applause. Dan moved away from the lectern, and gave an awkward bow. The RCMP head joined him at the front of the stage, clapping himself, and placed a strong hand on Dan's shoulder.

"Well done son," he whispered in Dan's ear.

"Thank you sir," replied Dan, his voice almost hoarse.

He shuffled back to his seat on the panel, the applause still ringing out. The after dinner party would be interesting. He checked his pocket for his business cards. It was time to start pumping the wealthy and the influential for funds and support. If he had the political support and the resources, there was no end to what he could achieve on this mission. Dan pursed his lips and nodded to himself as he considered the challenges ahead. He had a job to do.